GRASS ROOTS & SCHOOLYARDS

GRASS ROOTS & SCHOOLYARDS

A HIGH SCHOOL BASKETBALL ANTHOLOGY

EDITED BY NELSON CAMPBELL

THE STEPHEN GREENE PRESS
PELHAM BOOKS

THE STEPHEN GREENE PRESS

Published by the Penguin Group
Viking Penguin, a division of Penguin Books USA Inc., 40 West 23rd Street,
New York, New York 10010, U.S.A.
Penguin Books Ltd., 27 Wrights Lane, London W8 5TZ, England
Penguin Books Australia Ltd, Ringwood, Victoria, Australia
Penguin Books Canada Ltd, 2801 John Street, Markham, Ontario, Canada L3R 1B4
Penguin Books (N.Z.) Ltd, 182–190 Wairau Road, Auckland 10, New Zealand

Penguin Books Ltd, Registered Offices: Harmondsworth, Middlesex, England

First published in 1988 by The Stephen Greene Press
This paperback edition published in 1990
Distributed by Viking Penguin, a division of Penguin Books USA Inc.

10 9 8 7 6 5 4 3 2 1

Part openings illustration by Horvath & Cuthbertson

Library of Congress Cataloging-in-Publication Data

Grass roots & schoolyards : a high school basketball anthology /
edited by Nelson Campbell.
p. cm.
ISBN 0-8289-0641-6
1. Basketball—United States—History. 2. Basketball—United
States—Anecdotes, facetiae, satire, etc. 3. School sports—United
States—History. I. Campbell, Nelson.
GV885.7.G72 1988 87-19983
796.32′362′0973—dc19 CIP

Printed in the United States of America
Designed by Deborah Schneider
Produced by Unicorn Production Services, Inc.
set in ITC Cheltenham by AccuComp Typographers

CONTENTS

PART I THE LITTLE TOWNS

PART II THE BIG CITIES

PART III THE IN-BETWEENS

FOREWORD

The experiences of my boyhood and teenage years made it easy for me to relate to the stories of "The Little Towns" and "The In-Betweens" in *Grass Roots and Schoolyards.* I had the good fortune to be the son of a high school coach, and this, coupled with my personal aspirations to participate in all sports, created a natural interest in the stories of great high school games, outstanding players, and underdog champions during the '30s, '40s, and '50s in the state of Kansas.

My father, Alfred Smith, began his coaching career at Chanute (Kansas) Junior High School in 1919. In that same year the birth of Ralph Miller was recorded at the Neosho County courthouse in Chanute. Dad remembers Ralph as a legendary athlete at Chanute High School in the middle '30s and the origin of considerable lore in that part of the country. If the name Ralph Miller seems familiar, it is because he is one of the nation's leading basketball coaches. Now at Oregon State, Ralph is in the final years of a distinguished coaching career that includes highly successful tenures at Wichita State and Iowa.

Dad also made a contribution to "The In-Betweens" by coaching the Emporia (Kansas) Trojans to their only state high school basketball championship—in 1934. Though their accomplishments might not be material for a film such as *Hoosiers*, those members of the team who attended a 50-year reunion in 1984 might feel otherwise.

But what I consider to be wonderful basketball legends in Kansas are not known in North Carolina or even in states that border Kansas. History and lore at the high school level seem to stop at state lines. Fortunately there is now an anthology, *Grass Roots and Schoolyards*, to resurrect and perpetuate the most compelling stories from North, East, South, and West. I commend it to your reading.

—Dean Smith
Chapel Hill, North Carolina
June 1987

PREFACE

With each passing year basketball, the youngest and most totally native of American team sports, becomes more deeply entrenched in culture and folklore. While protagonists debate whether football has achieved "national game" stature alongside baseball, basketball is quietly building a case of its own.

Basketball has the most participants. It draws the most spectators. It is the only one of the Big Three pursued with equal enthusiasm in farm town, city ghetto, and suburb. It is the only one that the United States has exported with universal success. For Cinderella potential, cardiac finishes, community involvement, and lingering impact, there's nothing quite like a fast-paced team sport requiring only five regulars and a few reserves.

No other sport has achieved such geographical parity in interest and talent. It is said that to know where good basketball is played is to know where the streams cross the cornfields, where the buses stop between housing projects, and where the expressways separate the suburbs. Larry Bird, Jerry West, Elvin Hayes, Bill Bradley, and Willis Reed came from small towns. Oscar Robertson, Kareem Abdul-Jabbar, Bill Russell, Hank Luisetti, and Isiah Thomas came from big cities. George Mikan, Michael Jordan, Ralph Sampson, Jerry Lucas, and David Thompson came from "in-betweens."

Basketball is big in tropical Key West, Florida, just 90 miles from Cuba, where they fashioned a state championship in 1968. It's big in Barrow, Alaska, 330 miles above the Arctic Circle, where climate and long nights militate against outdoor activity and the high school team flies 27,000 miles a season to and from games. It's very big in the urban ghettos, where there'll be playground action in mid-August. And it's very big in the legendary Cinderella towns such as Hebron, Illinois; Duncan, Arizona; Milan, Indiana; and Waterloo, Ohio. In 1954 the French-born historian Jacques Barzun wrote in *God's Country and Mine*, "Whoever wants to know the heart and mind of America had better learn baseball—the risks and realities of the game—and do it by watching first some high school and small-town teams." Today, 33 years later, he might add basketball.

Every state has a rich basketball history, particularly at the high school level, the game's purest, most dramatic, and most nostalgic vineyard. Likewise, every state has a legendary schoolboy (or schoolgirl) team of otherwise ordinary kids who became magicians beyond compare once they stepped onto the floor, who ran up incredible records, and whose exploits have swelled with the ages. But prep lore, however compelling, tends to remain local. Hence this book, whose purpose is to uncover and share the best prep-oriented basketball stories from across the land, touching all aspects of the game and its relation to community life, mixing the bitter with the sweet, and covering all the regions and decades.

If there is a sport of the people, it is basketball. All a youngster needs is a pair of sneakers and a playground within walking distance. All a team needs is one ball that bounces. Equipment outlay is negligible when compared with football or baseball. All fifty states have postseason high school playoffs, usually with all teams starting from scratch. There are also tournaments for large and small colleges; AAU, YMCA, deaf, and wheelchair teams; and church, fraternal, and veterans organizations. No other American sport has so broad a base.

Blacks say basketball is their sport, and perusal of NBA rosters will quickly reinforce this. Basketball was a soothant in urban and rural ghettos alike long before it became a viable way out.

Farm and small-town people say it's their game. It's a sustainer during the tedium of a long winter. There were baskets on the sides of barns and garages in the hamlets long before the cities and television made basketball a "major sport."

Indians say it's their sport. One of Dr. Naismith's disciples introduced it to the Sioux in 1892, less than a year after its birth at Springfield College. Basketball has long been a cherished activity among various tribes, easing, it is claimed, the trials of reservation life.

Church groups say it's their game. The best teams in the early years came from the YMCAs, YMHAs, and settlement houses, where rosters were mixtures of high school, college, and adult players. Today basketball is the major sport at many denominational colleges.

The beauty is that everybody is right. The game has that much latitude. But it is at the high school level that it is most reflective of community spirit and most closely linked with the pleasant memories of youth. The players live next door, across the tracks, or down a country road. They're the rawest material, they represent all levels of academic ability, and they attend the public school that the law prescribes. By contrast, the college player is an all-star—at best a member of an academic elite, usually far from the roots that made him whatever he is, or at worst a hired gun.

Intellectuals may ask, "How can one in middle age care what happens to a teenage basketball team?" or, "With the world in flames, is it childish escapism to follow *any* sport with fervor?" Worthy questions, but perhaps we overdo our self-denunciations. At least one noted philosopher exalts sport as a civilized expression of war. Indeed he calls sport the most civilizing factor in society, because it best reveals the fundamental virtues of courage, equality, community, and excellence. In its communal innocence, grass-roots basketball represents perhaps the finest amalgam of these virtues. It's only a game, but then a violin is only a wooden box.

ACKNOWLEDGMENTS

Special thanks go to reporter-historian Kenn Hess of Portland, Oregon, who not only led me through the fascinating byways of his own state's athletic history but helped me unearth vital lore in other states.

Thanks are also due fellow journalists Jack Harvey of Alexandria, Virginia; Bob Lewis of Norwalk, Connecticut; and Bob Frisk of Arlington Heights, Illinois; who offered continuing encouragement while making suggestions instrumental in shaping the final product.

Still others made contributions similarly appreciated: Glynn Archer, Jr., the Bradley family, Jane Campbell, Al Claiborne, Mary Kay Connor, Erwin Crotts, Ray Crowe, Hayden Estes, Charles Hurley, Keith Johnson, the library staff at Lawrence University, Jerry Mathers, Bruce McIntosh, the Michigan High School Athletic Association, Dave Overpeck, Mrs. Milton Pashman, Kenneth Petz, William Plott, Ingen Richards, Walter Rubel, Sam Schapiro, Herb Schwomeyer, Sandy Singer, Jim Stinson, Linc Williston, and Barbara Zumwalt.

—N.C.

GRASS ROOTS & SCHOOLYARDS

PART I

THE LITTLE TOWNS

THE MOST UNFORGETTABLE CINDERELLA

Because of the "class tournament" system, now espoused in some form by every state except Indiana and Kentucky, most of high school basketball's Cinderella stories are from the distant past. But they abound, they touch the hearts of young and old alike, and they're as much a part of regional history as any political campaign or military battle. One of the most memorable, told by Fritz Howell of the Associated Press in 1959, extols Ohio's legendary Waterloo Wonders.

Just a quarter-century ago the Waterloo Wonders came nonchalantly out of the Lawrence County hills to set Ohio agog with their basketball legerdemain.

At least a million Buckeye fans in the interim have boasted how they saw the colorful kids win the 1934 and 1935 Class B high school championships with a 29–0 record the first year and 52–3 the second.

The old Fairgrounds Coliseum, antiquated and with a leaky roof which sometimes halted games because of wet floors, seated only 1,500. So some of the fans must be wrong about witnessing the legendary Wonders in action.

But come Saturday, March 21, they'll have a chance to make their boast come true. The Wonders—the original cast with fabulous coach Magellan E. Hairston—are coming back to where they enjoyed their finest hour.

At the suggestion of Dick Burdette of the *Portsmouth Times*, high school commissioner W.J. "Bill" O'Connell today invited the Waterloo veterans to the state interscholastic tournament as guests of the athletic association.

They'll be introduced at halftime of the state Class A championship contest and perhaps will put on a slightly slowed-down exhibition of their famed trickery.

In the 25 years since the five kids came from the village of 150 to capture the titles and the hearts of the fans, it's possible some frills have been added to their exploits. But all the frills and fancies of a faulty memory can't match the facts.

The Wonders had everything—class, poise, shooting ability, defensive strength and color in huge and gaudy gobs. No one who saw them will ever forget. Individually, there wasn't a standout in the lot, but as a team they were unbeatable.

That was in the days of the center jump when scores were low. But Orlyn Roberts scored 69 points in three games as the Wonders raced to the 1934 title, still high for a three-game tourney in the state meet.

Orlyn, pensioned as the result of service-incurred injuries, is still a Waterloo resident. So is his cousin and former teammate, Wyman Roberts, now a construction worker.

The others were Stewart Wiseman, now a school teacher in Ross County; Beryl Drummond, a Dayton industrial worker, and Curt McMahan, now employed in

Springfield. All except Wiseman made the 1935 all-tourney team.

Curly-haired Hairston, who coached the Wonders to the top of the world, has a garage and auto agency in Chesapeake.

Their entry to St. John Arena this time will probably lack some of the flavor of their descent on the old Fairgrounds Coliseum.

In 1934 they came to town in Hairston's ancient Model-T Ford. They wore bib-type overalls, and their uniforms—wrapped around their shoes—were tied into a bundle with baling twine. The packages were not wrapped in any outer covering.

They were late for their first tourney game as they became so intrigued by the Chittenden Hotel elevator that they were loath to leave its ups and downs.

But their saga began to unfold when they did go into action, and it was a thing of startling beauty. In the first 11 years of the state tourney, no Class B team had been able to score 50 points, and only seven had gone over 40. The Wonders went for a 58 to 29 win over Chandlersville in their debut, then nicked Lowellville, 43 to 32, and Mark Center, 40 to 26, for the title. The scores could have been bigger.

The first point garnered by the Wonders went to Drummond. He was fouled, and instead of tossing the ball through the hoop for the single point, he bounced it off the floor and into the ring. That set the stage for basketball's greatest scholastic show.

From then on everything happened. When one of the Wonders tired, he walked over and chatted on the bench with Hairston while the other four carried on. "Bunny" shots were passed up time after time as a Wonder donated, with a courtly bow, the ball to the frantic opposition. Half the time no one knew who had the ball, so fast and intricate was the Waterloo passing attack. Sometimes the tricks looked like feats of magic.

Anyway, they're coming back. Maybe a bit fatter and a bit slower, since a quarter-century has taken its toll. But chances are the 13,000 fans will test the new roof at the Arena as they try to raise it with their cheers in tribute to the most colorful, talked-about and improbable team Ohio has ever known.

From Fritz Howell, "Waterloo Wonders Return to State," *Toledo Blade*, March 8, 1959, Sports, 1. Reprinted by permission of The Associated Press.

FAREWELL TO SHANNON BROWN

Sometimes high school athletics seemed to be drawing American Indians into the mainstream, there to find opportunities for a better life. Sometimes nothing seemed to work, perhaps because the conquerors can never fully cope with Indian pride, sensibilities, and devotion to the past. Against this background, St. Stephen's School in west central Wyoming has done yeoman work. This story by Barbara Heilman from a 1961 issue of Sports Illustrated *tells some of it.*

The flat Wyoming country between the Wind and Little Wind rivers and the Wind River Range is bleak in winter. The sagebrush patches the snow and the tumbleweed is caught disconsolate in the fences as the land rolls somberly back until it achieves the beauty of the mountains. This is the Wind River Indian Reservation, and it takes 100 acres of it to support a horse.

"No water," said Father Kurth as we lurched along the winter-rutted roads on a tour of the reservation. "Only one family out of 25 even has a well—the rest have to come to the mission for water. It's about 125 feet down. Our well is big, and we had to go down 500. Costs about $5 a foot to sink one, depending on the width. Some of the Indians wash their clothes in the irrigation ditches and hang them along half a mile of barbed-wire fence to dry. . . . I've never known how they got them off again," he mused. "All in one piece, I mean. There's where Shannon lives." He pointed, and I could see the house a long way down the little side road, mean and boxy, like all the Arapaho houses in the flatlands. I couldn't see the rusty frame of the abandoned three-year-old car, or the outhouse or the dogs, but they probably were there. For the next few miles I watched the sides of the road and looked into passing cars, hoping for Shannon Brown on his way home, but he eluded me again.

He was not my business any more, strictly speaking. I was visiting St. Stephen's, a small Indian mission, to find out something about the mission teams as such. St. Stephen's Father Torres had written us:

> *Last year our high school teams lost only one contest in the three sports in which they compete. Unlike many parochial schools, we do compete in league competition against public schools. The one defeat was a 14–13 loss to the state football champion. Our basketball team was undefeated in 28 games, winning the state final game by a 71–55 score over a team that had won 25 straight. The track squad also won the state championship, and this year our football team. . . .*

Straight achievement, duly respected. But about Shannon the letter had said:

> *. . . might be the Indian angle. A good example is Shannon Brown. This boy has been an All-State basketball player for two years and*

is one of the greatest in the history of the state. And yet he quit school this year with his third and greatest All-State season undoubtedly coming up. He is a real paradox.

On the court he is poised far beyond the average high school athlete. He has never played a poor game in an important situation. Last year in the state final before over 10,000 fans in the Wyoming U. field house he scored 30 points, rebounded beautifully and generally demoralized the opposition. Yet he is so shy off the court that it took him about a year to get to the point where he would speak extended sentences to one of his teachers.

Once he split his trunks in a game and walked off the court without calling time, without saying even a word to his coach. When the coach noticed we were playing with only four men he looked down at the far end of the bench and there was Brown, looking straight ahead. "Shannon, for heaven's sake what are you doing off the court?" All Brown did was point stoically at his seat. That's all he would do when the coach questioned him further. Finally one of the other boys on the bench told the coach what had happened. Brown was rushed to the dressing room for a quick change, for to play without him is like Cincinnati playing without Robertson. The coach waited. He waited. Finally he asked one of the fathers to please see what the holdup was. Shannon was seated immobile in the dressing room. His explanation: there were no more white trunks with red trimming left. Only white with no trimming. If he put these on, the people would notice that he was different and would guess that he had split his pants. Father had to run to the laundry here at the mission, sew his pants and run back again, and then Brown went back into the game.

Yet the Wyoming press writes of him only in superlatives (the dancer-graceful Indian, the fabulous Shannon Brown, the much-discussed Brown, etc.) and, as I have written, besides his remarkable accuracy his forte on the court is his poise. His failure to return to school this year was almost the death of his coach, but it was only one of a long series of harrowing experiences. The coach is a 28-year-old named Bill Strannigan who tells anyone who will listen to him, without a trace of jokefulness, that Shannon has made him prematurely grey. For one thing, Shannon likes to break wild horses. For another, up until last year, Strannigan never knew him to show up for a game more than 10 minutes before the beginning. . . .

Shannon had looked out at me from innumerable newspaper clippings, solemn and shy under his astonishing hair—brushed back on the sides, forward in front, in a sudden and complex swoop, his own invention and particular pride. He was 6 feet 2 and except in the action shots was shy up and down every inch of it.

But if Shannon wasn't my business any more, he was not an irrelevancy either. In him were typified the problems and condition of his nation and what the mission was trying to do about them—and what the mission was trying to do about them was the explanation of the mission teams. So everything was really safely of a piece.

Shannon's nation is the Arapaho. They share the Wind River Reservation, unenthusiastically, with the Shoshoni—about 2,200 Arapaho in the flatlands to the east and 1,600 Shoshoni to the west, against and into the mountains. Though the land lacks water it was found to have oil, which yields the inhabitants approximately $40 a month apiece. This would probably be enough, if saved and applied wisely, to irrigate the land and allow something toward the purchase of farm machinery, but it is seldom so saved and applied. The Arapaho and Shoshoni have for the most part subsided into that apathy, almost an ethnic despair, which so often marks the grand job the U.S. has done on the Indian. It is rare that one of them here summons the spirit for a sustained try at anything. The successfully cultivated land or the healthy herd of sheep is almost invariably the work of a white man leasing the land. ("What is Shannon doing now?" I asked one of the sisters. "Nothing," she said. "When Sister says an Indian is doing 'nothing,' " I asked one of the fathers, "what does that mean exactly?" "It means nothing—staying in bed and reading comic books, going into town and standing on the corner. . . .")

St. Stephen's is concerned physically and sociologically with its people, as well as spiritually, and has for years been trying to help them up and out of this sort of "nothing." It is a small mission, which has been on the Wind River Reservation since shortly after the government designated it as such, where Jesuit fathers and Franciscan sisters minister to the Indians, Catholic or not. A great many of the Arapaho are Catholics, having been converted in the late 1800s by a Father Jutz and continuing in the faith in their own erratic fashion. The specific dictates of the Church regarding marriage, for example, are somewhat less specific in the minds of the Indians than they are in the minds of the fathers, and liquor still brings on the old mayhem—as in the case of two boys who undertook to get a friend home and decided on tying him by one leg to the back of the car. "He was dead by the time they got to the Lander bridge," Father Kurth said gloomily. "But the boys meant well."

The first step on the road to anywhere is always the education of the children. The fathers have undertaken it, but they do not regard lightly the idea of transposing a people from one culture to another. The mission is a most active force for the preservation of Arapaho skills and traditions. It encourages the old dances and the powwows; the interior of the mission church is decorated in vivid Indian designs and colors and so, on occasion, is the exterior of Father Kurth, in vestments magnificently worked in Indian beading. Father Torres has said he wonders, sometimes, what they are doing, training the placid Indian to the "hurry, hurry-up pace of the white." But the Arapaho cannot go back, or even stay where he is, and, that being true, all that those trying to assist him can do is to equip him to go forward. Hence the work of educating him and the opening of the mission school to white children, as was done several years ago.

> *We are cooperating with the government in its effort to integrate the Indian into American society. In order to spare him the shock of coming into sudden contact with the white man upon leaving the reservation we brought the white man to the reservation so that our Indians can become accustomed to white ways under less disturbed circumstances. . . .*

St. Stephen's had figured out the best thing to do. The only trouble was hanging on to anybody long enough to do it. The Indians didn't stay very long in school.

By nature the Arapaho are a shy, quiet, good-tempered people, eager to please. But they are also proud and not to be put upon, and not given to doing anything they don't care to do. To maintain a relationship in which anything is hoped or required of them takes a great deal of experience, delicacy and infinite patience. If you rant at an Arapaho at Mass, he is less apt to repent than he is to simply leave and not come back. If you chide him too harshly in class, he may give up coming to school. And he may give up coming to school anyway, since he doesn't care for schooling particularly, and who's to make him come? Indian parents love their children extravagantly, and deny them little. They aren't apt to force school on them when it may seem as unnecessary to the parent as to the child, and as unnecessary to the Indian truant officer as the parent. "They just drift away from school," Father Zummach said, a little tiredly. "Nobody is sure why. Some teacher may have bawled them out and hurt their feelings, who knows?"

It is schooling, therefore, pretty much by consent of the schooled. This means that the fathers, in addition to devoting their lives to teaching and their spare time to building the school to do it in, had to find something that would draw the children to school and keep them coming and get them to study the lessons that didn't interest them. However intelligent, the Indian is not extremely quick and responsive—his heritage is one of reserve. And though the functioning of his culture may be out of date, his nature is still rooted in it, and the study of, say, geometry may not seem particularly applicable to life on the reservation. So the children had to be lured into an education predicated on the white man's goals, not on their own. It was Father Zummach who realized that the lure should be basketball.

Basketball already existed as a disorganized passion among the Indians. No Indian house was, or is, without its rim on a cottonwood tree in the yard. There is no backboard and no net, and the rim is often not regulation size but scaled to the proportions of the rubber ball a boy can have from the dime store. Philip (Little Star) Warren, St. Stephen's junior high coach, remembers practicing with a wire hoop and five-and-ten ball.

Father Zummach, as a start at mining this vein of motivation, began the Termite and Midget teams, for the 8-to-10- and 11-to-13-year-olds. Before long, boys so little that they had to be helped into them had their own uniforms and warm-ups. St. Stephen's exists by charity, which is to say it is poor, and the expense of uniforms for the present five basketball teams is no small matter. But they blaze in rows in the locker room of the new gymnasium, a powerful inducement to not cut school. ("It has surprised us that they get the 'no study, no eligibility' concept as effectively as they do.")

All in all, the Termite and Midget competition worked out very well, and in time the county athletic association adopted the classifications. More important, little St. Stephen's was laying in crops of ballplayers who reached varsity age with eight years of competitive experience behind them and, most important, boys who reached varsity age—and were still in school.

Then in 1957 Bill Strannigan arrived from the University of Wyoming to take over the coaching. It was his first job, and he was a spectacular success. There were only 50 children in the high school, 23 of them girls, but in 1959 and 1960 his varsity won the conference, district and state class B basketball titles. As for his track and football records, when Father Torres says of the mission teams that "last year they lost one game in the three sports in which they compete," he is understating the case, for "last year" was only the second year of existence for the football team, and the third for the track team that took the state championship. Strannigan got half his boys out for that first football team, and the fledglings won one game and lost six—the next year they won five and lost one. Football uniforms for the new team were begged from St. Louis University, which had given up football, and Rockhurst College in Kansas City, Mo., and the fathers made the football field. "It's where the plum trees were," said Father Kurth. "The plum trees never got to have any plums. The boys ate them green, or threw them. So we leveled the trees and seeded the field with Kentucky bluegrass. We fertilized it and took out the dandelions and the rocks by hand—it's the second most beautiful field in the Wyoming class B football league," he added, scrupulous in his pride. "It's bigger than a regulation field, so it doesn't get worn out. Of course, the little kids just running around in their bare feet aren't going to hurt it any."

The track team the first year had consisted of Mike Harris and Mickey Gamble, who picked up 23 points in the state meet. The next year the team was second in the state, and last year they took first.

As the basketball teams got better and better, boys drifted in from all over the reservation—down from Ethete, from Fort Washakie, to come to school where good ball was played, and the varsity was a championship team known all over Wyoming. It had been the right bait for St. Stephen's quarry. The fathers took Carl Patton with it. Carl was a Sioux. His parents had died, and he had wandered for years until he came to visit his uncle, Ted Charging Crow, who had married an Arapaho. Carl had never stayed for longer than 30 days in a high school, but he let Strannigan and St. Stephen's make an All-Stater out of him, and a high school graduate.

And down from Ethete came Shannon Brown. He had left school at Ethete, nobody knew why. It was presumed to have been the usual thing—harshness, an affront to his pride—and he showed up at St. Stephen's. There was a great deal of excitement about it. Everybody knew Shannon as a basketball player; his first game for St. Stephen's would be an event. The day came, and with it probably Strannigan's first gray hair. The game was with Morton High.

"Five minutes before game time," Strannigan recalls, "we're all there awaiting the unveiling of Shannon Brown, and he hasn't arrived at the gym. Two minutes from game time he showed up. We rushed him into the locker room and we waited, and he didn't come out. I finally went in and there he was, sitting in his regular clothes. I asked him what he was doing, and he said he wasn't feeling good. 'You were O.K. at school all day. What's the matter now?' I said. He wouldn't tell me. I wasn't reaching him, so I got another Indian, Lloyd Jenkins, to go in. He came out and said, 'Shannon doesn't want to play. He looked at the other team, and they weren't good enough. He doesn't want to play against little kids.' "

He didn't, of course. "Well, he would have killed them," Philip Warren said about it, but I couldn't tell whether he thought Shannon should or shouldn't have.

It was par for that early course. His first year Strannigan had to put in some time blundering around amongst the Indian sensitivities, finding out what, in their pride, would spur them on and what would make them quit. The time-honored "All right, you guys, if you don't want to play football, why don't you leave?" had, for instance, sent the football team home. "The basketball court is really the only place where the boys will take a scolding," Father Zummach observed. "They love it too much to quit. That's important—if they go out and get jobs, they'll have to know how to listen, and maybe be scolded." Occasionally the boys will quit even basketball, though. Sometimes Strannigan knows why and sometimes he doesn't, but he knows *when* they will. "It's their tennis shoes. It's all right if they take them home before a game, but if they take them home on a Monday, watch out!"

But progress had set in. A few of the Indian boys began to take showers without their underpants. A few of them parted with the knee pads (which the fathers had finally figured out they were wearing over dirty knees). Three years ago there had been one graduate from St. Stephen's, the year after that, two. Last year there were 14; and now at St. Stephen's there is George Spoonhunter. George is 17, characteristically shy, but very obviously a quick, bright boy. He is an all-round athlete—a pillar of the football, track and basketball teams. And an eager student. George Spoonhunter is thinking he would like to be a lawyer. The mission has almost an air of holding its breath, like a child who planted the seeds and did all the things it said to on the package. . . .

The difficulty is that Shannon wasn't planted soon enough. When he got to St. Stephen's he could hardly read, and it hurt his pride. He fell behind in English and would have had to make it up in summer school. And his 20th birthday fell on March 8—he would have been ineligible for the state tournament in any case. Father Dillon went to his house from time to time to bring him back—followed him down across the creek, into the brush, across the hedgerow, where Shannon would have gone looking for his father's buckskin horse—but still the mission lost him.

Of course, he's no more lost just because he was almost saved, I tell myself. And after all, it's not the most important thing. The mission is on the way to succeeding with the children and doing the whole community a great deal of good, and there is George Spoonhunter, who may go to college, maybe even beyond. So I congratulate the mission and wish the best for George—but somebody, give my love to Shannon Brown.

THE LEGEND OF CARR CREEK

It's sheer fiction that Carr Creek's 1928 players were all related and practiced barefoot in bib overalls on a frozen outdoor court with one basket attached to a tree and the other to the schoolhouse. But it is true that the tiny mountain school with an enrollment of eight boys lost to eventual national champion Ashland in a four-overtime 1928 Kentucky state final, capturing hearts from coast to coast in the process. Carr Creek won the state title in '56 and went out of existence in '74. Dave Kindred traces the story in his 1976 book, Basketball, the Dream Game in Kentucky. *It follows.*

I tried to find out when the first basketball game was played in Kentucky. It would be impressive, even scholarly, to say the game reached Kentucky on Nov. 19, 1892, when a young Kansan named Adolph Rupp nailed up a bourbon barrel and threw a Hereford into it. I found nothing of the sort (possibly because Rupp wasn't born until 1901). History freaks who pick up this book must be satisfied with the one date I consider important and memorable in the love affair Kentucky has with basketball. On March 18, 1928, the Carr Creek High School team lost to Ashland, 13 to 11, in four overtime periods in a game at Lexington for the state championship. Carr Creek was Cinderella in sneakers, and whenever romantics speak of small-town teams like Tolu and Heath, Corinth and Sharpe, Cuba and Brewers and Inez—all those ragged urchins who won our hearts—we can never forget the Creekers.

In '28 Carr Creek was a community of maybe 200 people. The school sat on a ledge carved out of the side of a mountain in Knott County. Of the 15 students, eight were boys.

Mules pulling shovels dug out a level place for the boys to play basketball. One goal was on a chicken shed, the other on a railroad tie. Ellis Johnson, a star player for Ashland in '28 and later an all-America at Kentucky and a successful college coach, once said he knew why the Carr Creekers handled the ball so well: "The sides of their outdoor court dropped off a hill maybe 75 to 100 feet down. If a kid threw a ball away or fumbled it, he had a long climb. That pretty much discouraged careless passes."

Carr Creek had no gymnasium. There was an auditorium. "That's where we had chapel every day, reading the Bible and all," said Gurney Adams, a guard on the '28 Creekers. "We had baskets in there, in case it rained or snowed outdoors. Only trouble was, the durned ceiling wasn't but 12 feet high. You couldn't put much arch on a shot." For games, Carr Creek traveled by mule-drawn log wagon as far as the dirt roads went. They then proceeded by foot over the mountains, maybe five or six miles. It was an event of everlasting moment when the Creekers caught a train to Hazard, 20 miles away, and stayed overnight in a hotel.

They had no basketball uniforms. Legend says the mountain men played in bib overalls, which sounds quaint enough, but another report has them wearing white undershirts and khaki pants. The team's coach was Oscar Morgan, a grade school teacher whose basketball credentials consisted of attendance at a few games while studying at Centre College.

Through the semifinals of the 1928 regional tournament at Richmond, Carr Creek had won 14 games without a defeat, and its run-run-run style of play, both on offense and in a man-to-man pressing defense, so captivated the people of Richmond that they pitched in to buy the Creekers real uniforms, at a cost of $55, for the championship game. Victory there sent Carr Creek into the state tournament at Lexington.

The tournament then was in its 11th year. Lexington and Louisville schools had won nine of the first 10 championships, and in '28 the favorites were Louisville St. Xavier, Lawrenceburg and Ashland. That changed quickly enough, for the Creekers promptly dispatched their first three opponents by scores of 31 to 11, 21 to 11 and 37 to 11. Meanwhile Ashland, also undefeated, won, 16 to 8, 25 to 13 and 22 to 13.

The night of March 18, 1928, came up foul. It snowed and sleeted. Yet more than 4,000 customers stuffed the University of Kentucky's 3,500-seat Alumni Gym for the state championship game. Carr Creek led at halftime by the score of 4 to 3, which was unusually low even in those days of the center jump. The lack of scoring was attributed to Ashland's zone defense and Carr Creek's man-to-man press. Neither team had been up against the like before.

Ashland moved to a 9 to 6 lead early in the fourth quarter. But with three minutes left, Gillis Madden sank a long shot for Carr Creek. Then, with 30 seconds left, Shelby Stamper's free throw tied the game at 9–all. Through three overtime periods neither team scored.

Ashland took an 11 to 9 lead early in the fourth overtime on Gene Strothers' layup. Unable to penetrate Ashland's zone and growing desperate, Carr Creek missed a long shot. Then Ashland's Ellis Johnson began killing the clock by dribbling from one end of the floor to the other (there was no mid-court line then). Eventually Johnson worked loose for a layup, and Ashland led, 13 to 9. Carr Creek retained a measure of hope when Stamper made a long shot with a minute to play, but Ashland controlled the subsequent tip and Johnson dribbled away the time.

Forty-six years later a visitor to Carr Creek asked Gurney Adams about that defeat. "It was rough," Adams said. He twisted his face at the sour memory. "I'd have liked to play 'em again up there in Chicago."

The Creekers visited the Windy City. Cinderella went big-time. Both Ashland and Carr Creek were invited to a national high school tournament at the University of Chicago. The Creekers had taken their first train ride out of Kentucky, and now they were to see a moving box called an elevator. In the 40-team tournament they quickly became the favorite of the crowd, which included a young Illinois high school coach named Adolph Rupp.

Carr Creek won its first two games. It beat the U.S. Indian School of Albuquerque, N.M., 32 to 16, and Austin, Tex., 25 to 18. Another victory would have produced a rematch with Ashland, but the Creekers lost to Vienna, Ga., 22 to 11. Ashland went on to win the tournament, finishing the season undefeated in 37 games.

Basketball in the mountains of eastern Kentucky, basketball as Carr Creek played it, once was the standard of excellence for the state. In the 17 state tournaments from 1940 to 1956, mountain schools won seven championships: Hazel Green in '40, Inez in '41 and '54, Hindman in '43, Harlan in '44, Hazard in '55 and Carr Creek in '56. But in the 19 state tournaments following Carr Creek's victory, not a single mountain school even made it to the championship game. Louisville schools won 11 titles in that time and finished second six times.

"I have a theory on that," said R.B. Singleton, once a player at Carr Creek and principal there when the school closed down in 1974. "People say the kids nowadays have other things to do. Cars and that. But, really, around Carr Creek there's *nothing*—except basketball. My theory is that we were ahead of our time back then. We had kids playing basketball in the fifth grade. A feeder system. Well, now Louisville does that, too. And they have so many more kids to choose from."

There are other ideas. Integration, for one. Carr Creek's championship was earned in the last year that Kentucky kept black high schools out of the state tournament. Once allowed to play, black teams have been dominant. The last all-white team to win was Shelby County in 1966. From 1970 through 1975, the state champions did not have a single white player on the starting team.

"The day of the small school is over in Kentucky," said Jock Sutherland, a veteran of 20 years in high school coaching. "The black element has changed the game—black quickness, black endurance and the black athlete's ability to be uninhibited.

"Whether anyone wants to admit that or not, it's so. Especially in the metropolitan areas. Outside the metropolitan areas, Kentucky high school basketball is not as strong as it was. But in the cities it's much stronger than it's ever been."

Soon there will be very few small schools. Consolidation already has reduced the number of Kentucky high schools from over 500 to about 300. Cinderella's time has passed. A man went to Carr Creek in March of 1974 for the school's last basketball game. The next year Carr Creek students attended Knott County Central High.

"It's sad, to know this is the last year," said Dale Combs, whose husband, Morton, coached the '56 Creekers. The Combs' home was a bounce pass away from Carr Creek High.

"Morton's and my whole life has been in that building," she said. "Morton raised money himself to build toilets and to add a home economics department. And the gym—the people built it with their own hands."

Warren Amburgey played on that '56 team. So his son could play where the father's dream came true, Amburgey quit his job of 16 years in Louisville, borrowed money and bought a plumbing business between Hindman and Carr Creek. Donnie Amburgey was Carr Creek's leading scorer in '74.

"Donnie lived down here with his grandparents for his freshman year," Amburgey said. "We thought he'd come back to Louisville, but he never did." The father seemed proud of that.

Amburgey came to Carr Creek every weekend that next year. It's a 460-mile round trip. "I worked the night shift. So I'd look for a job here until Monday noon, then head back to Louisville."

Donnie Amburgey kept his father's scrapbook. "We used to talk about how he played for Carr Creek," he said. "And I wanted to, too."

With 14 seconds to play and Carr Creek behind, 77 to 62, in the last game the school would ever play, Dale Combs touched a finger first to her left eye, then to her right, as if wiping away tears.

"I was," the coach's wife said. "I hoped nobody would notice. I sat there thinking, 'No more Carr Creek.' "

Warren Amburgey was in the top row of the bleachers. "It's the end of the Creekers," he said. He spoke softly. "It's hurtful."

From Dave Kindred, *Basketball, the Dream Game in Kentucky* (Louisville, Ky.: Data Courier, 1976), 23–29.

GIRLS WIN, BOYS LOSE

Iowa girls' basketball was a high-caliber, fever-pitch activity long before ERA and Title IX. The state's first tournament series for girls occurred in 1920, the year of woman suffrage. Iowa teams have always favored the original six-player rules, under which only the forwards are allowed to shoot while the three guards are restricted to their half-court. This is a high-scoring game and deeply traditional. The fans in the farm towns like it that way. In 1984 Iowa relaxed its rules: its girls' teams could thereupon opt for either the six-player or the five-player game, leaving Oklahoma temporarily the only state still going the six-girl route exclusively. But tradition prevailed; the old rules were too ingrained on the prairie to be scrapped by a vote. The following story, by Douglas Bauer, captures the spirit of Iowa's intertown rivalries, equally ingrained. It appeared in Sports Illustrated *in 1978.*

The trophy case in the old Prairie City, Iowa gym was of light pine, shellacked to a deep glaze. It was tucked into an alcove inside the front door, the statues and plaques crowded into it arranged in tiers like a chorus. Stylized halfbacks, forwards and sprinters, perpetually frozen in midstride, midmotion, stared through the glass. The largest trophy was in the center of the second row. Adorned with pennants and a couple of eagles, it stood at least six inches taller than the others, and it was topped with a figurine of a woman raising a basketball, about to go in for a layup. Her uniform had a lot of folds and pleats, and there was a certain timidity about the modeling, which brought to mind old anatomical drawings in health textbooks that fade to pastel blanks in certain areas. But she was clearly female, clearly moving to the basket. The base of the trophy was emblazoned:

GIRLS' DISTRICT CHAMPIONS
1948
PRAIRIE CITY HIGH SCHOOL

No Prairie City team before or after has played its sport as well. Following its 1948 district championship, Prairie City competed in the Iowa High School Girls' State Championship, one of 16 teams from rural villages with populations in the hundreds to do so that year. Prairie City was beaten in the first round by the team that became state champion and, according to enduring local belief, would have been the champion itself if its coach had not stayed with a strategy so plainly wrong that the memory of it still rankles many of those who watched the game.

"He put Mona out front where she couldn't. . . . Guy's about as smart as a board fence. . . . Couldn't rebound out there. . . . Four fouls. . . . Fellow's brains wouldn't cover the bottom of a coffee cup." That's the sort of thing you hear if you bring the subject up at the co-op filling station when Dick Zaayer or Don Sparks is there.

For those too young to have been witnesses, it has never been clear just *what* the coach did, beyond losing the championship. But what's important to know is that a powerful feeling about it has survived; that in this remote central Iowa town the idea of girls playing basketball can heat a conversation with emotions free of any condescension. One could grow up in the town in the late 1950s and early '60s, as I did, watching girls' sports without the least notion that there was anything prophetic about a custom that in small Iowa farming towns is as deeply embedded in the psyche as the suspicion of skies and the certainty that a stranger is a Democrat.

Prairie City's girls usually had better seasons than its boys. When I was in grade school and went with my father to watch Janet Wilson release her fluid hook shot, the girls' team nearly always won. The boys, playing afterward, usually lost. And so we drove home with predictable dispatches. Mother, in a cone of reading light in her living-room chair, looked up as we came into the house and said, "Well?"

"Girls won, boys lost."

Girls won, boys lost. Girls won, boys lost. Tuesday and Friday nights. Season after season.

In fact, most nights the boys had their best moment while the girls' game was still being played. Almost all the high school students sat together in a section near the southwest corner of the gym. At the end of the third quarter, those boys who played basketball rose up like suddenly blooming plants. Because the game had stopped, attention was directed to the stir in the bleachers, and the boys played to it for all it was worth, stretching to full height with elaborate indolence. There seemed to be the hard-bitten courage of soldiers in their rising: "Love to stay but the Huns are waiting." They slowly walked in single file the length of the floor, took a right, walked the width of the floor and disappeared into their dressing room.

After the girls' game was over, the boys came out and got beat 68–37. But, Lord, they walked like champions. Naturally, then, my grade school heroes were Janet Wilson; Joellen Wassenaar, a quick, knife-thin girl, her limbs milk-white stems, who faked a jumper and drove to either side; Margaret Morhauser, the powerful guard. I took notice of the way Judy Kutchin folded her sweat socks—down, then up again—so they formed snowy tufts above her shoes, and I resolved to wear, as Joellen did, only one (left) knee pad.

I was not alone in my adoration. In Iowa the girls' state championships draw better than the boys' tournament, invariably filling the 15,000 seats in Veteran's Memorial Auditorium, Des Moines, for five days in March. One could argue that the scheduling of the girls' games before the boys' in Prairie City implied the girls were a warmup act, a preview. But I have a clear memory of looking up into the balcony, its bleachers rising like a cliff wall, where the farmers and merchants, the town's strongest fans, sat in the dim, atticy light. Many of them put on their coats after the girls' game had ended. They knew they had just seen the best basketball they would watch that evening, and they were going home. Let the boys lose in front of their parents and their girl friends.

As it's played in Iowa high schools, girls' basketball differs significantly from the boys' game. There are six players to a team: three forwards who remain all evening on one half court, with the sole responsibility for the offense, and three guards who do nothing but guard the opponent's forwards.

After a score, the ball returns to mid-court, is handed to the other team, and a second half-court game begins. No one crosses the midcourt line. It is inviolable. Stepping over it or on it constitutes a turnover. With a half-court of momentum, a player must brake furiously once she reaches the line. Frantic ballets are danced all along it. A girl often looks as if she's teetering dangerously at a roof's edge as she strives to remain on her side of the court.

The other distinctive rules include one that stipulates that a girl must stop after two dribbles and pass or shoot. The game takes on a high syncopation. Bounce, bounce, pass. Bounce, pass, shoot. The two-dribble rule is the 24-second clock of the game; it accelerates it, raises its scores. Only a few seconds elapse between shots. The best teams frequently score 100 points. The best players sometimes score 100 points.

Various factors—the rules, the range of young women's accuracy—keep the game near the basket. Twelve-to-15-foot jump shots predominate and field-goal percentages are consequently high. A girl who cannot shoot 60% has a future as a guard.

But there's more, some believe, to the girls' accuracy than the short distances from which they shoot. (From the free-throw line, eight of 10 or nine of 10 is routine. A girl who expects to win the annual state free-throw contest cannot afford to miss any of her 25 attempts. After a first perfect round, she will advance to a playoff.) One of the state's most successful coaches once claimed that girls have a unique sensitivity in the tips of their fingers.

"They're born with it," he says fervently. "They have something in their fingers boys don't have. Call it a gift, a feel, a fine tuning. Look at a girl's hands—soft, delicate. They're just better shooters. That's a fact that's clear as a sparrow's dew."

The Pentagon recently issued a report that says women soldiers throw hand grenades more accurately than men. Thousands of Iowans were, no doubt, not at all surprised.

Year after year the Prairie City girls fought Colfax for the Rock Lake Conference title. Only six miles of undulating farmland separates the towns. Their teams had played each other—all sports, both sexes—for many years, and were nearly always closely matched. Colfax, which is the larger of the towns, with a couple of thousand people, had a legacy of railroads and coal mines and a reputation as a rough and mean-spirited place. Its inhabitants, many of them no further than a generation removed from the dead mines, drank and cursed and took menacing energy from the phases of the moon. And so, with the passing of genes, did the children who were the members of Colfax' teams.

Prairie City was reserved and humorless, predominantly influenced by a Dutch Reformed faith that found sin in dances, movies and playing cards. Secular happiness came from one's work, and if one hadn't felt a blood-rushing joy after lifting 80 bales of hay, then he should lift an 81st.

Three sour-faced Colfax guards, a kind of delinquent malice in their manner and expressions, remain memorable. They had sallow complexions and bags under their eyes that hinted of late hours and bad diets. Their hair was black, short, tucked behind their ears like matted wings. They had names like Flo and Martha Lynn and Irma. They were sinewy and quick, and they worked together with the precision of the machinery in a watch. It seemed to me as if they played for Colfax for about 12 years, a running presence through all the seasons of my memory. They were mean.

Here is a moment from their play, from the countless heated evenings of claustrophobic tension that Prairie City vs. Colfax inspired. Judy Kutchin stood with the ball at the top of the key, a teammate positioned on her right near the sideline. Her center, stationed beneath the basket, is swinging now parabolically toward the free-throw line. Kutchin passes to her teammate on her right and cuts for the basket. Right-sideline passes to center, ball and girl arriving simultaneously at the line. Center looks for Kutchin racing by. Give and go. A formulistic score. The classic maneuver of the game. Prairie City's fans are up to cheer, having already finished the play, having added the two points.

No! Flo springs from a crouch behind our center and roughly strips Kutchin of the ball. Martha Lynn comes rushing over like a vulture. Irma is angling upcourt, a receiver. Unanimous action against the grain. Martha Lynn sweeps up the ball and fires to Irma, who passes to one of her forwards waiting at the center line. It's done in a split second and with the timing of conspiratorial street thieves. Flo, Martha Lynn, Irma nod cooly. No doubt they'll committee-lip a cigarette after the game.

But just as often, Kutchin took the pass, deftly moved past the mugging and scored. Two for Calvinism.

When I was in high school, I sat in the student section, stood melodramatically at the end of the third quarter, walked the length of the court, took a right, walked its width and entered the dressing room. I was a bad basketball player, having neither size nor speed. Yet the school was so small that I won a uniform, a place on the 12-man squad and made the ceremonial walk with the rest of a mediocre team. I played perhaps three minutes and 12 seconds of high school varsity basketball. But I wore a knee pad, left knee only.

I was in love all the way through high school with Sue. She had a clean, petite beauty. She had a lilting laugh. She had large green eyes and soft, light-brown hair. She had breathtakingly shapely legs. She also had very quick feet and hands that could slap at a basketball like a rattler's tongue. She was an all-conference guard. When she graduated, she was given a trophy as Prairie City High School's best female athlete.

On the eve of a game, we would drive from school to her home in my 1951 semi-automatic Dodge. We would park in front and look out into the early-falling dark toward her unlit house. Sue's mother, a widow, had a job in Des Moines and did not get home until an hour or so after school was dismissed.

"Can I come in?"

"Not tonight," Sue would say, smiling. "Coach says we should rest. If we win tomorrow night, we'll be tied with Pleasantville."

"Just to talk?"

"We're talking right here." Not only her feet were quick.

"What do you want to do this weekend?"

"Depends. If we lose, Coach says we might have Saturday practice."

"Who you guarding tomorrow night?"

"Sandy Sampson. She's good. Has a good jump shot from the side of the lane. But she can't drive to her left. I'll overplay her, force her to the left, and it should be all right. Of course, if she's hot from out. . . ."

As she talked, I would gradually incline my head toward hers.

". . . it won't be as effective, and I'll have to try to keep a hand—what are you doing?" And she would execute as neat a head fake as Pete Maravich.

No one cheered louder than I did during the girls' games, not only for the good of the school but also for the hope that Sue would have Saturday night off and could journey 25 miles to the blinking neon of Des Moines. Streetlights, movies, pizza afterward. "None for me. Coach says it slows you half a step." I cheered as well for Sue's mood that followed a win, because she was not an athlete who left her game in the dressing room.

It mattered little to me who won the boys' game. We were at best a .500 team and another loss could not set back nonexistent title chances. And, as a substitute who had been given a place on the team mostly for the sake of symmetry, I became insulated from events on the floor. So after an evening's exercise that consisted of warming up twice and, if the outcome of the game was settled early, playing the final 27 seconds, I left the dressing room showered and eager for companionship.

Sue's play, however, always had an important influence on the outcome, and she was in the lineup—working, stealing, fighting through picks—every second. If Prairie City lost, she was disconsolate and exhausted. If the team won, she was thrilled and exhausted. Neither condition allowed me much companionship, except to help her ease her spent body onto her living-room couch.

One night we sat on the couch in her darkened living room, close but not touching. There was a gap between us, one as narrow and nearly as inviolate as the center line in the game she had just played. Outside, students' cars were ritualistically roaming the streets after the game, their glass-packed exhausts deafeningly resonant. Her gloom was on every surface like a dull wax.

"It's O.K. It's O.K.," I said. "You played great. It wasn't your. . . ."

"I played lousy. Sampson got 38 points. She drove on me like I was nailed to the floor."

"You couldn't hold her by yourself. You forced her to the left. You should have gotten some help from Ramona on that side."

"Coach told Ramona to stay put in the middle. Coach figured if we could keep Sampson going left, I would be able to handle her one-on-one."

Minutes passed. Outside, the engines throbbed at full volume. Finally, hoping against hope that the fog of her mood had lifted, I turned to her and whispered, "Whatcha thinking?"

"Oh, if I'd played *up* on her, nose to nose, hassled her as soon as she got the ball, then she wouldn't have had time to set up. She might have forced a shot."

There were lessons to be learned from those nights on the sagging maroon couch trying to console an all-conference guard who believed her play alone had led to a loss. Among the lessons were some first tentative feelings for the full equality of the sexes, for responsibilities. Free of any blame for the boys' team's performance,

I said whatever comforting words there were to say and, mostly, listened. At the same time, I suppressed a deep wish to be able to trade the reserve's sweat-free innocence for the exhausted burden of Sue's talent. How great it would be to be so good that a bad night was the reason one's team had lost.

In the past dozen years, Prairie City has grown to a population of 1,200, an increase of 25%. New homes dot the streets, mixed in among the old ones like young buds. There is new construction everywhere, notably the new school building and its gymnasium.

The team's most recent star was a senior forward, Virginia McFadden, and her play was favorably compared by the men gathered in Harold (Hoop) Timmons' office beneath the co-op grain silos with Janet Wilson's, with Judy Kutchin's, even, hyperbolically, with Mona Van Steenbergen's. Mona was the leader of the 1948 state tournament team and is a member of the Iowa Girls' High School Basketball Hall of Fame. Virginia was shorter, smaller, one heard, but quick and tough and a shooter pure as back-porch butter.

"I'd say she's got it over Mona," said a farmer seated near a whining space heater. He placed both hands inside the bib of his overalls and his arms flapped for emphasis like a dwarf's.

Hoop thought about it. "I ain't so sure," he said. "The game's a whole lot faster now, so you think of Mona being slow, but she could move. Those long legs of hers."

"Smooth," said another farmer. "Smooth is what Mona was."

"This girl scores more points," said the first farmer.

Hoop, an air of verdict about him, said, "You could argue it till you're silly as a pet coon." He looked up and saw a tractor hauling grain heading for his silos. "You gentlemen are free to stay," he said, looking as he spoke for the Folger's coffee can, bottom-lined with kernels, on the floor near the heater. His spittoon. He found it and wet the kernels with a stream of Red Man. "I got to go to work."

Outside, Hoop waited near the deep grate-covered hole into which the grain would be unloaded. The tractor came up to him and moved past, big as a house, pulling two wagons with mountains of grain sloping above their tops. The tractor roared and then abruptly quieted as it negotiated the narrow space between the silos. Idling, it came to a stop precisely above the hole. Most farmers bringing their grain in brake too abruptly, setting their wagons into clangorous jerking, but this movement was clean, light, agile. Hoop raised the wagon doors, let loose the hissing fall of grain and waved to the driver. A broad, comradely wave, appreciative of the skill that made his own work easy: over the hole, open it up, let it drop.

From inside the tractor's cab, the driver, Virginia's mother, returned Hoop's salutation. She had shown where Virginia got her touch. "Call it a gift, a feel, a fine tuning. . . . They have something in their fingers a boy doesn't have."

Like all games, girls' basketball has become swifter and surer with the years. But all that has fundamentally changed is the size of the schools playing the game. The larger Iowa cities, some with three and four high schools, now have teams, and there is fear that these schools, with more money, better facilities, a greater pool of players, will dominate the tiny farming towns. The New York Yankee syndrome. In the face of that fear, coaches in the small schools place their belief in the enduring will of the rural athlete. "It seems to me," said the coach of a small Iowa school that almost always makes the tournament, "that a farm girl still knows how to *hurt* a little more."

At the north end of Colfax, near the junction of Highway 117 and Interstate 80, there is a diner popular with long-distance truckers and farmers. On a recent visit, I pulled in for Iowa eggs and bacon before going onto the interstate. As I walked inside I saw three women clustered around the cash register. They were huddled, as if planning some strategy. They wore the pink cotton uniforms of the diner. Sallow complexions, bags beneath their eyes. Lithe and poised for play. Flo, Martha Lynn and Irma.

"Scramble two, whole wheat, extra sausage," yelled the cook from her window at the back, placing a plate of food on a serving sill. The waitresses broke from their huddle. "Hot pork on white, mashed, extra gravy," yelled the cook, placing another plate beside the first. Flo picked up the eggs and headed for her customer on the left side of the horseshoe-shaped counter. Martha Lynn, sweeping up the hot-pork plate, fell in a step behind her. Irma, with a coffee pot, worked the right side, moving down the counter of empty cups, dipping the pot as if she were watering a row of plants.

"Hiya, Flo," said a trucker, frisky with sleep or pills to fight it. "Howya doing?" He reached a hand for Flo's hip as she swished past with the haste of a woman at work. Flo gave the trucker a quick move and left his hand pinching air. Martha Lynn, a step behind, knowing the move, did not break stride. "Watch the hand, honey," she said to the trucker, " 'less you want hot pork in your ear." And she moved on swiftly with her plate, handing, as she walked, another customer's check to Irma, who had finished her coffee refills and stood up front at the register, waiting for the pass.

Girls win, boys lose. Girls win, boys lose.

From Douglas Bauer, "Girls Win, Boys Lose," ***Sports Illustrated*****, March 6, 1978, 34–40. Reprinted by permission of the author.**

"BLACK NEWS AIN'T NEWS"

That was the prevailing sentiment in many newsrooms and among other segments of society a generation ago. It helped shape the attitudes of Elvin Hayes as he grew up in Louisiana in the fifties and sixties. This story is from They Call Me "The Big E" *by Hayes and Bill Gilbert (Prentice-Hall, Inc., 1978).*

I was headed down the path of so many others by the time I was in the seventh and eighth grades. I was running with a bad crowd and getting into minor scrapes that would surely lead to more serious trouble as I grew older. That's the path to a life of working on a cotton farm and getting drunk every Saturday night and maybe winding up shot and killed. That's the way I could have gone. But I didn't, for two reasons: Reverend Calvin and basketball.

Rev. John Calvin was one of the teachers at Eulah Britton High School. He was also a Methodist minister. He knew my mother and all my aunts and uncles, and he knew all my brothers and sisters who had gone through Britton ahead of me. I must have set a new Britton record for getting sent home. I was forever getting into trouble in class. One day in the eighth grade I was on my way to the office after getting kicked out of class—again—when Rev. Calvin spotted me in the hall. He went with me to the office and stuck up for me, mostly as a favor to my mother. Then he did two things that probably changed the course of my life. He arranged to have me transferred to his room, and he put me on the eighth-grade basketball team, which he coached.

He didn't do it without a warning, though. "I'm going to put your tail in my classroom," he told me, "and if you ever give me any trouble, I'm going to beat you or kill you." He wouldn't have, but I got the message. Rev. Calvin drew me away from the bad crowd I had been running with. He turned me around.

The following summer I started getting some fun out of basketball. When Rev. Calvin put me on his team at school, he made me a guard because I was still on the small side. It really wasn't that much fun for me, because I didn't have any idea what I was doing or why I was doing it. But that summer I began to acquire some of the basic skills and learn a little about the rules, so things started to make sense and added up to fun for me.

For the first time in my life, I started to play basketball instead of baseball in the summer. I was still running out the back door, hoping to escape Mrs. Menthy's eyes across the street and jumping over our 6-foot fence instead of opening the gate, only now I wasn't headed for that oat field. Now I was headed for the basketball court.

We weren't allowed to go over to the white school and play on the outdoor court there. We had to use the one at Britton. The white school was forbidden territory for us. It was against the law for us to walk on their grass, and we'd get arrested if we ever tried to play on their basketball court, but they could come over to Britton and rip out the windows and nobody said or did anything about it. They had seven or eight baskets on their outdoor court, with real chain nets and a tin backboard and a paved playing surface. We had just one raggedy old wooden backboard nailed to an old light pole with a flimsy rim that wobbled every time a shot hit it. The wooden backboard seemed to become more warped every time it rained, and our playing surface wasn't paved. It was plain old Louisiana dirt. But we played there and had more fun than you can imagine. We had only a few balls. The Ricks boys down the street had one, and Larry Ward had one—outdoor rubber balls. I never had one, but as long as one or two families could afford one, that's all we needed.

I'd get up every morning that summer and shake off the rats which crawled into bed with me every night and race down to play some more basketball. By the time I was a junior in high school, I was building my ability and my confidence and I was suddenly 6 feet 2 inches tall. My mother's side of the family had finally taken over, just in time for high school.

Our high school gym was a joke, but it was home to us. It's "The Crackerbox," and it's not one bit better than the gym Bill Cosby talks about in one of his comedy routines. He and his buddies in Philadelphia weren't any worse off than we were in Louisiana. The floor was cement tile. If you were brave enough—or stupid enough—to try a layup, you went crashing into a brick wall right behind the basket at either end. Pads? That was for sissies and rich schools. No pads for us, just that hard brick wall staring you in the face when you came driving in for that layup. It didn't bother us. We were a fast-break team, and all of us were on very close terms with those walls.

You wouldn't believe how much basketball we were playing by the time I was a junior. We were in tournaments every weekend, plus our regular weekly schedule. Sometimes we'd play three or four games in one day in a weekend tournament. We'd get to the site of the tournament at 8 in the morning, play a game at 9, another at 12, another at 4 and the championship game—which we were always in—at 8. It all added up to 55 or 60 games a season. It also added up to a lot of stamina for me, as I became used to playing a lot of games, and almost every minute of each game, running that fast break all the time. I'm sure that's why I'm able to be among the NBA leaders every year now in minutes played and can keep on running every minute I'm in there. That's my nature, and all that playing in high school developed it.

Basketball was a maturing process for me emotionally as well as physically. I learned to endure adversity, like my deep disappointment in my junior year when we went all the way to the state finals and played the championship game over at Grambling College just 50 miles from home—and lost, to DeQuincy. I cried on the bus going home, and the knowledge that we were losing three seniors from our starting five didn't do anything to stop my tears. I didn't think we'd have nearly that good a chance to win the state championship in my senior year, so I cried some more. It was a long bus ride.

Things have a way of evening up in athletics. We fielded a team at least as good as the previous one, strong and fast with a lot of talent, including my best friend,

Ronnie Jenkins. We raced our way through 53 straight wins, running up and down the cement floor of "The Crackerbox," avoiding those brick walls at either end and winning every weekend tournament we could find all over the state.

At the end of the season, there we were, still undefeated and playing in the final game for the state championship, just like the year before. Only this time we were playing in Baton Rouge, the state capital, our opponent was DeRidder and I was about to learn something.

The night before the championship game, after both our teams had won their semifinals, I was in a malt shop when DeRidder's center, Jessie Marshall, came in. Now I was used to seeing all types of players in those state finals, like the 30-year-old ringers who were recalled from retirement every year to play for their old high schools. But Jessie Marshall was the biggest high school player I had ever seen. He was 6 feet 8 inches tall—3 inches over me—and he weighed 230 pounds, 40 pounds on me. He was as intimidating with his mouth as he was with his size. He confronted me and threatened to blow us out the next night and shut me down. I was so scared I couldn't sleep that night.

The championship game came, and Jessie Marshall picked up where his mouth left off the night before. He was scoring over me, blocking my shots and making me totally useless. Our coach finally had his fill of my performance—and Jessie's—and called timeout. He spent almost the whole 60 seconds chewing me out and demanding to know if I was going to let Jessie do that to me all night.

"You going to let him do that?" he hollered. "Are you scared of that big old boy?"

Then he slapped me in the face.

The timeout ended, and I took the court again, knowing I was on the spot. I decided to put my tormentor on that spot, so I started taking the game to him. I became much more aggressive than I had ever been, scoring over Jessie and around him and behind him. I scored 45 points and dominated my opponent even more by grabbing more than 20 rebounds. My pants were too big, and every time I went up for a shot, my pants started to fall off. I spent the rest of the game shooting with my right hand and holding my pants up with my left. A few times I made a lefthanded layup to prove I could hold my pants up with either hand.

It all ended like a perfect dream. We won by more than 20 points, and I was voted the tournament's most valuable player. The next day the Baton Rouge paper carried a long story about the finals, and the first paragraph said something like:

> *Elvin Hayes scored 45 points as Eulah Britton High School of Rayville defeated DeRidder for the state AA championship last night.*

It was the first time my name was ever in the paper. I was so excited I was almost jumping out of my skin. I bought all the copies I could carry. Back home in Rayville, no black player ever got his name in the paper. Never, including this time.

The lesson I learned that night is still with me. I take the floor for every game confident I can beat my man and determined to do it. This feeling grew in intensity when I started playing freshman ball at the University of Houston. Don Chaney was my teammate, and we were the first two black players in the history of the school. We knew we couldn't just be as good as everyone else—we had to be better because we were black. I took the court for the first two games that season with a vow to destroy my opponent. And that's still my vow before every game.

Winning that state championship made me a celebrity at home, even though the papers around Rayville and Monroe never printed one line about it. It didn't make any difference. Everyone knew about it. They didn't run a story the night I scored 67 points for Britton in one game either, but everyone found out about that, too.

The one difference it could have made was in my chances for a scholarship to college. An athlete's career success depends not only on his or her ability but other people's knowledge of it. While Kareem Abdul-Jabbar, then going by the name of Lew Alcindor, was getting even national attention playing for Power Memorial High School in New York and other high school stars were getting publicity in their own parts of the country, here I was scoring 67 points in one game, averaging 35, playing on a team that was to go undefeated in 54 games and win the state championship, and I couldn't get my name in the paper, not even once.

I was convinced more than ever after my junior year in high school that I just had to get out of Rayville, and a basketball scholarship was going to be my ticket. All my sisters and brothers had been salutatorians or valedictorians of their graduating classes at Britton, and I had been on the honor roll every semester in high school and had scored the highest mark in the history of the school on our aptitude tests, but I chose basketball as my way out. It would help, though, if some of those colleges were reading about me.

Well, it turned out that they were hearing about me through their own grapevine and they didn't need newspapers. The scouts were in the stands every game I played in my senior year. It was always easy for me to know they were there. All I had to do was look at the crowd. They were the white guys.

I was shooting every kind of shot imaginable and from every spot on the floor. I played forward, guard and center in high school, and I could hit from anywhere. So could the rest of the guys. We played 8-minute quarters, and there I was scoring 67 one night and the team topping 130 another night. I was shooting from the corners, the top of the key, all over, with jumpers, hooks and layups. Other teams tried to stop us with a zone, but it never did any good. I'd shoot them out of it.

All this time I was working by myself on what today is my trademark—my turn-around jumper. I guess I really didn't invent that shot, but I'm sure I developed it. Now the writers and announcers identify it with me. When they talk about the sky hook, they say Kareem Abdul-Jabbar. When they talk about the slam-dunk, they say Wilt Chamberlain. And when they talk about the turn-around jumper, they say Elvin Hayes.

I developed that shot because I wasn't real strong in putting up a shot when I was away from the basket. I was scoring from the outside, but I still thought I needed more power. It occurred to me to try to get up in the air and turn around at the same time, then put it up, all in one coordinated act of shooting. All summer long between my junior and senior years in high school I worked on it—every day on that dirt outdoor court at Britton, always banking the shot off those tin backboards and through the crooked hoops. Gradually the coordination came, and so did new strength through my shoulders. By the time I started my senior season at Britton,

I could hit on the turn-around jumper often enough that confidence was developing along with the ability.

You can't stop that shot. Everybody tries, but nobody can—not if you shoot it right. Your back is to the basket, which means your back is also to your opponent, so he can't get to the ball. Your man doesn't see the ball until you've turned around and you are going up with the shot, the ball over your head. By then it's too late. The only thing he can do is foul you.

The funny thing is that after I developed that shot, I didn't really need it my last year at Britton because I had become stronger and was able to hit from anywhere on the floor. But the turn-around jumper became extremely valuable to me during my freshman year at Houston, because so many of my opponents were bigger and stronger than I was. So I resorted to the turn-around jumper and kept right on scoring—zip, zip, zip—over their heads. When I was a senior at Houston, I scored 62 points in one game against VMI, and I was shooting nothing but the turn-around jumper—zip, zip, zip—all night long. As a matter of fact, I became too dependent on it in college. In my early years in the NBA, I forced myself to start taking other kinds of shots as well. Now I'm back to shooting from outside more than ever, from the corners and just off the circle, but the turn-around jumper is always ready whenever I want to use it, and I do—every game.

With no publicity, the college scouts still managed to find out about me, and they kept sending letters to my coach, which I never saw because he didn't want me to feel the pressure. I received 75 to 100 offers of scholarships, mostly from schools in the Southeastern Conference, the Southwest Conference and the Big 10. Grambling was too close to home, and enough of my brothers and sisters had already attended Southern University, so I selected the University of Houston. It was one of the best decisions I ever made.

I disagree with the practice of college recruiters putting a great deal of pressure on high school kids. I felt entirely too much of that. Kids just shouldn't be exposed to it. I had to go to my girl friend's house out in the country for two days just to get away from the recruiters. They promised me cars, money, clothes, all those fancy things. They didn't seem to understand that what I wanted most out of college was an education.

I also disagree, emphatically, with all the pressure from coaches and even parents on a kid's college choice. The kids should be free to make that choice themselves. When I was being recruited, I felt safe as long as our season was still on. It was as if I were behind a protective glass shield and I could see all these recruiters scratching and clawing, but they couldn't reach me because you can't sign a player while his season is still on. But the moment that final buzzer sounds, that protective shield vanishes and you feel like saying quickly, "I'll take you!" to the first one to reach you so you won't have to fight off all the others.

The offers of all those material things give high school kids the impression right away that college sports are commercial, like a business. They enter college thinking the school owes them something just because they've been recruited. But the school doesn't owe them a thing. In exchange for tuition and books, all I ever wanted from any college was an opportunity to get a good degree and play basketball in return. It was a fair and even trade.

The Houston people offered me an education and a watchful eye, promising to help me out if I ever needed it in making the adjustment. I never did, but I always knew the help was there if I needed it. At the U of H, I also knew I wouldn't have to prove anything. San Francisco offered me a scholarship, but I knew that if I went there, I'd be compared with Bill Russell. The same at many other schools. That was another reason for choosing Houston. They had never had an outstanding basketball player. I wouldn't be compared with anybody.

I left Rayville, and I've never gone back to live—only for an occasional visit over the summer after my freshman year at the U of H. I fell in love with both the school and the city of Houston. When I'd visit Rayville, it was altogether different. But I knew it wasn't changing—I was. I was seeing it as it really is, with no opportunity and nothing to do, and I could understand then why I wanted success so badly. The people there were the finest in the world, and they still are, but Rayville was Rayville and it would never be the same for me, not the way it was during my Tom Sawyer years. It was gone, and there was no sense in trying to re create that happiness in Rayville. It would be like looking for a penny in a muddy river. You'd never find it again.

So I headed for the University of Houston, where—just five years earlier—one of the co-founders had said, "No nigger will ever set foot on this campus."

From the book *They Call Me "The Big E,"* by Elvin Hayes & Bill Gilbert © 1978. Published by Prentice-Hall, Inc., Englewood Cliffs, NJ 07632. Reprinted with permission.

"GENERAL STORE, GAS PUMP AND BROWN CHURCH"

It was possible to win both A and B Oregon championships in the 1930s, but only one school ever accomplished the feat and it no longer exists. Bellfountain residents recall they even made the New York Times. *"Bellfountain" is a regional symbol for "Cinderella." Every season its 1937 story is retold—in print and by word of mouth—throughout the state. This one is my composite of stories written in various anniversary years, notably 1977, the fortieth.*

Two hundred people gathered Sunday afternoon in the gym of old Bellfountain to sing their alma mater. They were here to celebrate the day 40 years ago when the unincorporated farm community with no post office and only one store became historic. They came to relive a moment in March 1937 when their no-longer-existent high school with a student body of twenty-nine and a team of eight boys startled the Oregon sports world by winning both the A and B state tournaments in one swoop. The assemblage included all seven living players, both the championship-year and predecessor coaches, and the referee of the big game, who brought his whistle.

As the only school ever to accomplish this feat, Bellfountain became a "David-Goliath" and "Cinderella" symbol far beyond the boundaries of Oregon. The Bells were "Davids" in more ways than one. They averaged 5′9″ in height, and their center, Richard Kessler, had to stretch to make 6 feet. At that time the state tourney was a consolidated sixteen-team event played at Willamette University in Salem. Since the four qualifying Class B schools were bracketed together, one would automatically reach the semifinals. The other three semifinalists would be Class A schools.

United Press described Bellfountain as "a general store, gas pump and brown church." A Portland writer called the team "the boys from somewhere in Benton County." The community's population was 300. The gym, heated by a potbellied wood-burning stove, was so small that the "over and back line" was in the opposite court. The old high school is now a grade school; high school students are bused to Monroe, 7 miles away. But the trophy case, with scorebook and other championship season mementos, is still there.

Among the notables present Sunday were coach Bill Lemmons; Ken Litchfield, the coach from 1930 to 1936; and referee Ralph Coleman, now the retired Oregon State University baseball coach. The players were Kessler, Cliff Larkin, Harrison Wallace, and Norman Humphreys, all of whom remained in Benton County to pursue logging or farm-related occupations; Frank and Stan Buckingham, farmers in Washington and California, respectively; and Lynn Hinton, a phone installer residing in Sherwood, near Portland. The eighth, John Key, was killed in World War II.

With Coleman officiating, the '37 vets played a brief exhibition game against some youngsters from the neighborhood. It was recalled that Lemmon, a former all-stater at Stadium High in Tacoma, succeeded Litchfield just in time for the '37 heroics. The third-place state Class A finish of Litchfield's '36 team should have stripped the "mystery men" veneer from the Bells, but the human mind sees quantum distance between third and first places. The '37 team compiled a 25–2 record, its victims including Salem and the Willamette University freshmen. Its triumphs included a 72 to 15 rout of Harrisburg, 62 to 10 and 56 to 9 shellackings of Shedd, and a 48 to 4 job on Alsea.

The gym, school, and nondenominational Bellfountain Community Church sit on a knoll where the westward view blends the Willamette valley and the Coast Range into a riot of green. In this setting the old grads turned back the pages of time, reliving the old days and a Cinderella scenario which, because of the modern "class tournament" system, can never happen again.

On Wednesday, March 17, 1937, an aviatrix named Amelia Earhart took off from Oakland on her last flight, Glenn Cunningham beat Archie San Romani in what the Associated Press called the "dazzling" mile time of 4:08.7, and eight rock-jawed kids from Bellfountain took the floor against Amity in the opening game of Oregon's "Sweet 16." The Bells ran up a 20 to 3 lead, played around until it got sticky at 34 to 28, then closed with 9 straight points to win, 43 to 28. Kessler was the big gun, hitting nine of twelve shots from the field, most of them from under the hoop, and totaling 20 points. Wallace contributed 10, Larkin 9, and Stan Buckingham 4.

On Thursday, March 18, a gas explosion killed 425 New London, Texas, youngsters in the worst school disaster in American history. Lou Gehrig signed a Yankee contract for $36,000, and the Bells took the floor against Chiloquin in the Oregon quarterfinals. They won, 39 to 31, after leading 16 to 5 at the quarter, 24 to 9 at the half, and 32 to 13 at the three-quarter mark. One writer said they "substituted freely" in the final period, or as "freely" as a squad with only three reserves can substitute. Another said "42 percent of the male student body" cooperated in the victory. Kessler again led with 16. Wallace had 11. Bellfountain stood supreme over the state's Class B schools. Now it was time to play with the men. Surely the Bells were at the end of the trail. Every sports writer in Oregon was predicting an all-Portland final—Franklin versus Lincoln.

And so on Friday, March 19, with the Portland city council announcing plans to experiment with a new gadget called a "parking meter" and the *Portland Oregonian* advertising a five-room house with basement for $1,950, the Bells felt the tug of destiny as they took the floor for their semifinal against mighty Franklin. Having talked Eugene out of contention with face-to-face jibes in an earlier game, the Franklins tried this ploy on the country boys. For a quarter it worked; the score stood 4 to 4. Then they razzed Kessler, and he sank a short one. They worked on Wallace, and he sank a long one. The half ended with Bellfountain out in front, 16 to 9, and it was to get worse. In the second half Franklin managed only two field goals. For 13 minutes the city boys were held without a single point. The final score was 39 to 13, and all the doubting Thomases in Portland, Salem, and Eugene now had to take the lads from Benton County seriously.

On Saturday, March 20, shortly after college basketball coaches, in "radical action" at Chicago, voted to eliminate the center jump after each field goal, the Bells had adrenaline flowing at fever pitch as they took the floor for The Big One—against Lincoln.

It wasn't even close. Bellfountain led 9 to 4 at the quarter, 20 to 8 at halftime, and due chiefly to 15-of-17 proficiency at the free throw line, won the Oregon championship, 35 to 21. Kessler pumped in 13, Stan Buckingham 9, Wallace 5, and Larkin and Frank Buckingham 4 each. In another combination phenomenon that can never happen again, Kessler and Wallace were selected to both A and B all-state teams.

In an editorial headed "Down Went Goliath," the *Oregonian* commented: "It scarcely seems probable that coincidence arranged for a concentration of basketball talent in a small high school at a Benton County crossroads. Much larger schools have such an abundance of equivalent material from which to pick and choose that on a merely physical basis Bellfountain might reasonably have been discouraged at the outset. Nor can one account for such phenomenal behavior by considering that Bellfountain must have an exceptional coach. That much is evident. There must have been, there must be, something else. This something is glowingly undefinable. Sometimes we call it 'class' or 'it,' but never do we quite describe it. It is so difficult to define a spiritual quality."

Settled in the 1840s on donation land claims, Bellfountain was named for the Ohio town of Bellefontaine. One of the state's oldest logging sites lies a few miles west. Ralph Hull, an area lumber mill operator who helped organize the fortieth reunion, said, "Everyone here has his roots in the soil, one way or the other. Most of them come from pioneer stock, and they have fortitude. They didn't ask for anything. Neighbors helped, but you never had to ask."

Under the auspices of the Eugene Active 20-30 Club, co-host of the state tournament since it was transferred to the University of Oregon in 1957, the seven Bells had been assembled for a previous reunion, their twenty-fifth, in 1962. The deceased Key was represented on that occasion by his mother. The affair took place in the Empire Room of the Eugene Hotel, with the press on hand for pictures and interviews. Afterwards the teammates and wives went to the university's McArthur Court where they were introduced at halftime of the championship game.

Larkin watches all the basketball he can on television and rarely misses an Oregon State home game. "The players today are much bigger and stronger," he concedes, "but I believe we could match them in conditioning and quickness. I think we were in better condition than some of these teams I see." Others recall that "we ran to school, and the penalty for making a bobble during practice was 100 laps around the gym."

Hinton represents the consensus when he admits winning the state championship has been the highlight of his life. "I say this, even though I was a spectator," he laughs, alluding to his role as substitute.

"Every so often someone brings it up, either in a newspaper or in conversation, and the memories come back in a flood."

The above was written by Nelson Campbell, based on the following: "And Down Went Goliath," ***Portland Oregonian*****, March 26, 1937, 10; B. Mulflur, "Bellfountain**

Relives State Hoop Title," *Oregon Journal* (Portland), March 7, 1977, 13; "Fifty Years . . . ," 1967 state tournament program, Oregon School Activities Assn. (Tigard, Ore.), 16–17; R. Friedman, "Oregon Profiles: Lynn Hinton," *Senior Profile*, December 1979, 16.

ONLY IN INDIANA

Indiana has been virtually synonymous with basketball since World War I. It's a prairie land where small-town gyms are huge, basketball is the undisputed major sport, the annual state tournament draws almost a million and a half fans, and folks recall historical events in their time relation to "the year we made it to Indianapolis" or "the year we were 25–1 but got upset in the sectional."

Tourney time is universally characterized as "Hoosier Hysteria." College administrator Herb Schwomeyer of Indianapolis wrote a book, the ultimate reference on the state's high school basketball history, bearing that title. So did Bob Williams, an Indianapolis newsman who took a depth-interview, literary approach to history, except that his title bore an exclamation point. When Bob Oates of the Los Angeles Times *was sent to Indiana in March 1976 to soak up the flavor of tourney madness, he produced the following story for his more blasé readers. From the vantage point of Cloverdale (population 1,050) he saw how prep basketball permeates life and commerce at every Hoosier crossroads. His work was headlined, yes, "Hoosier Hysteria."*

Eight years later—on July 9, 1984—an all-time indoor record 67,000 fans jammed the new Indianapolis Hoosier Dome to watch a doubleheader featuring the men's and women's Olympic teams. Only in Indiana could 67,000 people show up for a summertime basketball game, in the certain knowledge that half of them would be seated in a "twilight zone" and thus be unable to see much action. Only in Indiana would a coach seek competitive advantage by assembling his squad at midnight on opening practice day as Mike Copper of Warren Central did on October 8 that year. Now back to Bob Oates and Cloverdale in '76. . . .

The man on the radio, killing time before tipoff, was reciting what he called the facts of life about Indiana.

"The biggest thing in this state," he said, "isn't Notre Dame football or Indiana University basketball or even the Indianapolis Speedway. It's high school basketball. The thing that turns us all on is the state tournament."

In Indiana this month it's hard to argue with the man.

This is hysteria month here. In hundreds of Indiana towns and cities, the four-week state high school basketball tournament touches most lives.

Everybody attends or tunes in, and basketball regularly outranks women as a conversation subject everywhere, at least until the home team is eliminated.

In many communities there have been instances when most of the population packed into cars, trucks, campers or buses for the trip to Terre Haute or Indianapolis to see a tournament game.

The record-holder is the southeastern Indiana town of Milan, which played in the state finals 22 years ago. That day the fire department from a nearby town volunteered to run Milan's emergency offices, including the police and fire departments. Thereupon the shopkeepers locked up, the gas station closed and 1,173 of Milan's 1,174 residents made the game. One poor guy had the flu.

High school basketball in Indiana is like college basketball elsewhere except more so. The season lasts four and a half months, starting in mid-November, and the community focal point is commonly the high school gym. Capacities range from 2,000 to 9,000, with an average of nearly 5,000. The climaxing tournament each spring has been big news in Indiana since it began in 1911, sweeping politics and earthquakes and even the Hearst trial off Page 1.

"Every guy in the state is a basketball expert," Betty Sizelove, secretary of the Indiana High School Athletic Association, said one day recently. "I think that's why it's so exciting here. Everybody played basketball in high school.

"If you're born in Ohio," she said, doubtless thinking of Woody Hayes, "the first thing they do is weigh you. If you're born in Indiana, they measure you first. I don't know why it is, but every time I go to another state the kids all seem to be playing cowboys and Indians. Driving back through Indiana, they're all shooting baskets."

For four March weekends annually the Indiana state tournament is an exercise in democracy. Every high school in the state is eligible to enter, and most do. There are no B or C classifications. All Indiana high schools are Class A. And because of the nature of basketball, it often happens that a school with an enrollment of 300 can overpower one with 3,000. All this sets up a series of David and Goliath bouts, and in the David communities particularly, the excitement builds each week as their boys continue to win. The year Milan won it all, its team represented a student body of 150—against a city of 60,000, Muncie.

At its 1942 peak, 820 prep basketball teams competed in the Indiana tournament. Consolidations have reduced the number of schools to 411, of which 403 are competing this month. Six of the eight high schools that didn't enter are girls' schools, one is a trade school in Indianapolis and the other is the Indiana School for the Blind.

The tournament is actually 85 tournaments, starting with 64 sectionals in 64 of the state's largest high school gyms. At intervals of a week the winners next proceed to 16 regional tournaments and then to four semi-states, Evansville, Lafayette, Ft. Wayne and Indianapolis. The schools in the last round—called the Final Four—meet in Indianapolis on the last Saturday of the tournament. The setting is the new Market Square Arena, seating 18,000. There are two afternoon games, with the winners playing for the championship that night. No game for third place is scheduled. This is a single-elimination tournament in which you either win or you're gone.

Throughout the state nonetheless it is considered a great honor to make the Final Four. Indeed, in many Indiana communities time is reckoned that way.

"Let's see, we bought the north 60 (acres) the summer before we made the Final Four," an Indiana farmer will say.

An Indianapolis druggist: "I haven't been to Europe since the last time we were in the Final Four."

In Cloverdale, a western Indiana town 200 miles south of Chicago, only two really important things have happened in the past 150 years. James M. Rockwell, founder of the Rockwell Fund, was born here in 1863, and Cloverdale High School made the Final Four in 1966.

A Californian visiting Cloverdale in 1976 discovered that they still talk about both events as if they happened yesterday.

Ruby Barnett, who runs the smartest women's shop in this part of Putnam County, said the saddest thing about the game was that the Clovers were only a point down with a minute to play when they missed a one-and-one free throw. If the boy had made both, she pointed out, the Clovers would have won.

The pain is still such after 10 years that she didn't want to embarrass the player by naming him.

Barnett said the final score was 58 to 51, but it really didn't tell the story. The story, she said, was that Cloverdale, with a student body of 225, got to the Final Four that winter and came within two free throws of beating Indianapolis Tech, a high school with an enrollment of 5,000.

The intervening years have brought some changes.

"When the team isn't as good, there isn't as much interest," Barnett said in a lament as old as Sparta when Athens dominated the Olympics. "Besides, we have other sports now. We even have football."

The Barnett fashion shop is at Main and Market, the only intersection with a traffic light in Cloverdale (pop. 1,050). On an occasional corner nearby, however, you can still see an ancient hand-operated fire pump with a big bell on top. On the night of a big fire, the strongest man in town used to coax the water up, providing a show that was even better than basketball.

The Main Street business district here is two blocks long, ending at the railroad tracks, and at present it is almost garish. The storefront windows, Barnett's and all the others, are a mass of purple stripes and colorful signs commanding: "Hold That Tiger" and "Beat the Tigers." Extending a 50-year tradition, the windows were decorated by groups of Cloverdale High School girls the day after their team drew the Greencastle High School Tigers in the first round of this year's state tournament. Greencastle, the next town over, is a university town (DePauw, Buzzie Bavasi's school), and the rivalry with Cloverdale is intense. The girls worked all hours on the decorations.

The truth is that at Cloverdale, as at many Indiana high schools, girls still do most of the rooting and boys most of the playing. CHS girls compete in three sports with two coaches. The boys have nine coaches for seven sports.

But at boys' games, strangely, few boys are there as spectators. On a recent Tuesday night, when Cloverdale met Mooresville in a key regular-season-ending conference game, both rooting sections were four-fifths girls. They faced each other across one end of the floor with all-girl cheerleaders, six on one side in short blue skirts, four on the other side in short green skirts. In a closely played game the constant cacophony of high-pitched screaming and yelling was at the nether end of aural endurance. When the girls let up, the CHS pep band filled the void with a 14-year-old rock drummer named Larry Bault, who seemed to be most talented kid in town, on court or off. The stands seating 2,200 were about half full, testifying to the fact that the Clovers are 15–23 in their 38 outings since winning back-to-back sectional tournaments, when they regularly sold out.

The Cloverdale principal, Forrester Ison, a Berea college graduate with a master's from Indiana University, said basketball is the biggest thing there is in an Indiana high school.

"Morale depends on a winning program," he elaborated. "All extracurricular activities are important today, of course—the students have to have something to look forward to besides studies—but athletics reach more kids than anything, and there's more interest in basketball than any other sport."

Although CHS didn't play football until six years ago, its basketball program has been as sophisticated for years as any in the state. The Cloverdale school district competes with others on five basketball levels: seventh, eighth and ninth grades, high school reserves and high school varsity. There is a good college-trained coach for each of these five teams, even the seventh graders, and there are assistant coaches for some. Intramural basketball starts in the fourth grade, Ison said.

By the time he's ready to graduate, a Cloverdale boy has been so intensively trained that he needs only two qualities to step onto a university team, coordination and height. The unfortunate thing about basketball—in terms of all the time put into it in Indiana—is that it's a hard sport to compete in these days without unreal height.

When the game was first played in this state, men of normal size had a chance with tactics like the two-hand set shot. The leaping one-handers have made it a different game, in spite of which the state's traditions live on. And so it is that Indiana high schools now graduate mostly 5-9 and 6-0 second guessers, fellows who know as much about basketball as the 6-4 types but can't find a college team to play on.

In Cloverdale basketball this season, on Coach Al Tucker's 11-man varsity, two of the athletes are 6-3, four 6-2, three 5-10, one 5-7 and one 5-4. Competitively, Tucker's basic problem is that every player on the team lacks height or agility. If the 5-7 guy were a foot taller, he'd be headed for Indiana University.

The reason so many small towns win the Indiana tournament over the years is that all it takes in a five-man sport is a group of three or four kids the same age growing up together with above-average height and coordination. One year they have them at Marion or Milan and the next at New Albany or Connersville or Gary.

Some of the losers, frustrated, are beginning to try other sports, and it is now possible at CHS to compete athletically in nine consecutive months and win four letters in one year without going out for basketball. There is varsity competition in football and cross country in the fall, wrestling in winter and baseball, track and golf in spring—but significantly basketball underwrites the whole program. Even football loses money although it brings in a few dollars. The others don't bring in anything. Cloverdale's athletic budget is wholly financed by basketball revenues from the sale of $1 tickets to students and $1.50 tickets to adults. Thus the budget for all seven sports at CHS is $9,000 when the basketball team wins big and $6,000 in a year like this one.

By law, no tax money can go for sports in Indiana.

On the wide, white door of the red-brick garage attached to their house in Cloverdale, Al and Joan Tucker have posted a large green clover, the CHS sports symbol. As basketball coach, Tucker would be expected to have one, but he isn't alone. The symbols are all over town.

"Life revolves around the high school in a community like this," said businesswoman Ruby Barnett.

In Indianapolis, athletic commission secretary Betty Sizelove said: "The thing that really makes a community in this state is having just one high school. Everybody rallies around. It gets everybody pulling together. You see, people are very interested in children they know. They get involved."

This is the spirit that attracts them to places like Cloverdale, a small old town whose older sections are lined with narrow residential streets edged by big shade trees fronting big, old white-frame houses with wrap-around verandas. Front and back, the yards are unfenced, and in March the wind sings through the bare branches of the tall trees. Often there isn't an auto in sight. For a different kind of relaxation, rustic Cataract Lake is only five miles away, offering fishing, boating and other pleasures summarized in the nostalgic expression: a summer cottage on the lake.

So everybody works in Indianapolis or Terre Haute, 40 to 50 miles away, but lives in Cloverdale. The Cloverdale school district estimates that 50 percent of its parents commute to Indianapolis and 30 percent elsewhere. The 20 percent from Cloverdale includes farmers.

Much of Indiana is like this, factories here, residences there. In most of the state the commuting is palatable. Forests and parks are abundant, at least in southern Indiana. The storied Wabash River winds around, with tree-lined banks and a few covered bridges. And Indiana farms are pleasant to look at.

What's more, in March there's that basketball tournament. Last year it drew 1,250,659 paid fans—in four weekends. Even the Dodgers would settle for that.

From Bob Oates, "High School Basketball Takes Over a State," *Los Angeles Times*, March 11, 1976, sec. III, 1f.

"LOOK WHERE THEY'RE PLAYING THAT GAME"

Basketball manifests itself almost everywhere in Kentucky. Hoops are on telephone poles in Appalachia, barns in tobacco country, and garages, even stores in the towns. Keeping in mind Dr. Naismith's feelings for the game he invented in 1891, Dave Kindred journeyed to the state's remotest hollows preparatory to writing his 1976 book, Basketball, the Dream Game in Kentucky. *This is a work so steeped in the game that it features full-page cameo illustrations possessing a rubber texture remindful of a basketball. Excerpts follow.*

James Naismith played in only two basketball games. "Just didn't get around to playing," he said. With six other Springfield YMCA instructors, he played against seven students on March 11, 1892, in the first public game ever. The students won, 5 to 1, the instructors being saved from total humiliation by a short, stocky young man named Amos Alonzo Stagg, who dressed in his old Yale football uniform and played with such passion that he acquired a black eye. "I wish Lonnie could have made the point without fouling everybody," Naismith said to a reporter from *The Springfield Republican*. Not that the burly, walrus-mustached Naismith was innocent. With a background of wrestling, boxing and football, he, too, used tactics that he intended to keep out of his new game. "Once I even used a grapevine wrestling clamp on a man who was too big for me to handle," the Father of Basketball confessed.

More than 150 million people pay to see basketball games in the United States each year. Kentucky accounts for maybe three million customers. Just as Naismith would tremble in agitation should he see a basketball game today with its incessant physical contact, so would he grumble at the sport's commercialization. "He thought it should have been only a playground activity," said one of his daughters, Mrs. Helen Dodd of Westcliffe, Colo. "He didn't totally approve of it as an intercollegiate sport . . . and he would have been appalled by the present emphasis on professional basketball."

Naismith liked his game the way he dreamed of it. Mrs. Dodd said, "He started collecting pictures of some of the odd places in which he would find baskets: in alleys, farmyards and gosh knows where else. He would get quite a chuckle out of those pictures, and he almost always would say, 'Look where they're playing that game.' "

Goals are everywhere in Kentucky. Customers at a grocery store on the Mountain Parkway can shoot 30-footers from the bread shelves. At Red Fox, a gas station best serves its clients during timeouts. At Jackson, a funeral home has a hoop next to the hearse's parking spot.

A goal need not be storebought. A clothes basket, with the bottom still in it, is tacked to an abandoned church near Hazard. Not far from Monkey's Eyebrow, a bicycle tire rim (with spokes removed) is the accomplice of a boy's imagination.

New nets, no nets, ripped nets, nets of chain, nets of clothesline rope, red-white-and-blue nets, just plain nets. Nailed to trees, telephone poles, garages, worksheds, great white mansions (Joe Gregory, first owner of the pro Kentucky Colonels, built a gym next to his place, and Ellie and John Y. Brown, later owners, have a basket over their three-car garage). Whether grafted onto a dog house in Hardinsburg or attached to a housewife's clothesline pole outside Mayfield, no matter if the rim is a reworked clothes hanger like the one outside Balltown or if the backboard is corrugated tin like the one in Elizabethtown, whether the shooter has to stand on the railroad tracks in Burnaugh or in the street in Wurtland—no matter what, they all are basketball goals, and in the end they are all the same as the one Terry Lee Thomas built outside Vine Grove when he was 14.

Terry Lee and a neighbor boy, Tom Phillips, went over to Gilbert Young's land to cut down two trees to use as supports for the backboard and rim. They used axes, and it took them a day to down and trim the trees. They carried them, one at a time, the half-mile to home. Using a posthole digger, they made holes four feet deep in an open lot between the boys' houses.

They made the backboard from 3/4-inch plywood that Terry Lee's brother, Dicky, didn't use in his new house in Louisville. They bought a rim at Jones' Variety Store in Vine Grove, paying $2.98, and attached it to the plywood with screws. After the goal had been up six months, the boys didn't use it much. The ground in front turned to mud a lot. Another thing was that the rim was 12 feet high, two feet higher than Jim Naismith suggested. "We messed up, I guess," Terry Lee Thomas said.

"Look where they're playing that game," Naismith said. In Kentucky they play basketball in places you've never seen. Places like Kingdom Come . . .

Driving down KY 463 in February, 1968, you pass through Delphia, which isn't much more than the Delphia U-Wash Laundry on the right. Over a hill and you're in Letcher County in the mountains of southeastern Kentucky, 225 miles from Louisville. At a sign that says "Cumberland 5 miles, Hot Spot 15 miles," you turn left and go down a narrow road four miles—past Dollie's Place, which is a cafe with good hamburgers and a six-foot pool table—and you have found Kingdom Come High School.

It's a sandstone building, three stories high, built in 1925 and named Kingdom Come after the book, "The Little Shepherd of Kingdom Come," which they say is about this area.

Some 80 kids are in school, and most of them were upstairs the other night for a game with Red Bird High School.

Yes, upstairs. The gymnasium is on the third floor. From one end to the other it is 61 feet long, but the builders left a foot and a half at each end for out-of-bounds room. So the playing court is 58 feet long instead of the regulation 84 feet. This year they put big cushioned mats on the brick chimneys where the baskets are attached. Junior Halcomb, a Kingdom Come player, said, "One time ah like to busted mah brines out agin' that chimney, comin' in for a layup."

The court is 30 feet wide, which is 20 feet less than regulation. The out-of-bounds line on one side is painted against the wall. You're out of bounds if you go through the door in the corner.

On the other side, where there are three rows of bleachers for the fans, people's feet hang onto the court. Not that it matters much. Basketball in Appalachia is informal. During the pre-game warmups the other night, a Kingdom Come player had to wrestle a fan for the basketball. Given half a chance, the fans shoot baskets. So do the referees. The "B" team boys, who sit on the bench for the varsity game because there are only five varsity players, eat popcorn and drink pop during the game.

The action is sometimes strange. The basket rims are too high by maybe six inches. The old wooden floor, which dips and winds as much as KY 463, has spots where the ball just won't bounce. When somebody asked Junior Halcomb what it's like to play at Kingdom Come, he said, "It's hail, man."

Yet Junior is in his junior year and doesn't intend to follow the example of his coach, Jerry Coots, 22, who played half his freshman year at Kingdom Come and then moved to Whitesburg High, the city school. "Ah wouldn't be able to play ball over there," Junior said.

Playing ball means something to him. He has nine brothers and sisters, just one younger than he. Besides shooting pool (he likes the eight-foot table at Mary Jane's Grille across from the school, even though they use rolled-up napkins to support the cushioned rails), Junior said there isn't much to do in the narrow valley that holds Line Fork Creek.

"During the summer when it's up aroun' a hundred-and-somethin', Ah'm in this gym shootin' baskets for five hours and more," Junior said. He is Kingdom Come's leading scorer. He gets about 23 points a game, mostly on set shots from mid-court.

Kingdom Come doesn't have a good team. It has lost all 12 of its games and is last in *The Courier Journal*'s Litkenhous Ratings of the state's 350 high school teams. It has an 0.1 rating.

Coach Coots, who is called "Coots" by everyone in school, says Kingdom Come has problems it likely will never overcome. Only 30 percent of the fathers in the valley have jobs, he said. Boys leave school to join the army. They go to Cincinnati or Detroit to work.

"These kids have been losing for so long they're used to it," Coots said. "They joke it up just as big if they lose as if they'd just won a game."

Maybe.

When Red Bird moved ahead, 70 to 68, and was holding the ball until the final seconds ticked off an electric alarm clock (the scoreboard had shorted out), a Kingdom Come senior named Sharon Gentry shouted at a Red Bird fan:

"Don't you sound off about winning, or I'll come down and scratch your eyes out."

And when Junior Halcomb left the floor, after missing two late free throws that would have tied the game, the tears in his eyes were not from joking it up.

From Dave Kindred, *Basketball, the Dream Game in Kentucky* (Louisville, Ky.: Data Courier, 1976), 9–11, 19–22.

THE CHEERING NEVER STOPS

There will never be another Hebron in Illinois basketball. The one-class state tournament was abandoned in 1972, but ever since a March night in '52, the word "Hebron" has been a symbol and inspiration to Little Davids far and wide. In 1980 the University of Illinois was playing at South Carolina, 700 miles away. The fieldhouse custodian, noting "Judson" on an Illinois jersey, walked up to the lad and asked if he were related to the Judson twins of '52. "I'm Phil's son," Rob Judson answered. "My gosh, has it been that long?" the custodian sighed.

Tales of the Big Year are legion. At the "Sweet 16" in Champaign, the boys received a well-wishing telegram bearing the names of most of Hebron's 600 inhabitants. Large numbers of them were in Champaign's old Huff Gymnasium or outside trying to get in. The aged and the stewards of essential services hung by their radios in Hebron. The team nickname was "Green Giants"—after the area's corporate farms. In later years when Hebron needed a new water tower, one was constructed in the shape of a basketball. It bore the giant-sized words "Home of 1952 State Champions." Let Jerry Shnay's silver anniversary story from a 1977 Chicago Tribune *take you back.*

The cheering never stops. Tiny Hebron made high school basketball history 25 years ago, and the Green Giants' story has grown in that quarter-century.

"We're always reminded who we were," said Phil Judson, starting forward then and basketball coach at Zion-Benton High School now.

"We always bump into people who know us, or know about us," he continued. "I guess we caught everyone's imagination. You know, the kids from the small school winning the state championship. Like a story book."

Some story. The school just minutes from the Wisconsin state line won 35 of 36 games during the 1951–52 season, including a 64 to 59 overtime victory over Quincy for the title. And all this with a student body of 99, 48 of them boys.

Nothing like this had happened before. And it will never happen again since two classes now separate big from small schools. Braidwood in 1938 and Cobden in 1965 came close. But Hebron will remain unique.

The names are legends. The Judson twins, Paul and Phil; 6-10 center Bill Schulz, Ken Spooner, and Don Wilbrandt. They seldom were challenged.

The first time we got together in more than 20 years was at the funeral of our coach, Russ Ahearn, last November. I was surprised. I could hardly recognize the Judson twins.

—Bill Schulz

It was Russ Ahearn who groomed and guided the Green Giants. He also was principal of Hebron and saw to the care and feeding of his players.

"He was a great psychologist," said Schulz, now in marketing and sales for a television manufacturer. "When we got to Champaign for the state meet, we weren't even allowed to watch any other games. He kept us in our rooms. That was the first year the tourney was televised, but I don't think we cared about that. We did what the coach told us to do."

Ahearn had a great team but a terrible gym. "It was 34 feet wide and 74 feet long. I couldn't believe it," Schulz recalled. "We were all on the floor, for the first time in 25 years, just a few weeks ago. I kept thinking how small the gym really was."

The coach realized the limitations, so he scheduled only six home games. "That helped us," said Paul Judson, now Dundee High School baseball coach. "We were able to get used to big crowds and strange gyms."

Don Wilbrandt, who overcame the handicap of being born with one ear, recalled Ahearn was strict about diet. "We never ate pie or ice cream or things like that." The diets were even posted in each home.

At the time we didn't think we were doing anything special. We knew we were good, and we expected to win the state. We did. I really didn't comprehend what we had done until I was in college.

—Paul Judson

That 1951–52 season was extraordinary. The previous two years Hebron was 23–5 and 26–2. Schulz entered the school as a sophomore when the even tinier community of Alden was consolidated with Hebron.

"Russ wanted a sense of identity," Paul Judson said. "He refused to put 'Hebron' on our uniforms, so we had only numbers that year. No school name."

The Green Giants won their first 15 games, then dropped a 71 to 68 decision to Crystal Lake as Fritz Schneider scored 34 points for the winners. It was the only team to score more than 60 points against Hebron that season. The early streak included winning the Kankakee holiday tournament over Danville, a highly regarded team paced by Ron Rigoni.

"We won, 67 to 53," Phil recalled. "And then we all began thinking how good we really could be."

Hebron beat Elgin, 49 to 47, in the regionals. Then it romped past Barrington and De Kalb in the sectionals to reach Champaign.

When I first came to Hebron, I had a fairly clear vision of what would happen to us this year. I figured that by hard work we could make the state tournament in the not-too-distant future. The spirit was there, dormant perhaps since the great teams of Hebron just before World War II.

—Russ Ahearn in 1952

Howie Judson was in California, getting ready for spring training with the White Sox, in 1952. In 1940 the twins' brother helped Hebron reach the state tournament.

Judson, like the rest of the town, was caught up in the state tourney. He was kept up to date by telegrams from Ken Lopemann, a Hebron grocer, and Louie Wilbrandt, Don's father.

Townspeople stuck to their radios during the tourney. The pressure was enormous. Lopemann suffered a heart attack. H.A. Freeman said two listeners fainted.

But Hebron was prepared, even though Paul Judson couldn't recall what offense the team ran.

"If they played tight, we drove. If they played us loose, we shot from outside. We didn't play a sophisticated game, but we had speed, height, defense and good shooting. That will win for any team, even today."

The pressure built up for Hebron in old Huff Gym in Champaign. The Giants beat Champaign, 55 to 46, Lawrenceville, 65 to 55, and Rock Island, 64 to 56. Then they faced Bruce Brothers and Quincy in the final.

With two minutes left, Hebron led, 58 to 55. But Jack Gower scored three points in the final minute to send the game into overtime. Brothers, however, fouled out after scoring 20 points. That was all for Quincy. Schulz was hot, totaling 24 points on 12 of 16 from the field. Paul Judson tallied 13, Phil Judson 12 and Wilbrandt 10.

That association with Hebron, that reminiscing, never fazed me. But now that we're getting older, maybe it was *something special. Maybe it was more than going through the motions of winning a state championship.*

—Phil Judson

The final buzzer ended the tournament. The team was cheered that night, and the cheering didn't stop the next day. Crowds lined both sides of Ill. Hwy. 47 back to Hebron. Each town wanted to honor the team. It began at Morris and continued in every community that had cheered for the little town against the giants.

Morris was first to celebrate with a parade. Then came Yorkville, Elburn, Huntley and Woodstock, which had a parade complete with floats and bands. In Hebron 3,500 cars crammed the nine streets.

"The cheering didn't stop until the next week," Phil Judson recalled. "The sheriff would drive us to different schools in the county so they could honor us."

I was in Spain three years ago, and someone tapped me on the shoulder. "I remember you. Aren't you Bill Schulz? Didn't you play for Hebron?"

—Schulz

They still honor Hebron. For every small school and tiny town the Green Giants are a touchstone, a symbol of the great dream.

"It's amazing," said Spooner, who now teaches at Hebron. "No matter where you go, if you mention Hebron, people remember."

"We were a fairly naive group of kids," Paul Judson recalled. "But the state championship game gave us all college scholarships. We had three-hour practices four years in a row, and we were never tired."

Brother Phil added, "When you're growing up, you have a dream, pretending you're playing in the state tournament. Going to Champaign was always in the backs of our minds. And Ahearn insisted that if you point for things, you usually get them."

Two weeks ago the starting five went back to the gym for the first time since graduation. They held the trophy they had raised in triumph 25 years ago in Champaign.

"Things came back to me," Schulz said. "I saw the same lockers, the same science tables and the same seats in the gym. But what I recalled most was Ahearn and his notebook. He had a spiral notebook, and he told his assistant to write things in it to tell us at timeouts. Once he got so angry with us that he tore up the book. Walking through the halls, I remembered that torn notebook."

> *After Hebron beat Champaign in the tournament, a Champaign newspaper reported the losing coach would like to play Hebron five games instead of one. "That would be all right with us, but only if we could play 'em all the same day."*
>
> *—a Hebron fan*

THE ONLY GAME IN PANGUITCH

When the movie house and pool hall are a small town's only winter diversions, high school basketball assumes cultural significance. In a community that is 95 percent Mormon such as Panguitch in the Bryce Canyon country of southwestern Utah, it's a virtual religion within a religion. John Underwood's 1963 story from Sports Illustrated *tells how the game is woven into a social fabric.*

The only thing that stood between Donald Ortman and basketball was his terrible modesty. Lank, limby and obviously cut for the game, Don Ortman would gladly play for Panguitch High, he told the coach in 1936, but not if it meant taking off his long pants. The coach, equally inflexible, could not agree ("Long pants?" he shrieked. "Out there on the court? *Long* pants?"), and Panguitch, Utah, had to wait until Don's son Wally grew up before it could fully appreciate the Ortman family.

Nowadays, unabashed by the sight of his bare legs, Wally Ortman wears the conventional blue-and-white briefs of the undefeated Panguitch team and receives vast quantities of Panguitchian appreciation. This includes being a principal conversation topic on U.S. Highway 89 (Main Street) and at the Latter-Day Saints Social Hall and around the corner at Daly's pool and billiard retreat. Rhyming couplets are composed by adoring teenage girls: "The score goes up, that player, golly! / He's real neat, his name is Wally." His younger brothers, Kenny and Dennis, bask in his prominence and beg him to teach them to back-dribble. They consider the time golden when Wally gets with them at the make-do court in the vacant corral across the road. His girl, Barbara, has promised to retrieve the ring and picture she gave to another boy after the Panguitch coach, Bob Davis, a purist, got the team to swear off girls for the season.

Wally's gray-haired mother is still his most devoted fan. She recounts Panguitch basketball lore—like the time the "sore losers" from Marysvale set fire to a neighbor's car—while she struggles with the heavy batter for Wally's favorite boiled-raisin cake or punctiliously launders his uniform. Sometimes she cries to herself as she watches him disappear up the gravel road, walking, bag in hand, to the Panguitch gym on game nights. "It's sad for parents, the way time flies," she says. "We're content and we stay. Where can we go now? But when the children get out of school, they always go. There's nothing here to keep them."

Panguitch, Utah, is a blinking amber light at a dogleg on U.S. 89, 170 miles southwest of the nearest big town, Provo, and roughly along what Salt Lake City sensationalists imagine to be the beeline taken by itinerant bank robbers and high rollers heading west for Las Vegas. A brush with such glamorous villains was suspected in Panguitch last winter when the drugstore was robbed, but other than that, Panguitch doesn't qualify as much of a sin town. The local *Garfield County News* reported some time ago that when a woman in nearby Escalante called to report a robbery, the sheriff (since retired) instructed her to please get the name and address of the crook and he'd be over to make the arrest.

Panguitch (Ute Indian for "big fish") squats in a water-scarce trough between the Parowan Range on the west and the Panguitch Plateau, a branch of the Wasatch Mountains, on the east. Deer are plentiful in the hills, and no self-respecting Panguitch boy will go a season without getting his buck; venison is, therefore, staple fare in Panguitch. The area is 6,560 feet above a sea most Panguitchians have never seen, and is crisscrossed with irrigation ditches partly filled with snow this time of year. It is a gray land studded with cottonwood, ponderosa pine and native fir, but mostly there is sagebrush, uninspiring, mile after mile. The beauty is in the mountains, where there are vivid streaks of red beneath peaks that seem to have been confected with Reddi-Wip.

Because of the water shortage the population of Panguitch—1,435—has remained almost constant since the turn of the century. The people are interested in outsiders ("I have never seen a Negro," said the mother of one of the basketball players) and inquisitive about their tastes, yet they are at a loss to explain the red in their own mountains. The state's largest sawmill is at Panguitch, and there are alfalfa farms and small cattle ranches that vie for the water, but the lifeblood of the community is a million dollars' worth of tourists and hunters each year. There are 13 modern motels and nine gas stations to snare the traveler within the town limits. In summer the principal attraction is Bryce Canyon, a sort of Grand Canyon in miniature 25 miles to the southeast (Grand Canyon itself is only 175 miles south). The hunters come by the hundreds in the fall. The sign outside town discriminates only against "peddlers and hawkers" (licenses required) and "noisy mufflers and cutouts." Panguitch café food is hearty and the hospitality is, too, despite regiments of big-city parking meters. (This winter a second-string Panguitch High basketball player called Whips is famous for his fancy dribbling and fakes between and around the meters.)

The town's religious preference is Mormon, by 95%—which makes it a challenge for a visitor to achieve a social cup of coffee. The town's passion is basketball, and it is a challenge for anybody to talk about anything else. Bill Coltrine, a high school sportswriter for the *Salt Lake City Tribune*, stopped in Panguitch while vacationing last summer and was assailed by a delegation of townspeople eager to stuff him with details on the great team Coach Bob Davis was going to have. "But friends, this is July," protested Coltrine. "Nobody talks basketball in July."

"We do!" chorused the delegates.

The Panguitch team had won its 16th straight and appeared well on its way to the state Class B championship when Photographer Rich Clarkson and I checked into the New Western Motel down the street from the school the other day. We had driven the 71 miles from Cedar City, the nearest airport town. "You'll find people in this part of the country are very friendly," said the proprietor of the New Western, a native named Clarence Cameron. "Now, you'll be in rooms 15 and 16. But before you unpack, let me tell you about our basketball team. They've won 16 straight.

Could be better than that '57 bunch that won the state championship. And *that* was an exciting team. Never knew what they were going to do.

"Anyway, this could be the best we've ever had. They're fine boys, too, all of them. Joe Riggs is our little guard. We call him the Little General. Smart, very sensitive kid. His father runs the AG market in town. Just built a new house. Brent Turek is the big boy who scores so many points. His dad works for the state parks. Good job. Wally Ortman's dad has had a lot of bad luck. Been very sick. Wally's a great shooter. Lou Tebbs's dad is a rancher and a state legislator. Ned Richards' dad is the postmaster. They're big boys. Seem to get bigger every year. But listen. Let Bob Davis tell you about how they got to be the first five in the first place. Quite a scandal. Took a lot of courage on Bob's part."

Mrs. Cameron passed out dishes of peanut butter fudge ("It's my specialty") and said it wasn't unusual of a game night for Mr. Cameron to run back and forth from the motel to the gym, huffing and puffing, to get progressive accounts of the scoring. "We play Bryce Valley tonight," she said, "but there's not a seat to be had. The gym is sold out for the year. All 250 seats."

"We're getting a brand-new gym next year," said the proprietor. "Blueprints are already in. It'll cost $380,000 and will seat 2,300 people, which is 2,000 more than it'll seat now and 1,000 more than we've got people. But we're aiming to bring in the Region 9 tournament.

"Basketball," he said, "is really *it* in this town. Look around you at all the nets and goals in the backyards. There's as many backboards as there are TV antennas. In some places there was a basketball goal before there was indoor plumbing. Some of them still don't have indoor plumbing."

"Actually, there's no other diversion in the winter," said another Panguitch man. "Except the movie house and the pool hall. And the movie screen has a big slice in it where a kid threw a piece of cardboard. The slice always shows up on the hero's nose. And as for the pool hall, that's no place for a youngster."

"The pool hall is the blight of the community. Always has been," said a third man. "The idle brain is the devil's workshop."

Down the street there was only a handful of cars in front of the high school though it was 2 o'clock. This, it was explained, was because only a handful of Panguitch High School kids could afford cars. The bright yellow-and-silver Chevrolet, souped up to 250 horsepower, belonged to Dr. Sims Duggins' son Rodney. The Studebaker with the bongo drums in the back belonged to the marshal's son, and it was given to him because his father didn't want him flitting around in the patrol car.

There were sheep and cows in the yard across the street from the school. (Panguitch zoning restrictions, said the hotel proprietor, maybe aren't what they ought to be.) The school is a compact, two-story, buff-brick building built to last in 1937. It is right next door to the older Panguitch Junior High, which is condemned but still in use. Standing on the steps out front, one can feel the throb of the phys ed students pounding around in the gym upstairs, can smell the pastry being burned in the home ec oven and can hear, from somewhere, a struggling cornet soloist playing *The Nutcracker Suite*, or is it *Bye Bye Blues*?

Enrollment at Panguitch is 110, of which 64 are boys. The principal, Clifford LeFevre, a bright, middle-aged man, says he gave up ranching to return to education, and this explained the huge hide of a Hereford steer that covered one wall of his tiny office. He has a staff of only 13 and therefore requires double duty from some faculty members. In addition to his own job, LeFevre teaches biology and speech; Wrestling Coach Allen Smith is also the music teacher and directs the 30-piece band; and Basketball Coach Davis instructs in math and makes a stab at trigonometry. Davis will be qualified in chemistry as soon as he completes the biweekly course at Cedar City. Teachers get nothing extra for coaching, so Davis, father of five, with a sixth due in June (his annual salary is $4,750), works summers at the slaughter-house in Kanab and is always on call when somebody in Panguitch needs a pig butchered or some linoleum laid. "Bob can do just about anything he sets his mind to," says Principal LeFevre.

Coach Davis is a tall, curly-haired, handsome man of 32 with a crank-and-go voice and a knowledge of basketball gleaned mostly from books ("I didn't play when I was at Brigham Young, you see"). Sitting in Principal LeFevre's office, he talked about the intricacies of his offense and how he had decided to use a double post this year. Then he was asked about the basketball scandal he'd cleared up, and about his moratorium on dating. How did a coach cope with such explosive issues?

"A couple of years ago," he said soberly, "I discovered some of the boys on the team—all of the first five, in fact—were smoking and drinking. I passed on a warning and let it ride, hoping they'd see the light. Well, there was this party. Cigarettes and beer. A couple of the boys joined in only because they knew if I found out and was going to do anything I'd have to go against them all. That's what I did. I made a clean sweep, and the next thing you know we're starting a bunch of soph-omores—Brent and Wally and Joe and Lou. It was tough going for a while. I don't imagine I was too popular a fellow down at the pool hall. But it was a blessing in disguise. This team found itself. You'll see tonight. And I didn't have to worry about them. They made their own training rules and they abide by them. They're good boys."

Did they honest and truly give up girls on their own?

"Well, not exactly," said Davis, clearing his throat. "But rules are rules. Even now I have to get after them for standing around the halls mooning. There'll be plenty of time for that after the state tournament."

Principal LeFevre and his visitors stepped out into the hall. Basketball star Turek, tall and blond, and basketball star Riggs, short and brunet, were lounging by the locker of Cheerleader Melanie McEwen, soft and dreamy. "See what Coach means?" said LeFevre. On the bulletin board there was a huge chart divided into 40 squares. The first few squares had been crossed off with bold black strokes. "Count-Down Calendar," read the title, and LeFevre explained that the girls had put up the poster as a reminder of that day of salvation when the ball boys, as they are called in Pan-guitch, would be freed from Davis' clutches. "Happy days are here again!" said the caption under the last square.

As part of the general displeasure with the rules, Sophomore Sandra Crofts had written a poem (English Teacher Irene McEwen, Melanie's lovely mother, is very strong on poetry). The poem was called "Ball Season," and it portrayed the grim life of the boyless world of Panguitch girls and the girlless world of basketball players. "In bed every night, right at 10," Sandra had written sagely. "Being on the team is like being locked in a pen." She went on to say that all a girl does every day is go home to mother, and predicted that soon the girls will be dousing their hair with Brylcreem for something to run their fingers through.

The Panguitch gym was filled to popping for the game with Bryce Valley. In a front-row seat Hot Rodney Duggins, the doctor's son, pointed out that on both sides the fans were sticking out onto the playing court. This was all right, he said, because it made it impossible for a Panguitch player to go out-of-bounds. Rodney's father leaned over to say that in days past, when crowds were not so orderly, the corners of the playing floor would actually round off with people.

The Panguitch junior varsity players won the preliminary game as the key decisions by the two officials, both Panguitch High faculty members, consistently went in their favor. "Think they're prejudiced?" said Rodney, winking wildly. Dr. Duggins said that this was, after all, just the preliminary, but he remembered a Panguitch varsity game in Marysvale when the timekeeper kept the clock between his knees, hidden from view, and the last 17 seconds took half an hour. "Then there was the referee who gave the opposition the ball while Panguitch was out getting a drink of water. The other team scored," said Dr. Duggins, "and one of our lady fans fainted on the spot." By this time the preliminary game was over and Official Maloy Dodds came over to join the conversation. When he was playing for Panguitch, he said, the ladies of Escalante used to line the street outside after a game and throw their high-heeled shoes at the Panguitch players.

The varsity game began, and Dr. Duggins noted with pride that he had delivered every boy on the starting team. "The starting teams of *both* schools," he added. Melanie McEwen and her cheerleaders soon had the metal-roofed Panguitch gym, the exact acoustical equivalent of a rural mailbox, rocking with repetition: "Baskets! Baskets! Baskets, boys! / You make the baskets, we'll make the *noise*!" The boys responded, after a slow start, and soon were making baskets as fast as Melanie's group could suggest them.

Still, Bryce Valley, which had won only once previously, clung to the lead. It was sacrilege, said a Panguitch father. Coach Davis called for time. "Posing," he said to the Bobcats. "You saw a photographer out there and you started posing." He sat back down. "Slow starts, slow starts," he muttered. "Times like this we couldn't throw the ball into the Great Salt Lake." Lou Tibbs slumped beside him, momentarily relieved of his job at forward. "Have you ever seen a worse basketball player than me?" he asked. "I think I probably have," said Coach Davis absently.

The tide, inexorable as it always is for the better, taller team, began to change. Joe Riggs made six straight points, and Brent Turek and Wally Ortman seemed to get every rebound. Six, eight, 10, 20 ahead. The Bobcats piled it on.

They were every bit up to their credits. The 6-foot-3, 180-pound Turek played with exceptional basketball sense, timing and touch. His rebounding was superb. Wally Ortman's back dribble evoked many a long ah, and little Joe Riggs — "inspired," his mother said afterward when the parents got together on the floor — scored 16 points on long one-hand shots. "Unh-unh, Unh-unh, those Bobcats can't be beat!" cheered the cheerleaders. Bryce Valley became Panguitch's 17th victim, 71–48, and the state tournament was just five games away.

"Now what do we do?" I asked Hot Rodney as the crowd filed out. It was barely 10 o'clock.

"Nothing to do," said Rodney despairingly. "Unless—" He brightened. "Unless you want to ride up and down Main Street a couple times."

The next day, training rules notwithstanding, there remained the question of whether little Joe Riggs or big Brent Turek was in the lead with the beautiful Melanie. Between classes, Mrs. McEwen discussed this, but first she brought out a bundle of papers, the classroom compositions of Joe Riggs. One was entitled "Marriage Before Education?" and in it Joe wrote: "To a teen-ager of a small country town who has any foresight into the problems of the near future, the bonds of matrimony is a dread."

"Look at the others," said Mrs. McEwen. There was a poem, "Panguitch," in which Joe vowed to stay in his home town "forever," and a thesis on the multiple horrors of opiate analgesics. They were well written. On one of them, Mrs. McEwen had scribbled, "You're such a *swell* guy."

"This is a smart, sensitive boy," she said. "But, most important, he realizes there's more to this world—and should be more to Panguitch—than basketball. Oh, they know how I feel," she went on, eyes flashing. "I'm still as much a fan as anybody. Go to all the games. But I'm also the oldest teacher here. My husband has done well in the motel business and we have been many places and seen many things. We're going to Hawaii next month and we're going to send Melanie to Paris to school if she wants to go. What I'm driving at is this: as a teacher, I want a great deal more for these kids, these very fine, wonderful kids, than just a score and a winning streak." Her voice had been rising. She stopped.

"Now," she continued quietly, "Melanie was named after that fine young woman in *Gone With The Wind*, the one with such high character. I'm pleased to say Melanie has lived up to the image. And as for her love life, that's pretty much her own business."

Brent Turek, the third corner of the triangle, lives in Hatch, a village of 198 people, 16 miles south of Panguitch. In "My Story," a composition for Mrs. McEwen, Brent depicted himself as being initially amazed by how fast the crowd was at Panguitch High and how dumb he must have seemed. The night after the Bryce Valley game Mrs. Turek, a large, friendly, pink-faced woman, served a dinner of venison, rice, pear salad with strips of cheese, great slices of homemade bread baked in a wood-burning stove and milk. "I'm really very sorry," she said, "but there's no coffee." She said they didn't get much company in Hatch, and coffee-drinking strangers are rare. "It was funny last fall," she said. "Two bandits were supposed to be on the loose and the man on the radio said to lock your doors. Nobody in Hatch owns a lock."

It was suggested to Brent that he obviously had a talent for basketball and would surely get a scholarship offer. But what of the fair Melanie?

"Oh, gee, she's Joe's girl now, I guess," said Brent modestly. "I'm no heart smasher. Besides, girls are plenty destructive. 'Come on, come on, you don't have to be in training *all* the time,' that's what they say. Not Melanie, mind you, but some of them.

"Say, listen, I'd like to tell you a few things about the Mormon religion. I won't try to convert you or anything, but you'd be surprised how important it is in our lives and how much we help each other. It's a good feeling to be in touch with people. Tonight I'm going up to the Little ranch to give them the monthly lesson. As a priest—you get to be a priest when you're 16—I'm supposed to give a lesson to two families a month. Come along and see."

The Little ranch was another five miles south and apparently had fared poorly in the last 100 years. A simple unfrosted light bulb illuminated the tiny living room. There were pictures of old people on the walls, and a frayed Indian blanket covered the sofa. Mrs. Little, a painfully thin, bright-eyed woman of 77, sat rocking in a misshapen black chair, her fur-lined boots unbuckled after a long day. As Brent gave the lesson—"Honor thy father and thy mother"—she nodded approvingly, interrupting on occasion to test him with a question.

When the lesson was over she said, "He's a fine boy, isn't he? And a fine Mormon. And isn't that a fine basketball team he's on? Undefeated, you know."

PROPER PERSPECTIVE

Bill Bradley was different in many ways. The son of a bank president in Crystal City, Missouri (population 3,618), he became a two-time all-America and National Honor Society student in high school; a three-time all-America and history major at Princeton University; star of the U.S. Olympic gold medal team in Tokyo; winner of the Sullivan Award; a Rhodes scholar; a 10-year member of the twice-NBA-champion New York Knicks; coauthor of the critically acclaimed Life on the Run; *a U.S. senator from New Jersey; and from age 17, one of the best ambassadors without portfolio the nation ever had.*

As a player, Bill Bradley is a legend. On December 30, 1964, he received a 2-minute ovation in Madison Square Garden when he fouled out with 4:37 remaining and Princeton leading eventual NCAA runner-up Michigan, 75 to 63. He had outscored his man, 41 to 1. (With Bradley out, Michigan—led by Cazzie Russell, a Knick teammate-to-be—salvaged the game, 80 to 78.) Later, when Bradley poured in 58 points against Wichita in the third-place NCAA game, the Wichita fans set up a chant, "We believe!"

In southeast Missouri they still talk about the night in March 1961 when Bill almost pulled the Crystal City Hornets, with an enrollment barely into the largest class, to the state championship against four-time-winner St. Louis University High. He hit 33 of his team's 51 points and was generally heroic, but the city boys salvaged a 1-point victory in one of Missouri's most memorable finals. U High defensed Bradley well inside, and Crystal City answered by moving him away from the basket. Robert L. Burnes of the St. Louis Globe-Democrat *wrote that "it was a splendid chess match between two well-schooled teams, and one regrets that all this finesse wasn't preserved for future use."*

How U High avenged an earlier 1-point loss at Crystal City is told in the following story from the Fes-

tus Democrat, the daily newspaper in Crystal City's larger sister town, population 7,530. Not all epics are triumphs.

HORNETS LOSE STATE CROWN BY ONLY 1 POINT, 52–51

Crystal City came within a step of high school basketball's top rung as it was tripped by St. Louis University High, 52 to 51, in the state Class L final Saturday night at Washington University fieldhouse.

The one-point setback was a real heartbreaker and one that will be remembered for a long, long time.

The Hornets, led by all-America star Bill Bradley, led throughout most of the game and seemed ready to capture another spine-tingler and the school's first state crown. However, the experienced Junior Bills, four-time winners of the crown, showed their poise and all-around balance in the final minutes. A free throw by Joe Gegg, who was tough on defense all night and was picked to guard Bradley man-for-man in the second half, proved the decisive margin. Bradley tallied his 32nd and 33rd markers with six seconds left, but the Little Bills managed to stall out the clock.

Crystal City started strong, and in the first few minutes it looked as if Bradley was going to whip the Bills single-handed. He scored the team's first six points of the game and nine of the first 10 as Crystal City kept two and four points ahead. Late in the first half the Hornets went ahead, 25 to 20, but the Bills came back and at halftime it was Crystal City, 32 to 30.

Both teams played cautiously in the third quarter, each managing 10 points, and the Hornets had a 42 to 40 lead going into the final quarter. With two minutes remaining, the Bills tried to stall, only to have the Hornets intercept but miss a costly layup. The Bills got the ball, and Gegg was fouled, then to sink the decisive free throw.

The box score:

UNIVERSITY (52)	fg	ft	p	tp
Gegg	6	2	2	14
Curran	0	0	0	0
Zuchowski	7	3	2	17
Grawer	1	0	1	2
Zinselmeyer	4	2	2	10
Steube	4	1	0	9
Totals	22	8	7	52

CRYSTAL CITY (51)	fg	ft	p	tp
Trautwein	0	0	0	0
Mall	1	0	1	2
Bradley	15	3	3	33
Haley	3	0	1	6
LaPresta	0	0	2	0
Lucas	4	1	2	9
Hardin	0	1	0	1
Totals	23	5	9	51

If the final hadn't been such a classic city-country confrontation, Crystal City's semifinal might fill history's bill just as well. There the Hornets survived a three-overtime ordeal against Mercy of St. Louis. The win-

ning, sudden-death basket was on a lay-up, off a feed by Bradley.

Bill, 17 years old at graduation, took a trip to Europe that summer, an experience that gave him the first of many opportunities in international goodwill. (Four years later, his athletic, scholastic, and goodwill achievements would merit an official commendation from the Missouri legislature, preserved in a document known as House Resolution 157 of the 73rd General Assembly.) Following is another Festus Democrat *story, written after Bill's return from his post-high school European trip. Remember that the subject is a 17-year-old boy.*

MORE EFFORT NEEDED TO BUILD REAL WORLD FRIENDSHIP, SAYS BRADLEY

Bill Bradley, who hopes to enter the foreign service and who already holds the unofficial title of Crystal City's ambassador to Europe, discussed his travels on the Continent last night before the local Rotary Club and their wives and guests.

His theme was a serious one: the importance of individual friendships in building international goodwill. He took the audience on a whirlwind tour, by means of color slides, of seven countries, his running commentary describing the old colleges of England, the ancient churches and ruins of Rome and much in between. But he said he most enjoyed meeting the people of Europe.

The attitude of some American tourists, he said, hurts the country's reputation overseas. These persons feel everything in the United States is better and everything in Europe is second-rate. Many expect to have all the conveniences and foods to which they are accustomed at home. Others fume when they find nobody in a particular place speaks English.

Bill cited an incident in Florence, Italy, to demonstrate what he means by personal contact.

When he had a few free hours there, he sought a basketball court. With the aid of the son of a hotel man, he found a Catholic school so equipped and got permission to practice. As he shot baskets, boys gradually began to appear in twos, then threes, then fours. Finally a crowd was watching. Bill then organized a game among some of the boys. The next morning he returned to play with them again.

"I may be the only American some of them will ever see," Bill commented last night.

As he was leaving the court, a youth came up to Bill and said, "I no Communist." The friendliness of one American had made this Italian a friend of the U.S.A.

"If we do not call the people of other nations friends, someone else will call them comrades," Bill concluded.

It was said of Bill Bradley that his teammates were his greatest fans. He was a selfless, thinking player who could have scored more than his already prodigious totals and who believed that a foul is an adverse reflection on judgment and skill. Both Bradley and the Crystal City team were in a sense community properties. This was evident in the citation attending retirement of Bill's jersey, number 52, which—along with his picture and school record—was permanently showcased in the gymnasium foyer. The Crystal City community stands on a bluff in a mineral region 30 miles south of St. Louis and a mile and a half from the Mississippi River. The name "Crystal" derives from the area's high-quality white silica sand, once a required ingredient in the glassmaking process of the town's main industry. Part of Mississippi Avenue, which passes the plant, is cobblestone. But time changes things. Employment at the plant, once totaling several thousand, is way down at this writing, and reduced enrollment has dropped the high school to Class 3A, the second largest classification. All this makes memories of the Bradley era even more dear.

From "Hornets Lose State Crown by Only 1 Point," *Festus* (Mo.) *Democrat*, March 20, 1961, 1; "More Effort Needed to Build Real World Friendship, Says Bradley," *Festus Democrat*, August 1, 1961; letter from Sam Schapiro, Jefferson County Newspapers, (Festus, Mo.), May 28, 1984. Reprinted by permission of Jefferson County Newspapers.

WRONG TURN

If you're a Kentuckian over 45, you'll know that before he ran afoul of the system, Kelly Coleman was bracketed with Oscar Robertson and Jerry West on the all-America prep team. He averaged just under 47 points per game. Today Robertson and West are household words. Coleman isn't. This story is from Basketball, the Dream Game in Kentucky *by Dave Kindred, published in 1976.*

Kelly Coleman scored a record 50 points in the first game of the 1956 state tournament in Lexington's Memorial Coliseum. The next game he made 39 and, in a semifinal defeat, 28. Following that, he scored 68 in the third-place game. So he averaged 46.3, which is good for mortals, but for Kelly Coleman it was under his season's average of 46.9. When the third-place game ended, celebrants carried Coleman off the floor—against his wishes. He dressed hurriedly without benefit of a shower, left the Coliseum, hired a taxi and was in a tavern drinking beer (three mugs) during the championship game. He was 17 years old, already a legend: King Kelly Coleman, a coal miner's son, the greatest scorer in Kentucky basketball history, a man-child given to girls, basketball, bragging, beer and trouble although not necessarily in that order.

Nothing Kelly Coleman ever did, on the court or off, surprised his intimates. Ralph Carlisle said of him, "Gosh almighty, he was just the best." Coleman's coach at Wayland High School, deep in the mountains of eastern Kentucky, was Copper John Campbell, who said, "Adolph Rupp told me Kelly was a combination of Alex Groza, Frank Ramsey and Cliff Hagen." Copper John, a diplomat, also said newspapers used too much ink on Coleman: "It made him feel his Cheerios, if you know what I mean."

Coleman came to be called King Kelly when an imaginative sports writer decided coal was no longer king in eastern Kentucky, that it had been replaced in the hearts of the mountain people by a basketball player whose exploits, even 20 years later, seemed incredible. A dozen times in his senior season Coleman scored over 50 points. Once he made 75 (and had 41 rebounds the same night).

The mailman in Wayland grew weary of toting Kelly's mail that year. Daily he would leave a large canvas bag of letters outside the Colemans' $15-a-month house on the right fork of Beaver Creek. From Utah and California, from Ohio and Indiana, from everywhere people sent Coleman money, a dollar maybe, $5, even $75 once. Girls pursued him, and he often made certain they caught up. King Kelly the student? Some days the high school principal, Lawrence Price, telephoned the Coleman home and asked the player's mother, "Rusha, is Kelly out of bed yet?" Coleman, from his second-floor bedroom, would shout down, "Tell him I'll be there in time for practice."

As a freshman at Wayland High, Coleman averaged 19 points a game. He raised that to 26 the next year, and he broke the state scoring record his junior season with a 32.6 average. In basketball parlance Kelly was a gunner. He shot a lot. The Machine Gunner, they called him. No rawboned example of spartan living, Kelly was 6 feet 2 and weighed 215 pounds. Genes alone didn't account for his considerable size. They had help from hamburgers ("25 or 30 a week," he said), chocolate milk shakes ("one for each hamburger") and beer.

The night King Kelly scored 75 points against Maytown High, he was said to be playing under the inspiration of Milwaukee's famous export. A Maytown athlete complained to his coach that Kelly was drunk, and the coach said, "Be sure you find out what brand he's using; I'll get you some." It was Wayland's custom to carry its own drinking water in large bottles wrapped in tape. Few people believed Kelly's bottle to contain only water. "That's a myth," Coleman said of the Maytown report. "My senior year, *before* a game, never. *After* a game, well . . ."

Kelly was a 10th grader, he said, when he discovered it was difficult to play basketball after a bout with spirits. From his house to the Wayland gymnasium, it was a mile and a half walk. A buddy gave him a ride and asked if he'd like to share a fifth of tequila. Kelly was 14 years old. "At that time, the most I ever drank was three or four beers. I had four or five drinks of that tequila and then went to play a basketball game. My head was buzzy. That night I couldn't put one in a truck bed. I got two goals."

During games Coleman was not Little Lord Fauntleroy. He denied a story that he put opposing free throwers out of sorts by pulling hair on the backs of their legs, just as he denied he ever scored on a fast break and continued to the concession stand for a hot dog and Coke. ("I did have two or three hamburgers and a milk shake at The Fountain about 45 minutes before every game. If it bothered me, I didn't notice.") Many of Coleman's baskets came on shots put up after running over people. One writer said Kelly had moves previously used only by Sherman tanks. "Ninety-nine percent of the time the defensive guy tried to jump in front of me, but I was too quick for him and he'd stick a shoulder into me. The foul was on him."

Coleman said players trying to contain him took hold of his uniform shorts. Sometimes they stood on his toes. They threw body blocks at him. "I'd see 'em coming and stop on a dime. They'd fall down, and I'd step over 'em for the basket." If a defender persisted in his harassment, King Kelly might talk to him in this manner: "Hey, you're wasting your time. You're not gonna stop me. When I get the ball, you ain't even gonna *see* me." Or Kelly might embarrass the poor fellow by first holding the ball out toward him. Then, when the taunted defender lunged for the offered ball, Kelly bounced it between the guy's legs, caught it on the other side and scored. "It's a lot of fun when it works," he said.

Coleman was an outside shooter, mostly from the top of the key. He depended on an extraordinary change-of-pace move, first at full speed, then dead in his tracks, then at speed again, to free him for the instant he needed to put up his jumper. The shot was not textbook perfect in that he launched the ball from above his right shoulder instead of from the top of his head. He was a good rebounder, mostly because of his bulk and an uncanny ability to determine where the ball would bounce from the rim. "I'd just look and know where the ball was going," he said. "I don't know how."

On nights when it was all working—at Maytown, for instance, when he made 31 of 49 shots—Coleman played a game unknown to people less favored by nature. "I felt kinda like Cassius Clay. Floating like a butterfly. If I had to, to score, I felt I could jump over anybody."

When Kelly Coleman walked out of the Phoenix Hotel in Lexington on March 14, 1956, to play for Wayland High in the state tournament, pieces of paper fell from the sky and people scurried after them, curious. An airplane, circling the city, had dropped thousands of leaflets announcing the presence in town of King Kelly Coleman, "the greatest prep basketeer in history." Kelly saw people picking up the papers and talking about the wonder of it all. He paid little attention, for by then he had been the subject of so much publicity that one more piece of propaganda, no matter how ingeniously delivered, meant nothing. He was thinking only of the state tournament. He once said he had no particular ambition in life except to win the state championship.

In March 1956, some of the big movie stars were Alan Ladd, Joel McCrea, June Allyson, Audie Murphy, Yvonne deCarlo. Hamburger sold for 29 cents a pound and milk for 39 cents a half-gallon. In Hopkinsville the school board voted to expel any student who got married or pregnant. The South Carolina general assembly passed a bill ordering the firing of all public employees who were members of the NAACP. Integration, the legislators said, was not in the best interests of peace and tranquility. President Eisenhower said he'd "be happy to be on any political ticket" with Vice President Nixon, who'd been a source of discontent among some Republican leaders who wanted the young Californian out of office. On the radio The Lone Ranger, Fibber McGee and Molly, Groucho Marx and Gangbusters were in competition with the state tournament. Too bad for the stars of the airwaves. For Kentuckians it was time to tune in King Kelly.

The Coleman house on Beaver Creek was put up on seven logs in an attempt to escape the rising waters every spring. The family often moved everything from the first floor to the second until the waters receded. In March of '56 Beaver Creek was far out of its banks. The people of Wayland left in boats to see the King play. Coleman's mother, a Baptist who had nothing to do with fun and games, never saw her famous son play, save in a film. His father, Guy, moved from Wayland when the Elkhorn Coal Company, the town's creator and sustainer, closed down the mines. The elder Coleman, a strict disciplinarian who never allowed Kelly to go out at night, went to Cleveland to work in a steel mill when his son was a 10th grader. Of 11 Coleman children, Kelly was the first boy after four girls. A sister, Linda Carol, was in Lexington for the state tournament.

Kelly hadn't always been a basketball hero. Baseball was his game. When he tried out for the eighth-grade basketball team, he wasn't good enough to earn a uniform. "That really peeved me," he said, "because I knew I could beat everybody to death in baseball." So, for the first time and maybe the last, Kelly Coleman worked at basketball. With other Wayland boys he played day and night on a concrete, lighted court on the town's main street. "In the ninth grade I was all-district," he recalled.

"In the 10th grade it seemed like every game I was getting better. And my junior year—people don't realize this, but it's true—I broke the state scoring record. I was getting 30, 32, 40, 42 points. I could see that the next year it'd be hard for me to get *under* 40."

The game that earned Wayland a spot in the state tournament may have been Coleman's best ever. Wayland beat Pikeville, 96 to 90, in the regional final at Pikeville. Although Kelly fouled out with a minute and a half left in the *third* quarter, he had 44 points. "I would've got 80 if they didn't foul me out," he said. Coleman added that the game became a battle of referees, one working his whistle off for Pikeville, the other trying to keep things "honest." The box score shows, however, that six Pikeville players fouled out and that Coach John Bill Trivette's team played the last 39 seconds with four men. Trivette's wife, in a commentary on the officiating, socked the "honest" referee, Milford "Toodles" Wells, on the head with her purse. " 'Toodles' had a police escort out of the gym, out of town and out of the county," Coleman recalled.

On the night of March 14, the state tournament had a sellout crowd for the opening session. More than 13,000 people paid to see King Kelly Coleman. Many came attached by strings to helium-filled balloons bearing the single word, "COLEMAN." *The Lexington Herald* carried this headline:

"Kan King Kelly Kop Kommonwealth Kage Krown?"

As Wayland warmed up, eager patrons surrounded the mountaineers' end of the floor. "They were even counting the shots I missed in warmups, like I was really pushing to make 'em," he said. Though well aware of his fame, Coleman was shocked by this lavish attention. He wasn't feeling chipper, because he had the flu. And the goals, standing free in the vast open space at the Coliseum instead of being tacked to the wall as they were in the mountains, seemed small. Coleman thought, "How am I going to put one in *there*?"

The worst was yet to come.

"I jumped center for us, and from the first tip, when I tipped the ball to a guard and he gave me the ball back, all 13,000 people booed me," he said nearly 20 years later.

He couldn't figure it out. "I hadn't done anything to those people. I guess I'd gotten so much publicity that people resented it. Sports writers were looking for flaws. I wasn't on the sports pages. I was on the front page, and people were against me because of it. Hell, I wasn't responsible for those papers dropping out of the sky. I hadn't hurt anybody. I was just a little kid."

The booing took a pattern. "It stopped when I didn't have the ball, and it started up again when I got it."

Kelly scored 50 points despite the distraction. "But it kinda turned me off to the people in Kentucky, even to basketball really. Basketball lost its importance. It wasn't fun any more. It was a job, something I'd do just well enough to get by. I didn't even try after that. I didn't have the enthusiasm, the drive. I decided I didn't want to be a super-hero any more."

Wayland won that first game easily, then used Kelly's 39 points to beat Earlington, 65 to 58. That set up a game with Carr Creek, the tournament favorite. During the regular season, Wayland and Carr Creek played twice, each winning a close game. Wayland, winner in 35 of 39 games with a 91-point scoring average, figured to win the tournament if it defeated the Creekers.

As always, Carr Creek coach Morton Combs chose not to run with Wayland. To run with King Kelly was to invite him to score 50. So Coleman scored only 28 under defenses that often put three men against him (Wayland's other guard, Elmon Hall, scored 30 that night).

Wayland led, 67 to 66, with three seconds to play. Carr Creek's Freddie "The Ready" Maggard, whose 20-foot shot with seven seconds left in overtime won the Creekers' first tournament game, then launched a 30-footer.

"Maggard was looking for their star, Bobby Shepherd, and he couldn't find him," Coleman said. "So he shot it. It went straight through."

In the locker room Coleman sat on the floor in a corner, weeping. A Lexington sports writer, Billy Thompson, approached and then turned away. "Don't go, Billy, you're the only guy who's stood by me," Kelly said.

Pikeville's John Bill Trivette moved toward the pair. "Those people want your blood, Kelly," the coach said of the spectators.

Coleman turned to Thompson: "I'm going to give 'em the greatest basketball game they've ever seen. I'm going to get 60. And then, Billy, you tell 'em for me to drop dead."

That night Coleman scored 68 in Wayland's 122 to 89 victory over Bell County. "I could've got 90," he said. Excited fans hoisted Kelly to their shoulders in celebration. He only wanted down.

"I was mad. I left the floor, left the gym and went back to the hotel. I ran into a guy from Wayland in the lobby, and he gave me a brown paper sack with a fifth in it. I didn't drink it. Another guy from Wayland and I went to a little bar, and I had three mugs of beer. I gave the fifth to the other guys on the team."

Kelly says he was either in that bar or in his hotel room, reading comic books, when the all-tournament trophies were handed out at the Coliseum. His sister, Linda, accepted for him, explaining that the King was too "shy" to come forward. Carr Creek won the tournament, pleasing romantics who remembered the ragged urchins of 1928, and Ted Sanford, commissioner of the Kentucky High School Athletic Association, said it was the greatest state tournament ever. He never changed his mind.

As it was predictable that a drawn beer would have suds atop it, so it was certain Kelly Coleman would develop an intimate relationship with trouble. With the departure of his father for Cleveland, Kelly, then 15, was set free. His mother, Rusha, had her hands full with five younger children. Besides, Kelly confessed at age 36, "I think I must have a little Indian blood in me. I'd get a little wild sometimes."

Myth insisted that King Kelly left several gymnasiums to the accompaniment of gunfire. He denied it. He also denied he was ignorant. "If you look at my sixth and seventh-grade records, you'll see I got good grades," he said. "That was before I became an idiot. Girls, playing basketball, screwing around—that's all I was interested in. On an IQ test, I had the highest score in the county, 142. But school was a secondary thing. That's why Little Bo Peep called my house. Lawrence B. Price. His initials were L.B.P. Little Bo Peep."

Coleman's companions were not all Sunday School teachers. Because Wayland won so often with such ease, gamblers took to betting on how many points the King would rack up. In recruiting, one university sent a gambler to discuss with Kelly methods by which they could both grow rich. Pearl Combs, the old Hindman High coach, once bragged that his boys would hold Kelly to 21 points. The betting line was 35 points. "I had 39 at the half," Kelly said. "When I walked out of the gym, the gamblers all lined up and shook my hand. 'Nice game, Kelly,' they'd say. And every time I shook hands I'd pull back a $20 bill and put it in my pocket."

At the advanced age of 17 then, Kelly had been places and done things.

It was only the beginning.

Because it recruited Kelly with feverish zeal and greenbacks awinging, West Virginia University was punished by the NCAA even before Coleman enrolled. Part of that punishment was, in fact, that Coleman could never enter the university. At the behest of Coach Copper John Campbell, once an Eastern Kentucky University star and a buddy of its coach, Paul McBrayer, King Kelly signed up at Eastern—for six weeks. "And I stayed the last two weeks just to get my monthly paycheck of $250."

University of Kentucky zealots dearly wanted Coleman. They sent a 20-foot-long petition bearing thousands of signatures certifying their desire to see the King play for Baron Rupp. Frank Ramsey and Bob Burrow, both all-Americas at UK, whispered sweet nothings into Kelly's ear. Gov. A.B. Chandler said howdy, podnah. Coleman recalled, "Kentucky offered me four scholarships—for me and three of my sisters. They'd get me and my wife a place to live. They'd see we didn't need anything. They promised I would have a business opportunity open to me when I was done playing. They offered me the world."

How Coleman came to turn down Kentucky is a story we'll get to later. Likewise why he left Eastern Kentucky after six weeks. King Kelly made things happen. He worked a year in a steel mill in Middletown, Ohio, the home of his in-laws. He'd married his high school sweetheart, Ann Watkins, a majorette, shortly after graduation. From Middletown, he returned to Kentucky Wesleyan College.

"College beats manual labor," he once said.

Besides, Wesleyan did its best for the visiting royalty. "They couldn't give me the moon, but they made sure I didn't starve," Kelly said. "They got my wife a job at General Electric. We had one kid then."

At Wesleyan he was the nation's sixth leading scorer as a freshman (26.6 points a game). Later he walked off the court during a game, an action for which he was suspended and which led Kelly to put the team on notice that it needed *him* a lot more than he needed it. The last game of his college career was the semifinal of the NCAA small-college tournament. He refused to play in the consolation game because he had, he said, "several other things to do that night."

He was the second draft choice of the New York Knicks, the ninth player picked in the NBA's draft that year. But he never played a single regular-season game for the Knicks and wound up in the Eastern League on a team with Bill Spivey. Convinced that the Knicks had blackballed him in the NBA—we'll get to that story, too—Coleman joined the new American Basketball League, a venture financed by Abe Saperstein, owner of the Harlem Globe Trotters.

The ABL folded quickly, and to earn his full contract, Coleman played for the United States Stars, a stooge team traveling with the Trotters.

"We had one rule on the Stars," Kelly said. "Five of us had to be sober every day. I'd be sober Monday, Tuesday, Wednesday. Then not sober on Thursday, Friday, Saturday."

Other than that, nothing much happened since Kelly Coleman left Wayland.

Now those stories we promised . . .

First, why King Kelly said no to Kentucky:

The Elkhorn Coal Company home offices were in Charleston, W. Va. Word got there of the phee-nom at Wayland, and West Virginia University decided to make its move before Coleman was seduced by UK. The summer after his junior prep season Coleman was given a 1954 Dodge ("It helped my mobility with the girls"), a gasoline credit card and clothes ("All I ever had before was two pairs of pants. Suddenly I had 15 pairs of shoes, shirts, watches, coats—enough clothes to outfit our whole team."). In an attempt to hide the King from UK, West Virginia gained him entrance to the exclusive, $2,000-a-year Greenbrier Military Academy at Lewisburg, W. Va. The commencement speaker was perennially Dwight Eisenhower. Greenbrier, Kelly could do without.

"You had some 10th grader with rank pushing you around," Kelly said. "You had to have your shoes shined. Mine never shined good enough. Lights out at 9 o'clock. No girls. They arranged blind dates, but you had to be in by 10 o'clock. For every time you screwed up, you got 10 demerits. The maximum was 250, and they kicked you out. I had the max in six weeks."

Although the academy commandant offered to wipe the slate clean, presumably in deference to the King's 20-foot jumper, Coleman went back to Wayland for his senior year—after promising he'd still attend West Virginia.

Two lawyers came to Wayland that winter, he said, urging him to attend Kentucky. Besides offering Kelly the world, they said they'd pay back West Virginia all the money it spent on him. So Kelly told them all about his West Virginia dealings. "At the time I was thinking, 'To hell with Kentucky, to hell with all those people. They booed me at the state tournament, and all I ever did was play as hard as I could, the best I could.' I figured I'd been used and abused; it was time for me to use and abuse somebody."

The NCAA, snooping around on a tip from another school, uncovered West Virginia's illegal shenanigans in connection with King Kelly. "The NCAA man came to see me. He showed me the letter asking for an investigation of West Virginia. It was signed by those two lawyers on behalf of UK. That was it. They'd used what I told them. I was still thinking about UK in the back of my mind until I found that out," Kelly declared.

Adolph Rupp didn't remember it that way. He said King Kelly "wasn't a team player, like we wanted." Besides, the Baron said, "There wasn't any violent recruiting back then."

Next, why Coleman left Eastern after six weeks:

"McBrayer tried to operate like marine DI," Kelly said. "One time he told me to be in his office at 3 o'clock. I got out of class at 5 'til and went straight over. I got there at 3:05, and he said, 'When I say 3, I don't mean one minute past 3.'

"We ran in a cow pasture. I turned an ankle, and the trainer said to stay off it for two weeks. That was a Tuesday. McBrayer made me run on Friday. I had to hobble all the way, and I finished an hour behind everybody else.

"You had a spot to stand in practice. If I'm third in the front row, I better be in that spot or he'd make an ass out of me. If you were shooting in practice, you had your ball and your basket. If you miss a shot and somebody throws your ball back, he'd be all over you.

"He had me trying to change my shot—to get me to shoot it off the top of my head instead of the way I'd always shot. Well, hell. That nut. Six weeks was all I could take. They weren't paying me enough—$250 a month and room and board—to put up with him."

Next, why King Kelly didn't play in the NBA:

The Knicks gave him $2,000 to sign, a $1,000 bonus for reporting to camp under 210 pounds and an $8,500-a-year contract. In early scrimmages he played well, starting at guard opposite Richie Guerin.

Coleman had decided to reform. "Maybe I'll try to play," he said, describing his training-camp philosophy. "I won't drink. I won't anything."

The conversion didn't take. "Guerin one night said let's have a beer at this bowling alley. Well, we got to going. I never was one to control my drinking. And I got in a little dispute with a player who had a lot of pull with the coach, Carl Braun.

"I got no way of proving it, but I never started again, so that must have had something to do with it. Another time I was driving into town and waited 30 minutes for this big wheel. I called his room. Then I left him in bed. He got hot about it, and we, shall you say, exchanged words. Then, another time, something happened in the locker room."

After a good year in the Eastern League (18-point average on the championship team), Coleman was the third leading scorer in Saperstein's ABL. The league folded then, "and guys who couldn't carry my shoes onto the floor went right into the NBA. So I called a friend of mine, Harry Gallatin, who was coaching the St. Louis Hawks. He said, 'Kelly, find yourself a good job and forget about the pros.' The NBA had pegged me not to play."

It was September of 1975. In two weeks Kelly Coleman would be 37 years old. He lived in the Ramblewoode subdivision, a new community of $35,000 homes in suburban Detroit. Then an elementary school physical education teacher, Coleman in the years since pro basketball (1) worked three years in a steel mill in Cleveland; (2) returned to Wayland, bought a gas station and ran for the Kentucky House of Representatives ("I wasn't a politician; I thought all I had to do was get my name in the paper once a week; I didn't know I had to beat the bushes and lie a lot; I carried two precincts out of eight"); (3) sold the gas station to finance a final year of college at Pikeville and Wesleyan, and (4) moved to Detroit, where he first taught, then worked in the promotion department of *The Detroit News* and in 1974 returned to teaching.

"I turned down two high school coaching jobs this year," he said. "I'm too old now."

Coleman weighed 260 pounds. He carried the weight easily. As he moved about the living room, he was light on his feet. His eyes were a flame blue, and his brown hair was thick and wavy. He had four children: Terri, 18; Beverly, 17; Kelly, 12, and Mary Anna, 9. His son didn't play basketball. Hockey was his game.

If King Kelly had it all to do over, would he do it differently?

"I'd cut out the partying, I guess. But, back then, I just didn't care. I'd try a little more."

Regrets came occasionally. "I was the No. 1 man on the high school all-America team. Ahead of Oscar Robertson and Jerry West. Now I see them on television, making commercials. They're rich, and I'm still a poor guy."

What about 1956? Almost 20 years later, did it, looking back, seem real? Or a dream?

"I sometimes wonder *how* I scored so many points," Coleman laughed. "I watch games on television now, and I say, 'How could I score that many? How could I have been that cocky, to think that way?' "

From Dave Kindred, *Basketball, the Dream Game in Kentucky* (Louisville, Ky.: Data Courier, 1976), 31–34, 36–42.

NO CURE BUT NEVER FATAL

This is about a malady that is widespread, predictable, and peculiar to a sport. It affects all socioeconomic groups, and strangely, its positive aspects almost always outweigh the negative. Jim Stinson of Spokane, Washington, describes it.

There is an unusual disease which is caught by numerous residents of the state of Washington at the same time every year. It starts to appear in mid-February and lasts through the first few weeks of March. It is highly contagious and has been known to infect entire towns.

Symptoms of this illness vary according to the age of the victim. Students become extremely nervous and jumpy, eat irregularly, become disinterested in homework, develop cases of laryngitis and have a strange desire to travel to Spokane. Adults share many of the same symptoms, but they assume a disposition uncommon to most of them: they slip into new childhood, acting unusually relaxed and carefree. Many excuses are given to justify a few days off from work, and the only place people seem to want to be is the Spokane Coliseum where they can sit and watch basketball games. Authorities compare the disease with one occurring every October called World Seriesitis, which caused wholesale absenteeism until weekday afternoon games were shifted to evening.

No extensive research has been undertaken in the quest for a cure to the late winter illness, and the people who catch it would rather have it this way. The illness is accompanied by a form of amnesia. All is forgotten for a few days. Problems of the family, the economy, the farm and the world in general are far from the minds of the victims. Medical students can find no reference to the disease in their books, but those who have been stricken call it "Tournament Fever."

There are several degrees of The Fever. Some manage to catch it every year, but they are prepared for it. They schedule their vacations so they can see every one of the 26 state B tournament games without having to concoct an excuse for missing work. Others contract the disease only if their team qualifies. Still others go to the Coliseum without the fever, but once in the building cannot escape the germs in the air.

The strain of the fever common to Washington has four classes—AAA, AA, A and B. Type B is the most serious. Thousands of people seek group therapy at the Coliseum, and the people from the small towns, the chief carriers of the strain, traditionally infect a large segment of the population which would normally contract the fever on the AAA level.

In 1976 a new variety of the B malady was discovered in Ellensburg. It was caused by the appearance of the female of the species in tournament play. At first, the disorder seemed to be safely in quarantine. However, just when all cases were thought to be diagnosed and treated, new outbreaks were reported. They spread in epidemic proportions to obscure places like Bickleton, Mansfield and Soap Lake where the fever had never raged so strongly before. Since that time, the new ailment has branched to all corners of the state and appears to be just as excitingly incurable as any previous strain.

Tournament Fever has been passed down from generation to generation, and 38 epidemics have been reported since 1931. The Washington Interscholastic Activities Association, which is the authority on such diseases, says there is no way to control the Fever and that the number of infected people grows every year. More than 800,000 persons are known to have contracted the B strain.

The Fever has never been known to be fatal, but it does leave some scars. These scars are not hidden by those who receive them but are proudly displayed in order to be seen by all. Marks such as sportsmanship, pride, teamwork and congeniality are sported. Veterans and new recruits are identically marked and share the same joy, which is the Fever's major consequence.

From Jim Stinson, *Tournament Fever II: A History of the Washington State "B" Basketball Tournament* (Spokane, Wash.: Stinson, 1980), 7. Reprinted by permission of the author.

THE WEIRD AND THE WONDROUS: VINTAGE LITTLE TOWN

Superlatives, oddities, and memorable anecdotes I've collected over the years from communities with populations fewer than 5,000.

If you think you've had selection problems, consider the predicament of Oregon officials in 1919, their first state tournament year. There were no qualifying tourneys. The officials simply divided the state into eight regions and selected the most deserving team from each. Seven of the eight were easy—Portland Lincoln, Marshfield, Ashland, Astoria, Eugene, Salem, and Silverton. The eighth was tough. Hood River rated a shot, and both Madras and Prineville clamored for recognition. The latter two were to play off, with the winner meeting Hood River at the University of Oregon for the eighth spot. Instead of playing, however, both Madras and Prineville sent teams and rooting sections to Eugene. A pitched battle was narrowly averted before the teams agreed to toss a $20 gold piece for the privilege of facing Hood River. Madras won the toss, and the bitter Prineville folk remained to cheer their heads off for Hood River, which won easily, 63 to 12.

The term "barnburner," as descriptive of a nip-and-tuck struggle, is believed to have its origin in the central Indiana village of Wingate (population 400), the Midwest's earliest Little David. Its high school, which won the national interscholastic championship at the University of Chicago in 1920, used a livery stable as gym until it was consolidated out of existence. The gym was heated by potbellied stoves tucked in the corners, the bleachers seated 187 fans, and in the beginning the players cleaned up by stepping into a galvanized tub. Barn rentals were $3 per practice, $6 per game. Most memorable to Montgomery County old-timers are Wingate's back-to-back state titles in 1913–14. Those teams, led by the legendary Homer Stonebraker, had no gym at all. For practice they drove 6 miles by buggy or Model T to New Richmond. Their uniforms were baseball trousers, long socks, and sweatshirts. In 1913, with a squad of seven and a male enrollment of twelve, Wingate nipped South Bend, 14 to 13, in a five-overtime final. The next year it manhandled Anderson, 36 to 8, for the trophy.

Growing up in poverty in Silver City, Mississippi (population 400), Spencer Haywood played outdoor basketball without a basketball. They nailed up an old rusty hoop, and at first they threw tin cans at it. Then they got sophisticated and stuffed socks to make a ball. They pretended to dribble by saying, "Bop, bop." The guy with the ball got two "bops," then had to shoot or pass off. Later a star at Detroit's Pershing High, on the Olympic team, and in both ABA and NBA, Haywood says basketball saved him from becoming "an alky, an addict, or a hood. It was the way out."

After its first-round defeat in the state of Washington's 1967 B finals, Pe Ell (population 582) lost its coach, Alan Allie, to tonsillitis. Confined to his motel bed with a consolation game against Klickitat coming up, Allie seemed out of things. But no; they rigged a phone line for him, direct to the bench. He listened to the radio play-by-play and phoned instructions to assistant coach Warren Land. Pe Ell won by one point. The next day Allie returned, only to have his team lose by 24 to Liberty. Sports Illustrated *succumbed to the natural kiss-off: "He should have stayed in bed."*

It happened in North Dakota in 1949. With three seconds to go and Anamoose leading Rugby, 40 to 39, in a district Class B final, George Razook of Rugby fired a leaping underhand flip from 60 feet. It was good, but was it? No, according to the wall clock. But its hand habitually failed to stop when the buzzer sounded, slipping several seconds past the designated mark before coming to a halt. The referees were in a quandary; they couldn't hear the terminating horn due to the screaming of the crowd. They whisked to the timer's table where the nod was "yes" and the "count it" signal was flashed. Pandemonium reigned. The Rugby players danced with joy while the Anamoose partisans wept and pounded the floor. No silent-movie melodrama could have topped this scene.

When Sharpe won the Kentucky state championship in 1938, tournament officials found no phones in the community (population 250) to receive the news. Result: the nearest town was phoned. A man on horseback thereupon rode to a swollen river where he yelled to a boatman, who rowed and passed the word to another man on horseback. The latter galloped over the hill to Sharpe, bearing the glad tidings from Lexington.

The ultimate in scheduling headaches belongs to Barrow, Alaska, a treeless community on the Arctic coast 330 miles north of the Circle. Its high school, averaging a little over 100 students, is North America's northernmost, and its nearest athletic rivals, Fairbanks and Nome, are each a 1,000-mile round-trip away. Its teams travel 27,000 miles a year by plane and spend $100,000 doing it. Students themselves raise $10,000 to help out. The school sponsors track, cross country, wrestling, gymnastics, badminton, and volleyball, in addition to basketball.

Fans in Utica, Nebraska, thought they were receiving a raw deal from referee Rudy Voegler in their 1929 home game against Waco, and they booed continuously. Voegler stopped the game and warned the crowd. A short time later he called a one-shot foul on Utica. As the Waco player toed the line, a Utica fan yelled, "Give him another!" Voegler did. Another Utican shouted, "Give him two more!" Voegler did. Before Superintendent L.S. Smutz could quiet the throng, the Waco lad had been awarded twelve free throws. He missed eleven of them, but Waco won anyway—in overtime.

Texas's 1922 state tournament became known as "The Case of the Missing Trophy." Little Lindale (population 1,700 today) won the championship by routing giant El Paso, but the beards on the Lindale players wrinkled official eyebrows and there was an investigation. The boys weren't too smart; they should have shaved. One beard would be natural enough, two or three would arouse suspicion, but an entire team? The probe revealed that the Lindale superintendent's brother was an Oklahoma high school coach known as a recruiter partial to Indian players. The Lindale star was an Indian. Eventually both the superintendent and the coach admitted the charges. The governing association asked that the trophy be returned, but it was missing. Hidden in a store, it was said. "Try and get it," officials were told. After a year's suspension, Lindale High applied for readmission but was told in effect, "OK, but where is the trophy?" This scenario was repeated three more times. Finally, 5 years after the fact, the now battered cup was forwarded with the school's application for readmission. The controversy was ended. Meanwhile, El Paso, a finalist in every Texas state tourney from 1921 through 1924, had been awarded a substitute cup.

When they consolidated Duncan, Arizona (population 773) and Virden, New Mexico (population 246) into a single school district, they married two of the nation's richest small-town athletic histories. Eight miles apart in the farm-copper country along the Gila River, these schools were the basketball scourges of their states in the Depression-war period from the mid-thirties to the mid-forties. With an enrollment of only 180, Duncan became Arizona's eternal Cinderella by winning three consecutive state titles (1938–40). Its victim in the 1940 final was mighty Tucson, which had an enrollment of 2,216. Virden, with a student body smaller than Duncan's, won New Mexico titles in 1934 and 1944. Today Virden youngsters cross the state line to attend Duncan, the smallest school in the Eastern Arizona Conference, which embraces Globe, Safford, Clifton, Miami, Thatcher, Pima, and Morenci. "You have to live with it to realize what high school sports mean to a small town," observed a Duncan faculty man who coached until age 77 and remembered the Dust Bowl days.

The records of Iowa's Denise Long are to girls' prep basketball as Wilt Chamberlain's are to the men's pro game. Under six-player-team rules she amassed 6,250 points from 1966 to 1969 at Union-Whitten, including 1,968 as a senior. These were 1,147 and 201 superior to her nearest contenders. In the classic 1968 state final, won by Union-Whitten over Everly, 113 to 107 in overtime, she scored 64, opponent Jeanette Olson 76. Her single-game record is 111. But Denise was born too soon—before women's college ball got off the ground. She turned pro but rebelled against the intramural atmosphere, quit, and enrolled at the University of Iowa with these words: "In our state finals we had over 15,000 people screaming and jumping around in their seats. We were televised in nine states. Then I go to San Francisco where the only audience for the entire tournament is a handful of parents. I can't play basketball that way; I have too much respect for myself and the game. A team sport needs the support and the emotion of the crowd to make it exciting. Without that there is very little."

When Elvin Hayes was a seventh grader in Rayville, Louisiana, he didn't know much about basketball, but it was beginning to excite him. One day he slipped into the gym to watch the local girls' team play Tallulah, the winner to advance to a major tournament. It was great fun. The ball came bouncing toward him, sailing out of bounds, and he fielded it well, proudly throwing it back to the referee.

"Where are you from?" shouted the referee.

"Rayville," Elvin answered, again proudly.

"Technical foul on Rayville!" shouted the referee.

The poor kid didn't know the rule. Tallulah made the free throw, and that was the margin of victory. Elvin was harassed for months after the incident. Each day he tried to slip out of school early. He'd thought he was doing officialdom a favor.

Francis Scott Key High of Union Bridge, Maryland, was playing a possession game against Mount Airy. In the third quarter the score was only 12 to 9, and Key had frozen the ball for 7 minutes. Thereupon David Zentz, a reserve, shot a question at Coach Buzzy Lambert: "Coach, may we have a couple of balls and go shoot at the basket that isn't being used?"

Dedication was personified in spades by Marion Pierce of Lewisville, Indiana (population 530), the state's all-time scoring leader with 3,042 points over the period 1957–61. Described as a shy youth who needed an outlet, Marion would practice in the rain wearing a raincoat and shoot baskets at night, using the headlights of an old car until the battery went dead. Since his father operated a salvage yard, the boy had an endless supply of cars.

High point in Lewisville basketball history was its sectional final victory over the Henry County Goliath, New Castle (population 21,000), in '61. A power failure delayed its semifinal with Knightstown for almost 2 hours and when a snowstorm stranded the team in the New Castle fieldhouse and blocked all *roads, the final was postponed until Monday night. Lewisville won, 56 to 49, in the nation's largest high school gym.*

The town has lost its athletic identification. Its school was consolidated in 1969 with Spiceland and Straughan. The result is Tri High. But thanks to Marion Pierce, the Lewisville legend lives on.

To peruse Montana's roll of past state champions is to take a journey through the Old West and dabble in the glowing history of the Big Sky State.

There's Chinook (1930 and 1968), namesake of the warm, eastern-slope winter wind immortalized in painting by Montana's revered cowboy artist Charles M. Russell. Prompted by the disastrous winter of 1886–87, Waiting for a Chinook *depicts a lone cow, standing knee-deep in blizzard snow and near death from freezing while wolves circle in anticipation. The work revealed louder than any words the vast destruction wrought and the impracticality of open-range ranching. The Chinook community is just north of the Chief Joseph Battleground Monument, commemorating the 4-day Battle of Bear Paw in October 1877, the Indians' last stand.*

There is Fort Benton (1950), once the Missouri River's navigational terminus, debarkation point for tenderfeet bound for the gold camps, and military post until 1882.

There is Wolf Point (1941, '44, '52, '53, '61, '68), on the edge of the Fort Peck Reservation, named for the infamous episode early this century in which hide-seekers poisoned 2,000 wolves and left their carcasses on the frozen Missouri.

There is Bridger (1982), named for Jim Bridger, the trapper-guide-scout and most celebrated of the mountain men of the early 1800s.

There are the championship schools from Indian reservations—Lodge Grass (1980–82) and Plenty Coups (1981–83) from the Crow on the plains; Ronan (1960) and St. Ignatius (1956) from the Flathead west of the Continental Divide; and Browning (1980) from the Blackfeet just east of the Divide. Lodge Grass is on the Little Big Horn, a few miles upstream from the Custer National Cemetery. Plenty Coups, in the village of Pryor (population 329), is named for the last of the Crow war chiefs, a man who became friendly with whites and in 1921 delivered an epic war-and-peace oration at the Tomb of the Unknown Soldier.

There is Shelby (1955), where the Dempsey-Gibbons fight was held in 1923. The promoters took a bath—only 7,202 spectators occupied the specially built 45,000-seat arena, the town went bankrupt, and Gibbons didn't receive a cent despite going fifteen rounds with the great champion.

There is Miles City (1923, '29, '31, '35, '61, '78), one of the last of the cow towns, site of the Range Riders Museum and out near the Powder River, often described as "a mile wide and a foot deep."

There is Outlook (population 153), 8 miles from the Canadian border and probably the northernmost state champion town in any mainland state. Its boys won Class C in 1978 and 1980; its girls won Class B in 1976 and 1977.

There is Great Falls (population 60,000), "the big city" at the confluence of the Missouri and Sun rivers, where artist Russell's log cabin is preserved as a museum and a high school named for him won the AA title in '77. Great Falls High, across town, owns six state crowns (1936, '38, '44, '62, '65, '76).

And there are just plain frontier names like Cut Bank (1937, '38, '57, '66), Big Timber (boys, 1913 and 1940; girls, 1981–82), Bearcreek (1939), Three Forks (boys, 1974; girls, 1979–80), and Medicine Lake (1975).

Such are the characteristics of the nation's fourth largest state, one with twelve national forests, seven Indian reservations, a national battlefield, a national wildlife range, the Waterton-Glacier International Peace Park, both plains and mountain traditions, and a 550-mile common border with Canada.

Officials of the National Interscholastic Tournament, hosted by the University of Chicago from 1919 to 1930, regarded their event as a giant clinic, showcasing the various playing styles in a day when the sport was young and transportation was limited. But they were equally proud of the sportsmanship displayed. In 1927 Florence, Mississippi, defeated Huron, South Dakota, 19 to 16, in a bitter battle for third place. Shortly thereafter the Mississippi River flooded, causing great damage, and Florence was one of the towns hardest hit. The Huron lads read of the disaster and started a ball rolling. A few days later the town of Florence received a $1,000 check from Huron "in appreciation of our association on the basketball floor."

Florence (population 404) is typical of the small towns that dominated Mississippi boys' and girls' state championship rolls in the early pre-consolidation days. Some of them, listed here with current populations, had picturesque names: Duck Hill (706), Jumpertown (472), New Site (30), Vimville (75), Hurricane (later Esperanza, 150), Pine Grove (50), Potts Camp (450), Mossville (180), Shady Grove (150), Center Hill and Runnelstown (just plain "rural"), and Beat Four and Camp Ground (no longer listed).

Forever identified with Kentucky, where his University teams won a national record 874 games, Adolph Rupp was actually from Kansas, born on a farm 7 miles from Halstead (population 1,700). He played his early basketball either in the dirt at a one-room school in Harvey County or at home where the boys rigged a barrel-stave hoop with a grain-filled gunnysack for a ball. He was a 6'1" center at Halstead High, and when the coach went off to World War I, Rupp took over. The home floor was the city hall where the ceiling was only 3½ feet above the hoop and eight 300-watt bulbs, protected by wire baskets, provided illumination. At Sedgwick the boys played in a general store with a burning stove in one corner. At Burrton the court was a garage; cars were pushed out to accommodate basketball. Rupp attended the University of Kansas, where he saw limited action but associated with two of the most distinguished members of the Basketball Hall of Fame—inventor James Naismith and coach-innovator "Phog" Allen.

In 1962 a farmer from Yoder, Wyoming, placed this ad in a newspaper: "Wanted, man with high school age son, 6 feet or over, interested in basketball. Man must know cattle, irrigation, general farm work."

The Sioux Indians of St. Francis Mission, off the Rosebud Reservation in South Dakota, were automatic crowd darlings whenever they appeared in the National Catholic Tournament hosted by Chicago's Loyola University from 1924 to 1941. Featuring names like Leonard Quick Bear, Emil Red Fish, and Clarence (Thunder Cloud) Packard, they first captivated city folks one night in March 1934, when they flashed a wide-open style to eliminate Ursuline High of Youngstown, Ohio, 29 to 24. Their performances reached a crescendo in '41 when they lost the final to Leo of Chicago, 49 to 41, in overtime.

Long unknown to the outside world, South Dakota Indians had a distinguished basketball tradition. Henry Kallenberg, a student of Dr. Naismith, introduced the game during a Sioux conference at Big Stone Lake in 1892. Led by Stanley Big Bear, later a star at Haskell (Indian) Institute in Kansas, Oglala High School—from the Pine Ridge Reservation—won the state B championship in 1936. One of its two losses was to Rapid City, an A semifinalist. The other was to St. Francis. In 1962 the consolidated Pine Ridge High School captured the state B title with an aggregation including Wilmer Kills Warrior, Marvin Red Elk, Edgar Ghost Bear, and Donald Standing Elk. In the interim the Cheyenne Braves, off the reservation of the same name, had won the '59 B crown decisively.

The Pine Ridge Reservation is more than 4,000 square miles of dirt buttes and "cheet" grass. Originally treaties with the U.S. government guaranteed the fertile Black Hills to the Sioux, but the discovery of gold and an influx of settlers from northern Europe changed that. What was left for the Indians was long on acreage and short on productivity. One of the Pine Ridge landmarks is the Wounded Knee Monument where a sign commemorating the 1890 massacre reads: "Unrest on the reservation was due to a reduction in beef rations by the U.S. Congress and to the ghost dancing of Chief Kicking Bear and Sitting Bull, who said that by wearing the ghost skirt and doing the ghost dances of Wovoka, the Paiute mystic, the warriors would become immune to the white man's bullets, could openly defy the soldiers and white settlers, and could bring back the days of the old buffalo herds."

Among memorable Indian teams in other states have been:

- *Fort Yates, from the Standing Rock Reservation in North Dakota, which took state B titles in 1956 and 1964, then won Class A in 1973, nipping powerful Minot in three overtimes after overcoming an 8-point regulation-time deficit with only 1:07 remaining.*
- *The 1982 Crow Reservation team from Lodge Grass, Montana, which compiled a 24–0 record and won the state B. The coach's name was Real Bird. His players included three boys named Not Afraid, two named Good*

Luck, and one each named Big Hair, Little Light, Bright Wings, Rides Horse, Pretty on Top, Left Hand, Don't Mix, and, curiously, Whiteman.

- *Big Sandy High School of Dallardsville, Texas, whose teams of Alabama and Coushatta tribesmen reached the state B finals eight times between 1949 and 1958, winning in '52 and '57. Operating a successful tourist economy, the Creek Nation folk were publicity conscious. The entire reservation would follow the team, and the women would appear in traditional attire, papooses on their backs. Federal control of the Alabama-Coushatta Reservation ended in 1954 when it was replaced by a state trusteeship.*
- *Tuba City (Arizona) High, a 1A school on the Navajo Reservation near the Painted Desert that owns the nation's second largest treasury of state girls' basketball championships — nine — a feat accomplished in the 15-year period 1964–78.*
- *St. Stephen's, an all-sport power from the Arapaho-Shoshoni reservation in Wyoming's Wind River region (see "Farewell to Shannon Brown"), and the neighboring Indian School at Ethete, the 1985 state boys' 2A champion.*

It happened in Salyersville, Kentucky, in the 1940s. Veteran referee Sid Meade was sitting in the gym rest room at halftime when a man walked up to him with pistol in hand.

"Look, ref," the man said, "I've got my mustering out pay on this game, and the complexion better change."

Host Salyersville, unbeaten that year, was 4 points behind Sandy Hook.

"Mister," Meade countered, "you don't have enough money to buy me or enough guns to scare me. So get out of here."

The gods were with Sid. Salyersville came back to win.

When the Washington B tournament was moved from Cheney to Seattle in 1947, the trip across the mountains was regarded as a treat for the eastern teams. One of these was defending champion Colfax, just 15 miles from the Idaho border. For Colfax the best way to Seattle was an all-night train ride from Spokane, which in turn was a 90-minute bus ride away. But the school bus developed electrical problems and kept blowing light fuses. When the fuse supply was exhausted, the driver flagged down a motorist who agreed to pilot the bus into Spokane. Five miles outside the city the car wandered too far ahead. In the darkness the bus driver lost sight of the road, causing the vehicle to slip onto the shoulder and topple on its side. Since it was moving less than 10 MPH, injuries were confined to a few bruises and scratches. Motorists who came upon the accident took the boys into Spokane, and all hands made the "midnight special" to Seattle. Colfax successfully defended its title with four straight victories.

Central Catholic of Hartington, Nebraska, started five Wieseler brothers in a 1975 game against Plainview. They were Gary, a 6'5" senior and the only regular starter; Larry, a 6'2" junior; Rick and Roger, 6'1" sophomores, and Danny, a 5'8" freshman. They played 5 minutes together and led by 6 points at one time. At Polk, Nebraska, all six sons of Mrs. Hannah Hahn played for the local high school team during the period 1938–62. Their names: Donald, Dwayne, Doyle, Delano, Dolan, and Darwin, who led his mates to a state Class D, believe it or not, title.

With only Kentucky and Indiana remaining in the single-class tournament fold, it's noteworthy that the smaller schools are still contenders reasonably often in those two outstanding basketball states. This is particularly true in Kentucky. Given the new metropolitan school strength, the championship likes of Carr Creek (1956, population 150), Inez (1941 and 1953, population 469), Cuba (1952, population 200), and Brewers (1948, just "rural") will probably never be seen again. Still, almost half of the state's finalists since World War II have been from towns of fewer than 4,000, or county schools. In 1963 Carlisle County High of Bardwell (population 1,049), out near the Mississippi, lost the final to Henry Clay of Lexington (population 187,500), 35 to 33, in three overtimes before a crowd of 19,500. There were three and a half times as many people in the stands as there were in all of Carlisle County.

PART II

THE BIG CITIES

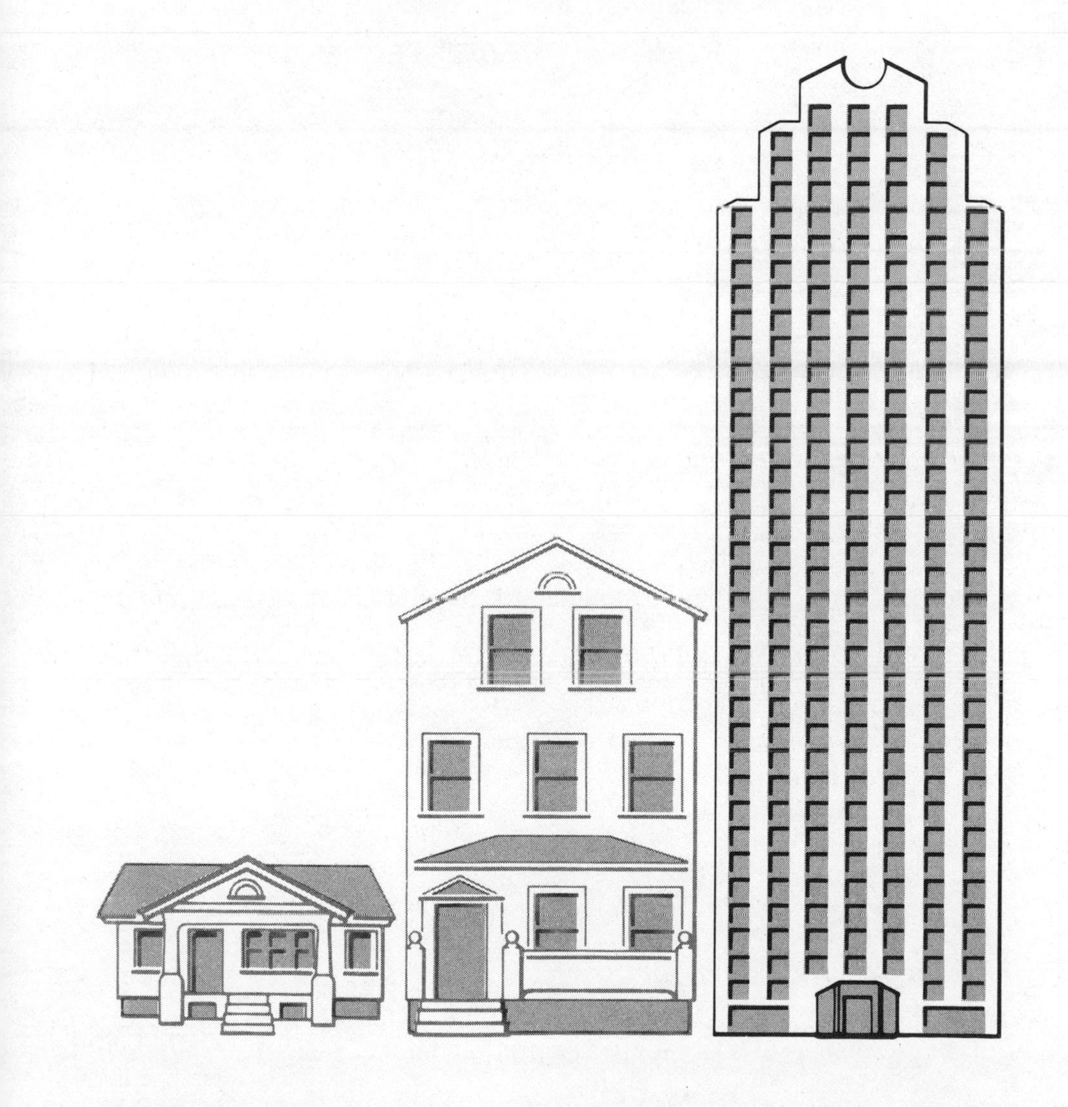

CHANGING NEIGHBORHOOD

Basketball can be a looking glass through which one can explore the people, history, and trials of a changing city neighborhood. The following work—about the Bensonhurst section of Brooklyn and written by Mark Jacobson for New York *magazine—does it all. It was adjudged the best magazine entry in* Best Sports Stories of 1976.

It seemed like a typical spring-fever Friday at Lafayette High in Bensonhurst, Brooklyn. Stillwell Avenue was clogged with punks wheeling the old man's Buick. The schoolyard fence was lined with Italian chicks picking at their Blush-On and smoking Marlboros. Whew! The way they poured themselves into their Wranglers made even the skanky ones look like they had bursting soccer balls for buns. Tempting. But as Ronnie Chisholm, the strongside forward of the basketball team, walked by, he didn't check out the action. He even pretended not to notice as the girls' boyfriends, brutal-eyed kids in brown leather, shouted, "Hey, Chisholm, you crazy nigger, win tomorrow or don't come back on Monday." Great school spirit, Ronnie thought. If this had been an ordinary day, The Chiz, being a crazy nigger, would have most likely replied with an obligatory variation on "What kind of crap you talking, guinea mother?" But not today. Today the pressure was too heavy for that kind of risk.

Today it seemed as if everything was coming together. Soon, maybe next week, it would be time to sit down and bust his brains about how to play the college scene and face, if it came to that, the withered prospect of a future without basketball. But today everything seemed to be riding on tomorrow's game with Canarsie. The "City Champs" was at stake.

Tomorrow was for glory—a crucible to test Ronnie's "game." A "game" is what comes from hours of dribbling basketballs on asphalt, shooting for crooked rims attached to reverberating steel backboards. It was on courts like that in South Brooklyn that The Chiz practiced until he had a corner jump shot as rare as radium and twice as deadly. It was also where he learned the deceit of making his eyes go one way and his feet another. It's a quirky, searing and deceptively stylish way to play, not unlike The Chiz himself. In the playgrounds, everyone's "game" has a personal stamp; there's identity in the way you go to the hoop. And when Ronnie and his friends took the subway to East Flatbush and Fort Greene to challenge kids for courts, the news of The Chiz' "game" spread, just as the reps of other schoolyard stars had. But it would take tomorrow to see if his "game" would be remembered.

There were other incentives. Last year, when The Chiz was a junior, Lafayette High had been in the City Champs, too. Easily the fastest team in the city, they had blitzed through the season undefeated and were 10 up on Taft High, bad dudes from the Bronx, with less than a half left in the final. Then came misery. Faced with

Taft's impassive consistency, Lafayette broke down. They threw the ball away when they should have held it, kept running when they should have stalled. In the last minutes, egos clashed and fatally wounded their chances. When Taft won, 74 to 70, some said Lafayette had blown the game. But others postulated that they'd never had a chance, that the team was too emotional and schoolyard-bred for its own good, that when the big spotlight came on, their confidence was bound to turn to stagefright. For The Chiz it had been a nightmare; he'd watched his coaches, Gil Fershtman and Ditto Tawil, cry, and he'd sat in front of his locker feeling like death.

Tomorrow would be the payback. For Ronnie it had been another year of moron classes like Applied Physics that he just didn't seem to have any head for, another year of three-hours-a-day practice learning to cram his flowing "game" into structures like "box and ones" and "triangles and twos," and another year of hour-long train rides to Twenty-fifth Avenue, where he'd had to deal with the Italian kids who would love to straighten his hair if they could.

Right now it seemed worth it. Twenty-three games into the PSAL season, Lafayette had won 22. No matter that Canarsie, the team from down the Belt Parkway, had won 23 of 23 and was thought to be the best high school team in the country. Or that Ronnie would have to pit his skinny body against Curtis Redding, a 6-foot-5 bruiser. After waiting a whole year to get respect, The Chiz wasn't about to be denied. And if the *Post* sports page was calling the game a battle for the Kingdom of Brooklyn, that was all the better. The Chiz didn't give a damn about Brooklyn, but being the king of anything sounded good to him.

Time was when the City Champs was the hottest ticket in town. It wasn't long ago (1960) that thousands packed the Garden to watch playground wizard Connie Hawkins of Boys' High go one-on-one with Wingate's fabulous Roger Brown. That was when the PSAL championship was recognized as a glittering celebration for the kids who labored so well at their "games" that New York was considered the basketball capital of the world. Besides Connie and Brown, any number of schoolyard kids went to the pros: Tony Jackson and Leroy Ellis, who played for Jefferson; Billy the Kid Cunningham, who did it all for Erasmus Hall, and Kareem Abdul-Jabbar, then known as Lew Alcindor. Those days you'd check the mug shots of the All-City team in the *News* and know that these cats could burn the Knicks on the half-court.

Later, great players still came, but things had changed. People who remembered Boys' and Jeff as good places to learn trig and get your first kiss began to shudder at the mention of the old alma mater. So many schools they would say "down the drain." Besides, there wasn't much need to watch high school basketball any more. Sanitized pro ball was all over the tube. Maybe the Cleveland Cavaliers and the Seattle SuperSonics didn't put their egos on the line every time they handled the ball, but you weren't afraid you'd find one of the players trying to steal your car after the game. The Garden didn't want any part of the high school crowd either. When wine bottles flew out of the balcony during the 1964 Boys'-Franklin final, that was it. The City Champs was banished to seamy high school gyms where not more than 500 people could squeeze in to breathe the old sweat.

Some reward for a million head fakes! Out in the sticks like Indiana, kid ball players have starched uniforms from birth and state tournaments are sold out for years in advance. But in the Apple, where the moves really are, no one seems to care. When the money crunch came, the white-socked accountants went straight to the athletic budget. Out of an already tight budget of $2.4 million, they cut $980,000. The entire PSAL program, including the City Champs, could be in danger. Groups like the Save Our Sports Committee have been formed to raise funds, but the future looks shaky. This year the Garden, apparently convinced that the high schools have cleaned up their act, was going to let the City Champs back in. At the last minute, however, scheduling conflicts—in the form of the high profitable Rutgers-St. John's game, set for some time—came up. The City Champs was shunted off to the St. John's Alumni Hall—not exactly a toilet, but not the Big Top either.

Out at Lafayette, though, The Chiz and the rest of the starting team they call "The Five" don't care about that. They'll play out their drama in a closet if they have to. You don't spend a year on the B train hearing about how you choked on the big one without getting obsessive. Besides, they know they're a special team. They can feel it on the floor. They're all seniors, all veterans of the Taft disaster, and have played together for years and know each other's "game" by heart. On a fast break—with Chiz and smooth Bobby Bishop hitting from the sides, Earl Nesbit and Vinnie Fuller snake-handling the ball up court, and Stretch Graham, one sweet 6-foot-7 center, muscling the middle—The Five fly. It could be magic; sometimes during a hot practice on the school's crummy court the ball would move so fast that Chiz would lay one up and then turn to Stretch with amazed exhilaration.

Those nights The Five would hit the subway with burning palms, and it seemed that no one could play the schoolyard game as well. They said they were a year older now and not so crazy, but watching them practice you could still see the wages of flying so high. Around Brooklyn the team had a rep for showboating and a cocky streak of meanness. They still screamed at each other in tight situations. Theirs is a schizzy game, and the bettors' line on The Five still said they could collapse as easily as explode.

If The Five play edgy, it makes sense. Lafayette is an edgy school. Walking through the scuffy hallways, you may not think high school has changed all that much. The desks still have BOOK YOU carved in them. Kids with wood-block "passes" scurry to the "lav" for a quick smoke. Signs on cork bulletin boards say things like VOTE FOR ANGELA NAPOLITANO—THE GIRL WHO DID THE MOST FOR LAFAYETTE. But this school has its own special tensions. You get a whiff of it when you listen to a "guidance session" that begins with a kid saying he needs a car "so I can get laid more" and ends with the teacher explaining, "You know, Sal, if you spent the energy you use to chase the black kids in the hall on your schoolwork, you'd be a goddamned brain surgeon by now."

Over at the Trieste Salumeria on Bath Avenue, "the white kids' hangout," things are more to the point. Talk to any kid with a blow-dried pompadour and slack mouth, and he'll tell you, "We're gonna fight. For what's ours. We don't want the niggers coming here . . . yeah, call it our turf."

Turf's the trip. At one time Lafayette, a red-brick box built at the tail end of the Depression, was virtually an all-white school, primarily Italians from the Bensonhurst and Bath Beach neighborhoods. Then low-income housing projects attracting black residents were built adjacent to the school. Other blacks came on the subway. The composition of the school shifted to an approximate split of 70 per cent white (almost all Italians), 30 per cent black.

For the people of Bensonhurst it was alarming. The old men in front of the Holy Ghost Knights of Columbus hall and in the restaurants under the Eighty-sixth Street El muttered about the invasion of the "melanjohn" (a corruption of the Italian word for eggplant, indicating that their new neighbors were "big, black and shiny") and how they weren't going to let their neighborhood go down the drain.

Bensonhurst is an oldline neighborhood. If you ride around, you'll see several substantial brick houses that people say belong to the "big families." And here the generations still talk. Consequently, the young "bulls" of the nabe have adopted Lafayette as the setting of their vendetta.

The Italian kids see "sociology" in their stand. "Yeah," they say, "the blacks think you're weak if you're white; we're showing them we're not that way. We'll get the respect." And watching the scene, you begin to understand why middle America feels so secure with Italians playing cops on TV. It's probably safe to say that Lafayette is the only New York City high school where the blacks are afraid of the whites. Chiz says it all: "Man, these are the roughest, toughest, craziest white dudes you can run up against. I saw that they were cold-blooded in the Godfather movies, but I didn't expect this."

For The Five, who are all black, it makes things tough. Stretch already has several offers of a new face if he doesn't pull down hundreds of rebounds against Canarsie. But not all the whites dump on the team. Today in Gillie Fershtman's tiny office The Five are hanging out, rapping about how Pumas just might be taking over from Converses and arguing about the merits of Burger King and McDonald's. A bunch of cheerleaders, all of whom are white, come in, dressed in tight denim. From their necks dangle crucifixes the size of tire irons. They sit down and go through a cheer especially designed for the Canarsie game. It goes: "Canarsie don't be blue, Frankenstein was ugly too." The Chiz cackles, "That's rank. That's the dumbest thing I ever heard." Insulted, a couple of the girls say if Chiz is so smart, why doesn't he teach them "some more of your expressions." "Yeah," coos Diane through her spreading blue eye makeup, "bad means good, right? That's right, isn't it, bad means good?" Stretch says he's not giving away any secrets, but private lessons could be arranged. All of a sudden the room is awash with pungent adolescent glances. Two Italian guys burst in, looking like boyfriends. "Let's go, girls," they say; "come on out of there." Reluctantly they get up, one saying, "Just don't rush me, Frankie." The Chiz cracks up. Stretch, too. They slap hands, and there are congratulations all around.

When The Chiz first got here, he had a thing about whites. Bensonhurst should have pushed him over the line, but somehow it didn't. The Chiz is still a moody guy; only a couple of weeks ago he was temporarily kicked off the team for merciless bitching. But when he was a sophomore, he was "really crazy. I was out of control then, I think; I ran around and failed everything." Playing ball for Ditto and Gillie hasn't turned The Chiz into a credit to his race, but it has mellowed him out a bit. Ditto told Chiz if he didn't go to classes, he'd "kill him." At first Chiz was all resentment, but later he was amazed what a little structure could do for your peace of mind. Later there were incidents that taught him tolerance. The week before the Champs, the Taft players were calling Chiz, who is very light-skinned, a "white boy."

He came back to the bench and told Ditto Tawil. Ditto suggested, "Fix 'em, call 'em nigger." Chiz laughed, because for once the whole race thing seemed so stupid.

Now Chiz still snaps, "Do I look like your son?" when Ditto or Gillie calls him that. But he smiles when he says it. And when Stretch moans, "Dad, Dad," to Gillie after someone "murphs" his money, no one makes fun of him. After all, Stretch's parents aren't around—his mother died last year and at 17 he's trying to bring up the family. Bobby Bishop lives with his grandmother. The Chiz doesn't have the foggiest idea what his father does for a living.

Ditto knows The Five have it tough; he understands. "I know stuff, bad stuff, about these kids that could break your heart. Maybe Gillie and I don't know exactly what to do for them, but we really try. They bitch, but I think they love us. I know I love them."

Local passions are not lost on Ditto Tawil. Years ago, "when Jewish jump shots were big in Manhattan Beach," Ditto, soon to be captain of the Lafayette varsity, used to go down to the courts looking for a game. That's when the king of the playground was Mark "Whitey" Reiner, already a star at Lincoln and on his way to NYU. The first time Whitey saw Ditto he told him to beat it and crashed his head into the chain fence. Now Whitey is the coach of Canarsie, and Ditto laughs about the incident. But you can see that Brooklyn boys don't forget.

Whitey Reiner is a winner—probably always will be. And compared with Lafayette, Canarsie High School is a winner, too. The kids have a newer building, a classy white-brick job with a courtyard and fluorescent lighting. They also have much more success with their problems. When Canarsie opened in the early sixties, there was heavy racial trouble. The blacks who came from Brownsville and East New York on the LL train took on the neighborhood Jews and Italians. It got dangerous enough to make the front page of the *Times*. Now, however, the "mix" is about 60 per cent white, 40 per cent black, and there has not been a major disturbance in years. Currently Canarsie is the kind of place where both blacks and whites come over to tell you that the school is "sixth ranked academically in Brooklyn." There's no razzing of the team in the schoolyard either. Even the subs are heroes. And today, the day before the City Champs, more than half the school has turned up in blue to show spirit. Even the principal has a blazer on. At Lafayette no one knows who the principal is; they think he must be a troll who hides behind bulletproof glass.

Whitey, who used to be boys' dean, says the relative tranquility has come from "organization and discipline," and that's the way he runs his team. The Five's practices are mental battles to weave five roaring "games" together, but at Canarsie it's all Whitey's show. There are no jokes. No back talk. Whitey doesn't have much use for schoolyard ball. He's here to teach basketball, not to feed egos. And throughout Brooklyn, kid players know that Whitey can take your jitterbug double-pump and turn you into a pro. Guard Tyrone Ladson got a "language variance" (a school change to take a course not offered by the school in your district) so he could play for Whitey. Counting to 10 in Italian is strange stuff, but who cares? Whitey is one of the most successful coaches in the city. In his office, where signs like HUSTLE IS ANOTHER WORD FOR SURVIVAL hang, Whitey keeps a detailed file on most local teams. Today he's standing in the corner of Canarsie's spacious gym with his "Lafayette" folder in his hands, making sure his charges know how to drive the middle against Stretch and put pressure on Chiz in the corners. The team is awesome. The backcourt men, Ty Ladson and Tee Waiters, travel with icy assurance. The forward line of Jesse Massey, Charlie Gipson and Curtis Redding looms like three tight flesh triangles. All biceps and churning feet, the Canarsie five powered through the PSAL schedule, winning games by 30 and 40 points. And as Whitey watches them noiselessly assault the basket, he says, "When Lafayette gets a load of the pressure we'll put on them, they'll fold. They're too crazy. I feel sorry for them—we're going to kill them, you know."

For the Canarsie players, being part of the best team in the city does more than just look good in their yearbooks. Being No. 1 brings the recruiters. All year long people from places like Texas and Missouri have been finding their way out to the ass-end of Brooklyn to watch Canarsie practice. Today two fair-haired guys in pastel suits and patent leather are here to look at forward Jesse Massey's "perimeter shooting." They are from Centenary College, your average basketball school. Until recently Centenary was an unremarkable liberal arts school on the Texas-Louisiana border. A couple of years ago it secured the services of Robert Parish, a fantastic basketball player (the kind recruiters call "program turners"), and Centenary became one of the top 20 teams in the country. Little matter that the NCAA found that Centenary's signing of Parish was in violation of its recruiting rules and placed the school on a six-year probation. Centenary was now on the map and alumni contributions flowed. This year, however, Parish will graduate, so Centenary has its recruiters out, trying to restock the team. "Yep," drawls Riley Wallace, the school's assistant coach and top recruiter, "we've been all over, looking for a muscly guard. This Jesse looks nice. I always like New York City boys. They never just stand around like a lot of them others."

Recruiting practices have cleaned up a bit since the days when "free-lance agents" used to roam the schoolyards with a briefcase full of "contracts," but under-the-table money still flows, and shady deals of all types are still conducted. Coaches try to keep on top of the recruiting scene, but sometimes it's difficult. What kind of advice do you give an 18-year-old kid like Canarsie guard Ty Ladson, who has offers from more than 200 colleges ranging from Dartmouth to Texas junior colleges?

Over at Lafayette there are offers, too. Stretch has hundreds of them. The funniest one is from Oral Roberts University. Recently Oral Roberts has been coming on strong, basketball-wise, with several top-rated teams. Last month the school sent Stretch a free plane ticket to come down for a chat with Oral himself. Stretch says the good reverend didn't convince him. "Too much praying. My mother used to be very religious, you know. She'd sit in front of the radio listening to those preachers. Nearly drove me insane. Naw, unless he comes up with a blessing for rebounds against Canarsie, I think I'll pass."

Wherever Stretch goes, it'll be outside the city. Taking the subway to St. John's sounds a lot like going to Lafayette—all the hours of working on your "game" should pay off with more than that. Besides, even if you become a star in New York, you go into A & S, and who knows you? Better to go to New Mexico and be a B.M.O.C., play in front of 20,000 and have the governor take you to dinner. Stuff like that blows Ditto's mind: "Here I am telling this big dummy I'll break his nose if he doesn't get to class, and he's talking to Oral Roberts—it's crazy."

For some of The Five, the future's not so sure. The Chiz would love to get out of the city, too. "No money here," he says. "No legal money, I mean." But there are problems. He doesn't "predict"—which means his high school grades indicate he is incapable of doing four years of college work. He'll have to go to a junior college somewhere and then transfer, which will be a drag—and a shame because everyone knows The Chiz is the sharpest guy on the team. Sharp enough to write a touching and evocative article for the *Post* about what hanging out with The Five has meant to him. And if he makes out in classrooms, maybe it was due more to contempt than to an inability to remember the dates of the Spanish-American War. But try to tell that to a college admissions officer. Gillie and Ditto say they know of a good junior college in Pensacola, Fla., but Chiz isn't into it. Not much chance for glory in Pensacola. Besides, Chiz hears it's cracker territory, one thing he doesn't need after Lafayette.

But that crap's for later. Business now. The Five are in the locker room at St. John's Alumni Hall, getting into their red-and-white uniforms for what will be, no matter what, their last game together. The seasick-green room alternately resounds with rowdy screaming and dead silence, as if The Five are all manic-depressives with extremely tight sine curves. Still, you can feel the arrogance. People ask Chiz if he's nervous. He crosses his eyes, shakes like an old man and shouts, "I'm tense, I'm tense." When Whitey comes in to wish The Five luck with some hokum about "It's for Brooklyn, boys, remember that," Chiz can barely suppress a smirk.

Outside, the frenzy whips. The Lafayette cheerleaders, their thighs flashing beneath pleated maroon skirts, lurch into their "Lafayette . . . boom, boom . . ." cheer. The wooden benches are filled with young blacks with stainless-steel combs sticking out of their Afros and white kids in marshmallow-heel clogs. Even on the Lafayette side they're talking to each other. Everyone stomps his feet as the teams run onto the court.

Going through their warm-up drills, The Five look woefully thin standing next to the Canarsie squad. Ditto, although acknowledging that once again Whitey has the power on his side, tries not to notice. "We'll fly over and around 'em," he says. Up in the stands the recruiters are not so charitable. "Speed and size," says a chubby who brags that he was assistant at a Louisiana college at the time the school was hit with "228 violations, a record." Money comes out of pockets. Immediately Canarsie is installed as a 10-point favorite.

From the opening tap, things look inevitable. Everyone expected The Five to have trouble off the boards, but this is ridiculous. Jesse Massey and center Charlie Gipson crush Stretch away from the ball. When Chiz comes over to help, Curtis Redding blasts him with an elbow to the eye. Canarsie's all over the place. They hover like air pollution, grasping until The Five cough up the ball. It's a first half of horrors. For Chiz, there's no room to crank up the feather touch; Curtis' hands are so close he can read his palms. Lafayette's only bright spot comes when the PSAL officials order the Canarsie cheerleaders to sit down, sparking a tearful protest. And after playing like sludge for two quarters, The Five are lucky to be behind only 38 to 27.

In their locker room the raucousness is gone, and panic is setting in. Gillie is trying to tell them how to keep the ball away from Curtis, but he is drowned out by recrimination about who's to blame. For the first time The Five's natural edge is melting into nerves. It's as if all the near-death scenes in the playgrounds and the kids in the Buicks promising "five white-knuckle sandwiches" have taken their toll. But two years in a row? This couldn't really be happening. Maybe everyone was right in saying The Five were too crazy to win. The Chiz begins to feel the desperation as he slams his fist into the locker.

It is time to collapse, but The Five, sons of entropy, choose to explode instead. As soon as the second half begins, you can feel the heat. Earl and Vinnie touch the pulse first and begin to force Ladson and Waiters into mistakes. Stretch rips the ball from Charlie Gipson, and the charge is on. Chiz and Bobby, their eyes flashing like tops of police cars, find their "games" and fill the hoop. The schoolyard magic was pumping now, dizzying methodical Canarsie with its recklessness. The Five close in. The Lafayette cheerleaders, near suicide at halftime, call for "AC-tion, AC-tion, BOYS!" Italian kids with megaphones scream, "Tonight we own Brooklyn!"

At the end of the third quarter, The Five have moved within two points, 48 to 46. As Ditto says, they are flying, and across the court Whitey is sweating. In the huddle, The Chiz, his blood pressure doing double time, can't sit down. He sneers out at the crowd, as if to give a big stiff one to everyone who said he'd choke. But when Waiters steals the opening tap in the fourth quarter, bad things begin again. The mad spasm has been just that, and it has fallen short. Three times The Five come down the court with a chance to tie. They never do. As the recruiters said, you got to go with size and speed—even against magic. Canarsie has opened the score to 57 to 52 by the time Vinnie fouls out. There are four more minutes to go then, but essentially the game is over—once you break up The Five, forget it. By that final buzzer the Canarsie cheerleaders have returned from the grave and are pointing at The Five, screaming, "U can't beat the blue, U can't beat the blue." The Canarsie players hoist Whitey on their shoulders and hold up their index fingers to show that they are "No. 1." PSAL people search desperately for Brooklyn Borough President Sebastian Leone and Comptroller Harrison Goldin, who are supposed to give out awards. It is quite a parade. And The Chiz, staring at the ceiling and feeling like death still another time, almost gets trampled.

A few days later, back in Bensonhurst, things are only a little better. Yesterday the Converse Rubber Company gave a dinner and The Five had to sit around and watch Canarsie get trophies twice as large as theirs. The Chiz is happy to report that The Five didn't wind up with cement shoes after losing. But as they walk down the halls, they are continually followed by people who make gagging, choking sounds. No doubt it will go on until June.

But The Five will try to ignore it. They're too busy dealing with the mundanities of American history and study hall to fight anyway. Stretch has it easier than most; today he got another plane ticket, this one to Southern Methodist University. "Those religious boys are really after me," he says. He might even go to Oral Roberts after all. But for The Chiz it's eight straight classes. With Ditto watching over you it's crazy to cut. Maybe he'll "predict" yet and avoid Pensacola. But as Chiz sits in Lafayette's dump auditorium, where there is no curtain, only a backdrop that says "asbestos," he's thinking of alternatives. The *Post* guy loves his story and wants him to write again, perhaps the story of his life this time. That's something. He will think about it a little more tonight; he's got a date to meet the rest of The Five to shoot some hoops.

From Mark Jacobson, "Rebound for Glory," ***New York*** **magazine. Reprinted by permission of the author.**

THE GREATEST HIGH SCHOOL GAME EVER PLAYED

Morgan Wootten is to high school basketball what John Wooden is to the college game. Wootten may be the most inspirational coach ever. His teams at DeMatha, a Catholic school in Hyattsville, Maryland, just outside Washington, D.C., have won more than 800 games in 31 years for a near-.900 percentage. His products include Adrian Dantley, Kenny Carr, Hawkeye Whitney, Sid Catlett, Adrian Branch, Bob Whitmore, Danny Ferry, and both guards on North Carolina State's 1983 NCAA championship team, Dereck Whittenburg and Sidney Lowe. He turned down the State job in 1981 for family and labor-of-love reasons.

DeMatha's schedules are among the nation's strongest and most cosmopolitan. In 1983–84 the team opened at Georgetown University, handing Baltimore Dunbar, the nation's Number 1 prep team the previous season, its first defeat in sixty games. The following week, Wootten's men won Baltimore's Beltway Classic via victories over Calvert Hall of Towson, Maryland, the Number 1 U.S. team in 1981–82, and New York's St. Nicholas of Tolentine. Seven days later, DeMatha participated in the Hillbrook Classic at Lexington, Kentucky, losing this time to Clay, the defending Kentucky champion.

In 1965 at the University of Maryland, Wootten's team snapped the seventy-one-game winning streak of Lew Alcindor's Power Memorial juggernaut from New York. Alcindor (now Kareem Abdul-Jabbar) was 116–1 in high school en route to the Hall of Fame. This story is about that memorable game and the events leading up to it, as described in From Orphans to Champions *by Wootten and Bill Gilbert. Wootten speaks first.*

Sometimes we take the floor before the other team, sometimes after, sometimes at the same time. It depends how I see the psychology of the situation. That night we took the floor first because I knew the crowd would be with us. I wasn't able to hear the reaction, however, because I never hurry out with my team. I lag behind on purpose, in order to say a silent prayer that I will be a good coach in this game, that I won't cheat the kids with a poor performance on my part, that I'll conduct myself like a gentleman and that God will be with me. An assistant coach takes charge of the warm-ups, and I walk onto the floor a few minutes later, usually after stopping at a water fountain for a drink, talking to a friend or two and generally in no hurry to reach the bench. When I got out there that night, I asked Frank Fuqua, then my assistant in charge of warm-ups, "What was the reaction?"

Frank's answer was the kind every coach likes to hear: "We have the crowd, and we'll have the game." That's the only way to go into a game, athlete or coach. Any other attitude and you're beaten before you start.

Again we stayed with our usual routine. As in every other game, we took the final minute before the opening whistle to say our usual prayers:

Remember, O most gracious Virgin Mary, that never was it known that anyone who fled to your protection, implored your help or sought your intercession was left unaided. Inspired with this confidence, I fly to you, O virgin of virgins, my mother. To you I come; before you I stand, sinful and sorrowful. O Mother of the Word Incarnate, despise not my petitions, but in your mercy, hear and answer me. Amen.

Hail Mary, full of grace, the Lord is with thee. Blessed are thou among women, and blessed is the fruit of thy womb, Jesus. Holy Mary, Mother of God, pray for us sinners, now and forever. Amen.

Saint John DeMatha, pray for us.
Our Lady of Victory, pray for us.

My starting five walked out to their positions, in front of that huge capacity crowd and the longest press table any of us had ever seen, not to mention the newspaper photographers and television camera crews lining each end of the court. We were only a few miles up the road along Route 1 from DeMatha, but the real difference was immeasurable.

I looked at the first few rows behind me and found Kathy, my wife, only days away from the birth of our first child. It could have happened at any time, even that night, and I had an ambulance standing by just in case. We exchanged glances, then I looked around and up the aisles of that huge college fieldhouse and heard the ear-splitting noise as the referees moved to center court with the ball for the opening jump. Suddenly the thought struck me: "What's a kid from Silver Spring who used to coach at an orphanage doing in a spot like this?" But the thought was only fleeting. The game was about to start. It was time to go to work.

Both teams started slowly, feeling each other out, as you might expect in that kind of game. Both were playing superb defense, which made me confident, even though people were missing shots. We knew defense would win for us if anything would. If our defense was working against Power, we knew we had a real chance. By the half, nothing had changed: still a low-scoring game, still close. We were ahead,

23 to 22. We walked across the floor toward the dressing room, and I looked back for Kathy. Still there.

As before the game, I let the players have their privacy in the dressing room at halftime. I never follow them into the dressing room. I let them go in alone and have a few moments to themselves—to wind down and talk among themselves. While they're doing that, I get the halftime stats and look them over, then go to each assistant coach and ask his opinion on what went right, what went wrong and what we should concentrate on in the second half to win. I am emphatic about telling them that I want their honest advice, even if they think I made some mistakes out there myself. Being a coach doesn't mean you can't make mistakes. It only means that maybe you won't be aware of them, especially if you have made your staff of assistants afraid to tell you about them. I tell my assistants, "I want your opinion *now*. I don't want you telling me after the game what we should have done at the half. That doesn't help anybody. Tell me now, while it can still do some good."

Nobody really had anything to suggest at that halftime, though, because we had played an excellent half. Consequently, when I went into the locker room for the final few minutes before play started again, I simply told my team, "Fellas, you're doing a good, solid job. Our field goal percentage is not too good, but theirs isn't either, and that just reflects the excellent defense by both teams. Our job on the boards pleases me. There are no major areas of your performance I can criticize, but we have to do even *better* this half. We have to do an even *better* job of rebounding, we have to do an even *better* job of running our plays and we have to do an even *better* job of outhustling Power at every turn—diving for loose balls, for instance. Basically, we're following the game plan perfectly. Just keep right on doing what you've been doing—only push yourselves to do even *better*.

"If that seems impossible, remember one thing: you've got a half to play and a lifetime to remember it. Now let's go."

The second half was just as tight. With a minute and 40 seconds to play, we were still leading, but only by two points, when Sid Catlett hit on a long jump shot and added a free throw to put us up by five, 41 to 36. A layup by Power closed it to 41 to 38, but Mickey Wiles sank two free throws, Sid tapped in a rebound and we were up by seven, 45 to 38, with less than a minute to go.

Suddenly the speakers boomed, and the public address man came on with the same announcement as the year before—once again, he said, the crowd was watching the two most outstanding high school teams in America. And once again 12,500 people jumped to their feet with a deafening ovation.

And Kathy was still there.

With six seconds left and our lead at five points, Power called a timeout. I walked to the scorer's table, my millionth trip there that night, it seemed, and said, "I just want to be sure. Is that their last timeout?"

That was essential information. If it wasn't, the Panthers could throw a long pass and make a layup, cut our lead to three, then quickly call another time-out, still with four or five seconds left. It would still be possible for them to make a three-point play somehow on a steal and tie this thing after all. You can't *think* you know the situation in a spot like that. You have to *know* your information is correct.

The answer came back: yes, that was Power's last timeout. I knew then we had the game won.

As I headed back down the court to our bench, I spotted Johnny Jones, a star on our 1961–62 team who would later go on to two years with the champion Boston Celtics. He had come down out of the stands during the timeout and was talking to my team, standing in front of them as they sat on the bench. I wondered what the heck was going on. "Johnny," I said, "what are you doing?"

"Morgan," he said, "don't worry about a thing. I got it from here."

It broke me up, and while I was roaring with laughter, the greatest high school basketball game in history ended. The crowd sprang up, and I reached for my victory cigar, just as I always do after a win. I hadn't known Auerbach all those years without learning something.

The classic of '65 was a natural, because its predecessor was a huge success. But the '64 game almost never happened. Father Louis, DeMatha's moderator, had serious doubts about it and called me into his office.

I was on the spot. Father Louis laid it out for me. He knew I had agreed to pay Power's traveling expenses—train, room and board—about three thousand dollars. "Morgan," he said, "we're going to lose our shirts on this game." He said we had to move it from the University of Maryland to Catholic University in Washington. We'd save a lot of rent money. The only problem was we'd also lose close to 10,000 spectators, since Catholic had a much smaller gym.

I was opposed to the whole idea. DeMatha was trying to make a national name for itself and we were so close; this was no time to pull up scared. I had scheduled the game because of Power's tremendous national reputation and because every coach knew all about Lew Alcindor. We had proven in the past few years that we could beat the good teams, not just in our county or our metropolitan area but in the whole East. We were playing—and with success—against the best teams in Washington, Baltimore, Philadelphia and New York and making believers everywhere we went. Now I wanted to take on the biggest national name around. I wanted to show that we could beat the best, and to do that you had to *play* the best. That's why I had scheduled our meeting in 1964, and that's why I wasn't going to move it to a small gym. I wanted as many witnesses as possible.

Father Louis made it clear that he didn't see it that way. I knew all I needed was a little time, to raise some money, so I said, "Father, just give me one day." He gave it to me but was plainly skeptical. "I'll be happy if we can just cut our losses to five hundred or a thousand dollars," he said.

This was a job for Rodney Breedlove. Rod and I had gone to the University of Maryland together where he had been a football star following a great high school career in Cumberland, Md. We became great buddies at Maryland and still are. He was an usher at my wedding and traveled with us on our road games. Later we formed the Washington Redskins basketball team together.

In those years, though, Rod was playing football for the Redskins, not basketball, and was their standout linebacker, good enough to make all-pro. I got him on the phone. "How would you like to get involved in a business venture with me?" We had a quick meeting later that day during which I gave him the details and told him we could buy the game ourselves and be its sponsors. All it would take was three thousand dollars each. He'd never miss it from that fat pro football salary, I said. As for me, I'd wipe out my savings account and mortgage everything if necessary, but I just knew we could turn a comfortable profit if we kept that game in front of 12,000 fans instead of 3,000.

Rod asked the decisive question. "Will the game go?"

"It can't miss."

We had a deal. Now all I had to do was convince Father Louis to let us do it, then figure out where I was going to get three thousand dollars for my half of the deal. But first things first.

I went back to Father Louis the next day, well within my deadline of 24 hours, and gave him the good news. "Father, I have a sponsor."

"Who is it?"

"Rodney Breedlove and a friend."

Father Louis always wanted all the information, not just most of it, and he always asked the right questions to get it.

"Who's his friend?"

"Me."

He didn't hesitate, never even batted an eyelash. "Morgan, if you think it's a good deal, then I'm not about to let you buy the game. It's still DeMatha's game, and we're still playing it at Maryland."

Which was exactly what happened, and, of course, the place did sell out, all 12,000 seats of it. On the night of the game, tickets which had cost two dollars were being scalped for twenty-five dollars. DeMatha's profit—profit, mind you, which would have gone to Rod and me if Father Louis hadn't been so alert—was twenty thousand dollars.

We didn't win the game; we lost by three in the last minute, but we gave them everything they could handle. Now the world knew we belonged right up there with anybody, and it just made me hungry for more. Now that we had proved we could play evenly with the best teams in the country, we had to prove we could beat them. Power's coach, Jack Donahue, and I agreed immediately to play again in 1965 at Cole Field House.

[The following words are Bill Gilbert's:]

What Morgan Wootten wants to produce, far more than rounded athletes, is well-rounded human beings. He touches people's lives. He works hard at teaching, finds genuine satisfaction in it and is especially gratified when he learns that he has influenced a person's life in a helpful way without ever knowing it.

Folded away in the back of a book in the Wootten household is a letter received in 1976 from a John M. Fantone, operations officer of the First National Bank of Tampa, Fla. Mr. Fantone never knew Morgan well, never played for him, never even went to DeMatha. Morgan can barely remember what he did for the man. Still, there is this letter in tribute:

I was a player for another school, and I will always be grateful to you for seeing to my needs in my senior year at Saint Anthony's. If it hadn't been for your efforts, I would not have been able to attend college and possibly would not hold the position that I do now. I often wonder how much more successful I would have been if I had attended DeMatha High School.

And then there is this letter, from a boy named Michael O'Brien at Coffeyville Junior College in Kansas, received in 1964:

Dear Morgan,

I want to express my deep thanks to you for showing the confidence in me to provide an opportunity for a college education. Your call to Tulsa University on my behalf opened the door for me here at Coffeyville.

I'll be the first in my family to receive a degree. My parents came from Ireland and have always hoped their children would go to the university. I called my mother yesterday and she is receiving radiation treatments for her cancer. When I told her I wanted to come home and be with her, she told me, "Don't let Coach Wootten down. Stay out there and do your best."

Well, Morgan, I know if I do well on the team and in the classroom, you will be able to call Coach Ball and recommend another city kid for a scholarship and a chance for an education.

Thanks again for extending your hand in friendship to someone who wasn't even on your team but someone who you believed would be a credit to you and the program at DeMatha.

Sincerely,
Michael O'Brien

That's the Morgan Wootten story—in only four paragraphs.

LINGERING BITTERNESS

If basketball has an Achilles' heel, it is the subjectivity of officiating. At a critical juncture, two bodies collide; did the defensive player have position or didn't he? Two giants soar basketward; did the defender block the ball or the shooter's arm? On the decision of a moonlighting, probably underpaid mortal rides the outcome of an historic game. Given a borderline case and a difficult crowd, perhaps the mortal cannot be faulted for leaning toward the home team, thus raising the specter of a corollary Achilles not found in other American team sports, the home-floor advantage.

There were several close calls in the waning moments of the 1954 Illinois final at Champaign between a pair of classic opposites, DuSable from Chicago's South Side and Mt. Vernon from the farm-oil country 280 miles downstate. DuSable was an unbeaten, all-black, black-coached, fast-breaking, pressing, flamboyant team bidding to become Chicago's first state champion in 47 years. Mt. Vernon was a thrice-beaten, pattern-playing, mechanically sound, white-coached team led by a single black and buoyed by a school tradition of two state titles and a third place in the previous 5 years. Two of the calls were for traveling, thus nullifying DuSable baskets. Two were for charging—against DuSable—sending Mt. Vernon to the line and fouling out the playmaker. Result: Mt. Vernon won in a massive upset, 76 to 70, and 4 more years would pass before Chicago was to have its first state champion, Marshall.

But should it have been this way? Ira Berkow explores all sides of the matter in his 1978 book, The DuSable Panthers; the Greatest, Blackest, Saddest Team from the Meanest Street in Chicago. *It's a sociological and human study as well as a search for athletic truth without conclusion. It's a tale of discrimination and ongoing tragedy that took 24 years to surface in the world beyond the ghetto. It's a tale of eleven high school boys, ten from DuSable and one from Mt. Vernon, born a generation too soon.*

I saw the game but, while surprised at two calls, suspected nothing. Was I a victim of the folkway that said state tournament referees, known to have received good marks or they wouldn't have received the assignment, were above reproach? Or was the whole thing a case of overreaction, improperly correlated with accompanying acts of racism? Veteran Chicago writers, hungry for a state champion, never raised a questioning voice in print. Were they simply in shock at seeing DuSable play a flawed game? Or were they outraged but held their fire in order to avoid "sour grapes" charges? After the messy 1962 Nebraska title game between half-black Omaha Tech and all-white Lincoln Northeast at Lincoln, protests and furor lasted for weeks, letters and calls poured into the media, and the tourney site was moved. In the Land of Lincoln in 1954, why, if the charges had any validity, wasn't there at least some public discussion? And if they had no validity, how could they haunt the losers all their lives?

There are these foods for thought:

- *The referee who made the key calls in the final minutes, respected and later swearing no favoritism, was banned from Big Eight, Big Ten, and Missouri Valley college officiating after his handling of a suspicious Oklahoma City–Seattle game. In a lawsuit against* Sports Illustrated, *which had alleged he associated with known gamblers and rigged some games, he asked $50,000. He got $9,000 out of court. Was he on solid ground in the Mt. Vernon–DuSable game? Was he simply enforcing a traveling rule that in the eighties, to be sure, is winked at? Were the fouls based on a tendency of southern section officials to call 'em closer than their northern counterparts? It was common knowledge that there was a mild difference, just as there was between eastern and midwestern college officiating. Or, sensing the possibility of a completely unexpected Mt. Vernon triumph, did the referee at issue unconsciously succumb to a desire to help his fellow downstaters across the threshold?*
- *Shortly before the championship game, a white man slipped through DuSable security to warn Coach Jim Brown that "while you have the better team, you*

will not win tonight. It's not in the cards." Was this man just a scare merchant, or did he know something?

- *Brown, the first black coach in an Illinois final, feels veteran Mt. Vernon coach Harold Hutchins avoided him at handshake time after the game. Was Hutchins, so highly respected that he was immediately recruited by the University of Idaho, simply caught up in a melee? Or was he embarrassed because he suspected favoritism if not outright taint? Mt. Vernon's black star, Albert Avant, did embrace Brown, actually apologizing for doing what he had to do.*

Several factors kept the game close. First, DuSable backcourt wizard Paxton Lumpkin, an eventual Globe Trotter, had a bad game. In the pressroom afterward, one sports editor blurted to me as he raced to a phone, "I have a story in type that says Paxton Lumpkin is the greatest high school guard of all time; I'm praying I can pull it." Second, Don Richards, Mt. Vernon's "other" guard, scored 25 points, his season high. Third, Mt. Vernon's defense was one of the toughest DuSable had seen, and its offense, with Avant leading the way, was able to break through the Chicagoans' vaunted press frequently.

The following excerpts from Berkow's book tell what happened to the principals in the 1954 game, how the survivors from both sides look back on it, and the deep pride future DuSable generations have taken in that season. One of the Panthers, McKinley Cowsen, later a DePaul star, died of cancer at 36. Another, Shellie McMillon (called "Reggie Henderson" in the book), who starred at Bradley and had four good years in the NBA, died of a heart attack at 44, reportedly haunted to death by the events of 1954. Meanwhile, Chicago, "the nation's most segregated city," has undergone at least some change. It has its first black mayor, Harold Washington, himself a DuSable graduate. Paxton Lumpkin has noticed some changes, too. He sees the white referees giving a few extra breaks to black players and the black referees doing likewise to white players, each perhaps to avoid any suspicion of prejudice. He also finds downstate officials calling their games a little looser. Time heals.

On Saturday night, Apr. 27, 1974, twenty years after they just missed winning the state championship, the DuSable High School basketball Panthers of 1954 were honored, along with a recent state championship team and several individual players, by being voted into the Illinois High School Coaches' Hall of Fame. Lumpkin, Henderson and Sweet Charlie Brown were named as individuals to the Hall. A banquet was held in a large hall in Normal, Ill. Not a single DuSable player showed up.

Sweet Charlie Brown was the leader behind the decision to boycott the banquet. The players hesitated about going. They met in a South Side bar on the Friday before the affair. Charlie Brown contended that it was an indignity to be asked, as honorees, to pay for the dinner, regardless of the price. (It was $12.50 per person.)

He also felt that since they had not been sent invitations individually (only Lumpkin among the players even received one phone call from a committee member), they were not really wanted, just as they felt in retrospect that they had not been really wanted at Champaign twenty years before.

In a way, surely, the players' decision was vengeance of a sort for the injustice they believed they suffered at the hands of white society (and white referees) twenty years before, when they were too young to understand what was happening at the moment, and helpless to do much about it.

"Whatever it was," said Coach Brown, "it was embarrassing. I really didn't know what to tell anyone at the banquet." Coach Brown had urged the team to come, not to wallow in the resentment of the past.

Coach Brown stood on the dais and accepted the plaque commemorating the team's achievements in, as the inscription read, "pioneering the fast break, the full-court press and pro socks in Illinois basketball . . . and (tearing) down racial barriers of select hotels, motels and eateries."

Ironically, Mt. Vernon's 1954 championship team had not been elected to the Hall of Fame.

Coach Brown and I sat one night in the summer of 1974 in his apartment on the ninth floor of a building in the fashionable Hyde Park area. I had come to see the highlights film of the '54 state tournament.

Brown's broad face, quick-shifting eyes, slight gap-tooth smile and his affable but firm manner made the 56-year-old Brown appear a cross between a benign James Earl Jones and a strict Vince Lombardi. In short-sleeved shirt and Bermuda shorts, he looked beefy now but still formidable.

"I was out of town all the week that discussion was going on among the players about whether to go to Normal," he said. "I understand they tried to reach me but couldn't. I don't feel it was a slap in my face. I mean, I'm still close with most of them, still hear from them from time to time. They are adults, capable of making adult decisions."

Brown, however, was clearly disappointed. He felt that the Hall of Fame induction was a gesture of good will.

"You know," he said, "every weekend for 17 years I'd be either going to campuses where I had sent boys or I'd be writing them letters. It started with the '54 players, of course. It was hard for me to let them go off and to forget them. We were close, and I felt I knew them. I was hoping for the best. I know where they had come from, from the lowest ebb of poverty. It was a heavy task for them just to keep out of jail, stay off drugs and maintain their sanity."

He continued, "But you can't control their lives. And maybe sometimes you can do too much, shelter them too much. Maybe I should have left the kids alone a little more, let them solve their own problems. Maybe the results would have been greater.

"A number of the boys had troubles in school—and some dropped out, but others stuck it out. The trouble stemmed in part from the insecurities that are developed from life in a racially segregated neighborhood and a racially segregated school. These insecurities—that they just may not be able to compete with whites—manifested themselves when these fellows went to college.

"Since Reggie and Paxton and Charlie and Karl (Dennis) were going to schools that had had very few blacks, it was a culture shock—no question about it. But America was growing. These were new times. Someone had to be first to shoot through the grease. And the time was about to pass when the only place a graduate from a black high school could go was to a black junior college.

"It wasn't just the transition from a black to a white environment that created problems. In some cases, such as Paxton's, it was a matter of not mastering the disciplines required. Not to condemn Paxton, either. He had his special problems. He was married just before he went off to school, and his wife exerted a pull on him to return home to Chicago as much as she could. She lived in Chicago while he was in school at Indiana.

"For some of the boys, the start of a whole new way of looking at life began with that state championship game. They met up with the realities of the integrated world. And for some of them, that championship game was very damaging. I think it's something that in one way or another they are still trying to overcome.

"And when you view their lives, there are the tragedies—the dilemmas in college, the deaths, the lost ways. But there have also been success stories. Charlie Brown is doing fine. And Paxton? Maybe not in financial terms, for he might have made half a million dollars from basketball if he had stayed in school and then gone on to the pros, but he is a success if you consider that he has a kind of missionary spirit. Karl Dennis does, too. Brian Dennis, he owns a good business. But once I thought Mack Cowsen would make a great minister, that the Dennis boys would make great lawyers, that Sweet Charlie and Paxton and Reggie would make great pro players and then go on to success in some kind of business.

"You think of the long road these kids had before them, and, after all, you have to salute them for going as far as they did. It would have been much easier for them to turn to something like crime. They pulled themselves up by their bootstraps when they didn't even have bootstraps.

"You look at the lifestyles they came from—where their home lives were often despairing: little food, few comforts, a minimum of hope. Even the history books in school helped perpetuate the myth of their inferiority. This is 1954, remember, and blacks were hardly even *mentioned* in history textbooks. And if they were, it was before 1976, and they were shufflin' Uncle Tom stereotypes. This type of educational pounding was like being strapped in a chair and having drops of water trickle from a hole in the ceiling—it was a brain-washing designed by the political power structure to keep young blacks in their place. I'm convinced of that. In essence they were told that only certain jobs were open to them after high school graduation. They could be cab drivers or bricklayers or waitresses, but not lawyers or doctors.

"Things began to change slowly after 1954 and *Brown versus Board of Education*, but these kids were brought up in the ghetto mentality, and one can never forget it. So when you deal with white society—as you eventually must—with the banks and businesses, there has to be a remembered sense of inferiority. It is some hurdle."

Coach Brown clicked off the large lamplight and snapped on the movie projector. We were to watch for 45 minutes the state tournament of 1954 in black and white on his living room wall.

A breathless announcer took us winging through snippets of first-round play, the quarterfinals, the semifinals and, with two of the 16 teams remaining, the finals, with "the high-scoring and crowd-pleasing DuSable Panthers!"

None of this was new to Brown. He had seen this film and run the game through his mind many times. At the end of the film, the young, strapping Jim Brown accepted the trophy for second place. He was wearing his bow tie and his "lucky" plaid vest and a brave but transparently sad smile.

Albert Avant never forgot the excitement he felt as he rode in the lead car of the motorcade that brought the state champions of 1954 home. In front of the school he stood front and center, as team captain, holding the winner's trophy. He stood hatless but wore a white winter raincoat in the cold, windy, sunny afternoon. He was the Mt. Vernon team's high scorer and its only member to make the all-tournament team selected by the coaches and sportswriters.

He was patted on the back and fussed over. He smiled and courteously accepted congratulations. That was Sunday.

On Monday he decided to do something he had never done before. He walked into a drugstore in the white part of town and sat down at the soda fountain.

"Hello, Al," said the owner. "Great game."

"Thank you, sir," replied Avant.

"What can I do for you?"

"Like to order a milkshake."

The druggist looked at Avant and after a moment said solemnly, "Now, Al, you know we don't serve coloreds here."

Albert knew; he just wanted to see if it still held.

Except for the few trips he had made with the high school teams to various parts of southern Illinois, Avant had never been away from home. He now had received several college scholarship offers. From some of the older black fellows in the neighborhood he had heard that there were only two "free cities" in America, Portland and Milwaukee. When Marquette University in Milwaukee sent him an offer, Avant accepted readily since it was closer to home than Portland.

Neither Marquette nor Milwaukee turned out to be what he had hoped for, however. He was the only black on the basketball team. As a sophomore on the varsity, he was not a starter and thought he should have been. He could not shake the feeling of race prejudice. He had suffered a knee injury early in the season and felt the coach used that as an excuse not to play him as much as he felt he deserved.

He remembers, though, playing against the University of San Francisco, the national championship team with Bill Russell, and being so tight on his first shot that the ball missed the basket entirely. In the last two games of his sophomore year, Avant scored 24 and 18 points. But he felt discouraged. His grades suffered, and he decided to join the army for two years. Upon his return to civilian life, he enrolled at Western Illinois University where he became high scorer and captain of the team his senior year.

Avant also earned a teaching certificate, with close to a B average. He moved to Chicago, and one of the first persons he called was DuSable's coach, Jim Brown. Brown tried to get Avant a job at, of all places, DuSable. Only at the last minute were plans changed, and he became a physical education teacher at the neighboring high school, Wendell Phillips. But Avant was invited by Brown to work out with the DuSable teams, and, ironically, he did so for several years.

Avant was surprised to find totally black neighborhoods in Chicago and schools that were virtually segregated. He was stunned by the ghetto, by the poor quality of life. In comparison, he thought, Mt. Vernon was idyllic. It was clean and relatively enjoyable. There was an integration there that did not exist in Chicago. He *knew* whites because he lived next door to them. These Chicago blacks could only make *assumptions* about whites. He could see how black kids in cities could quickly grow despairing and be led "astray."

He tired of teaching after three years. He wanted something else out of life. He wasn't sure what and wasn't sure what opportunities would be available to him. It was in the early '60s. Pressure to hire blacks was being put on companies by the federal government as well as by black groups. Avant learned that the Borden Milk Company had a position open for a salesman.

"Twenty blacks were interviewing for this one little job," he recalled. "I was fortunate to get it. I was the only black in management at the time at Borden. They needed a token black man to serve them in the black community."

A few years later he learned that Amoco, the motor oil section of Standard Oil, was looking for a black in management. He applied and got that job. He became the first black sales manager for Amoco.

On a top floor of the enormous Standard Oil building in downtown Chicago, Avant has a desk in a cubicle with frosted glass separators. He is a conservative but natty dresser and favors vests with his suit. There are touches of gray in his hair. His body has filled out, almost to chunkiness. He lives in an integrated neighborhood in a comfortable home with his wife and 11-year-old daughter in Homewood, a southwestern suburb of Chicago.

He plays no more basketball. He used to play in pick-up games in parks with some of the DuSable players of the 1954 team, and his relationship with them is amiable.

On the South Side one day, some 22 years after the championship game, Avant ran into Reggie Henderson on a street corner.

"Hey, little ol' boy from Mt. Vernon," said Henderson, "I'll break your arm for stealin' the game from us."

Reggie got Albert into a soft, friendly bear hug, and they both laughed.

Dusting up around the caskets was part of Larry Whitlock's job at the mortuary. Whitlock, the Mt. Vernon center, went to nearby Southern Illinois University at Carbondale, then a relatively small school. He received a scholarship but had to work to supplement his income and got a job in a local funeral home. Whitlock lettered in basketball in each of his four years at SIU, was a high scorer and made honorable mention Little All-America his junior year. He tore ligaments in his leg midway through his senior year. That injury ended his basketball career.

Of the 15 players on the SIU team in his senior year, 11 were black. Whitlock became friends with several of them. In high school, Whitlock, like each of his teammates, had simply gone his own way after practice. But in college he was closer to his teammates. It was a time for racial consciousness-raising. Sit-ins, the struggle to integrate schools, the *tone* of the times made him rethink his own attitudes. One night at dinner with the basketball team in Owensboro, Ky., the restaurant owner refused to serve the blacks. That night Whitlock lay in bed thinking about that; his reflections returned to the DuSable game, and he saw it in a new light. The feelings against blacks in southern Illinois ran so deep. He felt pain at how unfair it was and wondered how this racism influenced the outcome of the game.

Whitlock became a physical education and English teacher in a junior high school and later a high school basketball coach and athletic director in suburban St. Louis, the same general area as the referees of the Mount Vernon–DuSable game, Przada and Moore, were from.

Whitlock was "shocked," he says, to find how prejudiced people are in the area. "It's ridiculous, but nine out of ten people here still say 'Nigger,' and not even the teachers say 'Blacks.' "

Larry gave up coaching and teaching to become chief negotiator for the local teachers' organization. "I have been classed," he says, "as a super-liberal. The only reason for that is that I have expressed distaste for the racial double standard."

Once every few years he will play the taped radio recording of the 1954 Illinois championship game, given to each member of the team by the Mt. Vernon radio station, WMIX.

"How we won that game," he says, "remains a mystery to me. I didn't think we had a prayer. I listen to the recording, and I remember thinking during the game that DuSable always seemed about to run off and blow the game right open."

"That game changed my life," he adds. "It provided opportunities for me that I might not otherwise have had. I was poor white, the bottom of the barrel. If I hadn't been recognized as a champion at something, I might still be out with the pigs." His three brothers are blue-collar workers: one is an oil truck driver, one a laborer in a factory and one a sandblaster.

There are souvenirs of the 1954 DuSable team. One is in the coaches' office, where several old brown blown-up photographs of the players and coach hang from the walls.

The current head basketball coach, Robert Bonner, came to DuSable in 1958. He says that the 1954 DuSable team remains an important part of the school. The team is legendary, he says, and all of the new players each season are told about it—like a piece of Homeric folklore. The school once had highlights films from the 1954 state tournament. No more.

"Wore out," said Coach Bonner. "We showed it so much that—you know how celluloid is—after 20-some years it got brittle and cracked. And splicing doesn't help."

So word of mouth must do. "That team established a tradition here," said Bonner. "It was the first Chicago team—the first all-black team—to win a state championship."

He was corrected: they didn't win.

He laughed. "In our eyes, they did win," he said. "By that I mean we consider just getting to the finals a victory, especially what they had to go through to get there. The racial prejudice. The ridicule, being called a five-ring circus and such. So in a sense it was a *great* victory."

He added that the influence of that team still is present—at DuSable, on the South Side and in the entire Chicago area.

"That was the beginning of the swing toward the northern part of the state's domination of basketball. Most of the state champions since then have been from the north. And many have been from Chicago, including the first, Marshall, in 1958. In fact, in the four years from 1973 through 1976, three of the state champions were black teams from Chicago and the fourth was from a Chicago suburb.

"What the 1954 DuSable team did was give all of us hope and inspiration. They showed us that it could be done. Kids here began to take greater interest in basketball."

Bonner added that besides good basketball, another tradition was started. Athletes in all sports began to consider going to college.

"Before 1954," said Bonner, "few of our athletes went beyond high school. The '54 team began a new trend, one we carry on to this day. And much of it had to do with Jim Brown—he's maybe the most prominent part of the legend. Jim kept pushing the athletes to get more and more education. He saw to it that they got to schools that would be good for them."

One other remembrance of the 1954 team at DuSable today is the gym itself. High on a wall at the east end is a large red-and-black piece of string art in a paper frame. The string has been worked to resemble a basketball. Inside the basketball is an inscription: DUSABLE HIGH SCHOOL, WELCOME TO MCKINLEY COWSEN PANTHER PARADISE.

Before each home game, a coach at the public address system asks the crowd to rise and pay tribute to Mack Cowsen. He explains briefly who and what Mack Cowsen was. Cowsen died before any of today's students reached high school age. Then the gym lights are shut off. A spotlight is turned onto the Mack Cowsen memorial art object way up on the wall. Everyone stands. A moment of silence. For most of the students in the gym the 1954 team is history, though prideful history. The thrills of the team of Paxton Lumpkin and Sweet Charlie Brown and Reggie Henderson and Mack Cowsen and Karl Dennis—the excitement and anticipation of going downstate, the tense drama of being black and the focus of attention in that uncertain white world, the agony of losing the game—these memories exist only as legend for the students sitting now in the floor-level bleachers, and in the balcony, and standing crowded behind the baselines and along the walls.

But that is the way of things. Generations go, but their foundations may remain. The coaches and teachers at DuSable do not want the 1954 team forgotten. It is perhaps the single richest period in the school's history. It is used and in a sense exploited to instill a measure of pride and possibility into succeeding generations. Such inspiration is still hard to come by in the ghetto.

But the students today, they have their own team to cheer now. And they *do* cheer.

The lights, after the Cowsen dedication, are switched back on; the voice on the public address system shouts, "Play ball!"; the cheerleaders kick up a dance; the crowd responds joyously; and the players run onto the court, filled with expectation.

A new game in the old gym begins.

"MASQUERADING PROS"

Bones McKinney is a basketball legend in a basketball-mad state. NBA regular. Star at both North Carolina and North Carolina State. Coach at Wake Forest. The man who recommended Sam Jones to the Boston Celtics. But some of his greatest glory antedated all that. He was the leader and "clown prince" of the Durham High School teams that won seventy-three straight games from 1937 to 1941, terrorizing opponents from New York to Florida. John Evans's 1980 story from the Durham Herald, *written on occasion of the '40 team's fortieth reunion, captures the flavor of those rollicking days.*

They were affectionately accused of being "a team of professionals that masqueraded under the name of Durham High School." From 1937 through 1941 they pieced together a 73-game winning streak. Forty years later the memory still lingers.

Coached by the legendary late Paul G. Sykes and anchored by a tall skinny kid named Horace "Bones" McKinney, Durham High put the city and state on the map with its winning streak. The Bulldogs not only won the first three of five straight state championships but traveled to Lexington, Va., and Glens Falls, N.Y., to take regional titles that imbedded their skills in the minds of many non–North Carolinians.

The winning streak, which ran from Dec. 13, 1937, to Jan. 3, 1941, included victories over several college freshman teams, a number of preparatory schools and a host of high school teams from 12 states.

The team gathered Saturday in Durham for a reunion of the Class of 1940. Thirteen of the players and managers from those teams traded memories of the second longest win streak in North Carolina prep basketball history.

McKinney and Bob Gantt are now members of the North Carolina Sports Hall of Fame. Marvin "Skeeter" Francis, the manager of the 1940 team who reported the team's progress as a *Durham Morning Herald* correspondent, is currently assistant commissioner of the Atlantic Coast Conference. Three other members of the 1938–39 and 1939–40 teams—Gordon Carver and brothers Garland and Cedric Loftis—later played basketball for Duke and, along with Gantt, comprised four-fifths of the starting lineup for the 1942–43 Blue Devil team. Gantt was also a first-team football all-America and played on Duke's 1941 Rose Bowl team.

McKinney, who dropped out of school for two years, was a 21-year-old high school senior during the 1940–41 season and went on to a storied basketball career. He played at N.C. State and North Carolina and was a pro with the Washington Capitols and Boston Celtics. He coached eight years at Wake Forest before turning to sportscasting for the C.D. Chesley Basketball Network.

McKinney's reputation as an amusing after-dinner speaker is well-known to ACC fans. Few, however, realize that his on-court antics during high school rivaled those of Meadowlark Lemon.

"Bones was a cut-up even then," said Carver, now a Durham physician. "He had been the leader and inspiration of the team all along, and that was primarily because he was such a character."

Carver recalls when McKinney played in the 1940 Eastern Interscholastic High and Prep School Tournament in Glens Falls, N.Y.

"They were really taken by Bones," said Carver, who was a junior at the time. "After the tournament they gave him a trophy that was bigger than the championship trophy, and on it was the inscription, 'The Clown Prince of Basketball.'

"Bones was something. Whenever the official called a foul on him, he would get down on his knees and beg. The fans went wild, but by the time the ref turned his back to see what was going on, Bones would be tying his shoes. He made a real monkey of the ref the whole tournament.

"In the semifinal game against Memorial of West New York, N.J., Bones played against this guy Mahnken (future NBA star John Mahnken) who stood about 6-9. He was even uglier than Bones. At the opening center jump, he looked at Bones and said, 'I'll call you Frankenstein, you're so ugly.' Well, Bones just looked up and said, 'Okay, Shirley Temple, let's play.'

"All night long Shirley and Frankenstein went at it, and we started the fourth quarter down by six. To open, someone whipped the ball to Bones under the basket, and he stuck the ball between his legs and faked a hook shot. The big guy fell all over himself trying to block the shot. Bones took the ball from between his legs and laid it in. That just tore the guy up, and the fans went wild. Shirley didn't play well the rest of the game."

The records show that Durham won the game, 44 to 35, and took the tournament the next night with a victory over West Virginia's Greenbrier Military Academy.

The '39–'40 Durham team was one of the first, college or high school, to initiate the fast break. It happened by accident.

"We were scrimmaging the second team one day in practice," said McKinney. "So we just started passing the ball among us. We ran their tails off. After watching us run over them for a while, Coach Sykes decided to put the fast break into our game plan."

"P.G. (Sykes) was always doing that, picking up stuff and putting it into the system," recalled Carver. "What was different about the fast break we used and the one all teams use today is that we never let the ball touch the ground. We had two big men on the wings, another big guy in the middle . . . and the guards, we'd pass it in, then out, then off to the guard. He laid it up, and the ball never touched the floor."

Cedric Loftis was unique. At age 3 he lost three fingers when one of his five brothers dropped an axe on his right hand. Undaunted, he went on to play four years of varsity basketball at Durham. During the streak he was the team's playmaker and top defensive player.

Loftis was responsible for one of the biggest wins of the streak—against Mossville (Miss.) during the December, 1939, Duke-Durham tournament.

"They had us down entering the fourth quarter," said McKinney. "But we came back, and the score was tied with less than a minute left. I don't remember exactly how much time was left, but I threw the ball to Cedric. He had his back to the basket, and he couldn't have been very far past mid-court. He just threw the ball up. It went in, and we won, 34 to 32. That was as close as we ever came to losing during the streak."

During that period Durham was nearly invincible on defense. In 1937–38 Durham outscored its opposition, 857 to 337. In 1938–39 the Bulldogs outscored their foes by an average score of 64 to 18.

"We played more defense than teams do nowadays," said Loftis. "Back then, you didn't score much, and the whole team shot maybe 40 times. Today you'll find one guy who will shoot 40 times."

The teams that produced the 73-game streak were awesome. With 6-7 McKinney, 6-5 Bob Gantt, 6-5 Sam Gantt, 6-6 Bill Gattis and 6-2 Carver, they were extremely tall for that era. And the guards, Cedric and Garland Loftis, were quick playmakers who could shoot from anywhere on the court. The 1937–38 season was the first in which the ball was put into play after each score as it is today. Prior to that time, a center jump started play after each basket. The 1937–38 team was also the first Durham High team coached by Sykes. It went 25–1 and won the first of five straight state titles. The 1938–39 and 1939–40 teams were undefeated, stretching the string to 69 games and two more appearances in the South Atlantic High and Prep School Tournament.

After a 54 to 14 victory over Daytona Beach, Fla., which marked the 50th win of the Bulldogs' streak, a reporter from the Daytona Beach paper wrote that Durham "was as big as they said they would be, as good as they said they would be and beat us by about what they said they would beat us by." The same reporter made the reference to the Durham team as "masquerading professionals."

"We were supposed to play Boys High of Atlanta and a team from Miami, Fla., on the same trip," recalled Carver. "But after they heard the score of the Daytona Beach game, they canceled their games with us."

McKinney, Bob Gantt, Sam Gantt and Garland Loftis ended their careers with a 69–1 record. Carver graduated the following year after playing on another state championship team. A third Loftis brother, Shuler, was a top reserve on the 1938–39 and 1939–40 teams. The only member to play during the entire 73-game streak was Bill Gattis.

Other members of the team during that period were Charlie Ferrell, Fred Moore, Ran Few, George Lipscomb, Harold McBride, Jack Garner, Norman Herndon, Ruben Whitfield, Elliott Pickett, Douglas Ausbon and managers Francis, Bob Lougee, Arthur Harris and Herbert Perry.

The winning string, which began with a victory over the Wake Forest freshmen in 1937, ended four games into the 1940–41 season. Ironically, it was the Wake Forest freshmen who snapped it—in January, 1941.

Shortly after Durham High's 73-game feat, the North Carolina High School Athletic Association put a restriction on the number of out-of-state games a team could play, ending the type of competition Durham had built its reputation with.

"There will never be another team like it," McKinney said.

From John Evans, "Prepsters Played Like Pros," *Durham Herald*, June 22, 1980, 1B. Reprinted by permission.

THE BREAKTHROUGH

If you tell your grade school youngster you remember a time when there were no blacks in the NBA and very few on major college or contender high school teams, even in the North, he may look at you as if you were the Old Man of the Mountain and ask two questions, "When was that?" *and "Why?" The first one is easy to answer; the transition wasn't really so long ago. The second one is tougher; every state has a different history, some of them agonizing. I've based this story on the reminiscences of a black coach who broke the "barrier," whose background is more mainstream small town than urban or rural ghetto, and who remembers how it was—before and after.*

In a sense the road to black domination of organized basketball started in Indianapolis, the night in March 1955 when a juggernaut from local Crispus Attucks High School, led by the legendary Oscar Robertson, became the nation's first all-black, black-coached state champion. After that, slowly at first, then like a runaway freight, came the other states, the NCAA, and the NBA.

Crispus Attucks, named for the black man who was the colonies' first casualty in the Revolutionary War, won two consecutive titles, the second with consummate ease, under Coach Ray Crowe, himself a Hall of Famer with a story all his own.

When it was over, two veteran white fans were overheard in socio-athletic conversation.

"I think we've been had."

"What do you mean?"

"There's no way these black teams got this good overnight. They must have had the ability all along, and we just didn't believe it or else operated such a repressive society that they were slow in building up confidence. I hear the same thing is happening in Illinois and Ohio, probably all across the country.

"I didn't know they enjoyed straight basketball. I thought they just naturally preferred entertainment ball, like the Globe Trotters."

"So did I. Maybe they've been secretly laughing at us. They clown and fancy-dribble, because that's where the money is and the role us ticket-buying white folks want to give 'em."

"Yeah, what other people say we think and want isn't necessarily what we really think and want."

"These guys are so quick, so fast, and so seemingly untiring that they're going to revolutionize the game. They can make what we think is a tactical or mechanical error and still score. Here's a prediction: very shortly there'll be a Crispus Attucks in every state."

"Not in the Deep South."

"Even there—eventually. When the guys down there get the monkey off their backs, they'll see what a great new dimension blacks can bring to their game, not to mention the economic potential, and go along. Basketball plays second fiddle to football in the South. This could give the game a needed shot in the arm."

"When you don't get an equal chance at housing, education, and jobs, does that make you more or less able to assert yourself on a basketball court before thousands of screaming fans, most of whom are for the other team?"

"I don't know, but it couldn't have made Crispus Attucks much less able tonight. I wonder how good those guys really are. I'd like to see 'em against some good, medium-size college teams. . . ."

A melodramatist might hope that the black basketball transformation occurred by mass anointment as players, coaches, and administrators gathered in a giant sunrise revival to hear "pride" exhortations from an earlier-day Martin Luther King. But that's not the way things work. Coach Crowe recalls that since black schools weren't admitted into Indiana High School Athletic Association (IHSAA) membership until 1947—and thus weren't subject to its travel limitations—they had been free to schedule other unaffiliated schools far beyond state confines. This was great experience, but since black competition was poorly covered by the general press and there were no meetings between IHSAA members and nonmembers, nobody outside the black community knew how good its teams were.

Crowe, an Indiana Central University immortal, came to Crispus Attucks in 1951 and developed Willie Gardner (Globe Trotters), Hallie Bryant (Indiana University), a Final Four team his first year, and a Final Eight team in '54 before the back-to-back championships. His '55 team, the one that opened people's eyes, had a close quarterfinal call with Muncie Central, but was devastating in a 23-point championship-game victory over a Gary Roosevelt team featuring Wilson Eison, an outstanding Purdue regular-to-be, and Dick Barnett, later a starter on the NBA-champion New York Knicks. In addition to Robertson, the '55 crew boasted Willie Merriweather, who broke the career scoring record at Purdue; Sheddrick Mitchell, who made the first five at Butler; and Bill Hampton and Bill Scott, who played at Indiana Central and Butler, respectively.

With Robertson again running things, the '56 team was even more storied. Merriweather, Mitchell, Hampton, and Scott were gone, but there was yeoman support in Albert Maxey, who was to star at Nebraska and play in the ABL; Edgar Searcy, who lettered at Southern Illinois after a fling at Illinois; Bill Brown, later of Tennessee State before he contracted polio; and Stan Patton. Their average victory margin over the final four tourney games was 24 points. Robertson had 18 field goals and a 39 total as Attucks downed Lafayette, 79 to 57, in the title game.

Crowe's greatest coaching satisfaction came in the next season, his last. Maxey and Searcy returned, to be joined by a 5′8″ spark plug, LaVerne Benson, but Robertson had graduated and the talent depth in no way compared with the championship years. This team posted the poorest record in Ray's 7 years, 25–7. Still, it had class. It clawed all the way to the state final, the school's third in a row, before succumbing to South Bend Central. At this juncture, Crowe retired to the athletic directorship, leaving a legacy of success—a 7-year 129–20 record for a percentage of .899—and the coaching reins to Bill Garrett, star of the 1947 state-championship Shelbyville team. His record for the back-to-back years had been 61–1, with the lone loss, a one-pointer, occurring at perennially tough Connersville under memorable cold-night conditions. During the second half the floor in the packed crackerbox gym was extremely slippery, caused by condensation forming when the doors were opened for fresh air at halftime and the frigid air outside met the ovenlike atmosphere inside. The demand for tickets was so great that night that the overflow crowd was ushered into the school auditorium where it heard the play-by-play over a loud speaker.

To those harboring black stereotypes, Crowe's career will come as a shock. A Republican who served five terms in the Indiana legislature, he is a former director of the Indianapolis Department of Parks and Recreation; a trustee of his alma mater, Indiana Central University; a former president of the Indiana Basketball Hall of Fame; and at this writing a GOP nominee for the City-County Council. He lives near a lake in a suburban setting in north Indianapolis and plays golf regularly with a few of his former charges. An autographed picture of President Reagan is among numerous political, athletic, and award mementos on his den wall.

He had a white roommate at Indiana Central, where he captained the basketball team, lettered in baseball and track, and graduated in 1938. In high school at Whiteland (population 1,500 today), 7 miles south of Indianapolis down Interstate 65, the Crowes were the only black family. Although Indiana was Ku Klux Klan country prior to Ray's grade school days in the late twenties, with both the governor and the mayor of Indianapolis supportive of Klan's activities, he recalls no real prejudice or discrimination until he began teaching in the inner city.

Ray was one of ten children and the oldest of seven brothers, six of whom went to college. His father was a farmer, up from Kentucky. Later the family moved from Whiteland to Franklin, a larger town a little farther south with a great basketball tradition. There his brother George played high school ball for the legendary Fuzzy Vandivier, who is in the national Basketball Hall of Fame in Springfield, Massachusetts. In 1939 George led Franklin to the Indiana final and became the state's first "Mr. Basketball." After winning four letters in each of three sports at Indiana Central, he joined the New York Rens, several-time world professional champions. Seven years later he turned to pro baseball. Also in Indiana's Basketball Hall of Fame, George was known as "Big G," decades before the names "Big O" and "Big E" were hung on Oscar Robertson and Elvin Hayes.

If Ray himself has an athletic regret, it's that he never had the opportunity to play football. Franklin High had a team, but Ray's school, Whiteland, with a male enrollment of only about 125, didn't.

Things are different now, but Ray recalls that in his Attucks era black players were always prepared for bad officiating, thus steeled against it. His most indelible memory is of a conversation with a newspaperman about a respected referee. The latter two had been speculating on the regional chances of the various sectional winners, and the newspaperman spoke glowingly of Crispus Attucks, the Indianapolis favorite. "They're not coming out of there," the referee countered. They didn't either. The speaker turned out to be one of the officials in that regional. Attucks lost to

Shelbyville by two. The official continued to ply his trade for years. "In the beginning the local referees were the worst on us," Ray recalls. "We were treated royally away from home. When the situation was touchy, we had two antidotes. One was to take a big lead so officiating couldn't affect the outcome. The other was to have a thick skin."

Scheduling was a problem in the late forties and early fifties. Schools were reluctant to schedule a probable defeat at the hands of a newly emerged black colossus. Veteran coach Howard Sharpe of perennially powerful Terre Haute Gerstmeyer opened the first door, and Crispus Attucks coaches and players alike have been forever grateful.

Like artists or musicians, some coaches remain in their vocation forever, never longing to stray. Others use the field as a stepping-stone, happy at last to escape the pressures. But Ray Crowe found he missed coaching and at various times during his athletic directorship and subsequent business years explored the market. Certainly his credentials and reputation were impeccable, and what school administrator couldn't recite the accomplishments of the Crispus Attucks juggernauts of the fifties? But he found no offers. The black coach at anywhere except a black school was an idea whose time had not yet come—a frontier for the next generation.

Most of the Attucks stars of the fifties have done very well. At this 1983 writing, Searcy is a CPA. Merriweather is vice-principal of a Michigan high school where he coached the famed George Gervin. Bryant is field representative for the Globe Trotters. Maxey is a police detective in Nebraska, Brown a fireman in Indianapolis. Hampton is an insurance agent, Scott a school teacher, Gardner a salesman for a beer distributorship, Benson a Miami (Ohio) University graduate now residing in Denver.

There were many others during the dynasty. Two of them—Bailey Robertson, Oscar's older brother, and Bob Jewell—starred at Indiana Central. Jewell, the 1951 recipient of the Trester Award for Mental Attitude, the ultimate honor in Indiana high school basketball, is now a chemist for a pharmaceutical manufacturing firm. Bailey compiled a career total of 2,280 points at ICU, was a Helms all-America in both '56 and '57, and saw pro service with the Cincinnati Royals, Syracuse Nationals, and Globe Trotters.

Gardner is perhaps the most unsung of all the Attucks greats. Though age limited his high school eligibility to only 2 years and a heart problem halted his Trotter career after only one season, Butler's Tony Hinkle, the grand old man of Indiana athletics, placed him on his "All-Time Indiana Dream Team" in 1972. (Other members were Oscar Robertson, George McGuinnis, John Townsend, Bobby Plump, Bob Ford, Fuzzy Vandivier, and Homer Stonebraker. Household names *not* on the team, all from Hinkle's era, included John Wooden, Stretch Murphy, Don Schlundt, Ralph Vaughn, Clyde Lovellette, Bobby Leonard, Jewell Young, and Junior Bridgeman.)

And Oscar? He came out of Public School 17 and was a predicted genius from the outset. He was the hardest worker on the squad, idolized by his mates and a sensation at the University of Cincinnati in a day when life was not easy for black athletes at predominantly white institutions. His heroics in the NBA are legion. He was master of every art and, like few before or after him, could control a game almost single-handedly. He is very possibly the greatest basketball player who ever lived.

Now a construction executive in Cincinnati, he recalls his youth in words preserved in *Echoes from the Schoolyard* by Anne Byrne Hoffman. They tell something about how far he and his contemporaries have come and how basketball helped them do it: "I used to look at airplanes and wonder where they were going and what it would be like to be in charge of something everybody needs. But at an early age I didn't have anything to dream about. I never had anything to miss." He does now. There have been so many basketball firsts in Indiana. It is perhaps poetic justice that the black basketball revolution, however thwarted, also had beginnings there.

By Nelson Campbell.

A LITTLE FRIENDLY CHEATING

As soon as you learn this is by that Philadelphia basketball raconteur Bill Cosby, you'll know what to expect. It appeared in Look *magazine in 1970. You'll find yourself wishing Bill's description of the game against Overbrook High and Wilt Chamberlain were available on tape. The story as a whole could be a trilogy companion for "Who's on First?" by Abbott and Costello and "What It Was Was Football" by Andy Griffith.*

When I played basketball in the slums of Philadelphia—outdoors on concrete courts—there was never a referee. You had to call your own fouls. So the biggest argument was always about whether you called the foul *before* the shot went in, or whether you had waited to see if the ball went in. See, if you yelled "foul," you didn't get the basket. You just got the ball out of bounds.

Sometimes you called a *light* foul. Like you have a guy driving in on you and you punch him in the eye a little. That's a light foul in the playgrounds.

Another light foul is submarining a guy who's driving in on you. He comes down on the concrete, and you visit him every two weeks in the hospital. Of course, there is always a pole sitting in the middle of the court. Something has to hold up the basket. So you let a guy drive in, and you just kind of screen him a little bit, right into the pole. This is where you visit him three times a week in the hospital.

There's always a big argument, too, about whether you stepped out of bounds or not. That's a four-hour argument. So usually you take another shot—20-minute argument. Another shot—20-minute argument. Out of bounds—four-hour argument. So this one game—the winner is the first team to score 20 points—can go maybe two weeks. The most important thing is to remember the score from day to day. Sometimes you argue four hours about *that.*

To play on any team outdoors, you have to have a pair of old jeans that you cut off and shred a little bit above the knees so they look like beachcomber pants. You get an old sweat shirt of some university—mine was Temple—and you go outside to the playground and play basketball all day, until dark and your mother has to come and get you.

Let me say something about mothers. When I was a kid, mothers were never really interested in sports. Even if you became a fantastic star, your mother was probably the last person to know. She was more concerned with you being on time for dinner.

My mother was a fantastic color changer. Whatever color my uniform was, my mother would always put it into the washing machine with different-colored stuff—

the red bedspread, the green curtains, the yellow tablecloth or the purple bathroom rug. And when the uniform came out, instead of being white, it would be avocado.

I've worn a pink uniform, and I've worn a running yellow-and-blue uniform, which, of course, startled my teammates quite a bit. One time I had to learn how to use karate in order to answer for a pale lavender uniform.

Later I graduated from playground basketball to indoor basketball. I played for a place called the Wissahickon Boys Club along with a very famous defensive back by the name of Herb Adderly.

Well, very few teams could whip the Wissahickon Boys Club on our own court, mainly because our court was different. First of all, the floor hadn't been varnished and the out-of-bounds lines hadn't been painted since the day the gym was built, about two weeks after Dr. Naismith invented basketball. We didn't have to see them. We could feel where they were. Our sneakers had soles as thick as a piece of paper. But it was hell on the other team.

So was the ball. We used a leather ball that had been played with outside—in the dark of night, in the rain, in the snow. It was about as heavy as a medicine ball and just as lively. There were stones and pieces of glass stuck into it, and it never had enough air because the valve leaked. You could wear yourself out just trying to dribble it.

Now about the basket. The rim was loose, and hanging, and shaking. And all you had to do was kind of lay that heavy ball up softly. The rim acted like a trampoline. It lifted the ball up and threw it through the center of the hoop and you always had two points.

Another thing about playing at the Wissahickon Boys Club. We would get ol' Weird Harold, who was 6 feet 9 and weighed about 90 pounds, to make black X's all over the backboard. Now only our team knew what each X stood for. See, we aimed maybe two inches under a mark and, zap, two points. If you followed our mark, you'd miss the rim. We always had something going for ourselves.

The ceiling of the gym was only 15 feet high. For those who may not know that much about basketball, that means our ceiling was only five feet above the rim of the basket itself. When other teams came to play us, they weren't aware right away that the ceiling was low. So when they shot the ball, they hit the ceiling, which was out of bounds. And we would get the ball. Meanwhile we had practiced shooting our jump shots and set shots on a direct line drive. No arch, no nothing—just straight into the basket. Sort of Woody Sauldsberry style.

We also had a hot-water pipe that ran around the wall, and the wall of the gym was out of bounds. If you touched the wall or anything, you were out of bounds. So whenever a guy on the other team would go up for a rebound or a jump shot, or drive into the basket, we would kind of screen him into the hot-water pipe.

At the Wissahickon Boys Club we graduated to the point where we had referees for the games. We had them because they were honest and fair and impartial. Which is what they teach at boys clubs. Also because we were playing teams from other neighborhoods and had to finish the games in one day. The referees cut down on the long arguments.

We had two steady refs whom we named Mr. Magoo and The Bat. You might say they did not have Superman vision. They more or less had to make their calls on what they could hear. Like if they heard a slap, and thought they saw the ball fly out of a guy's hands, they cried "foul" for hacking. So whenever a guy would go up for a rebound or something, all we had to do was just give him a little nudge, and boom! He'd wind up against the wall and probably that hot-water pipe. His screams would tell The Bat and Mr. Magoo he was out of bounds.

When new teams came down to play us and saw our uniforms, which consisted of heavy old long-sleeved flannel pajama tops over below-the-knee corduroy knickers, they'd call us "turkeys" and all kinds of chicken names. Maybe we weren't cool. But we were protected from that hot-water pipe.

One time Cryin' Charlie's mother had his PJ tops in the washing machine at game time, and we had to make him non-playing coach that day so he wouldn't cry.

In the middle of the court, we had five boards that happened to be about the loosest boards that you ever stepped on in your life. So that while dribbling downcourt on a fast break, if you hit one of those boards, the ball would not come back to you. Many times a guy on the other team would dribble downcourt on the break, and all of a sudden he'd be running and his arm would be pumping, but there was no ball coming back up to him. All we had to do was just stand around at the loose boards and, without even stickin' the guy, let him go ahead and do his Lamont Cranston dribble and we could pick up the ball, dead and waiting, right there. Whenever *we* went on a fast break, we dribbled *around* those loose boards.

One team I remember we lost to was the Nicetown Club for Boys & Girls. We played in their gym. They had a balcony that extended out over one side of the court about 10 feet. It was almost exactly the same height as the rim of the basket. So if you went up for a jumper, the balcony would block your shot. The defense of the Nicetown Club was to force the flow of your offense to the side of the court with the balcony. When we tried to shoot from there, the Bill Russell balcony would block the shot and the ball would bounce back and hit our man in the eye. Whenever *they* came downcourt, they would play on the free side of the floor away from the balcony.

I would say, on a home-and-home basis, the Wissahickon Boys Club and the Nicetown Club were even.

In high school I had one of the greatest jump shots—from two feet out—anybody ever saw. The only man who ever stopped me was Wilt Chamberlain.

We played Wilt's high school, Overbrook, and they had a guy on the team by the name of Ira Davis, who was a great track man. He ran the 100 in nine-point-something and a few years later was in the Olympic Games. Ira was great on the fast break. So Chamberlain would stand under one basket and growl at us. And when he growled, guys would just throw the ball at him—to try to hit him with it. And he would catch it and throw it downcourt to Ira Davis, who would score 200 points on the fast break. We lost to them something like 800 to 14.

My best shot was where I would dribble in quickly, stop, fake the man playing me into the air, and then go up for my two-foot jump shot. Well, I was very surprised when I found Mr. Chamberlain waiting under the basket for me. I faked and faked and faked and faked and faked, and then I threw the ball at him, trying to hit him. But he caught it and threw it downcourt to Ira Davis: 802 to 14.

So then we tried to razzle-dazzle him. But for some reason he could always follow the ball with that one eye in the middle of his forehead. And, of course, the only thing we could do was just throw the ball at him.

We had one play we used on Wilt that had some success. We had one kid who was completely crazy. He wasn't afraid of anything in the world. Not even the Big Dipper. He was about as big as Mickey Rooney, and we had him run out on the court and punch Chamberlain right in the kneecap. And when Chamberlain bent over to grab our guy, we shot our jumpers. That foul alone was worth our 14 points.

Now that I'm a celebrity making a million dollars a year, we have Celebrity Basketball. I play with guys like James Garner, Jim Brown, Don Adams, Sidney Poitier, Mike Connors, Mickey Rooney and Jack Lemmon.

In Celebrity Basketball you pull up to the fabulous Forum in your Rolls-Royce, and your chauffeur puts you in a beach chair and wheels you out on the court. And after each shot, you have a catered affair.

And the ball. The pros wish they could find a ball this great. It's gold-covered and has a little transistor motor inside, with radar and a homing device, and it dribbles and shoots itself.

A 60-piece orchestra plays background music while you're down on the court, and starlet cheerleaders are jumping up and down. After every basket, we all stop and give the guy who scored it a standing ovation.

Another thing about when I used to play basketball in the playgrounds: if you went to a strange playground, you didn't introduce yourself. You had to prove yourself first. No names.

"Over here, my man."

"Yeah, nice play, my man."

Later on, if you earned it, you'd be given a name: Gunner, My Man or Herman or Shorty or something.

Now, when we play the Celebrity games, they come out on the court and say, "Hi, my name is such and such. I'm from so forth and so on," and the whole thing. And I say, "Oh, very nice to meet you."

But later, during the game, I forget the cat's name anyway, and I just go back to "Over here, my man. I'm free in the corner, my man." And I'm back in the old neighborhood.

FREAK SHOT SPECIALIST

Basketball has an entertainment side not shared by football or baseball. Everyone knows about the Harlem Globe Trotters. Old-time high school crowds remember exhibition shooters like Bunny Levitt, who under AAU auspices sank 499 straight free throws, then 870 of 871, in 1935 before a large crowd in Chicago's Madison Street Armory. Californians debate the feat of Fred Newman, a computer programmer who claims 1,418 in a row in 1974 and has protected himself by passing a lie detector test. But not enough people know about Wilfred Hetzel, a consummate though unlikely master of the trick shot who was still on the road at 73, and it's too bad. Let Joan Ryan's 1974 story help fill the void.

Wilfred Hetzel, who bills himself as "The Freak Shot Specialist," was the halftime entertainment at a junior high faculty basketball game recently in Olney, Md.

It was hardly an ideal audience. Hordes of kids were migrating back and forth to the coke machine and the doughnut stand. Knots of self-conscious cheerleaders were combing their hair and rustling their pompons. The younger set was playing chase in the halls, oblivious to the faculty game, much less the halftime entertainment.

But Wilfred Hetzel had two things going for him, not the least of which was his startlingly unathletic appearance. He really looks like a Wilfred Hetzel, and that got the youngsters' attention right away.

A shimmer of laughter surfaced as Hetzel shuffled up to the foul line, his body bent under the weight of the basketball. He is 63 years old, but he doesn't look his age. He looks much older.

His basketball shorts billowed pathetically around his toothpick legs; his shins were badly bruised and scarred. Each knobby knee was patched with two enormous bandaids, now peeling and grubby. Black socks had begun to withdraw into his white hightop shoes. He ran one slightly shaking hand through his thinning white hair, carefully brushed in a military crew cut, and took aim.

Swish. Swish. One after another, his underhand free throws fell silently through the hoop. That was the second thing Wilfred Hetzel had going for him: he produced what he said he would produce, one freak shot after another. The youngsters stopped laughing and gave him their whole attention.

Standing on one leg, first the right, then the left; on his knees; with his eyes closed; with his legs crossed; his tiptoes; on his heels; using his right hand, then his left, he always found the basket.

When the final shot, a dropkick from 30 feet out, sank, the kids cheered wildly. Wilfred Hetzel, a crepe-skinned oldtimer, was their hero.

Hetzel has spent the better part of four decades stumping the country to perform for just such hard-to-win audiences. He has appeared in 48 states, mapping out a schedule as he goes. Always prepared, he wears his uniform under his clothing, hustling to make as many as three appearances in one day. His usual fee is around $40.

"I missed the Metro in Wilmington, Del., this morning, trying to make Riverdale, Md.," he said ruefully. "I was standing on the center platform, and they didn't open the doors on that side."

In some ways life has treated Wilfred Hetzel with the same disrespect as Wilmington's Metroliner. As a teenager in Melrose, Minn., he was taunted by his basketball teammates (they stole his uniform twice) and was cut from the team despite his free throwing accuracy. When he bragged that he had converted 98 out of 100, no one in Melrose believed him.

Rejected by his team and his town, he became a loner. He perfected his narrow art, adding the trick shots to break the monotony. Eventually he held more than 27 records in trick shooting: 144 straight on one foot, 35 straight bounce-back shots, 92 out of 100 on one foot and blindfolded.

That last record put him in *Ripley's Believe It or Not*. "I'm going to tell you a secret," he said, leaning closer to me. "The Ripley people said I did it one-handed, too, and that's not correct. I've never told anyone before, because I didn't want people to lose faith in *Believe It or Not*.

Despite Mr. Ripley's small goof, Wilfred Hetzel remains virtually unbelievable. He admitted to only two appearances on the court as a team player. In the first he drew two technical fouls for not checking in. The other time he was sent in to shoot two free throws. "I only made one," the recordholder said, sounding only a trifle crushed.

Now retired and living in Arlington, Va., Hetzel, a bachelor, devotes full time to barnstorming the high school circuit. But times have changed. "I had to eliminate my 70-foot over-the-rafters shot because my sciatica bothers me," he said, rubbing his shoulder. "And some of my longer bounce shots had to go when I had part of my lung removed for TB. But I keep busy," Hetzel said with a smile. "I keep busy."

IN AND ON COURT

The relative purity of high school athletics never shines so brightly as when compared with the "hired gun" conditions at major colleges. Public school district boundaries are generally inflexible. The coach is limited to youngsters residing within set lines on a map. He takes what he gets. He's a teacher, not a recruiter. The fans know the players are their neighbors. Nobody is bought.

At least that's the public school rule rather than the exception. Pressured by victory-hungry taxpayers, some public coaches—or their anonymous "booster club" agents—have found creative ways to enhance their personnel, and these cases become newsworthy far and wide. Meanwhile, a host of problems surface in the metropolitan areas where "transfers" may be an issue, parochial and other private schools have no boundary restrictions and sometimes award athletic "scholarships" or "guardianships," busing to the suburbs creates "exceptions," and with mass transit, every school is reasonably accessible to everybody. In inner-city parlance, a transfer to a public or parochial school in the suburbs is "breaking out." Various coaches have proved expert at helping the stars make "the break." All this is compounded when private schools belong to public school–dominated associations.

Proponents of the "scholarship" system say it "gives deserving kids a better education, thus a better shot at college." Opponents say, "Funny all the 'scholarships' are for star basketball players." The receiving coach says, "I have a reputation; the kids just naturally come to me." Sometimes rightly, sometimes wrongly, his have-not rivals counter, "It's recruiting, and it's illegal." Proponents of the suburban "guardianship" practice, as spotlighted by the 1980 Cambridge, Massachusetts, cases, say it has helped turn the lives of several disadvantaged ghetto youngsters. Opponents say it's essentially a subterfuge and that recipients have been unduly harmed by adverse investigative publicity. Com-

plications also arise when the recipient is found not to be living with his "guardian" or when he is over 18 and thus not required to stay with a "guardian," each a facet of the Cambridge cases.

The "magnet school" creates intra-city controversy. A school offering, say, the city's only dental technician course, as does Dunbar High in Baltimore, is happy to receive applicants from far and wide. Critics say they've never seen so many star basketball players wanting to be dental technicians.

The parochial/private schools say they have traditions, that they couldn't exist on a neighborhood boundary system, and that if this offends the state association, it should have made an issue of the "problem" at affiliation time. Public school critics often rebut, "We're glad these schools are in the fold; it makes the state championships really mean something. But their license to recruit puts us at a distinct disadvantage."

There have always been eligibility subterfuges. An Ohio steel company devised a particularly ingenious system. Under the cloak of "community relations," the personnel manager volunteered his services to the high school coach. Volunteer assistants then combed surrounding states for top junior high prospects (who aren't covered by high school association restrictions), concentrating on those fathers who were either unemployed or underemployed. The personnel manager offered each father a relatively good job, handled the real estate problems, and some promising ivory moved into town.

A tragic corollary of the "junior high system" occurred in Indiana. The only, and very important, difference was that the lads were already in high school, one a senior and the other a highly promising freshman. They were black. The father was offered a better job in a plant across the state line. The family moved, but somebody blew the whistle on the receiving school. The state association charged "recruiting," the case went to court, the school lost, the boys never played a game in their new community, and they lost their ticket out of a rural ghetto. There is no way I can be convinced that a minor, with no voice in the decision-

making process, should suffer 100 percent of the punishment for the maneuverings of king-making adults who go scot free. But that's the way it is.

The near-ultimate in residential subterfuge cropped up in Illinois. The father of a hot-shooting suburban star was at loggerheads with the coach. The boy "wasn't being used properly." Concluding that a conference school 6 miles away would better appreciate the youngster's talents, Daddy rented an apartment in that community, meanwhile placing the family home on the market at a ridiculously high figure that would never be met. The boy had a great season and received a scholarship to a Big Ten university. Daddy gave up the apartment and moved back home. The rival coaches sizzled.

Occasionally a school has an "untouchable," that is, a student of known ability whom coaches can't or won't use because of the youngster's previous brushes with eligibility dicta. My own school in Illinois had one, a handsome, gifted 18-year-old mystery kid who had no parents, lived above a business establishment, and worked nights in a gas station. His circumstances had made him fair game for recruiting coaches. Two schools, 150 miles apart, had been placed on Illinois High School Association probation because of the kid's presence on their teams, and whatever the case's ramifications, the coach, however needy, wasn't going to take a chance. The kid could have helped.

Though embellished by time and therefore not 100 percent reliable, some of the eligibility yarns of yore are worth brief mention. There were the orphans or foster youngsters who had been given arbitrary birth certificates because theirs "were burned in the courthouse fire," then declared "over age" the day before the Big Tournament. There were the country boys who returned to school after years of "servitude" on the family farm. There were the street-wise who alternated semesters of school with semesters of coal trucking. There were blacks who starred at all-white city schools when everybody knew no blacks lived for miles around. But perhaps the most dramatic, and most verifiable, eligibility lore stems from state tournaments.

In Oregon in 1921 they replayed three rounds after a finalist team was revealed to be using an ineligible player under an assumed name.

In Wisconsin 60 years later, the championship was declared vacant after a post-tourney protest uncovered a fifth-year player.

In Illinois in 1916 some "detectives" from DuQuoin undertook a "perils of Pauline" search in order to clear the age eligibility of player Ray Harrell in time for the tournament at Decatur. They rode a freight train to Harrisburg, his birthplace, but found no records. Referred to the county treasurer at Eldorado, they hired a horse and buggy, but it broke down, and they rode 5 miles bareback. Referred in turn to a rural grade school, then to the home of an aunt, they finally found their evidence—in a family Bible. Harrell was born in November 1895, making him under 21 and eligible under rules of the day. They got word to Decatur just in time.

The situation in metropolitan Boston in 1980 spotlights many of the current enforcement aspects of high school eligibility. No attempt will be made here to update the Boston picture, except to point out that all parties subjected their positions to re-examination and that the state association (MIAA) instituted a one-year moratorium on state tournaments for the school year 1981–82. Deeply concerned on its own, the Boston Globe *published the following material, prepared by Will McDonough and Walter Haynes, on March 14, 1980. Preceding it were these words from attorney Dan Harrington, investigator for the MIAA: "The headmasters have tried for years to run schoolboy sports on the honor system. They know now, with the Cambridge case, that those days are over. It's time to get a cop." Cambridge's Rindge & Latin School, led by the later nationally renowned Patrick Ewing, won its second of three consecutive state titles that night, but after a whole season in and out of the courts, the team had been freed to play only hours beforehand.*

For years they had buried their heads, choosing to ignore the seamy side of life that was building in high school athletics.

Coaches who worked for them were breaking the rules. Rules that clearly state a high school coach cannot recruit or induce an athlete to go to a school.

Athletic directors who worked for them had to know what was going on, and yet did nothing to correct the wrongs that were eroding their system.

"The rules were being stretched," says Dan Harrington, the Boston attorney who was hired by the MIAA (Massachusetts Interscholastic Athletic Association) to investigate recruiting allegations at Cambridge Rindge & Latin School, "and the people with the power to stop it didn't. To my mind there had to be times, when illegal recruiting took place, that the superintendent, headmaster, athletic director and coach all had to know what was going on.

"The problem was that they tried to handle it with the honor code. They tried to keep the problems in house; they didn't want to go to court. What they failed to realize till now is that the honor code has broken down. Times had changed. These kids are much more sophisticated now. They know how to beat the rules and get away with it."

Harrington was just a temporary cop. He was called on the scene after someone had finally blown the whistle. Coaches and administrators from the Boston schools and the Suburban League were pointing fingers at the Cambridge Rindge & Latin School basketball program and yelling thief. Harrington was hired as an independent fact-finder for a seven-person blue ribbon committee of educators.

He was called after a series of embarrassing public hearings on the case, in which the MIAA tried to handle the problem in house in the same indecisive fashion that had brought down much criticism on the organization in the past. They made rulings, changed the rulings and finally ended up where they never wanted to be—in court, where it was ruled that their association did not have the right to bar Rindge from this year's state basketball championship tournament. The balloon that was being stretched and twisted finally popped.

Here are two cases from recent years that have caused controversy because of the way things were done and the way the MIAA ruled . . . or failed to rule:

- In this school year Cambridge Rindge & Latin accepts anywhere from six to nine guardianship transfers who are athletes. All are thought to be basketball players. The headmasters ask for a complete list of the guardianship transfers, but at this writing none has been forwarded.

  In the entire state, in all sports, there is only one other guardianship waiver request. Karl Hobbs, who had been an all-Scholastic at the Jeremiah Burke School in Boston, transfers to Cambridge as a senior. Hobbs is not a guardianship transfer case because he is 18 years old and considered an adult. The administration at Jeremiah Burke protests, saying Hobbs was recruited under the direction of Cambridge basketball coach Mike Jarvis. Hobbs, after two MIAA hearings and a Massachusetts Interscholastic Athletic Council hearing, is allowed to play, but the case against Cambridge continues after protests by the Suburban League (of which Cambridge is a member) and others are made that some of the guardianship transfers were improper. The case goes into the courts.
- And then there's the case of Gary Burke. No one has ever brought recruiting or rule-breaking charges against the schools for which he played basket-

ball. No one is sure how many there were. They just know he was a superstar, leading Cathedral in Boston to a state title as a freshman, Notre Dame of Fitchburg to a state title the next year, and attending Burlington, Cambridge, Dorchester, Salem, Boston English and Brighton high schools. As for talent, it is said he had as much as any youngster to play around Boston in the past decade. Academically he never went beyond his freshman year, despite playing for two state championship teams. He is now incarcerated in a Massachusetts correctional institution.

ROCKY ROAD TO TITLE

Cambridge Rindge & Latin's battles off the court during the 1980–81 season are best dramatized by the following chronology:

Nov. 15—Jeremiah Burke school accuses Cambridge coach Mike Jarvis of recruiting Karl Hobbs.

Dec. 11—MIAA Board of Control rules Hobbs ineligible, because it believes he was recruited.

Dec. 27—MIA Council restores Hobbs' eligibility but says it believes he was recruited.

Jan 17—Reports circulate that Cambridge girls may forfeit 1978–79 state basketball championship because of guardianship question relating to Medina Dixon, and that boys may forfeit games because of waiver violation.

Jan. 31—Reports circulate that guardianship papers listed Dixon's mother as dead when in fact she is alive.

Jan. 31—After seven-hour hearing, MIAA Board of Control strips 1978–79 title from Cambridge girls, puts school on probation for a year but takes no further action against Cambridge boys.

Feb. 8—Suburban League, of which Cambridge is a member, asks MIAA to reconsider penalty against Cambridge.

Feb. 20—MIAA Board of Control votes to ask Cambridge to forfeit all games in which ineligible players were used.

Feb. 20—Cambridge headmaster Edward Sarasin declares Cambridge has not used any ineligibles and files appeal to MIAC.

Feb. 21—MIAA delivers letter to Sarasin that says Ladon Adair is ineligible.

Feb. 22—Cambridge seeks restraining order preventing MIAA from barring Cambridge from tournament. Judge William C. O'Neil takes petition under advisement pending Cambridge's exhaustion of relief within the MIAA.

Feb. 26—MIAC upholds MIAA ruling on Cambridge ineligibilities.

Feb. 27—Judge O'Neil turns down Cambridge request for restraining order.

Feb. 28—Cambridge takes case to State Appeals Court.

Feb. 29—Appeals Court Judge Frederick L. Brown enjoins MIAA from barring Cambridge from tournament.

March 12—Reports circulate that Hobbs and Adair were enrolled in Boston CETA program requiring Boston residency while listing Cambridge as domicile for enrollment and athletic participation at Rindge & Latin.

March 13—MIAA subpoenas and receives Boston CETA records and asks Appeals Court for reconsideration of Judge Brown's order based on CETA disclosures involving Hobbs and Adair. Judge Brown turns case over to Appeals Court Chief Justice Allan Hale.

March 14—Judge Hale turns down MIAA request for reconsideration, freeing Cambridge Rindge & Latin to play for state title.

From Will McDonough, "A Game Where Rules Don't Matter," *Boston Globe*, March 14, 1980, 33. Larry Ames, "A Rocky Road for Cambridge," *Boston Globe*, March 18, 1980, 33. Reprinted courtesy of the *Boston Globe*.

BOTTOMLESS RESERVOIR

When George Raveling coached at Washington State, he compared the Los Angeles area's athletic talent position with the Arabs' in oil; it's sitting on half the world's supply. A slight exaggeration, of course, but where else could a university like USC, with predominantly homegrown boys, win NCAA baseball, track, and tennis championships in the same season? What other area could stock the basketball and football squads of so many western colleges? What other city can boast a Fremont High, which has sent nineteen baseball players to the major leagues? And what other area ever produced eight future basketball greats like David Greenwood, Bill Laimbeer, Reggie Theus, James Hardy, Paul Mokeski, Brad Holland, Roy Hamilton, and Rich Branning in one season as metro LA did in 1975? Greenwood and Hamilton, each an all-America prep selection and future UCLA star, were teammates at Verbum Dei, a south central Los Angeles parochial school whose cage heroics fashioned southern California's dynasty of the seventies. During that period its products included six all-Americas, the others being Raymond Lewis (1971–72), Lewis Brown (1972–73), Leonel Marquetti (1978), and UCLA standout Kenny Fields, whose senior-year selection came in 1980, three months into the next decade. The huge L.A. metro area, with its city population near 3 million and eighteen suburbs over 80,000, has turned out many storied teams. There were unbeaten Compton in '70, unbeaten Inglewood in '80, and a string of Crenshaw aggregations that compiled a near-.900 winning percentage from 1972 to 1985, capped by state titles in '83 and '85. But the Verbum Dei saga is particularly absorbing. Jeff Prugh's story from a Los Angeles Times *of March 1973 captures some of the spirit.*

If you blink near the intersection of 111th Street and Central Avenue, you will probably miss Verbum Dei High School.

It reposes unpretentiously across the street from a body shop and a poultry market, hard by the Southern Pacific tracks where the "Watts Express," as the students laughingly call it, rumbles through the industrial yard of south central Los Angeles.

Perhaps the school's least laughable symbol is a sign over the stage of a multipurpose room which, almost as an afterthought, serves as a basketball practice gym: "Home of the CIF Champions: 1969, 1970, 1971, 1972, 1973."

"I was really tempted to carry that sign—even with the '1973' on it—in front of the crowd BEFORE our championship game a couple of weeks ago," said the Rev. Francis Shigo, the school's vice principal and director of athletics. "But then," he added, grinning sheepishly, "I chickened out."

As it was, Father Shigo's apprehensions about premature hoopla were misplaced. Verbum Dei is to Southland high school teams what UCLA is to the college game. The record is impressive: 141 wins, only 9 losses and 24 consecutive playoff victories over the past five seasons.

Along the way the school has turned out an almost unparalleled procession of all-Everything players: Raymond Lewis, the nation's No. 2 collegiate scorer at Cal State Los Angeles; Ricky Hawthorne, California's freshman playmaking guard; Keith Batiste and Bobby Walters, stars at UC Riverside, and 6-foot-9 Lewis Brown, the senior hero of this year's team (30–2) who has received scholarship offers from more than 100 colleges.

Such a success story becomes all the more astonishing when you consider that Verbum Dei's all-male enrollment is only 325!

How does a tiny school—which opened almost unnoticed barely a decade ago on 15 acres previously occupied by a Bethlehem Steel plant—find happiness competing against schools with enrollments of 2,000 and 3,000 and 4,000?

Well, for one thing, you attract players from the playgrounds of Watts and Compton, where in one afternoon you can round up enough budding Oscar Robertsons and Walt Fraziers and Willis Reeds to make a run at the NCAA title.

For another, you hire a bright, energetic coach who used to room with Walt Hazzard (now Mahdi Abdul-Rahman) at UCLA, played baseball there with Gail Goodrich and Keith Erickson and became a close friend of Freddie Goss (now head coach at UC Riverside) and an even closer observer of Bruin coach John Wooden.

His name: George McQuarn, 32, who for several years as Compton's full-time superintendent of recreation has all but wire-tapped every playground in quest of an encyclopedic knowledge of pre-teen kids with post-graduate skills.

Does he recruit?

The answer is "yes" if you believe accusations from embittered rivals who say Verbum Dei, a parochial school not bound by neighborhood enrollment restrictions as are public schools, has a sort of carte blanche pick of players from throughout south central L.A. and Compton.

The answer is "no" if you believe George McQuarn, even though he admits that "three or four players" live in north Compton. One is a youngster he befriended 10 years ago when he "lived around the corner" and attended St. Albert's grade school. His name: Lewis Brown.

"I have never contacted a kid about going to Verbum Dei, period!" says McQuarn.

Rather, he says, the kids—and their parents—recruit Verbum Dei. "When you win championships as often as we have," he said, "kids are attracted to our program, just as players are attracted to UCLA's." Another factor, he added, is the spread of gang violence, particularly in Compton where McQuarn played baseball and basketball at Centennial High and Compton JC. "A lot of parents," he said, "feel safer if they know their kids are going to a private school."

Actually, such charges by public schools are nothing new. They erupted a decade ago when Loyola was winning CIF football championships—and 33 games in a row—with players from as far away as Monrovia. They surfaced in Orange County during Mater Dei's football glory years. And they were rekindled recently when three of the CIF Southern Section's four basketball titles were won by Verbum Dei and two other Catholic schools, Daniel Murphy and Aquinas.

Rarely a month passes when a "they-can-recruit-but-we-can't" complaint does not cross the desk of Southern Section commissioner Ken Fagans. "It's always been a problem," said Fagans. "When Catholic schools win a lot, people write in and say it's unfair to the public schools. We heard them when Loyola set the record of 35 straight, but when Temple City broke it by winning 43 straight, nobody complained. The innuendos about recruiting are always there, but we say, 'All right, prove it.' It's difficult to get any proof."

Still, the CIF is not insensitive to the problem. A committee of public and parochial school representatives was formed last spring to investigate recruiting, which is illegal under CIF by-laws. "The Catholic schools are policing themselves and setting up more restrictive areas," said Fagans, who added that Chaminade Prep, a Canoga Park parochial school, has been barred from playoffs next year after allegations of recruiting.

And Verbum Dei?

"They don't recruit per se, but they do have a wide area to draw from," said Fagans, who knows the Compton area well, having coached Compton High to CIF basketball titles in 1951 and 1952. One of his former players, he said, was the father of Dwight Slaughter, a recent Verbum Dei star. "He told me he didn't want his son to go to school in Compton," Fagans disclosed, "because of the gang problem there."

Fagans said Verbum Dei's winning program "attracts" talented players and that its students come from "high class" families who can afford a private education.

Of all the ingredients that have put the Verbum Dei Eagles on the basketball map, however, perhaps the most significant is McQuarn.

He is gregarious off the court, tough and demanding on it. He also has not been immune to controversy. In 1970, when Verbum Dei pulled out of an Inglewood tournament because of what its players called "poor officiating," the CIF charged "breach of sportsmanship" and barred the Eagles from the 3-A playoffs. The order was rescinded, however, when McQuarn agreed not to coach the Eagles during the playoffs. An interim replacement, Caldwell Black, coached them to the 3-A title while McQuarn watched conspicuously from the bleachers.

McQuarn was catcher on UCLA's baseball team in the early 1960s and joined Compton's municipal recreation staff upon graduation from Cal State Long Beach. He moonlighted as Verbum Dei's freshman basketball coach, his first team going undefeated. His varsity teams have won CIF titles in 2-A play (1969), 3-A (1970) and

4-A (1971 and 1973). Verbum Dei also won the 4-A tournament, composed of the CIF's biggest schools, in 1972, with former UCLA guard Kenny Booker coaching the Eagles while McQuarn took a year's leave to establish Compton's Model Cities program.

At the moment no fewer than 10 Verbum Dei alumni are playing college basketball, all from the school's first four championship teams. Lewis, a superlative sophomore guard who scored 53 points in one game for Cal State L.A., may soon be the first to turn professional, that is, if he declares himself a "hardship case" under pro draft rules. At least two other starters besides Brown on this year's team—forward Michael Pyles and guard Eddie Williams—are regarded as college prospects.

With so many exceptional players, it is easy to minimize McQuarn's coaching skills. Longtime Verbum Dei watchers contend, however, that McQuarn's strong hand is evident in all those championships.

Like Wooden, he strongly favors discipline and defense, fundamentals and cohesion. Any player who insists on maneuvering to the basket one-on-one, playground style, gets a one-way ticket from McQuarn back to the 109th Street Recreation Center, a popular hangout for pickup games among varsity and non-varsity youngsters, assorted ex-pros, ex-collegians and dropouts, located just a double dribble from Verbum Dei.

His most celebrated pupil was Lewis, a stylish, flamboyant player who had to adjust, grudgingly, to McQuarn's smooth team-before-self offense. They clashed not unlike Sidney Wicks and Wooden at UCLA, with McQuarn benching Lewis for breaking on-court rules. It wasn't long, however, until, Lewis, like Wicks, became the leader in a team-conscious, poetry-in-motion attack.

McQuarn says that players of Lewis' extraordinary skill pose a severe challenge for every coach. "The hardest part," he said, "is getting such a player to understand his role, that he's part of a team and is not an individual. The reason is, he has so much great ability to begin with. He believes he can win games all by himself. He may not agree with you, but he's got to know where you stand. You can't let a player break a rule a couple of times, then bench him when he breaks it again. That's when he gets upset. You have to discipline him right away so he knows where you stand."

The glory years at Verbum Dei, he said, have not been without minor annoyances toward his discipline, but the championships have prevented any tremors from becoming full-throated explosions. "There's no substitute for winning," he added, "and I've known enough UCLA players to know that that's what has kept everybody fairly happy there over the years."

Lest anyone think Verbum Dei is strictly a basketball factory, a visit to the campus suggests that the school is academic and community-conscious, too. "Discipline" and "self-awareness" are words you often hear from the principal, the Rev. Fisher Robinson, as he conducts a tour through the quiet campus, with its white, California-modern buildings and semitropical foliage.

But he says it's not the kind of regimentation an outsider might normally associate with parochial schooling. Instead of uniforms, students are required to wear shirts and neckties of their own choosing. The only exception is Friday when seniors may go tieless. Classes begin at 8:15 a.m. and end at 2 p.m. Attendance at chapel and ethics classes is required, too, but the feeling is that Verbum Dei exerts as much effort toward ethnic awareness as it does toward religious and academic training.

"We insist on the parents working closely with us and with the youngsters—to reinforce their training in the home," said Father Robinson, a soft-spoken, bespectacled man who has been principal for six years. "Once they leave here, we feel they're prepared to make decisions for themselves, morally and intellectually."

Verbum Dei ("Word of God") High School was a dream of James Francis Cardinal McIntyre, the retired head of the Archdiocese of Los Angeles. It opened its doors in 1962, graduated its first class in 1966 and is just beginning to benefit from alumni returning from college to help with teaching and community work. The student body is predominantly black, with one-quarter from the Mexican-American community. The faculty is integrated—Father Robinson and McQuarn are black, Father Shigo is white—and about 30 percent of the enrollment is non-Catholic.

Father Robinson says 80 percent of Verbum Dei's graduates go to college, mostly four-year schools and some as distant as Northeastern (in Boston), Marquette, Xavier and St. Louis U. One has received an appointment to the Air Force Academy.

Tuition is nominal ($527 per year) and is heavily subsidized by the archdiocese and by private contributions. Enrollment has remained constant, although officials say facilities can accommodate 450.

Meanwhile the little school remains the Goliath of high school basketball. It overshadows such big schools as Pasadena (enrollment 3,700), which Verbum Dei has beaten in each of the past two championship games. But you don't hear Pasadena's coach, George Terzian, crying "foul" about recruiting or complaining that his school's boundaries are too limited.

A big part of Verbum Dei's success, he said, is the year-'round succession of pickup games at the 109th Street Recreation Center. "The kids who play there," he said, "go up against guys three to five years older—sometimes guys who played in the NBA. They learn the game differently from how our kids do. They learn the hard, aggressive style first, while our kids—who aren't exposed to that kind of play—learn basketball the way it was originally taught. Body position. No reaching. No hand-checking. They're coached the way most high school coaches teach it. But the Verbum Dei kids learn the rough stuff first, then are taught the fundamentals. They learn the game in reverse order from how our kids learn it."

All of which does not suggest, said Terzian, that Verbum Dei is guilty of unethical play. "They play very sound basketball, with very little rough stuff," he emphasized. "The difference is they know *when* to lean on the rebounder, *when* to hand-check the forward getting the lead pass. That's something they picked up early in life and it's easy for them to pull off later."

Terzian also praises McQuarn.

"They win," he said, "because of their coach. I know a lot of people discount that, but he's outcoached me both times we've played. It takes a tremendous coach to discipline those kids and make them play the way they do."

When will it all end?

Many observers, including McQuarn, believe Verbum Dei will likely relinquish its crown next year, even though it has an adequate reservoir of younger players to perhaps start another dynasty in 1975.

FALLEN IDOL

A few of the prep greats, for one reason or another, never make it to college. Unknown beyond the city limits while lesser contemporaries become household names as collegians, they nevertheless remain legends in their neighborhoods. Nothing tarnishes accomplishment, not even the drug-prison syndrome into which a few nice guys sink. This is the story of Earl Manigault, the Harlem one-on-one king and Franklin High star of the 1960s, as told by Peter Axthelm in The City Game *(reprinted by permission of The Sterling Lord Agency, Inc.).*

In the litany of quiet misfortunes that have claimed so many young athletes in the ghetto, it may seem almost impossible to select one man and give him special importance. Yet in the stories and traditions that are recounted in the Harlem parks, one figure does emerge above the rest. Asked about the finest athletes they have seen, scores of ballplayers in a dozen parks mention Connie Hawkins and Lew Alcindor and similar celebrities. But almost without exception, they speak first of one star who didn't go on: Earl Manigault.

No official scorers tabulate the results of pickup games; there are no composite box scores to prove that Manigault ranked highest among playground athletes. But in its own way, a reputation in the parks is as definable as a scoring average in the NBA. Cut off from more formal channels of media and exposure, street ballplayers develop their own elaborate word-of-mouth system. One spectacular performance or one backward, twisting stuff shot may be the seed of an athlete's reputation. If he can repeat it a few times in a park where the competition is tough, the word goes out that he may be something special. Then there will be challenges from more established players, and a man who can withstand them may earn a "neighborhood rep." The process continues in an expanding series of confrontations until the best athletes have emerged. Perhaps a dozen men at a given time may enjoy "citywide reps," guaranteeing them attention and respect in any playground they may visit. And of those, one or two will stand alone.

A few years ago, Earl Manigault stood among the loftiest. But his reign was brief, and in order to capture some feeling of what his stature meant in the playground world, one must turn to two athletes who enjoy similar positions today. Herman "Helicopter" Knowings, now in his late twenties, is among the most remarkable playground phenomena; he was a demigod before Manigault, and he remains one after Earl's departure. Uneducated and unable to break into pro ball, Helicopter has managed to retain the spring in his legs and the will power to remain at the summit after many of his contemporaries have faded from the basketball scene. Joe Hammond, not yet 20, is generally recognized as the best of the young crop. Neither

At the moment, McQuarn is rumored to be strongly in line to accompany his friend, Cal State Long Beach coach Jerry Tarkanian, to Nevada Las Vegas, that is, if Tarkanian decides to leave Long Beach. McQuarn won't comment on the rumors, but he looks back on his unprecedented CIF success in a way that would suggest—well, he will be glad to rid himself of all those charges and pressures of winning and having to play home games away from home, at Compton JC.

"It's like any coaching job, I guess," he sighed. "You win with black kids, and your critics say the only reason you win is because you've got great talent. You lose with black kids, and they say you're a lousy coach."

He gazed up from his shrimp sandwich, and his eyes brightened.

"I look forward to the day a few years from now when my son is 8 or 9," he said, "and I can coach him at the boys' club or playground level. That's where you can enjoy coaching and you don't have to worry so much about winning. That's where coaching can be beautiful."

You get the feeling, though, that George McQuarn is curious—and ambitious—enough to sample life in the volcanic world of the John Woodens and the Jerry Tarkanians before he returns to the courts of 109th Street.

George McQuarn did graduate into the college ranks. At this writing he is head coach at Cal State Fullerton, which makes him a Pacific Coast Athletic Association rival of Jerry Tarkanian.

From Jeff Prugh, "Verbum Dei: 'UCLA—South Central Branch,'" ***Los Angeles Times*****, March 22, 1973, sec. III, 1f.**

finished school and vaulted into the public spotlight, but both pick up money playing in a minor league, the Eastern League, and both return home between games to continue their domination of the parks.

The Helicopter got his name for obvious reasons: when he goes up to block a shot, he seems to hover endlessly in mid-air above his prey, daring him to shoot—and then blocking whatever shot his hapless foe attempts. Like most memorable playground moves, it is not only effective but magnetic. As Knowings goes up, the crowd shouts, "Fly, 'copter, fly," and seems to share his heady trip. When he shoves the ball down the throat of a visiting NBA star—as he often does in the Rucker Tournament—the Helicopter inflates the pride of a whole neighborhood.

Like Connie Hawkins, Knowings can send waves of electricity through a park with his mere presence. Standing by a court, watching a game with intent eyes, the Helicopter doesn't have to ask to play. People quickly spot his dark, chiseled, ageless face and 6-foot-4-inch frame, and they make room for him. Joe Hammond is less imposing. A shade over 6 feet, he is a skinny, sleepy-eyed kid who looks slow and tired, the way backcourt star Clinton Robinson appeared during his reign. But like Robinson, Hammond has proved himself, and he now stands as the descendant of Pablo Robertson and James Barlow and the other backcourt heroes of the streets.

The kings of playground ball are not expected to defend their titles every weekend, proving themselves again and again the way less exalted players must. But when a new athlete begins winning a large following, when the rumors spread that he is truly someone special, the call goes out: If he is a forward, get the Helicopter; if he's a guard, let's try him against Joe Hammond. A crowd will gather before the star arrives. It is time for a supreme test.

Jay Vaughn has been in such confrontations several times. He saw the Helicopter defend his reign, and he watched Joe Hammond win his own way to the top. He described the rituals:

"When I first met the Helicopter, I was only about 17, and I was playing with a lot of kids my age at Wagner Center. I was better than the guys I was playing with and I knew it, so I didn't feel I had anything to prove. I was playing lazy, lackadaisical. One of the youth workers saw how cocky I was and decided to show me just how good I really was. He sent for the Helicopter.

"One day I was just shooting baskets, trying all kinds of wild shots, not thinking about fundamentals, and I saw this older dude come in. He had sneakers and shorts on, and he was ready to play. I said, 'Who's this guy? He's too old for our games. Is he supposed to be good?'

" 'The coach sent for him,' somebody told me. 'He's gonna play you.'

"I said to myself, 'Well, fine, I'll try him,' and I went out there one-on-one with Herman Knowings. Well, it was a disastrous thing. I tried layups, jump shots, hooks. And everything I threw up he blocked. The word had gone out that Herman was there, and a crowd was gathering, and I said to myself, 'You got to do something. You're getting humiliated.' But the harder I tried, the more he shoved the ball down into my face. I went home and thought about that game for a long time. Like a lot of other young athletes, I had been put in my place.

"I worked out like crazy after that. I was determined to get back. After about a month, I challenged him again. I found myself jumping higher, feeling stronger, and playing better than ever before. I wasn't humiliated again. But I was beaten. Since that time, I've played against Herman many times. He took an interest in me and gave me a lot of good advice. And now, when I see he's going to block a shot, I may be able to fake and go around him and score, and people will yell, 'The pupil showed the master.'

"Then, of course, he'll usually come back and stuff one on me . . ."

"Joe Hammond was playing in the junior division games in the youth centers when I was in the senior games," Vaughn continued. "He was three years younger than me, and sometimes after I'd played, I'd stay and watch his game. He wasn't that exceptional. Just another young boy who was gonna play ball. I didn't even know his last name.

"Then I came home from school in the summer of 1969, and one name was on everyone's lips: Joe Hammond. I thought it must have been somebody new from out of town, but people said, no, he'd been around Harlem all the time. They described him and it sounded like the young kid I'd watched around the centers, but I couldn't believe it was the same guy. Then I saw him, and it was the same Joe, and he was killing a bunch of guys his own age. He was much improved, but I still said to myself, 'He's young. He won't do much against the older brothers. They've been in business too long.'

"But then I heard, 'Joe's up at 135th Street beating the pros . . . Joe's doing everything to those guys.' I still didn't take it too seriously. In fact, when Joe came out to Mount Morris Park for a game against a good team I was on, I said, 'Now we'll see how you do. You won't do anything today.'

"Now I believe in him. Joe Hammond left that game with seven minutes to go. He had 40 points. Like everybody had said, Joe was the one."

Many reputations have risen and fallen in the decade between the arrival of the Helicopter and Joe Hammond. Most have now been forgotten, but a few "reps" outlive the men who earn them. Two years ago Connie Hawkins did not show up for a single game during the Rucker Tournament. When it was time to vote for the Rucker All-Star team, the coaches voted for Hawkins. "If you're going to have an all-star game in Harlem," said Bob McCullough, the tournament director, "you vote for Connie or you don't vote." (Having been elected, the Hawk did appear for the all-star game and won the most valuable player award.) One other reputation has endured on a similar scale. Countless kids in Harlem repeat this statement: "You want to talk about basketball in this city, you've got to talk about Earl Manigault."

Manigault played at Benjamin Franklin High School in 1962 and 1963, then spent a season at Laurinburg Institute. Earl never reached college, but when he returned to Harlem he continued to dominate the playgrounds. He was the king of his own generation of ballplayers, the idol of the generation that followed. He was a 6-foot-2-inch forward who could outleap men eight inches taller, and his moves had a boldness and fluidity that transfixed opponents and spectators alike. Freewheeling, unbelievably high-jumping and innovative, he was the image of the classic playground athlete.

But he was also a very human ghetto youth, with weaknesses and doubts that left him vulnerable. Lacking education and motivation, looking toward an empty future, he found that basketball could take him only so far. Then he veered into the escape route of the streets and became the image of the hellish side of ghetto existence. Earl is now in his mid-twenties, a dope addict, in prison.

Earl's is more than a personal story. On the playgrounds he was a powerful magnetic figure who carried the dreams and ideals of every kid around him as he spun and twisted and sailed over all obstacles. When he fell, he carried those aspirations down with him. Call him a wasted talent, a pathetic victim, even a tragic hero: he had symbolized all that was sublime and terrible about this city game.

"You think of him on the court, and you think of so many incredible things that it's hard to sort them out," said Bob Spivey, who played briefly with Earl at Franklin. "But I particularly recall one all-star game in the gym at PS 113 in about 1964. Most of the best high school players in the city were there: Charlie Scott, who went on to North Carolina; Vaughn Harper, who went to Syracuse, and a lot more. But the people who were there will hardly remember the others. Earl was the whole show.

"For a few minutes Earl seemed to move slowly, feeling his way, getting himself ready. Then he got the ball on a fast break. Harper, who was 6 feet 6, and Val Reed, who was 6 feet 8, got back quickly to defend. You wouldn't have given Earl a chance to score. Then he accelerated, changing his step suddenly. And at the foul line he went into the air. Harper and Reed went up, too, and between them the two big men completely surrounded the rim. But Earl just kept going higher, and finally he two-hand-dunked the ball over both of them. For a split second there was silence, and then the crowd exploded. They were cheering so loud that they stopped the game for five minutes. Five minutes. That was Earl Manigault."

Faces light up as Harlem veterans reminisce about Manigault. Many street players won reputations with elaborate innovations and tricks. Jackie Jackson was among the first to warm up for games by picking quarters off the top of the backboard. Willie Hall, the former St. John's leader, apparently originated the custom of jumping to the top of the board and, instead of merely blocking a shot, slamming a hand with tremendous force against the board; the fixture would vibrate for several seconds after the blow, causing an easy layup to bounce crazily off the rim. Other noted leapers were famous for "pinning"—blocking a layup, then simply holding it momentarily against the backboard in a gesture of triumph. Some players seemed to hold it for seconds, suspended in air, multiplying the humiliation of the man who had tried the futile shot. Then they could slam the ball back down at the shooter or, for special emphasis, flip it into the crowd.

Earl Manigault did all those things and more, borrowing, innovating and forming one of the most exciting styles Harlem crowds ever watched. Occasionally he would drive past a few defenders, dunk the ball with one hand, catch it with the other, and raise it and stuff it through the hoop a second time before returning to earth.

"I was in the eighth grade when Earl was in the eleventh," said Charley Yelverton, now a star at Fordham. "I was just another young kid at the time. Like everybody else on the streets, I played some ball. But I just did it for something to do. I wasn't that excited about it. Then there happened to be a game around my block, down at 112th Street, and a lot of the top players were in it—and Earl came down to play. Well, I had never believed things like that could go on. I had never known what basketball could be like. Everybody in the game was doing something, stuffing or blocking shots or making great passes. There's only one game I've ever seen to compare with it—the Knicks' last game against the Lakers.

"But among all the stars, there was no doubt who was the greatest. Passing, shooting, going up in the air. Earl just left everybody behind. No one could turn it on like he could."

Keith Edwards, who lived with Earl during the great days of the Young Life team, agreed. "I guess he had about the most natural ability that I've ever seen. Talent for talent, inch for inch, you'd have to put him on a par with Alcindor and the other superstars. To watch him was like poetry. To play with him or against him—just to be on the same court with him—was a deep experience.

"You can't really project him against an Alcindor, though, because you could never picture Earl going to UCLA or any place like that. He was never the type to really face his responsibilities and his future. He didn't want to think ahead. There was very little discipline about the man . . ."

And so the decline began. "I lived with the man for about two or three years," said Edwards, "from his pre-drug period into the beginning of his drug period. There were six of us there, and maybe some of us would have liked to help him out. But we were all just young guys finding themselves, and when Earl and another cat named Onion started to get into the drug thing, nobody really had a right, or was in a position, to say much about it. And even as he got into the drugs, he remained a beautiful person. He just had nowhere to go . . ."

"The athlete in Harlem," said Pat Smith, "naturally becomes a big man in his neighborhood. And if he goes on to college and makes his way out of the ghetto, he can keep being a big man, a respected figure. But if he doesn't make it, if he begins to realize that he isn't going to get out, then he looks around, and maybe he isn't so big any more. The pusher and the pimp have more clothes than they can ever get around to wearing; when they walk down the street, they get respect. But the ballplayer is broke, and he knows that in a certain number of years he won't even have his reputation left. And unless he is an unusually strong person, he may be tempted to go another way . . ."

"You like to think of the black athlete as a leader of the community," said Jay Vaughn, "but sometimes the idea of leadership can get twisted. A lot of the young dudes on the streets will encourage a big-time ballplayer to be big-time in other ways. They expect you to know all the big pushers, where to buy drugs, how to handle street life. And if they're fooling around with small-time drugs, maybe they'll expect you to mess with big-time drugs. It may sound ridiculous at first, but when you're confronted with these attitudes a lot, and you're not strong enough, you find yourself hooked."

It didn't happen suddenly. On the weekends, people would still find Earl Manigault at the parks, and flashes of the magnetic ability were there. Young athletes would ask his advice, and he would still be helpful; even among the ones who knew he was sinking deeper into his drug habit, he remained respected and popular. But by early 1968 he seldom came to the parks, and his old friends would find him on the street corners along Eighth Avenue, nodding. "He was such a fine person," said Jay Vaughn; "you saw him and you wished you could see some hope, some bright spot in his existence. But there was no good part of his life, of course. Because drugs do ruin you."

In the summer of 1968, Bob Hunter was working on a drug rehabilitation program. He looked up Earl. They became close, building a friendship that went deeper than their mutual respect on a basketball court. "Earl was an unusual type of addict," said Hunter. "He understood that he was a hard addict, and he faced it honestly. He wanted to help me in the drug program, and he gave me a lot of hints on how to handle younger addicts. He knew different tricks that would appeal to them and win their trust. And he also knew all the tricks they would use to deceive me into thinking they were getting cured. Earl had used the tricks himself, and he helped me see through them, and maybe we managed to save a few young kids who might have got hooked much worse.

"But it's the most frustrating thing in the world, working with addicts. It's hard to accept the fact that a man who has been burned will go back and touch fire. But they do it. I have countless friends on drugs, and I had many more who have died from drugs. And somehow it's hard to just give up on them and forget that they ever existed. Maybe you would think that only the less talented types would let themselves get hooked—but then you'd see a guy like Earl and you couldn't understand . . ."

Some people hoped that Earl would be cured that summer. He did so much to help Hunter work with others that people felt he could help himself. Hunter was not as optimistic. "The truth is that nobody is ever going to cure Earl," he said. "The only way he'll be cured is by himself. A lot of people come off drugs only after they've been faced with an extreme crisis. For example, if they come very close to dying and somehow escape, then they might be able to stay away from the fire. But it takes something like that, most of the time."

Earl was not cured, and as the months went on, the habit grew more expensive. And then he had to steal. "Earl is such a warm person," said Vaughn, "you know that he'd never go around and mug people or anything. But let's face it: most addicts, sooner or later, have to rob in order to survive." Earl broke into a store. He is now in prison. "Maybe that will be the crisis he needs," said Hunter. "Maybe, just possibly . . . But when you're talking about addicts, it's very hard to get your hopes too high."

Harold "Funny" Kitt went to Franklin three years behind Earl Manigault. When Funny finished in 1967, he was rated the best high school player in the city, largely because he had modeled himself so closely after Earl. "We all idolized Earl in those days," Kitt said. "And when you idolize somebody, you think of the good things, not the bad. As we watched Earl play ball, we had visions of him going on to different places, visiting the whole world, becoming a great star and then maybe coming back here to see us and talk to us about it all.

"But he didn't do any of those things. He just went into his own strange world, a world I hope I'll never see. I guess there were reasons. I guess there were frustrations that only Earl knew about, and I feel sorry for what happened. But when Earl went into that world, it had an effect on all of us, all the young ballplayers. I idolized the man. And he hurt me."

Beyond the hurt, though, Earl left something more. If his career was a small dramatization of the world of Harlem basketball, then he was a fitting protagonist, in his magnitude and his frailty, a hero for his time. "Earl was quiet, he was honest," said Jay Vaughn, "and he handled the pressures of being the star very well. When you're on top, everybody is out to challenge you, to make their own reps by doing something against you. One guy after another wants to take a shot, and some stars react to all that by bragging, or by being aloof from the crowd.

"Earl was different. The game I'll never forget was in the G-Dub (George Washington High) tournament one summer, when the team that Earl's group was scheduled to play didn't show. The game was forfeited, and some guys were just looking for some kind of pickup game when one fellow on the team that forfeited came in and said, 'Where's Manigault? I want to play Manigault.'

"Well, this guy was an unknown, and he really had no right to talk like that. If he really wanted to challenge a guy like Earl, he should have been out in the parks, building up a rep of his own. But he kept yelling and bragging, and Earl quietly agreed to play him one-on-one. The word went out within minutes, and immediately there was a big crowd gathered for the drama.

"Then they started playing. Earl went over the guy and dunked. Then he blocked the guy's first shot. It was obvious that the man had nothing to offer against Earl. But he was really determined to win himself a rep. So he started pushing and shoving and fouling. Earl didn't say a word. He just kept making his moves and beating the guy, and the guy kept grabbing and jostling him to try to stop him. It got to the point where it wasn't really basketball. And suddenly Earl put down the ball and said, 'I don't need this. You're the best.' Then he just walked away.

"Well, if Earl had gone on and whipped the guy, 30 to 0, he couldn't have proved any more than he did. The other cat just stood there, not knowing what to say. The crowd surrounded Earl, and some of us said things about the fouling and the shoving. But he didn't say anything about it. He didn't feel any need to argue or complain. He had everyone's respect, and he knew it. The role he played that day never left anyone who saw it. This was a beautiful man."

From Peter Axthelm, *The City Game: Basketball in New York from the World Championship Knicks to the World of the Playgrounds* (New York: Harper's, 1970), 179–192.

THE WEIRD AND THE WONDROUS: VINTAGE BIG CITY

Superlatives, oddities, and memorable anecdotes I've collected over the years from communities with populations of more than 100,000.

It happened in Rio de Janeiro in 1977. The touring DeMatha High team from the Washington, D.C., suburb of Hyattsville, Maryland, was ahead, 58 to 52, with 6 minutes to play. Then it became a five versus seven game. Three personals and two technicals were called against DeMatha in quick succession. The DeMatha players walked off the court and assembled in a corner while Coach Morgan Wootten spoke to the referees. "Stop cheating or we're through," he told them in effect. The refs admitted they were and said they'd stop. Just like that. DeMatha won, 68 to 61.

The touring Original Celtics of 1931 had just finished a game in Macon, Georgia, and were stepping into the shower when they heard a knock on the dressing room door. It was a handsome young local man who just wanted to tell the famed pros how much he had enjoyed their play. He said his name was "W.L. Stribling." Then everybody knew. This was Young Stribling, America's Number 1 heavyweight boxing challenger, soon to battle Max Schmeling for the title. He'd played high school ball in Macon several years before and dearly loved the game. The Celtics were scheduled in Atlanta the following night, and just to make conversation one of them suggested that Stribling suit up if he wished. To their astonishment he accepted. When word hit the papers that Stribling would play with the Celtics, Atlanta was stirred. A huge crowd surrounded the arena for two blocks on all sides. Stribling saw 20 minutes of action and performed extremely well despite the long layoff. He lost to Schmeling in Cleveland on a fifteenth-round TKO, his only career knockout defeat and one of only twelve losses in an incredible 286 bouts. He died two years later of injuries suffered in a motorcycle crash.

Des Moines East and Waterloo West met during an Iowa snowstorm in 1962 before a paying crowd of one, an ex-East athlete home from college. Price Dahlstrom, a reserve, plowed 2 miles through 10 feet of snow and started when a regular didn't show up. The referees didn't show up either. The football and track coaches filled in.

The greatest comeback ever? In a 1971 San Diego, California, game Morse led Hoover, 70 to 50, with 2:40 to play. Hoover thereupon went on an unanswered 21-point binge (approximately 8 points a minute or a field goal every 15 seconds) to win, 71 to 70.

The East, which spawned basketball in Springfield, Massachusetts, as well as the great early-day YMCA and pro teams—notably the Buffalo Germans, the New York Celtics, and the New York Rens—also produced the top pioneer prep aggregations. Some were so strong they numbered colleges among their victims. Holyoke (Massachusetts) High won a "national" prep tournament at the 1901 Pan-American Exposition in Buffalo by defeating Mount Vernon (New York) and Pratt Institute. Flushing (New York) won another "national" at the 1904 St. Louis Olympics against teams from Chicago, San Francisco, and the host city. Eleven of the 159 straight victories amassed by Passaic (New Jersey) High between 1919 and 1925 were against college frosh or junior college teams. The first high school team? Some historians say Holyoke. Some say Philadelphia Central. In his book, I Grew Up With Basketball, Frank J. Basloe says Herkimer, New York, was playing as early as 1895.

Many coaches fought the jump shot in its early days, contending it's an off-balance delivery and "if you have to jump to shoot, you didn't have a shot in the first place." Or if you jumped on defense, it was "an invitation for the offensive player to go around you." Bill Russell, barnstorming with a California high school all-star team following mid-year graduation from Oakland McClymonds in 1952, met a particularly unbending purist on a Northwest tour. After each All-Star basket, the coach shouted, "Don't jump . . . give 'em the shot . . . it'll ruin 'em." It didn't. Russell's team, featuring jumpers, won, 144 to 41. The new shot revolutionized the game, opened the door to astronomical scores and gave the nervous shooter new hope.

When two state contenders are from the same neighborhood, strange things can happen down the postseason tournament trail. The 1979 scenario in Virginia, where tourney rules place a premium on regular-season performance and two district teams qualify for regionals, may be history's strangest. The Mount Vernon Majors from Fairfax County won the AAA (largest schools) championship, defeating the Norfolk Maury Commodores from Tidewater country by one point in the final. But should either have been there at all? Mount Vernon (9–1 in conference play) had lost to neighbor Groveton (8–2) three times; they split their scheduled home-and-home meetings before the Majors lost to their rivals in both the district final and a play-off for regional seeding. Meanwhile the situation was even more weird in Norfolk. Booker T. Washington was 4–0 against Maury, having logged two victories during the regular season, another in an automatic regional tourney berth play-off occasioned by the *teams' identical 8–2 conference records, and still another in the district final. As predicted, the Bookers and Commodores met again in the regional final, with the latter, down 10 points with less than 2 minutes to play, pulling it out, 74 to 73, on a basket at the gun. Mount Vernon was spared a fifth meeting with Groveton, which fell to Woodson of Arlington County in the regional semifinals. All of Maury's pre-state-final losses were to Booker T. Washington. All three of Mount Vernon's setbacks were to Groveton, whose supporters may have had a hard time developing enthusiasm as the Majors' victory parade rolled by.*

When St. Michael's and Walther Lutheran, rival Chicago-area schools, finally completed their 1977 Class A regional final, it was 6 days after tip-off and before empty stands. By court order, the second half was replayed.

Walther Lutheran had won the duly constituted game, 67 to 66, but top-seeded St. Michael's filed suit in Circuit Court after the Illinois High School Association failed to act on a protest. The issue was an alleged scoreboard error that gave Walther Lutheran 2 points too many, thus the victory.

At the halftime buzzer a Walther Lutheran player had been credited with a tip-in basket, giving his team a 38 to 32 lead. But after a discussion between St. Michael's coach Jim Roberts and the referees, the score was disallowed on grounds that the ball was not in the basket cylinder in time. Most of the participants conceded that the scoring discrepancy occurred when the basket was erased from the player's total but not from the running score.

St. Michael's deposed that the mistake was undoubtedly honest but that teams need protection against mathematical errors and the ultimate possibility that a discrepancy might not be honest. It sought an injunction that would (a) prevent Walther Lutheran from playing in the scheduled sectional tournament at Somonauk, Illinois, or declare St. Michael's the regional winner, with the IHSA prohibited from declaring a double-forfeit; (b) order a replay of the game; or (c) issue an injunction stopping the sectional. Also sought were $10,000 damages for the school and $10,000 damages for four players on grounds of "scholarship damage."

Walther Lutheran's position was that its team had won a regional, that no certainty existed that the running score was incorrect, and that this sort of thing opens up a can of worms for the future. Its squad was ready to board the bus for Somonauk when the phone rang with news of the injunction proceedings.

The IHSA's position was that Rule 2, Section 11, of the National Federation of State High School Associations states that "if there is a discrepancy in the score which cannot be resolved, the running score shall be official." Under IHSA by-laws, there can be no protest against a game official.

Circuit Judge Joseph M. Wosik, however, took another view, saying, "The issue here is not the protest of the ruling of a game official. It is one of mathematical computation." He reconciled the issue by issuing an injunction postponing the sectional game involving the St. Michael's–Walther Lutheran winner and ordering a replay of the second half of the disputed game on the original floor, Timothy Christian High School of Elmhurst, with new officials, a new timer, a new scorekeeper, no spectators, and the starting score of Walther Lutheran 36, St. Michael's 32.

Crucial testimony had been given by host principal Arnold Hoving, who said the scorekeeper had reported the probable error to him 2 hours after the game.

The teams took the Elmhurst floor at 10:00 A.M. In what might be called poetic justice from the winners' standpoint, Walther Lutheran won the compromise game, 64 to 63. Amazingly it ended with the same winner, the same victory margin, and the same player taking a charge and thus recovering the ball for his team in the waning seconds.

While still a student at Philadelphia's Overbrook High, Wilt Chamberlain outscored college all-America center B.H. Born of Kansas, "about 45 to 8," in a summer game in the Catskills. In a high school contest he piled up 36 points in a single quarter. He was in such demand that recruiters lost all reason. Red Auerbach wanted him to attend Harvard; that would give the Boston Celtics "territorial rights," then in effect. Eddie Gottlieb of the Philadelphia Warriors got the "territorial" rule extended to high school players for one immediate reason, Chamberlain. Other noted Overbrook products include Walt Hazzard, Wali Jones, Lewis Lloyd, Wayne Hightower, Andre McCarter, and Jackie Moore.

With pre-World War II fans Angelo "Hank" Luisetti was to basketball as FDR was to politics. At Stanford, before joining the navy and contracting spinal meningitis, he introduced the one-hand shot, revolutionized the game and set Pacific Coast scoring records which lasted 12 years. Yet at Galileo High in San Francisco from 1931 to 1934 he was more a master playmaker and defensive specialist. At Spring Valley playground he was remembered as the little kid who splashed through the puddles an hour before the director arrived, hurling the ball at the basket like a discus. A San Francisco Call-Bulletin *reporter wrote this after watching Luisetti's college swan song: "When future fans start talking about basketball stars of their days, those who witnessed the Stanford games of 1936–37–38 will shake their heads and say, 'My lad, you never saw Luisetti.' "*

Woodrow Crum had coached Kentucky teams to three "Sweet 16" appearances, but he was having trouble at Lawrence Central in Indiana. After his charges had suffered their thirty-sixth consecutive loss, an angry fan complained to the local newspaper that as a taxpaying citizen he wasn't getting his money's worth. Duly stung, Crum divided his salary by the number of taxpayers in the metro Indianapolis community and refunded the fan his share, 6 cents. Central snapped the losing streak in its next outing.

Nate "Tiny" Archibald had been cut at DeWitt Clinton High in New York when Floyd Lane, the community center director and former star on an NCAA- and NIT-championship CCNY team, interceded with the coach. It was a good move. Tiny made all–Public School as a senior, but at only 6 feet needed Lane's assistance again. He got a scholarship to Arizona Western Junior College at Yuma, which led to a scholarship at University of Texas at El Paso, which in turn led to stardom in the NBA. Tiny spent summers in the old South Bronx neighborhood, teaching, preaching "stay in school," and speaking against drugs. One of his prep teammates had collapsed and died on the court from an overdose.

Did it count, or didn't it? With time running out, Mercer Island High from a Seattle suburb was leading Shadle Park of Spokane in the 1981 Washington AAA final by one point. But Shadle Park scored from the field at the buzzer, and the officials could not agree. One said yes, the other said no, and the timer would not commit himself. Thus the basket stood; Shadle Park was the winner. Mercer Island then protested. At the WHSAA hearing the timer still would not render a judgment, and a video replay was inconclusive. Shadle Park went into the record books with a one-point victory.

Every state has a favorite come-from-behind legend, one against which all pretenders must be judged. Michigan's classic also features perhaps the most famous single shot in its state tourney history. In the 1959 Class A final, Hamtramck dominated Lansing Sexton well into the fourth quarter, holding a 60 to 45 lead. But suddenly Sexton went on a 27 to 12 scoring binge, forcing an overtime at 70–all. Hamtramck took a 79 to 78 lead in the final seconds on Art Reid's free throw, and Sexton came downcourt with one final chance. The gun sounded as Bob Davis's desperation shot was in the air. The ball hit the rim, took two distinct bounces back and forth, and finally rolled in to give Sexton an 80 to 79 triumph. Most epic rallies in key contests evoke immediate pandemonium. In this case there were several moments of stunned silence, then *pandemonium.*

When Richard Barry, Sr., father of Rick, was a high school player in Elizabeth, New Jersey, he loved basketball so much he sandwiched club ball into his schedule whenever he could. Though it was clearly against school rules, he made the rounds, playing for YMCA, YMHA, Irish, Polish, Italian, Spanish, Lithuanian, and Ukrainian teams. One afternoon he played in a city league game, then had to rush to meet the bus for home where he would get transportation to a high school contest that night. Unfortunately the family car had had an accident, and Barry had to run a great additional distance. He was late and dead tired. He fouled out, his team lost, the story came out, and he was booted off the squad. Later, on mass plea from his teammates, he was reinstated.

The 1957–62 teams at McClymonds High in Oakland, California, were so devastating that Paul Silas, a storied NBA rebounder for 17 years, was a forward rather than center despite 6′ 7½″ height, and they won 111 of 112 games, including a state record 69 straight from 1957 to 1960. Bill Russell, history's greatest defensive center, was never a regular during his 1947–52 career there! Other McClymonds stars during the 1957–62 period were Jim Hadnot, a 6′ 11″ center who played at Providence and in the ABA; Joe Ellis, who went on to the University of San Francisco and eight seasons in the NBA; and prep all-America Eddie Thomas. Hall of Fame baseball player Frank Robinson, Olympic sprint champion James Hines, and NFL luminary Wendell Hayes were also McClymonds products.

Three weeks after Madison High of Milwaukee defeated Wausau West for the 1981 Wisconsin A championship its bubble burst. Acting on a phone tip from a Milwaukee coach who had studied player pictures in a newspaper, the state association ruled that Madison had used a fifth-year man and declared the title vacant. The player was a reserve center who had attended four different schools. Because the association felt the offense inadvertent, it did not ask that the championship trophy or individual medals be returned. Madison's regional and sectional titles were allowed to stand, but the Wisconsin record books show no state A champion for 1981. (Nor does North Dakota show a B titleholder for 1942. Lakota nipped Elbowoods in the final but was also found later to have used an ineligible player.)

Mitch Chortkoff, Los Angeles basketball writer, told this one in 1983:

"One night I cover the Lakers against the Celtics. The next night it's UCLA versus USC. But the biggest thrills come on the third night—Bosco Tech versus nationally prominent St. Bernard in the L.A. playoffs. I'd never seen a game with three successful desperation baskets at the buzzer, but Bosco makes 30-footers to finish the second and third quarters and then another in the third *overtime. Final score: Bosco 49, St. Bernard 47."*

In what was surely a team conspiracy, Walter Garrett made all 97 of West End's points against crosstown Birmingham, Alabama, rival Glenn Vocational in 1963. He had 39 field goals and 19 free throws in a 97 to 54 victory.

Long before the dunk was conceivable, let alone recommended, giant basketball players occupied a much lower rung in society. Instead of being potential "franchises" who could lead the locals to the promised land, they were at best "unfortunate freaks" or at worst the targets of abuse because they were "ruining the game" or, "with limited real talent, taking unfair advantage."

Wade "Swede" Halbrook, whose 7′1″ height was accentuated by Portland (Oregon) Lincoln teammates standing 5′9″, 5′9″, 5′8″, and 5′5″, was subjected to vicious verbal abuse, crank calls, and occasional spittal during his 1952 state championship season. Halbrook poured in 51 points, running his four-game tournament total to 166, as Lincoln defeated Central Catholic, 66 to 44, in the finale. Though later a major college regular, his life has not been easy. He is living in purposeful anonymity, something a 7-foot basketball player might not have been able to achieve in the fifties.

George Mikan, 6′9½″ and "Mr. Basketball" of the first half-century, didn't play during his Illinois high school days but learned coordination under Ray Meyer at DePaul University, then dominated the NBA as a Minneapolis Laker. He recalls youngsters, apparently influenced by "big bad giant" fairy tales, running from him in terror on city streets.

Don Otten, a 6′11″ center at Bowling Green University and a Mikan contemporary, played only one year in high school. Bob Pettit, 6′9″, eventually all-America at LSU and an all-time NBA frontliner, couldn't make his Baton Rouge High team until his junior year and even after a distinguished college career was warned he was "too frail for the pros."

In the old, old days coaches took what they got. If you were coordinated, great. If you weren't, they'd find somebody who was. Today we start working with the physically endowed at an early age, interview their parents, computerize their measurements, prescribe weight training programs for virtually everybody, and send a select few to dancing school. If the giants lack coordination, we'll develop it for them. Meanwhile, we're receptive to 7-footers, high school or college, from Nigeria, Germany, Turkey, the Sudan, or wherever.

When Nancy Lieberman was growing up in Far Rockaway, her mother so despaired of her daughter's "no future" avocation that she took a screwdriver and punctured her basketball. Nancy didn't quit, of course. In addition to high school ball, she played for St. Francis de Salle in the CYO league, took the subway to Harlem for AAU competition, and played "radar ball" at night on the playground where the only illumination came from a distant street light. She later led Old Dominion to two NCAA titles and was a member of the U.S. silver medal team at the Montreal Olympics.

It took the girls' team from East Ridge (Chattanooga, Tennessee) sixteen overtimes to nose out Ooltewah, 38 to 37, in 1969. The boys of Boone Trail (Mamers, North Carolina) outlasted Angier in a thirteen-overtime 1964 game, 56 to 54.

Keith Dyk, star scorer at Northwest Christian High in Spokane, Washington, was like thousands of graduating athletes: he hoped to play college ball in the coming years. But Keith was different. He had a rare form of cancer, which after debilitating surgery and treatments went into remission, allowing him, with great rehabilitative effort, to play again. In 1982, against Darrington in a state Class B tournament game, he poured in 50 points, just 4 short of the tourney record. It was a philosophy versus heart situation for Coach Jim Stinson, who doesn't believe in hammering opponents (NWC won, 93 to 55) but wanted to give a deserving boy the fullest possible shot at a record. Indeed Stinson admits he had one of his players intentionally miss a free throw with 1 minute remaining in the hope that Keith would grab the rebound and pad his total. It's doubtful if any purist faulted him.

PART III

THE IN-BETWEENS

HE JUST FADED AWAY

One of the greatest high school players of all time was a perennial eighth grader who brought national championships in both 1929 and 1930 to the piney woods town of Athens, Texas. In those simpler days, Preacher Tompkins probably never even dreamed of college. This is Edwin Shrake's story as it appeared in Sports Illustrated *in 1967.*

Like its namesake in Greece, the town of Athens, in the pine woods and dirt of East Texas, has produced a number of citizens who think very big. So it was proper that when Athens decided to get itself a good high school basketball team 40 years ago, its high-thinking citizens went out and got the best.

In Grenado, Tex., they discovered Doc Sumner, later to become an all–Southwest Conference forward at Texas Christian University. In Pine Bluff in the neighboring state of Arkansas, they found Buster Brannon, who has recently retired from a basketball coaching career at Rice and TCU with six Southwest Conference championships to his name. But it was in the nearby hamlet of Brownsboro that the recruiters hit their bonanza—the Tompkins brothers, Freddie and Dennis, later all–Atlantic Coast players at the University of South Carolina, and their tall, uncommonly gifted cousin, Preacher Tompkins, who was, in the opinion of Buster Brannon, as fine a natural phenomenon on the basketball court as this country ever saw.

When Brannon met him, Preacher was in the eighth grade and, at 6-4, could not get his knees under the desk. Preacher endured the eighth grade for four years at Athens until he finally got bored and ambled out of town.

Meanwhile, though, Athens was winning about 30 games a year, which was all Coach Jimmie Kitts could manage to book. Athens went against college freshman teams, athletic club teams from the cities, other high schools, anybody with five players and a ball that would bounce. An Athens citizen, Ike LaRue, bought Kitts two new Model-A Fords, and the team took off on a barnstorming tour through Missouri and Illinois to earn expenses. Once, in Chicago where 38 states had sent teams to the national championships, Preacher Tompkins was touched with fame.

"The crowds and the newspapermen fell in love with him," Brannon recalls. "We told Preacher that if he looked good in the first two or three games, he'd be picked for the all-America team. He used all the fancy moves, color and shots, but still you could see he was just a lanky country boy.

"We'd go into a French restaurant and Preacher would peer at the menu, even though he had enough trouble reading English, and then he'd order scrambled eggs and sausage. Preacher enjoyed the tournament. He'd never read a book on basketball or listened to much coaching, but he knew instinctively that on a fast break you dribble high for speed and in a tight place you dribble low for control. He had more basketball savvy than anyone I ever saw. He knew every situation on the court and every shot. He really liked to go into a low dribble, put on the brakes and trip his defensive man. He loved seeing them fall."

In the finals Athens played Classen High of Oklahoma City, coached by Hank Iba. A Classen guard named Andy Beck, later three times all–Big Six, shot six times in the first half without missing, and Athens was behind, 12 to 11, at the intermission. Kitts told his team not to worry; Beck would cool off. "Listen, Buddy," said Preacher, who solved the problem of remembering names by calling everybody the same one, "that guy ain't gonna cool off. There's only one way to stop him. I'll play him man-for-man in the second half and the rest of you fellers play a zone." The strategy that Preacher proposed was radical for an era when the regular zone was the accepted manner of play, but Coach Kitts was wise enough to agree. Athens won the championship handily, and Preacher was named the most valuable player and rewarded with a gold watch.

The other Athens players were somewhat jealous of Preacher's notoriety. They kidded him about the watch. To top them, he would shove the watch into a teammate's face and innocently say, "I can't read this tew good, Buddy. Whut time do it be?"

The team traveled back to Athens in the two Model-A's and arrived after an absence of three weeks. Kitts was given a house and the two Fords. The citizens put a barrel in the town square in front of the drug store and filled it with $6,000 in bills and loose change for Kitts. Sumner and Brannon moved on to TCU, where Buster became a left-handed quarterback under the famous Francis Schmidt as well as a guard on the basketball team. In 1930 Athens again won the national high school championship, beating Gena, La., in the finals. That was the last year of the tournament, which was dropped because participating teams were missing too much school.

After the 1930 tourney, Kitts was promised a job coaching at the University of South Carolina. He sent Freddie and Dennis Tompkins and two other players ahead of him and then somehow failed to get the job after all. But the Athens boys won the Atlantic Coast Conference championship as sophomores. With his old friends gone, Preacher eventually wandered some 75 miles to the northwest to play for the Dallas Athletic Club. But Dallas was too big for him. Preacher began a letter to Kitts requesting advice. Stumped, he walked into a room where two teammates were playing cards and asked, "How do you spell Buddy?"

"B-U-D-Y," one replied.

"Naw, it's B-U-D-D-E-Y," said the other.

After waiting a while to see who won the argument, Preacher went back to his room. He soon left Dallas. He drifted into the oil fields as a laborer and was killed in a car accident. "If Preacher had ever gone to college, people would be talking about him today as one of basketball's immortals," Brannon says. "But he simply wasn't so inclined. It's a pity." However, they remember him that way in Athens, the only town in the country ever to have won two consecutive national high school basketball championships and certainly the only one to have done so with an eighth-grade star.

DEVILISHLY GOOD

One of the greatest prep dynasties of recent vintage belongs to Quincy, Illinois, a Mississippi River city of 44,000, whose Senior High fashioned a 132–6 record from 1978 to 1982, producing an unbeaten state championship juggernaut in '81 and a state AA record 64 consecutive victories. The '81 team, featuring Michael Payne and brothers Bruce and Dennis Douglas—later of the Universities of Iowa, Illinois, and Northern Illinois, respectively—toyed with most opponents, winning the state final by 29 points and earning Basketball Weekly's *Number 1 national rating. A third Douglas brother, Keith, later a South Florida regular, was the star of the '79 team, which went undefeated until losing the state final to Maine South of Park Ridge. Quincy has become known far beyond its orbit for an infectious community spirit and a uniform coaching program reaching down into the elementary schools. The following 1982 story, by Michael Davis of the* Chicago Sun-Times, *captures some of that spirit.*

There is a shrine in this Mississippi River town where they worship The Devil.

Townsfolk come out on Friday and Saturday nights for a rejuvenation of the spirit, a bolstering of faith for those who trust in him. It is a sight to behold.

Even on the frost-sheared winter nights, when a hateful wind whistles across the river from Missouri, his believers come without fail. They forge over snow-caked roads to partake in the ritual, 5,000 unrelenting souls conquering every obstacle that stands in the way of seeing him emerge from the darkness, his pitchfork spewing hellfire and his frenzied eyes ablaze.

"I've gone with a 102-degree temperature, I've gone with the flu, and I've even gone with diarrhea," says Dick Wentura, owner of the Volkswagen dealership on the edge of town. "Nothing could keep me from seeing that Devil." Wentura hasn't missed an appearance for 30 years.

The very sight of him strikes terror in the hearts of first-time visitors. Some run to an adjoining dressing room and hide. Others merely turn their heads. Only the bravest look at him squarely and return his savage taunts with angry words of their own.

The men from Collinsville did. And they paid dearly for it.

It is 11 minutes past 7 on a Saturday night, 49 minutes from showtime, and Brad Schrader is having a devil of a time straightening his costume so that everything is wrinkle-free and satin perfect. That is the way it must be when you are mascot of the Quincy High School Blue Devils. After all, you are the second-most-important person in town.

Jerry Leggett, the basketball coach, is the most important.

For Leggett is the silver-haired basketball evangelist who has made believers of all those Devil-worshippers chanting outside the locker room. After four decades of near-misses in the state tournament, Leggett finally brought a championship back from Champaign last year with a crack team that was 33–0. Despite losing its indomitable center, Michael Payne, to graduation and the University of Iowa, Quincy's unbeaten string remains intact, 55 straight after Saturday night's victory over Jacksonville. The Blue Devils are four games away from tying the Illinois record of 58 consecutive victories, set in 1972 by Thornridge High School, the team by which standards for greatness are measured in this basketball-rich state.

"When was the last time we lost at home?" Leggett asks the team in a down-to-business pre-game briefing. "The 1977–78 season," he hears in reply. "And who beat us that night?" he asks. "Collinsville," they say.

"It's a six-hurdle race until the end of the regular season, gentlemen, before we start worrying about the state playoffs," Leggett says. "There are six hurdles in the race, but two of them are just a little bit bigger than the others. Collinsville tonight and Galesburg later on. Now if you were running in a race and you came to a taller hurdle, what would you do? You'd put out a little more energy, a little more effort. And that's what we're asking for tonight. Quincy plays its best in big games, and this is one of them."

The starting five, including all-state guard Bruce Douglas and his brother, Dennis, a 6-5 junior forward, are sitting in the front row, the reserves directly behind them, and all eyes are affixed to Leggett and the blackboard behind him. To the left is the Devil's Graveyard, a collection of cutout tombstones that represent every team Quincy has snuffed out this season. To the right is a meticulously detailed chart chronicling every Blue Devil's offensive and defensive performance. There are symbols and artifacts everywhere in the locker room, a handsomely equipped facility by most college standards. In addition to the weight-training equipment, the wall-to-wall carpeting and the piped-in stereo rock, the players have a videotape screening room where they can drop in and replay any game from this season or last. This seeming luxury is all part of Leggett's "system" for winning, an all-encompassing philosophy of coaching that starts in Quincy's elementary schools and comes to full flower in the secondary grades.

"The kids in this town will do anything to grow up and be a Blue Devil," Leggett says. "All the coaches in the lower grades know my plays and how I want drills run in practice, so that by the time these kids reach high school, there's no time lost in teaching them the fundamentals. When I stand up from the bench and hold four fingers in the air for an out-of-bounds play, nearly every kid in the gym will know what's going to happen."

On this night, as always, the youngest Blue Devil fans are sitting in their own section, high above the sidelines. The high school student section is filled to overflow in the stands directly behind the Quincy bench on both levels of the 5,200-seat gym. The rest of the seats are sold to adults on a season-ticket basis, and there are more than 200 people on the waiting list, hoping against hope that they will someday own season seats to the Blue Devils.

"It's crazy," says Leo Henning, a former Chicagoan who moved to Quincy in 1973 to work at WGEM-TV and its AM and FM radio stations, all of which broadcast Blue Devil basketball. "Ever since I came here I've been trying to figure out this mania. And now, after all these years, I think I've got it. A basketball game in this town is our Picasso, our Sears Tower," he says. "When you ask people about Quincy, the biggest source of pride is its basketball teams. The biggest status symbol among the most prosperous and influential people in town is to have season tickets to all three games in town: Quincy High School, Notre Dame High School and Quincy College. And the best way for any newcomer in town to know who is and who isn't a big shot is to see how close the person is sitting to the floor."

Many of the wealthy of Quincy reside on Maine Street, in homes with hand-carved filigree and rounded dormers, touches of elegance that German immigrant craftsmen gave to houses built during a post–Civil War boom. The stone-mortared homes are as sturdy now as they were then.

In the sweet used-to-be, Quincy was a convenient stop between Rock Island and St. Louis, a welcome outpost on the winding way downriver. Now it is merely an isolated dot on the map, just a town across the water from Hannibal, Mo., and not the center of commerce and commotion it once was. Though hundreds of day-workers still punch in at the calcium carbonate mines and the Gardner-Denver compressor factory, the list of unemployed grows each week. Like so many smaller midwestern manufacturing centers, Quincy is a town in transition.

Though the mill wheels have slowed and the train doesn't stop as frequently any more, Quincy's heart beats strong and steady.

"We're isolated from the mainstream of metropolitanism in our own corner of the world, without a doubt," says Dick Wentura. "But our people have a lot of pride in everything we do. And because of that, we feel we have a great community."

No greater moment in the lives of the citizenry has come than on a Saturday night last March when the Blue Devils obliterated Proviso East, 68 to 39, for the Class AA championship. "It was the culmination of a community's pride," says principal Richard Heithold, a forward on the 1945 Quincy team that finished third in the state. "There was something unfulfilled in our community until we won that championship. It wasn't anything that was ever demanded, never a do-or-die situation. But in the minds of the people it was a goal that the community deserved: a kind of community prize.

"It was uncanny at Champaign that night. Since we were able to buy about twice as many tickets as we were allotted, with thanks from other schools, the Quincy contingent literally made a ring around the Assembly Hall. And a tremendous thing happened in the middle of the third quarter, when it was evident we were going to win the championship. The adult fans on one side of the gym started a yell: 'Q-U-I.' Then on the other side, spontaneously, they began answering 'N-C-Y.' It just went on and on like that, rocking the gymnasium . . ."

The fans were already on their feet at 7:59 as Coach Leggett and his team wound their way in a snake dance through the locker room to the entrance of the gymnasium.

The players were clapping in unison and singing a capella, "Q . . . Q City . . . uh huh . . . Q . . . Q City."

Leggett spots the peanut gallery, where the children are squealing in anticipation of the blackout, the spotlight introduction of the visiting team and the arrival of the Blue Devil himself. "That's the reason Quincy is going to keep winning," Leggett says, pointing to the Class of 1990. "There's the future."

At precisely 8 the lights go down, and it's bedlam. "I've never seen anything like this anywhere I've been," says Leo Henning, overseeing the production of the radio broadcast and delayed-TV broadcast of the Quincy-Collinsville game. "When the devil runs out on the court with that pitchfork aflame, it scares the living hell out of the opposition before they even throw the ball up."

Though the 10th-ranked Collinsville Kahoks scoffed in the Devil's face, the No. 1–ranked Blue Devils vaulted to a 17 to 2 lead and never looked back, winning 75 to 46.

The Quincy Blue Devil got his due.

A SCHOLARSHIP FOR JACKIE

When mature adults aggressively recruit teenaged athletes, using inducements that will not stand the light of day, are they really surprised when they warp a few minds now and then? The author of this 1957 case history, which first appeared in Sport *magazine, is the distinguished Furman Bisher. A period piece whose sordid details will shock few in these jaded days, this story has historical significance because it represents perhaps the "super recruiting" era's first in-depth investigation. The subject, who might have been an all-time great, didn't attend any of the colleges battling for him herein. Instead he wound up at Louisiana Tech, near home. There he performed creditably, then went on to 5 years in the NBA and 3 in the ABA. Jackie Moreland died of cancer in 1971. He was 31.*

All these years I've wanted to get on the inside of a college recruiting case, one involving a big catch. In this case I did it. I walked a gumshoe beat from the college (North Carolina State) to the farmhouse of Jimmie Moreland, daddy of the boy, Jackie Moreland.

I think I got as accurate a picture of how a major recruitment comes off as I can possibly get. I got, I think, as much gratification out of the actual leg work on the story as I did the writing. I talked to coaches, girl friend, storekeepers around his town of Minden, La., and sat in the family living room watching the tears of his distraught parents.

You may note one thing: that I never talked to the boy. I was sure that was one thing I should not do. As partial as I am to fine young athletes, and as much admiration as I have for them, I'd have been moved to such a point that the perspective I'd already gained might have been destroyed.

I've enjoyed the working-out of the story, I think, because it became the one recruitment about which I could talk with positive conviction and without having to depend on second-hand knowledge. And, too, because it convinced me it was a rare case, that most of the recruiting that goes on in college is on an honest-to-God level.

This is a story of athletic recruiting in college. The central figure is a very tall boy named Jackie Moreland, who lives on a farm midway between Minden and Homer, in the northwest corner of Louisiana, and who plays basketball.

Jackie high jumped 6 feet and broad jumped 21 feet 6 inches for the track team at Minden High, to which he commuted 10 miles each day. He hit .319 for the local semipro baseball team and played first base so skillfully that the Baltimore Orioles were prepared to offer him a $45,000 bonus to sign a professional contract.

He was more than just an accomplished athlete at Minden High, though. He was also a student who showed every prospect of becoming a worthwhile citizen. He was president of the senior class of 1955, president of the student council, staff member on the school paper, class favorite, "Mr. School Spirit" and salutatorian. He missed being valedictorian by less than one point.

Jackie didn't play football, but the Minden coach, George Doherty, a big, spirited fellow with a plump face and a love for boys, said he was the best statistician he'd ever had. "He fitted into everything that went on at the school," Doherty said. "If Jackie Moreland had a fault, I didn't know it."

But most of all Jackie was a basketball player. He was 6 feet, 7 inches tall, going on 8. For three years running he made the all-state Class A team at Minden, a never-never sort of thing in high school. College people who watched them both through critical eyes said that Jackie had class that Bob Pettit never had until he became an all-America at Louisiana State. Jackie was more than just big. He had finesse. He had a mind that functioned clearly, no matter how raging the heat of battle. He was completely ambidextrous and seemed to have a thousand different shots. In three seasons he scored 1,965 points. When a recruiting storm broke around his head and forced his name into the sports headlines prematurely, one famous college coach was asked why one boy should stir up such a furor.

"Simply," the coach said, "because he is the greatest basketball prospect in the country today."

Jackie Moreland's little world was about as orderly and as brilliantly promising as it could be. His family life was simple, for the Morelands are plain rural folk whose social life revolves around the church and to whom everything outside the unbordered trade area called the Ark-La-Tex is foreign.

That's how it was before Dec. 7, 1955, the date on which senior high school athletes became eligible to sign college scholarship grants. That was when the storm broke, when Jackie's world became muddled and confused, when his dreams were washed out and when the ideals he had lived by at Minden High tarnished like a 49-cent bracelet.

Jackie eventually enrolled at North Carolina State College in Raleigh, about 1,000 miles from home. Everett Case, a driving Indianan devout in his dedication to the favorite sport of his native state, has built a southern basketball empire at State. It takes a steady stream of incoming talent to keep the empire thriving, and Case ranges from the Rocky Mountains to the sidewalks of New York on his hunt for the finest of the breed.

The Moreland kid was a natural for Case's empire, but Jackie will never play for N.C. State. Last November the policy council of the National Collegiate Athletic Association returned State to the probation list from which it had been paroled only the year before. This time the sentence was for four years, the harshest penalty of its kind ever inflicted by the NCAA. The reason: State's conduct in its recruitment of Moreland.

At the same time, the NCAA refused to grant Texas A&M a shortened probation sentence it already was serving for a football indiscretion until it had been dealt friend to a college in Denton, Tex., $400 per month while in school, and a new car on acceptance and another on graduation.

The girl friend, a poised 18-year-old of statuesque build who is now a freshman at Centenary College in Shreveport, confirmed in an interview with this writer that a party representing N.C. State's interest had offered her a seven-year medical scholarship to a school of her choice, preferably Duke University in Durham, N.C. There she could be closer to Jackie.

"There was a lot of talk in my presence about money," said the girl, Betty Claire Rhea, a star witness for the NCAA. "I haven't told everything yet."

Why didn't she accept the scholarship, since Moreland did go to N.C. State? Why not choose Duke rather than Centenary, a little Methodist school of some 1,000 enrollment?

"If we had been married, or even engaged," Betty Claire said, "it would have been different. But too much can happen in four years at our age. I didn't want to be under any obligation."

Texas A&M did accept a boy named Joel Smith on scholarship. Joel and Jackie were close friends, farm neighbors and once teammates at little Harris High School, where Jackie played before transferring to Minden's golden frontier. The Southwest Conference ruled Smith considerably below basketball standards for that level, and after this investigation he transferred to Louisiana Tech in Ruston.

Thus there was more than circumstantial evidence on which the NCAA could build its case. Betty Claire was a focal point of the preliminary investigation. Later, after Jackie had enrolled at State, he was called before Byers and Weaver in a Raleigh hotel, confronted with the evidence, and was said to have signed a statement confirming all offers. Back on the campus later, he denied making a confession.

Fate allowed State just one good look at the vast potential of this Moreland boy. In a practice game against the varsity he scored 30 points. The next week he was declared ineligible, and to pour salt into the wounds the ACC fined State $5,000, remissable if Moreland stayed in school on his athletic scholarship terms and completed his non-athletic education.

The tall farm boy from Minden stood at the crossroads again. He could stay at State and be the greatest intramural basketball player in the country, or he could transfer to another school and play the kind of game he loves. Whatever he did, there was nothing in it for N.C. State.

How did all this come about? How did N.C. State, Texas A&M and Moreland get themselves hopelessly involved in this thicket of recruitment? What came over Jackie Moreland between December, 1955, and December, 1956? Where was the boy in whom George Doherty had been unable to discover a fault?

Jackie apparently had entered the danger zone of recruitment with clear-eyed resolution. It began on Dec. 7 with a visit from Jack Heldman, an assistant coach from Vanderbilt. Next in line at the farmhouse on Highway 43, almost before Heldman was out of sight, was Harry Lancaster, assistant to Adolph Rupp at Kentucky.

Here, with Lancaster present, Jackie fulfilled a boyhood dream. He signed a standard Southeastern Conference grant-in-aid with Kentucky. "He's always wanted to go to Kentucky since he was so big," said his father, Jimmie Moreland, holding his hand about four feet above the floor. "That was his ambition."

with on a Moreland charge. The Aggies, the NCAA said, had violated some rul and regulations of recruitment in their headlong pursuit of the young man fro Minden.

A few weeks later, Commissioner Jim Weaver of the Atlantic Coast Conferen of which N.C. State is a member, declared Moreland ineligible at the school whi had fought a determined recruitment fight for him and won. Another storm bl up. N.C. State, with Chancellor Carey H. Bostian as spokesman, rose up in righteo indignation. "It is our belief," said Chancellor Bostian, "based on the evidence kno to us at this time, that State College is not guilty of the violations as charged."

There is a clause in the athletic code of the Greater University of North Carolin of which N.C. State is a member, that any member of an athletic staff found guil of willfully violating recruiting regulations as set forth by the ACC shall be dismiss from his job. This projected two members of the State staff, assistant athletic direct Willis Casey and assistant basketball coach Vic Bubas, squarely onto the seat of jeopa dy, for they had been assigned to the Moreland recruitment campaign.

For that matter, the whole basketball program at State seemed in danger. Te years ago this program was nothing. Case had just arrived from Frankfort (Ind.) Hig School where he had been the scourge of the Hoosiers, and State played its gam in an antiquated gymnasium that could seat only 3,000. Now State plays in Reynol Coliseum, a palace that accommodates 12,500 fans in comfortable theatre-style seat In late December an invitational tournament called the Dixie Classic is played i the Coliseum and draws close to 60,000 spectators. Because of State's initiative, baske ball has taken a death grip on the Tobacco Belt. And State has taken a death gri on ACC basketball trophies. In seven of the past eight seasons, some covering th old Southern Conference, Case's men have won conference championships.

Ditch all this for one farm boy from Minden, La.? What kind of a set of value is this? Is this the kind of judgment that goes into college recruiting? Who says N.C State and Texas A&M are guilty of indiscretions? What kind of evidence does it tak to get put on ice for four years?

"I'll put it this way," said Walter Byers, executive director of the NCAA, one collegiate America's most unwanted positions. "We must have enough concrete ev dence to convince a board of 18 men from all parts of the country. In other word our decisions aren't based on hearsay."

The NCAA detective on the case was A.J. "Dutch" Bergstrom, former athle director at Bradley University. A mystery gumshoe artist turned up in Shrevepo 30 miles from Minden, one day last September and announced that he had be assigned to the case. He was an elderly man who identified himself as Billy Als of Atlanta, Ga., but who refused to identify his client. It was later learned that was working for the University of Kentucky. At any rate, private eye Alston's re fell into the hands of the NCAA and Commissioner Weaver of the ACC. It dealt b N.C. State and Texas A&M a critical blow. It said that State had offered More an unrestricted (five-year) scholarship, a seven-year medical scholarship for a friend from Minden, plus a $100 clothing allowance for the girl twice a year, $1,000 a year for Jackie.

The report said that Texas A&M representatives had offered Moreland a year scholarship, a scholarship to a friend of his choosing, a scholarship for hi

But the recruiters kept coming. The family guessed that representatives of 43 schools hovered around their Jackie. His Minden coach, Cleve Strong, a passive man with grey-tinged hair and ulcers, said it was more. "It got so bad," Strong said, "that Mr. Williams (the principal) quit letting them see Jackie at school."

Little Centenary, where basketball is the major sport, made a good pitch for Jackie. Jimmie Moreland liked the Centenary coach, a well-scrubbed, down-to-earth young man named Harold Mooty. They fished together. They found companionship in each other. Soon Jackie was saying he would go to Centenary.

Around the square in Minden, where Centenary is not a big favorite, cynics charged that the Shreveport school offered Jackie more money than anybody. A Centenary official quite frankly said: "We offered Jackie a good job in the summer, a very good job. We offered him the prospect of a good future when he was graduated. Somebody said that we offered him $36,000. I suspect that in the long run it would have meant a lot more to Jackie than that, should his future have panned out the way it might have. But Walter Byers knows all this."

Texas A&M made its sweetest overtures in the spring. Jackie had assured Centenary he would be there when the roll was called, but added, "I just want to look around a little more." A Texas A&M alumnus flew him to the College Station campus for some of this "looking around." By this time, it seems, Jackie had picked up some pretty worldly advice on the matter of how to be recruited. "The first thing he said when he got off the plane," said A&M coach Ken Loeffler, once the builder of national champions (with the assistance of Tom Gola) at LaSalle College in Philadelphia, "was, 'What's the offer?' "

" 'What do you mean, son?' I asked him," Loeffler reported.

" 'You know,' he said, 'an automobile or something like that.'

"I knew right then that we had hold of a 'hot' one. He was too big for A&M. He had indicated an interest in petroleum engineering, though, and we thought we might get him on that."

When Moreland actually did sign a Southwest Conference letter-of-intent with A&M, Loeffler was 1,000 miles away at a boys' camp in Wyoming. The Moreland pursuit, however, was being carried on by some active alumni in Shreveport, with the surprising assistance of Paul "Bear" Bryant, A&M athletic director and head football coach. Bryant and four A&M alumni of influence showed up one day last summer at the Moreland farm.

"Mr. Bryant seemed awful nice," said Mrs. Moreland, a hardy woman of stout structure and the mother of six other children besides Jackie. "He did most of the talking. He offered Jackie a scholarship. He said, 'If you want a car, your daddy will have to buy it for you, or your granddaddy.' "

The NCAA investigators, however, charged that A&M alumni in Shreveport had pursued Moreland with more financial ardor. One, a mining and gas company official named Harmon Egger, became so incensed at whispered stories involving him that he submitted to a lie detector test in self-defense. He had been in Bryant's party the day of the visit to the Moreland farm.

The summer passed with still no final, conclusive decision by Jackie. Kentucky, Centenary and Texas A&M all had his word that he was coming to their campus. N.C. State moved in at the climactic moment, setting up on Jackie's actual day of decision an almost fantastic series of concentrated uncertainty, promises, fast changes, bewilderment and, finally, the last emotional scene of an addled farm boy staggering barefooted the last few feet into the arms of N.C. State.

Jackie awoke that day, Aug. 31, 1955, packed and prepared to make a departure for N.C. State, whose basketball administration had moved an impressive task force to make the catch. The register at the Washington-Youree Hotel in Shreveport shows that Willis Casey, the athletic director's assistant; Vic Bubas, the basketball assistant; Harry Stewart, director of the Wolfpack Club, an alumni booster organization; and Ron Shavlik, all-American center at State the previous season, and his wife had set up camp there for three days. Together with a man named Dwight Laughlin, an ordinance plant employee who lives across the Red River in Bossier City and who is a relative of Casey's wife, a State crew had visited the Moreland home the day before. Jackie had promised that he would be ready to leave at 3 p.m. on the 31st.

First, though, he had to tell Betty Claire goodbye. According to the Moreland family, "she pitched a fit." Somehow Betty Claire swung him back to Centenary, and they drove off to Shreveport to give athletic director Buzz Delaney and Mooty the good news.

Here a blackout develops, but it seems that Jackie and Betty Claire stopped at the Washington-Youree for one final word with the State task force. Here also, it seems, some of the last desperate counter-offers took place, because it is known that Jackie left the hotel with $80 which had been handed him by Laughlin to pay for his plane fare to Raleigh. It was this $80 that finally brought the ACC house down on State.

The trail continued to Centenary, where Jackie happily announced that he would play for the Gentlemen of Centenary. His picture was taken with members of the athletic department and was splashed across the sports section of the *Shreveport Times* the next day, with an appropriately exuberant story of announcement. *Times* editions began rolling with a headline reading: "Moreland to Become Gent."

By the next morning the line had been changed to read: "Moreland to Become Gent?" For by that time he was on his way to Raleigh.

Throwing the $80 on Delaney's desk and asking him to get it back to the proper owners, Moreland and the girl friend set out for Minden. Before he got out of Betty Claire's sight, another change took place. "Mr. Shorty Long met him before he got around the corner," Betty Claire said. Long was Kentucky's agent, not an alumnus but a self-appointed recruiter set on corralling Jackie for the Wildcats.

A hot reception was waiting for Jackie when he reached the farm. The State group had made its 3 o'clock appointment and left empty-handed. Jimmie Moreland, driven to his wit's end by the bewildering change of pace, charged his tall son with these words: "Dammit, make up your mind right now, and let's get this mess settled once and for all. What do you want to do?"

Jackie pondered. What he wanted to do was to go to Kentucky. He said so. His father told him to call Shorty Long and tell him to come get the body. The Minden line was busy.

"That's how close Kentucky came to getting him," Jimmie Moreland said.

Before Jackie could call again, the State troops rode in again. In a few minutes Jackie said he was going to State again, and he stalked out of the house toward the guests' station wagon, without his shoes. Someone reminded him of his oversight.

His trunks were placed in the station wagon, and he was rushed to the airport at Monroe, La., not to be heard from by his family or the press for the next four days.

"It's a wonder he didn't have a nervous breakdown," his father said. "You don't know what all of us have been through the last year. It's been somebody on our doorsteps or on our telephone all the time. We just took to lying. We'd tell them Jackie wasn't here. I never did think I'd want him playing for that Coach Rupp at Kentucky, but now I'm sorry he didn't go there, where he wanted to as a boy. That Mr. Lancaster was a nice fellow, and Mr. Bubas was, too. But I never saw a bunch of people who seemed to hate each other so much."

The Morelands are unpretentious people of plain, humble, rural Claiborne Parish stock. Jimmie Moreland, in his middle 50s, works as a gauger in the oil fields near Homer. There is steel in his grip, honesty in his eyes and the undisguised trace of the out-of-doors life in his ruddy face. Two married daughters and a son no longer live at home. Another son is at Louisiana Tech. Two more, twins Joe and Ed, are juniors on the Minden High basketball team.

The Morelands are accustomed to a life without complexities. It is true that they had had a preview of this kind of turbulence. When Jackie was transferred from little Harris High School and its student body of some 60 students to Minden, the Louisiana High School Association declared him ineligible until a thorough investigation could be made, causing him to miss a few games as a sophomore.

"We left the farm and moved into town to make it all right for him," Jimmie Moreland said. He and Mrs. Moreland and a visiting daughter sat in the dimly lighted parlor of their home. They had just finished decorating a little pine Christmas tree on a table in the corner. Jackie would be home in a few days.

"I drove 20 miles to work every day. We've made sacrifices for him to be able to play, then all this . . ."

Jimmie broke into tears and rubbed his calloused hands together in a gesture of helplessness. Mrs. Moreland, tearful herself, patted his knee sympathetically. This was a family emotionally uprooted by recruiting grief. In some manner, everybody concerned had contributed a fault to it. In the course of events, Jackie had become the prize beef at a cattle auction.

"We never gave him guidance," his father said. "We didn't know about things like this. But nobody ever talked to us about money. If he got any big offers, we don't know about them. But nobody believes us. All they ever talked to us about was education and how much Jackie would like the school. We never knew it would be like this. Now Jack's ashamed to come home and face his friends."

Downtown in Minden, Jack Bridges' clothing store is the sounding board for local sports opinion. "Nobody blames the kid around here," Bridges said. "Everybody's for him. They know he made some mistakes. He shouldn't have told all those people he was going to their schools, but he did that to get them off his back. The kid's biggest mistake was that he didn't know how to say no. He would make up his mind he was going to one school, then somebody would come by and he couldn't tell him he'd already made up his mind."

" 'But they've come from so far,' he would tell me," Mrs. Moreland said.

Somewhere somebody in the background was giving the boy a good coaching job on how to be recruited. This is borne out in his shopping around after he had first signed with Kentucky, the pre-determined destiny of his ambition. There are plain, unvarnished facts, however, that would have eliminated this temptation to play the field, and they fall generally into the realm of the colleges' responsibility.

If no recruiter had offered more than the legal scholarship allows, the Moreland case would never have become an affair of notoriety.

If Kentucky's original grant-in-aid had been respected, the so-called cattle auction never would have come off. This is an argument for having the grant-in-aid, or letter-of-intent, be administered by the NCAA on a nationally recognized basis.

From Furman Bisher, "A Scholarship for Jackie," *Sport*, April 1957. Reprinted by permission.

PIONEERS AND BLOOMER GIRLS

The first state high school basketball tournament didn't occur in Massachusetts, where the sport was born. Or in New York, where its greatest early progress was recorded. Or in Indiana, where it found its most religious fervor. It happened in Wisconsin—in 1905. That was 9 years before World War I, 15 years before the first commercial radio broadcast, 40 years before the first commercial telecast, 32 years before rules makers abolished the center jump following each basket, and during a year when only 1,700 automobiles were on Wisconsin roads. It was just 13 seasons after Dr. Naismith hung peach baskets at Springfield College and introduced a game that he hoped might bridge the gap between football and baseball. This story, which I wrote in 1983, takes you back to those incredible pioneer times.

Winters can be cruel in upstate Wisconsin, and in the horse-and-buggy days they must have seemed even more so. Such was the background in March 1905 when athletic authorities at Lawrence University in Appleton, cognizant of rising interest in a 13-year-old indoor game called "basket ball" (then officially two words), decided to stage a postseason invitational high school tournament. Since the event was the first of its kind anywhere, historians accord it the mantle of "America's first state tournament," though its field was limited to ten schools in the state's more populous, more accessible eastern half.

This then was the granddaddy of the all-encompassing, fever-pitched Sweet 16, Elite 8, and Final 4 tourneys, along with their elimination rounds, sponsored today by interscholastic governing bodies in each of the fifty states, stirring communities at every crossroad, and attracting crowds up to 20,000. The Lawrence classic reigned until 1916 when the Wisconsin Interscholastic Athletic Association (WIAA) took over amid rebellion by southern-section schools against Appleton control. Lawrence officials had taken the only practical route in 1905, three years before the Model T. Transportation problems would have militated against any real statewide event in that era, even in warmer climes. As it was, Appleton citizens marveled that 200 rooters from challenging towns would descend on their city.

Participating schools in 1905 were Fond du Lac, Sheboygan, and Sturgeon Bay (which had made the loudest claims); West Division of Milwaukee, Oshkosh, Two Rivers, Antigo, Oconto, Grand Rapids (now Wisconsin Rapids), and hometown Appleton. The entry fee, "to cover forfeits," was $5. Mark Catlin, all-America football star from the University of Chicago, then a perennial gridiron juggernaut, was engaged as referee. Lawrence students "who possess practical knowledge of the game" were exhorted to volunteer as deputy officials. And "to save as much time as possible," team captains were asked to declare it a full game if one team were ahead by 15 points at halftime. Like a TKO.

With six successful intercollegiate campaigns behind it, opponents including the strongest colleges and National Guard teams for miles around, Lawrence University was well qualified to host a major prep basketball event. Lawrence was also one of the first institutions to field women's teams. Indeed one of its interschool women's contests in March 1905, a home engagement against Oshkosh Normal, became a regional cause célèbre. "The Girls May Wear Bloomers," a front-page story cackled, there being no sports pages per se in the smaller cities in those days. But a subheadline tempered the non-unanimous faculty decision with: "Must Themselves Sell the Tickets but Only to Those Before Whom They Are Not Ashamed to Appear Wearing Them."

"Them" refers to "Bloomers," not "Tickets," but you get the idea. All this constituted a daring first and not one to be allowed without well-calculated checks and balances. "Never has the foot of man been set in Alexander Gymnasium while the girls' basket ball team was practicing," declared one story in tongue-in-cheek discussion. "No eastern harem has been more closely secluded, more undefiled by masculine glance. How will the bloomered ones know that behind the big pillars there may not be prying masculine eyes?"

Prior to 1905, oratory had been the major wintertime interschool competition at many high schools and colleges, including those in Wisconsin's Lake Winnebago area. When Lawrence's oratorical team left by train for the 1905 state contest at Ripon, it was accompanied by a brass band and more than a hundred rooters waving pennants and shouting college yells. Special songs written for the orators were belted with such gusto that a large crowd was attracted at each stop. At the Ripon opera house, site of the competition, rooters were allotted time for organized cheering before the program got under way.

Tied to a slower, simpler, more restrictive time and a florid journalistic style, the atmosphere of the 1905 tourney can perhaps be better appreciated in the light of contemporary world and local events chronicled by such area headlines as:

- "Russians Make Final Stand in Manchuria," whose story describes the surprise Japanese drive, leaving much of America opining that if giant Russia can't handle a little archipelago like Japan, what could we ever have to fear from either?
- "The Women Can Vote in April," in which it is carefully explained that females may vote for superintendent of schools but, of course, not for judges or city officials. (The Nineteenth Amendment is still 15 years away.)
- "Maine Blowup All a Mistake," in which a convicted New York dynamiter says the U.S. battleship disaster in Havana harbor, a major factor in America's declaration of war 7 years before, was probably not the work of Spaniards after all.

• "Ministers to Kill Boxing," in which a "semi-authentic source" reports organization of an intercity clergymen's network to stop prizefights as soon as rumors surface.

• "Delays Graduation to Play Football," an example of early-day, self-imposed redshirting in which an unnamed high school senior is revealed to be deliberately flunking a subject in order to extend his eligibility another year.

At the prep tourney's eleventh hour, Sturgeon Bay was reported "getting cold feet" and might not show up. Manitowoc was poised to step in. But the rumor proved false; Sturgeon Bay did appear and won its opener against Grand Rapids. The Appleton–Two Rivers game was called at halftime with the former leading, 25 to 2. Led by a little forward named Dana (first names weren't used in local sports coverage), who scored 43 points in the final two games, favorite Fond du Lac defeated Sheboygan, 32 to 24, for the championship. A silver Spitz Cup was presented to the winning team. Gold medals were awarded to the five Fond du Lac regulars, there having been no substitutions in the finale. Silver medals went to the Sheboygan players, bronze medals to members of the third-place Milwaukee West Division team. Two Rivers received a special Schlafer Cup for "the best appearance and the highest marking in conduct."

The university publication *Laurentian* saw the good conduct cup as a future means of preserving order and sportsmanship. "Not infrequently in affairs of this kind, where there is considerable rivalry, there is also a certain amount of ill feeling," it commented. "The cup for good conduct and appearance had much to do with the absence [here] of this feeling."

The tourney was an instant success. Not a single complaint against an official's decision was heard, and observers were unanimous on two points: the event was here to stay, and it proved the wisdom of using out-of-town officials. Despite lack of representation from Madison, the dairy country, and the north woods, it had been the biggest secondary school event in Wisconsin history. A new activity breeds an atmosphere of awe, mutual respect, and a refreshing, innocent enthusiasm, perhaps never to be duplicated, and the Lawrence Invitational was no exception.

By 1915 the natives had become restless. As the October 23 editions of the *Fond du Lac Commonwealth* put it, "It looks as if the championship games will be played in either Podunk or Timbuctu. The high schools in the southern part of the state have thrown out a defy to Lawrence College and assert that they will not submit to Lawrence's 'hogging' these games or directing the why and what of elimination games." The Wisconsin Normal School Athletic Directors stepped in and ran the state tourney until 1920 when the WIAA took over. Today the 1916–19 tourneys are recognized as "official."

In the interim Illinois and Utah (1908); Indiana, Montana, and Nebraska (1911); Kansas and South Dakota (1912); Minnesota (1913); North Dakota, North Carolina, and West Virginia (1914); and Virginia (1915) had instituted official state tournaments. Fond du Lac, Wisconsin's original basketball scourge at all age levels and home of Company E, Wisconsin National Guard, which in 1900 had defeated Yale University for the "championship of the United States," not only won the first Lawrence Invitational but added the last pre-WIAA invitational title (1915), the first recognized WIAA crown (1916), and three of the WIAA's next eight. Fond du Lac still holds more state championships than any Wisconsin school, even though the Cardinals have made only one big-tournament trip in the past 57 years. That was in 1973, a venture ending in a 60 to 59 title-game loss to Beloit Memorial. Such are the vagaries of athletic history, explainable in part by coaching and demographic or sociological factors, but never quite completely.

Based on the following sources: "The Girls May Use Bloomers," *Appleton Post-Crescent*, March 18, 1905, p. 3; "High School Teams Arrive," *Appleton Post-Crescent*, April 6, 1905, p. 1; "Championship to Fond du Lac," *Appleton Post-Crescent*, April 10, 1905, p. 1; "The W.I.A.A.: A Capsule History" and "Fond du Lac High Swept to First WIAA Title in 1916," 1981 boys' state tournament program, Wisconsin Interscholastic Athletic Assn., Stevens Point, Wisconsin, pp. 56 and 58.

159 IN A ROW!

Sure, records are made to be broken. Babe Ruth's 60 home runs and Ty Cobb's 4,191 hits were records that lasted 34 and 57 years, respectively, but they finally fell. Jesse Owens's long jump mark lasted 25 years, but now it's more than 2 feet short. Some records seem untouchable, notably Lou Gehrig's 2,130 consecutive games and Joe DiMaggio's 56 straight safe-hitting games. Then there's the 6-year basketball winning streak of a New Jersey high school, which has prevailed for more than 60 years.

If complete domination of contemporaries in a six-state area over a 6-year period is the criterion, then the Passaic Wonders of 1919–25 were the greatest high school teams of all time. With a style far ahead of their era, they set the existing national record of 159 consecutive victories, averaging an incredible 60 to 21 margin, amassing 100 or more points twelve times and 70 or more thirty-four times in a period scarcely noted for big scores. They rolled over the state champions of New York and an all-star team from Philadelphia. Their opponents escaped with one-digit defeats only seven times during the streak.

If avant garde play is the criterion, it's still Passaic. The Wonders used a backcourt press, supposedly a brainstorm of the fifties. They fast-breaked, supposedly a phenomenon of the forties. Forward DeWitt Keasler had a twisting one-hander, a shot unknown or taboo most places until a generation later. The Wonders used the existing center-jump-after-each-basket rule to maximum advantage, once scoring nine straight field goals with the ball never touching the floor. In a day when basketball was barely budding, they were so storied that most of their home games were played in armories before standing-room-only crowds.

If superstars are the criterion, the Wonders give no ground. They had 'em in droves. They're the only high school team(s) in the National Basketball Hall of Fame. Even before they were admitted en toto, they had two individual enshrinees. One was John Roosma '21, later a 10-letterman at West Point, where he led the basketball forces to a 73–13 record, including an unbeaten season in 1923, and scored 44 percent of his team's points. The other was Coach Ernest "Professor" Blood, whose statistics are simply beyond belief.

The "Professor" was already 43 years old when he arrived in Passaic. He started playing basketball in 1892, just a few months after word of Dr. Naismith's invention hit his hometown, Potsdam, New York. In 10 years at Potsdam High (1906–15) he didn't lose a single game! Before embarking on the 159-game skein—on December 13, 1919—his Passaic teams won another 40 in a row before bowing to Union Hill in the finals of the 1919 state tournament, New Jersey's first. When he transferred to St. Benedict's Prep in Newark in 1925, his Passaic record was 199–1!

Coach Blood was a combination Amos Alonzo Stagg, John Wooden, and Nathan Bedford Forrest. He seemed to go on forever, coaching for 55 years until 1949, 6 years before he died on his birthday at 83. He is probably the winningest coach of all time, finishing with 1,296 victories against only 165 losses for a percentage of .887. Even Everett Case, with careers at three Indiana high schools, North Carolina State, and a navy preflight school on his record, falls 135 wins short at 1,161. At St. Benedict's Blood posted a 421–128 record in 24 years. Certainly he was "firstest with the mostest." He pioneered conditioning as a prerequisite for winning basketball. He drilled his teams to precision tempo when few of his contemporaries did. He developed a stream of tall centers to take advantage of the center-jump rule, and his teams featured a host of innovations that would have been too radical for most of the country.

But the Wonders had many other luminaries. Bobby Thompson '22 was the first American high school player to score 1,000 points in a single season. He hit 1,000 on the head—in thirty-three games for a 30.3 average. Under rules of the day, he shot all his team's free throws, but as an old-time Passaic fan observes, "He sure didn't do it all on foul shots." Thompson's 1921–22 gang was the highest scoring of all. It surpassed 100 points eight times and averaged 69. In 1922! Thompson later made his living in insurance.

Mike Hamas '23, brother of Steve, the heavyweight boxing contender of the early thirties, succeeded Thompson as the Wonders' premier scorer. He registered 873 points in twenty-eight games for a 31.1 average. Mike, who later graduated from Penn State and was with Western Electric all his working life, put up the first backyard basket in Passaic. It was in a vacant lot next to his father's tavern on Third Street. He saved money to buy a basketball, practiced all summer, and by his senior season was ready to take over. Prior to his initiative, the boys used a taped-up bundle of rags as an outdoor ball. Mike died in 1970.

Fritz Knothe '23, who became a major league third baseman with the Phillies and Boston Braves, is remembered as king of the floor men. He and Keasler are believed to be the only Wonders who saw or participated in all the 159 victories. Knothe joined the Passaic Police Department after his baseball days and remained there until his death in 1963. His brother, George, a second baseman, also had a major league fling—six games with the Phillies during the same and only year Fritz was there.

Milt Pashman '25, who became Passaic's assistant city attorney and court prosecutor, was New Jersey's leading scorer as a senior with an even 600 points, achieved without benefit of the one-man-free-throwing rule, by then repealed.

It is doubtful if any high school team ever met so many college or out-of-state secondary schools. During their streak the Wonders were 11–0 against junior colleges, college freshmen, business colleges, law schools, and what were then called "normal schools." They were 18–0 against high schools, high school all-star aggregations, and prep schools from New York, Pennsylvania, Connecticut, Massachusetts, and Rhode Island. In 1922 they whipped the Philadelphia All-Scholastics, 57 to 30. In 1923, in a challenge game engineered by Passaic and New York sports writers, the

Wonders, fielding a team composed of Hamas, Knothe, Keasler, Fred Merselis, and Moyer Krakovitch, routed New York's top team, St. Mary's of Ogdensburg, 59 to 38, before a packed house in the Paterson Armory. It was the team's one hundredth straight triumph, and it received attention as far away as San Francisco. Broadcast by radio station WBAN in Paterson, this may have been the first high school basketball game ever aired.

Some of the Wonders' most humbling scores were against out-of-state teams whose leaders probably had no idea what they were getting into. Attleboro (Massachusetts) was throttled, 111 to 5. Williams (Connecticut) Prep went down, 145 to 5. Jamaica (New York) learned about life, 89 to 19. East Greenwich (Rhode Island) Academy took a 68 to 13 drubbing. The one hundred and fiftieth game in the streak, a 73 to 33 rout of Arlington (Massachusetts) on New Year's Day, 1925, was filmed and shown at a Passaic theater 5 days later. This is believed to be the first prep basketball contest ever filmed for public showing.

Perhaps the weirdest coincidence during the 159-game skein was the home-and-away performance against traditional rival Ridgewood during the 1920–21 campaign. The scores were identical: 92 to 4!

Transportation was the hardest problem the Wonder Teams faced. The school didn't yet supply buses, and both cars and roads in those post–World War I days often proved unreliable. Thus the players used trolley cars, trains, and foot power to reach game sites.

Greatness allows for magnanimity and a freer flow of humor. During the 1921–22 season Passaic was whitewashing hapless Dumont, 72 to 0. As the final seconds ticked away, Knothe deliberately passed to an opposing player so he could get his team on the scoreboard. Final score: 72 to 2. A year earlier Coach Blood was unable to make the Leonia game and ordered Roosma to handle the team in his stead. Reporting afterward, Roosma apologized for a loss but said the team showed good sportsmanship. Thus eliciting the desired expression of bewilderment, Roosma revealed the truth. Passaic had won, 107 to 8.

Competent in six sports, Blood was a bear of a man. In this vein someone in Potsdam gave him a bear cub that the coach would wrestle. When the bear was refused admission by a bus driver in Paterson, coach and pet walked all the way home. The next day the *Passaic Daily News* ran the story under this headline: "Prof. Blood Walks from Paterson to Passaic with Bear Behind."

The 159-game streak ended in the Hackensack Armory on February 6, 1925. Hackensack High, which had lost by 17 at Passaic, prevailed this time, 39 to 35. Pashman led all scorers with 17, but it wasn't quite enough. By now, Coach Blood had been succeeded by his assistant, Amassa Marks, who regrouped his forces and a few weeks later guided them to the school's fifth state championship. Their victim in the final was Union Hill, the school that had done likewise to Passaic in 1919, snapping the forty-game streak. By the end of the twenties, Passaic had captured six of New Jersey's largest-school state titles and two runner-up spots—in 11 years. It hasn't reached a final since.

There is a special justice in the civic pride that the Wonder Teams' legacy still inspires almost three generations later. Once a wool and rubber manufacturing center, the city has lost its major plants to the South. The exodus has included the Botany

Worsted Mills, which dated to 1890 and constituted the world's largest complete unit for woolen manufacture. So the fiftieth anniversary celebration—in October 1969—was a real "pepper-upper." The Passaic/Clifton *Herald-News*, with staff writer Les Plosia producing reams of readable research and on-spot coverage, ran this banner and subbanner:

50 YEARS LATER—PASSAIC REMEMBERS
City Honors 'Wonder Team'

Streamers across streets read, "Welcome to Passaic . . . 50th Anniversary Wonder Team." An anniversary dinner at the local Pennington Club showcased one of the most distinguished speaker's table contingents in the sport's history. It was a microcosm of eastern basketball progress with a heavy Hall of Fame representation. The toastmaster was John "Honey" Russell, a pro immortal and coach of Seton Hall's 1953 NIT champions from South Orange 10 miles down the road. He was joined by members of the Original Celtics—Nat Holman, coach of CCNY's NCAA and NIT champions in 1950; Dutch Dehnert, the first great pivot man; and Benny Borgman—as well as Hall of Fame author-historian and Passaic graduate Bill Mokray and numerous others.

Twenty-two veterans of the Wonder Teams returned for the celebration. Roosma, by then a retired colonel with 30 years' service, was the center of attention. He was the Hall of Fame enshrinee and the player Coach Blood had called his greatest. Colonel Roosma and Thompson appeared on national television, and the colonel renewed his plea that the Hall admit all members of the Wonder Teams, a plea granted a few years later.

Colonel Roosma was at Pearl Harbor on December 7, 1941. Retired and living in nearby Verona, he was to lead Passaic's Memorial Day parade until age 80. He and fellow returnees were products of an age when college was not yet a social imperative or occupational necessity. A few had become wealthy or otherwise high-salaried executives. Others found niches in more routine jobs. Their generation saw the bubble of the Roaring Twenties burst. It weathered the Great Depression, then the biggest war in the nation's history. By the Rebellious Sixties they were set and approaching retirement. Many remained in the Passaic area. Keasler became superintendent of the Passaic Post Office, Krakovitch a Port Authority policeman. Sam and Phil Riskin became a local attorney and bank president, respectively. Chester Jarmolowicz worked in the county probation office. Meanwhile Ike Rumsey, one of Coach Blood's big centers, wound up as president of Tobin Packing Company in Rochester, New York.

The community's fiftieth anniversary celebration plans sparked high praise and extensive reminiscence in the Passaic City Council. City Clerk Anthony Martini, normally a quiet participant in such sessions and only a child when the Wonder Teams were running rampant, took the floor to review their exploits for 10 minutes. Echoing the lingering partisan view, he said the Hackensack Armory was as slick as ice on the day the streak was snapped.

"The Wonder Teams were the greatest thing that ever happened to the city of Passaic," Mrs. Fannie Fischer, who saw many of the games, said on occasion of the teams' admission to the Hall of Fame. "The day we lost to Hackensack I cried." Mayor

Gerald Goldman said he felt it "important for the city to get the fun and benefit from its history. The city must generate and continue the spirit of the Wonder Teams' successes."

"Passaic" is Indian for "peaceful valley." Because the falls of the Passaic River a few miles upstream offered ideal power potential, Alexander Hamilton chose neighboring Paterson as the United States' first industrial city. That was 1791. The textile mills brought wave after wave of immigrants to the valley, and at Passaic's peak Poles led its ethnic census, followed by Italians, Russians, Hungarians, Slovaks, Germans, Austrians, Scots, English, and Irish. As time went by, union strife belied Passaic's name, cheaper labor and tax incentives sent the mills southward, and the valley was forced to diversify. Some recovery had been accomplished when a $400 million fire in 1985 destroyed 3,000 jobs, nearly 25 percent of the city's industrial base, and the homes of 500 new immigrants. Once Passaic's population exceeded 70,000; at latest check it was 55,000.

The old-timers had plenty to talk about in 1969 besides basketball. They'd been through war and peace, through terrifying and inspiring times. Colonel Roosma had tasted early fame, served his country for three decades, seen social and military upheavals from a special vantage point, and come back home to a vastly changed community. O, what a book he might write!

Based on the following sources: "50 Years Later—Passaic Remembers," "Alumni Return from All Walks of Life," and "Hamas Recalls Building First Backyard Basket," by L. Plosia, *The* (Passaic-Clifton, NJ) *Herald-News*, October 8, 1969, pp. 49 and 51; and P. Soderberg and H. Washington, eds., *The Big Book of Halls of Fame in the United States and Canada*, New York: Bowker, 1977, pp. 94, 97.

HOAX

If a cloak-and-dagger hoax at a state tournament could cause a furor in 1921, imagine what it would cause today. The state was Oregon. The school was Baker—from the butte country near the Idaho border. The controversy's center was the outstanding Harry "Red" Blakely, later a college star, who died in 1973. The following is a composite of stories that appeared in Oregon papers, commemorating the fiftieth anniversary of the ploy.

It's poetic justice that the Baker Bulldogs are back in Oregon's "Sweet 16" on the fiftieth anniversary of the school's legendary 1921 masquerade. Hardly a Beaver State fan has escaped somebody's version of how superstar Harry "Red" Blakely played under an assumed name until discovered just before the championship game. Officials ordered the entire state tournament replayed, and Baker was thrown into an uproar.

Yes, replayed. The 6′4″, hook-shooting, generally avant garde Blakely, playing under the name "Roy Stoddard" while Stoddard took the name of substitute Raymond Luce, wowed fans and foes alike as he powered Baker to triumphs over Portland Franklin (22 to 15), McMinnville (39 to 29), and Molalla (25 to 17) in the big tournament, then held in the Salem armory.

"Roy Stoddard has been the sensation of the tournament and has the uncontested distinction of being the best man that ever played on a local floor," it was written in the *Salem Statesman*. "His keen mind and perfect ease practically won the games alone."

Decades later Chappie King, a member of the Franklin team that won the replayed tournament, called Blakely "a player 30 years ahead of his time." He was often bracketed with the Globe Trotters.

When reports of the Bulldogs' success reached Baker, 250 miles east, school principal George McIntire became suspicious and wired tourney officials: "If Stoddard is a big guy with red hair, send him home. He's ineligible."

Confronted with the wire, Coach George "Ad" (for "Admiral") Dewey admitted chicanery. Blakely had been declared ineligible by McIntire shortly before the team departed for Salem because he had overdue makeup work and lacked the necessary credits. Armed with $300 raised by appreciative, expectant citizens to help defray "Sweet 16" expenses, angry that he should be hit by critical ineligibility at the eleventh hour, and certain that Baker stood no chance without Blakely, Dewey concocted a ruse. A rumor was spread that Blakely had gone to Chicago. In reality he headed for Salem on his own and joined the team there, becoming "Roy Stoddard."

The joyride was over. The Oregon High School Athletic Association ejected Baker from the tourney and redrew the bracket. Franklin, Baker's first-round victim, won the title, 26 to 19, over defending champion Salem. One of the Franklin regulars was Howard Hobson, later coach of the University of Oregon's Tall Firs of 1939, the first NCAA champions.

Unfortunately Blakely, now 70 and living in Fargo, North Dakota, where he once starred for North Dakota State under his old coach, George Dewey, won't be on hand for Baker's current quest. He might clear up some long-standing controversies if he were. He insists he was eligible, a position shared by an alumni committee that investigated his school records shortly after the fact.

Back in Baker, fireworks really flew. The alumni report and principal McIntire's defense of his action were aired at an overflow public meeting in the high school auditorium. Chairman Leland S. Finch was "armed with a dummy rifle, which proved more effective than a gavel," the *Baker Herald* reported. Coach Dewey resigned in the turmoil.

"They almost killed the poor principal," recalls Vern Manary, the team manager in 1921 and now manager of the Baker County Chamber of Commerce. "He had to have police protection."

It's hard to imagine a high school athlete of the twenties with a more exotic background than Blakely. A former all-stater from Centralia, Illinois, where he had played on a state championship team in 1918, he had come to Baker after a 2-year navy hitch. His parents moved to Oregon during his enlistment, and he was 19 when school started, his twentieth birthday occurring a few weeks before the tournament. In age he was eligible. During regular-season play he cut a wide swath. He led the Bulldogs to a 62 to 4 rout of Weiser and a 39 to 14 shellacking of the storied Ogden Deaf team, then to a best-of-three regional play-off victory over Pendleton. He followed Coach Dewey to North Dakota State, where he became a household word and was recently inducted into that institution's Hall of Fame.

Generations come and go, but yarns like "The Masquerade of '21" never die

Paraphrased by the author from "Blakely Tells Story of '21 Baker Masquerade," *Oregon Journal* (Portland), March 24, 1971, sec IV, 3; C. Whitaker, "Red Blakely's Death Brings Back Memories," *Democrat-Herald* (Baker, Ore.), February 23, 1973, 6.

A TOWN DIVIDED

Sport can be a microcosm of life. In a medium-size industrial town like Hamilton, Ohio (population 64,000), class conflicts stand out indelibly in a hard-pressed economy. A basketball game in the late 1970s between public high schools from different sides of town, explored in social depth by Peter Davis in his book Hometown *(copyright © 1982), takes on much greater meaning than a mere box score. The following is reprinted by permission of Simon & Schuster, Inc.*

In repose, before their team has made its appearance, the Taft High cheerleaders could almost be mannequins. Care has made no crease on any of their six upturned faces. Their wholesomeness is marred only by the scent of their honey-licorice cough drops wafting from two of them who have colds. The girls are not, however, innocent of anxiety. One chews on her lip, another toys with an ear-level pimple she can only wish she had disposed of earlier. Perhaps they are not naive about the world but simply immune to it. At 16 and 17 they have known pressures equivalent to those to which board chairmen are subjected at angry stockholders' meetings. Selected after scrutiny far more rigorous than the members of the basketball team had undergone, the Taft cheerleaders have seen their every flaw magnified in videotapes of tryouts that were shown to a panel of judges with Olympian authority. Yet they are now placid.

Though no player has yet burst from the locker room, the gymnasium, redolent of sweat and wintergreen, is abuzz with the din of 2,200 voices, not yet in full yell but warming up like a symphony orchestra. The game is being played at Garfield on Hamilton's older, shabbier East Side, but the Taft fans have one side of the gym to themselves. The two stands emphasize the differences between the schools, the divisions in Hamilton. The Taft side is tweed and cashmere. Garfield tends toward chinos and leather jackets, dungarees and workshirts.

The Garfield side is divided between Appalachian whites, come north to man factories after their farms gave out, and blacks, who hope their children will break out of Hamilton to find money and equality in nearby Cincinnati, or Chicago, Los Angeles or Atlanta. A local character, whom I shall call Flatiron, a former steelworker whose nose was mashed in a foundry accident, describes the Garfield atmosphere: "On the big hill right above the school is the old home where the county has stashed its down-and-outers since the 1840s, and that's pretty much the Garfield story." With little to do but collect his pension and disability payments, Flatiron spends his time examining the social forces of the town. "What you get these days at Garfield," he says, "is peacetime teenagers whose parents both work, yet never see more than $11,000 between them in a single year. They send their young to a school at the foot of Poorhouse Hill in a neighborhood appropriate to that designation. The southern whites and the blacks have weak affection for each other. Sometimes right in the hallway they fight like bearcats, but for the game they hate Taft more. In 10 years, if they don't leave town, they'll be competing for the same jobs, working for the folks on the other side of the gym. Garfield teachers with kids send them to Taft, never the other way 'round. Now and then Garfield gets its mad up and gives Taft a run for its big bucks. Not this year."

For the students at Taft and Garfield, the game is a way of telling time, of establishing a relationship with Hamilton's past. Banners from old championship seasons drape the gym. The game between Taft and Garfield redeems a dreary record, settles ancient grudges. To the players and their classmates, the game is the season.

Not that the Taft-Garfield game assumes a larger importance only among Hamilton's adolescents. The community at large is aroused by the game, which inspires bets, office pools and barroom arguments. Because Hamilton doesn't have professional or college sports it's making no great claim to say that a ticket to the Taft Garfield basketball game is the hottest one in town, but extremes are reached that would be scarcely imaginable to those unfamiliar with the role of sports in America. Fistfights over seats have broken out among Garfield fans, and Taft parents have used basketball season tickets as courtroom pawns in divorce settlements.

Taft's practice sessions the week before the game had all the fervor of war councils. Coach Marvin McCollum paced the court, squinting intently at his varsity. It was a squint with a twinkle. McCollum's war council was also a play, and the play wasn't a melodrama but a kind of ethical romance with moments of self-mockery. The romance was in the love of victory, the ethics in the means by which victory was pursued.

McCollum was as calm as he was concentrated. When mistakes were made, he gestured a player to the sideline for quiet advice. He watched his charges making layups, trying hook shots, turn-around fadeaways, and then scrimmaging against the second team. McCollum is a moralist fond of trite sayings and mangled parables from sources as disparate as Lao-Tse and Tennyson. While practicing for Garfield, these flowed in a happy mixture of earnestness and whimsy. McCollum believed all of them, but he knew they were, after all, slogans and not the Sermon on the Mount. He seemed to use them for inspiration and as tension-breakers.

Having beckoned Mike Grubbs, a senior guard, to his side after Grubbs missed a bounce pass that should have led to an easy basket, McCollum gave a brief lecture on concentration. Then he interrupted himself with: *If you can't be a highway, be a trail./If you can't be a sun, be a star./If you can't be the best, be the best man you are.*

McCollum explained that he loved basketball, but he loved teaching even more. "If you do it right, coaching is teaching," he said. "If you don't, it's a crime against youth."

When one of McCollum's two top players, senior Andy Kolesar, a tall, muscular guard, lunged in the wrong direction for a pass that ended up behind him, McCollum intoned: *You can pitch a no-hit ball game,/Pass and run with easy grace,/But it's just another loss if a teammate's out of place.*

McCollum himself had played baseball and basketball as a high school student in Fairfield, three miles from Hamilton. He came out of World War II with a knee wound that gave him a permanent limp. Though he also had diabetes, he did well enough as a semi-pro pitcher that the Dodgers offered him a contract with a Class B farm team. "Which wasn't that hard to turn down," he said, "because all I had was control, and I knew it even if they didn't." McCollum became Taft's basketball coach in 1960, the year after the school opened. He's as different from the screaming drill sergeant coaches as Casey Stengel was from Vince Lombardi. But when his other top player, a rangy forward named Scott Grevey, loafed after a loose ball, McCollum enfolded him in an anthology of bromides. *Good, better, best./Never let it rest./ Until your good is better, and your better best.*

"I wondered which one I'd get. Sorry, Coach," said Grevey, both of whose older brothers had been coached by McCollum. The eldest, Kevin, now starts for the Washington Bullets. Scott had been around McCollum's parables most of his life. "We'll get them for you on Friday night, Coach. I promise," he said.

Located on the West Side, in Hamilton's newer residential area, Taft had a student body composed of the children of the town's first families and its upper middle class as well as some of its poor just up from Appalachia.

Across town at Garfield's last practice before the Taft game, Coach Don Gillespie's problem was completely different from McCollum's at Taft. Where McCollum had to make sure his team (2–1) would be sufficiently inspired against the crosstown rivals they were supposed to beat easily, Gillespie had to find out if he could field a team at all. His top player, a graceful guard named Robbie Hodge, had been in a Volkswagen accident the week before that had left him with a whiplash. Two of his starters had been lost because of suspensions. One had been a truant; the other had told a teacher to kiss his ass. Gillespie, 35, was Hamilton's first black head coach and had played football for McCollum in high school. He was very fond of his old coach, but he didn't think the genial way McCollum handled players would work at Garfield. "The homes my fellows come from," Gillespie said, "they simply don't *hear* anything softer than a holler."

On the court Hodge moved with ease and confidence among his taller teammates, showing no effects of the accident. At 5-9 he was the shortest member of the squad, but he could outjump everyone else, including a 6-3 forward. Most of the players were black, but Hodge, a white senior, managed to be the star and everyone's friend at the same time. Gillespie would shake his head and say, "Taft averages three inches taller among the starters. All we've got are quick hands and fast legs. If we can't hang onto the ball, we're dead." When Hodge or his most talented teammate, a 5-11 black forward named Calvin Chapman, tired of the rest of the squad's mistakes and began to play tricks with the ball, Gillespie shouted, "Hodge and Chapman, I warned you, no more razzle-dazzle! Drop for 10!"

He would yell to keep order, but behind his loud voice Gillespie wasn't stern. Where McCollum was fatherly, Gillespie was brotherly. He also worked as a probation officer and was co-owner of a carpet business. And besides coaching boys' basketball and girls' track, Gillespie taught vocational training and was chairman of the Occupational Work Experience Department at Garfield. With all his duties and outside jobs, he still had found time to move his family out of Hamilton to Forest Park, a Cincinnati suburb. Even though his ties to Hamilton were so strong that he and his family attended church there each Sunday, he moved because he wanted his children to go to an integrated school. Garfield was integrated, with 37 per cent black students, but Hamilton's feeder schools—both elementary and junior high— were predominantly white or black. If he stayed in Hamilton, Gillespie's children could attend all-black schools for the first nine years of their education or else be token blacks in the upper-middle-class schools on the West Side.

"The situation in Hamilton is socially stagnant," Gillespie said as his basketball players took their final practice shots. "This is a status quo town and not just for black people. But the young blacks say, 'Hurry up and get me old enough to move out of here.' I had roots here and wanted to stay; in fact, I still hope to move back some day. When I was a kid, I served parties at the homes of rich white families, which gave me advantages later. I felt I knew the whole community. I didn't resent being a servant; it was just an apprenticeship. My father is a businessman himself. We lived in the Second Ward ghetto when I was a kid, but it seems poorer now, more hopeless. Some of my students who come from there have a very dim view of themselves. The black junior high allows them to practice stupidity as long as they don't become discipline problems. They get good at dumbness. We have to try to correct the junior high's mistakes when they come to Garfield, but teachers make up their minds on certain students who have a bad rep, and they stick to their initial impression."

There was a sense that Gillespie didn't quite belong away from his hometown because he still cared too much about it. He had the objectivity of an outsider, having grown up black in Hamilton, yet this was combined with the insight and affection of an insider. Knowing the town's problems so intimately, he was wary of plunging back into Hamilton as a contestant for community stewardship. Gillespie summoned his players. They were slow to assemble, Hodge horsing around with his best friend, a black guard named Tony McCoy, while some other players tried long, idle hook shots from well past the key. Hodge and McCoy were partners on and off the court, known to everyone as salt and pepper. "Fellas, I said get your asses over here!" Gillespie bellowed. Now they crowded around him. "I don't know what I can tell you," he began. "Taft figures they're going to kill us. They're thinking state tournament, and we're just a little pebble in the road they can roll right over. The paper says, I quote, 'The Taft Tigers should encounter no difficulty with the Garfield Griffins.' End of quote, end of city rivalry, end of our self-esteem. Men, and that's what you are, I appeal to your competitive instincts. Most of all, I appeal to your pride."

Waiting for the game to begin in the steamy Garfield gym, Flatiron muses on the relationship of the sport to its environment. "Basketball has always been a perfect game for the Midwest," he says. "This is a vast area of small towns that were tied together at first by interurban tracks and later by Model T's that enabled fans to follow their teams from town to town. There wasn't a damn thing to do in most midwestern towns once the hunting season ended, so the local gym became the town hall for a few months. This crosstown matchup only goes back 17 years because before that Hamilton had just one public high school, the Big Blue they called them, and they won several state championships. When they built the two high schools, they split the town but they started a pretty hot rivalry. It should just about end tonight. Taft could win this by 30 or 40 points."

The gym explodes as the Taft team breaks onto the court, each player leaping dramatically through a paper banner held up by cheerleaders. Next, the Garfield players do a loop around their own gym, and the crowd volume turns to thunder. There are a few boos for the Tigers, because they are in enemy territory, and for the Griffins because they have a dismal (1–4) record.

The opening jump ball sets off a furious scramble until a Garfield forward seizes the ball, dashes for the basket and misses. Taft's Kolesar controls the rebound and slows down the play, setting his team's preferred pace. Taft scores first on an easy shot by Grevey. The Tigers lope to their end of the court while the Tigerettes—Taft's cheerleaders—give the yell that signals that their boys have drawn first blood. The Garfield Griffins, named after the mythical hybrid between a lion and an eagle, retaliate with a long jumper by Hodge, admirable not only for its accuracy but its trajectory. High school ballplayers, when they shoot a jump shot, often fire the ball straight at the basket, making a score impossible unless their aim is perfect. Hodge's shot, taken when he was high off the court, described an arc like the dotted line on a globe showing a great circle route across the North Atlantic.

With the score at 2 to 2, Taft's full-throated cheer is simply "Go!" repeated 10 times, though the Tigerettes pronounce it "Geaow." A free lance cheer wafts down from the Garfield stands: "Tiger thinks he's cool, but Griffin ain't no fool. We gonna get 'em, you just bet 'em. We got the jive-ass school!" The city's racial partition is reflected on the court and the sidelines. Garfield has three black starters, Taft none. Four of the six Garfield cheerleaders are black, only one of the six on the Taft side.

Taft controls the game easily at first, not yet hot, passing the ball too much, waiting to shoot until after the best opportunity has passed, but still in command. Garfield, by contrast, is disorganized, inconsistent in its shots, but always hustling. By fighting for every loose ball, the Griffins keep the game even until it is tied at 10, Taft scoring each basket first and Garfield responding. A pattern is established in a personal duel. The 6-2 Kolesar, Taft's leading scorer, cannot shake the player assigned to guard him, the 5-9 McCoy. It's a matchup between Mutt and Jeff. McCoy will hound Kolesar all night, crowding him, blocking his drives, stealing passes intended for him. He becomes Kolesar's shadow, his ghost, his tight-fitting glove.

Grevey fills the void left by McCoy's neutralization of Kolesar. According to McCollum, Grevey had been improving every week; as a 6-2 junior, he appeared ready to join the family tradition of high school stardom and a college scholarship. Maybe there would even be the NBA. Hodge and Grevey personified the differences between Garfield and Taft. They shared one characteristic—both fathers wanted them to play basketball. Beyond that, their lives were completely different, beginning with the fact that Hodge was short and Grevey tall. The Greveys are a prominent Hamilton family. Norm Grevey, Scott's father, is a successful lawyer who in one three-day span flew to South Carolina to see his son Bryan play college ball, then up to Washington to watch Kevin with the pros and finally back to Hamilton to be at one of Scott's games for Taft. The fourth Grevey son, Norm Jr., was then only nine years old, and his father liked to say Normie hoped to quit junior high to turn pro as a hardship case.

Hodge's father was traveling all around the country installing safes for the Mosler Safe Company. One of Robbie's older brothers had been in trouble with the law. Robbie himself was a nervous, inattentive student who at times seemed to have a crush on every girl at Garfield. According to Gillespie, Robbie's father hoped to restore the family's reputation, sullied by the older son's juvenile delinquency, through Robbie's becoming a great basketball player.

While Hodge doesn't score any more in the early going, Grevey does find his rhythm and his eye; with him leading the scoring, Taft opens a 16 to 10 lead. Garfield has prepared for Kolesar; its defense against him is almost perfect. When Grevey takes command, Garfield seems to lose its bearings. He leaps past several defenders for a twisting layup. A few seconds later, before the Griffins can get the ball to midcourt, Grevey steals it, heads toward the hoop but is quickly surrounded. He lunges away from the basket to free himself of the defenders and arches up a long hook that swishes through. When Hodge has a pass picked off, Garfield looks out of it.

Hodge is mad at himself. He brings the ball downcourt with a dribbling display that leaves three Tigers springing at each other instead of him. He seems less interested in scoring than in maneuvering the ball between a defender's legs, which he does as the fans laugh. In his folding chair on the Garfield sidelines, Gillespie covers his eyes. How many times has he cajoled, ordered, threatened Hodge about this? Just play straight basketball; never mind the hotdogging. We all know you can bounce the ball. But Hodge's dribbling gets most of the Taft players out of position, and he passes to a wide-open teammate who easily scores. Then Hodge steals the ball as soon as Taft brings it into play and lofts himself over a defender to sink another basket. Hodge doesn't appear to jump, but float. When Taft misses its next shot, Hodge goes high over a 6-3 opponent to get the rebound. For just an instant, with everyone else frozen, Hodge appears to be a pink streak among the white and black beanpoles who populate the rest of the floor. Once downcourt, he sets up a play for Chapman, who is fouled while making his layup. Chapman sinks his free throw, and Garfield takes its first lead when Hodge steals the ball once more and passes long to a waiting forward, who dunks it.

Grevey and 6-1 forward Sam Marcum lead Taft back in the second quarter, but the tempo is much faster than McCollum likes it. "The height on this court belongs to us; Hodge has the speed," McCollum says to his starters during a timeout. "Slow down and play your own game."

Taft settles into the rhythm McCollum has prescribed, and the Tigers leave the court at the half with a 32 to 25 lead. Garfield has shown more spunk than expected, but Taft has now found its pace and forced the game to fit it.

Halftime reflection: the bond issue.

This came about because of birth control and all the factory jobs that left Hamilton when the South rose again in the 1960s and '70s. In 1970 Hamilton had 3,000 high school students, but six years later the total was around 2,200, and the projection was that there would soon be fewer than 2,000. Many Hamiltonians felt that the two high schools, once necessary because of the World War II baby boom, should be unified.

Superintendent Peter Relic, a young Ed.D. from Harvard, was determined to modernize the schools and schooling of Hamilton. "We have a wonderful cooperation within our neighborhoods," he said, "but almost none at all between one neighborhood and another. That's why, with our loss of students, we can take the opportunity to unify the entire town by consolidating the two high schools into one. We'll be able to offer more varied courses; art, music, drama, dance are all secondary now, but they can be primary in a single comprehensive school. We can have far better teams. Hamilton used to have very, very powerful football and basketball teams on the state level; that's impossible while we have split high schools. It can be argued that pragmatically this country was built by segregation, but our ideals have always moved toward integration. Blacks should be spread equally throughout the system, and one high school will do that. Blacks are locked into the Second Ward ghetto. For all practical purposes, the Supreme Court's integration decision has never been implemented in Hamilton. With a single stroke, one high school will solve all these problems."

A special vote was scheduled for September 1976. The new, unified high school would cost $17.5 million; the money would be raised through a local bond issue whose fate would be decided by the balloting. Once the new high school was ready, Taft and Garfield would be used as junior highs, giving the community in effect, three new schools. Opponents said the tax bite was too large, that discipline and learning were needed far more than buildings and that Taft and Garfield—both only 17 years old—were perfectly decent high schools. It was said quietly that those opposed to the bond issue also didn't want their children going to school with blacks.

To defeat the bond issue a good deal of money was spent by a swiftly formed group called the Butler County Taxpayers Association. It placed ads in the *Hamilton Journal-News* and made numerous radio appeals against the bond issue. *The Journal-News* itself took a pro-bond stand, and its publisher, Chuck Everill, was a vigorous backer of the cause. "Hamilton is very much in need of this improvement, both for its own sake and as a symbol," Everill said privately. "This is a vote not just for a new central high school but for a solution to our racial problems and for a civic enterprise to combat the loss of pride that went along with the loss of industrial jobs. The school will give Hamilton a new image of itself, which we need badly."

Proponents tended to be liberals, blacks and those like Everill who felt a new school would help the community's self-esteem. Their adversaries tended to be poor whites, who felt overtaxed already, the elderly on fixed incomes and fiscal conservatives, all of whom the Butler County Taxpayers Association purported to represent. The bond issue became a community litmus test. Mayor Frank Witt, who owned a supermarket, preferred to stay out of the fight. He didn't want to confuse the two institutions of city council, of which he was head, and the school board, of which he was not a member, and he had doubts about asking the citizens of Hamilton for $17.5 million. But the vociferousness of the Taxpayers Association propelled Witt into action. First, he personally placed an ad in the paper, urging passage of the school bond issue. Then he agreed to appear with Relic at a town meeting to support a single high school. The meeting was held in the auditorium of the Hamilton branch of Miami University.

Thirty citizens showed up in a hall that could hold over 450. For Witt, the politician, the meeting provided a rare opportunity. Without notes, he mounted the podium for a speech he had no idea he was going to give until he gave it. "The new community high school is not an extravagance for the taxpayer; it is an investment in Hamilton's future," he said. "It can end the isolation of our neighborhoods, heal the lesions in our community. It can unite East Side and West Side, black and white, rich and poor and middle. They're telling us to watch out for bogie men; I say watch out for *them*! Watch out for those who would isolate ourselves from each other. Watch out for those who sneak around inciting fear and race hostility. They tear the fabric of a society that needs mending. They serve ignorance, not knowledge, and knowledge is the purpose of all schools. A progressive educational system is the foundation and backbone of our youth, and our youth are the backbone of the future. I urge you to support a single, consolidated high school for the city of Hamilton." When he left the rostrum, there was only scattered applause.

The voters rejected the bond issue by more than three to one. Not long after the balloting, Relic announced he was leaving Hamilton for Washington and a long title—Deputy Assistant Secretary for Education. "I couldn't turn down the opportunity, but I feel very frustrated," he said candidly. "I started a lot here and finished nothing."

As play resumes, Garfield gets only a single free throw by Chapman while Kolesar shakes off McCoy and combines with Marcum to make four unanswered baskets for Taft. The 40 to 26 score indicates the embarrassing mismatch Flatiron predicted could come to pass. Although Hodge strikes back with two quick baskets and a free throw, he's unable to set up his teammates, who are smothered by the taller Tigers. Nine points look like a hopeless chasm that can only grow wider.

The gap has increased to a seemingly unclosable 12 points when Hodge intercepts a Marcum pass. He laterals to McCoy who converts the turnover. The stolen ball fires up Hodge and the rest of the Griffins, and they step up the pace to Hodge's rhythm. Taft goes cold, and Hodge lifts the pace still further. He swarms all over the Tigers—on offense, defense, forecourt and back, out of position, stealing the ball, setting a pick, making the play. Once he even passes the ball to himself. When McCollum sends both Marcum and Grevey to cover Hodge, Chapman, McCoy and a 6-3 sophomore named Jeff Jones score in turn for Garfield. At the end of the thir period, Chapman takes a long jumper that hits the rim and springs away. In th scramble for the rebound, Hodge bats the ball through the hoop at the buzzer. Ta is on top only 46 to 42.

The last quarter begins with Hodge stealing the ball and making an easy lay to bring his team within two points. Grevey strikes back with a long set shot, a the game stabilizes, which is to say that the pace returns to Taft's liking. Garfi can get no closer than four points. Hodge cools off, looking tired. Time is on Tigers' side. With two minutes left, they make a free throw to go ahead by five. Ho is fouled but misses both shots. From the Garfield fans comes a cheer, "Hey sweat, the game ain't over yet." But it really looks as if it is.

With 30 seconds remaining in the game, Grubbs shoots for Taft and the caroms off the hoop, then against the backboard and finally bounces crazily t side. The two players nearest it are the 5-9 Hodge and 6-5 Mike Grammel, center. Hodge makes a soaring jump, but eight inches are too many to give and Grammel comes down with the ball. Hodge comes down onto Grammel's which accidentally catches Hodge underneath an arm. A harmless, mome painful jab, it has the effect of an injection of adrenaline. Hodge doesn't sc take the ball out of Grammel's hands as leap it out. In one motion, as if t had been planned all season, he hurls the ball downcourt to Chapman, who dribbles twice and scores. Chapman is fouled as he scores, and he makes the foul shot, closing the gap to 59 to 57 with 19 seconds to play.

Crossing midcourt into Garfield territory, Marcum juggles the ball for an instant. McCoy swipes it, and suddenly there is a loose ball squiggling around the court. Garfield's Mike Hardy grabs it and passes it to Hodge, who calls time out. Thirteen seconds.

Gillespie chooses the play. Hodge is to bounce the ball into Chapman and break for the corner. Chapman will be guarded now by the talented Kolesar, but Gillespie wants only his two best ball handlers to touch the ball. After Hodge has faked toward the corner, he's to cut inside to the key. Chapman will throw the ball near the key in the desperate hope that Hodge has managed to get there.

Like any good coach in the final seconds of a close game, McCollum believes in giving his players only the most fundamental instructions. Once a game is actually under way, he dispenses with his platitudes, but what he tells his team now is as obvious as his corniest slogan: "Keep the ball away from Hodge." Reading Gillespie's mind, McCollum adds that since Hodge is the best Garfield passer, he will probably throw the ball inbounds and then try to position himself to get it thrown back. He also tells Grammel to make a wall in front of Hodge on the inbounds play so Hodge won't even be able to see his teammates, much less get the ball to one of them.

Grammel looms over Hodge while Hodge looks for somewhere to throw the ball. Grubbs comes over to help Grammel. When Hodge feints a bounce pass, Grubbs and Grammel are a jungle of legs. When he considers throwing over them, they seem a forest of arms.

Urgent, possessed, Hodge catapults himself above the defenders. In the air, he hangs for what seems a full second, as though a platform had suddenly sprung up to hold him. Chapman has faked himself clear of Kolesar for an instant to receive the ball Hodge rifles to him. Surrounded, Hodge darts for the corner as Gillespie has directed. Then he cuts toward the basket. The key is so crowded he cannot get near it. Chapman looks for his own shot but there is none. He dribbles out toward midcourt while waiting for Hodge to get open. Hodge breaks away from the key, heading in the wrong direction with four seconds showing on the clock. Chapman releases the ball. Hodge dives for the pass and catches it. He's smothered by the Tigers. He fights loose, throwing hips and elbows, and dribbles once. Falling away from 30 feet out, he airmails the ball. It smacks the rim and caroms straight into the air. Jones, underneath the basket, leaps and tips it in. The final buzzer brays.

The gym detonates, 2,200 throats in peril of rupture. The town's best game in years is tied 59 to 59 at the end of regulation play, Hamilton equaling Hamilton. The crowd owes the night to Hodge, and no one begrudges him the credit. From the Garfield side comes "Hodge! Hodge! Hodge!" and the Taft side echoes. The sound builds until no words at all can be heard. It's almost like silence, the gym roaring for a performance that on Broadway would get 10 curtain calls and in Madrid two ears and a tail.

Hodge, who had scored 21 points, seems propelled not by hunger for victory but for excellence. Often he has performed almost alone, not ignoring his teammates as ball hogs do but using them to express his own impulses.

The overtime is anticlimatic and unsuspenseful. The score remains close enough, Garfield getting two more baskets, Taft three. But Grammel and Grevey are now in charge of the game that winds down like the clock itself. With two seconds to go, Garfield gets the ball under its own basket. Never surrendering, Hodge yells at the teammate with the ball, "Call time out!" Hodge's teammate has already flung the ball in a desperate full-court arc toward the Taft basket. The ball is stopped by a girder at the top of the gym as the buzzer sounds, with Taft winning, 66 to 64.

As the Taft and Garfield cheerleaders line up together at center court, both teams and their coaches envelop Hodge in congratulations. A Tiger and a Griffin momentarily carry Hodge on their shoulders. He blinks in embarrassment and slithers down to the floor. Gillespie puts his arm around Hodge as the assembled cheerleading squads send out a last yell:

We're from Hamilton, couldn't be prouder;
If you can't hear us, we'll shout a little louder!

In 1980 Taft and Garfield merged to become Hamilton High School, with an enrollment of 2,054, in the building that was formerly Taft High. Garfield is now a junior high school.

Marvin McCollum officially remains the coach at Hamilton, although he has been on sick leave since last September and last week announced plans to retire in June. Don Gillespie continued working as a vocational counselor in Hamilton until December 1981 when he left to take a job as government rep for a company in Cincinnati.

Scott Grevey went on to play basketball, though not as a star, at Pitt where he's now a senior. Andy Kolesar graduated last spring from VMI, where he was captain of the basketball team and a two-time academic all-America. He is now doing graduate work in engineering at Ohio State.

None of the Garfield starters went on to college. Robbie Hodge, who still lives in Hamilton, is a senior production specialist for Boise Cascade Corporation. He's still friends with Tony McCoy, who's in the Army.

Last year, in its first season after the unification, Hamilton's basketball team finished with a 25–1 record, losing in the regional final of the state AAA tournament.

"DANCE FLOORS, THICK SMOKE AND LOPSIDED BALL"

This is about two New York State high school–age boys who never went to high school. The city boy, Joe Lapchick, became a national immortal, reaching the heights as both player and coach. The small-town boy, Frank Basloe, made his first mark as a teenage player-entrepreneur in a turn-of-the-century day when youngsters grew up fast and basketball was in its helter-skelter infancy. Of only regional stature, Basloe is mildly controversial among historians, but his career is part of a rich pioneer lore that ought to be preserved.

Imagine a 15-year-old playing for a top semipro team between 10-hour shifts in a factory. That was Joe Lapchick of Yonkers, New York, a household name to all basketball diehards over 45, center on the Original Celtics, noted college and NBA coach, and two-way member of the Hall of Fame. His formative years were "the good old days" prior to 1920, when the pro game was played with a lopsided ball in a barn or on a slick dance floor surrounded by a cage to insure continuous action. Basketball scholarships were unheard of, and family pressures ended many an education at grade 8. Today we have laws requiring high school attendance until age 16, it's fashionable for everyone to try college regardless of scholastic record, and we're spellbound when a Moses Malone or a Darryl Dawkins leapfrogs college and goes directly to the pros.

Imagine, too, a 16-year-old sixth grader organizing a semipro team and managing a tour at a profit. That was Frank Basloe, perhaps no longer a household name even in his native Mohawk Valley of upstate New York but one of the game's real pioneers upon whom history might look with favor. Basloe spent 45 years in the game, barnstorming for 20—from barn to armory—across the Upper East and Midwest. Those were the bizarre "old, old days," beginning in 1903 and perhaps forever to be shrouded in at least partial mystery. Basloe conceded that Dr. Naismith invented basketball and that he mailed a descriptive pamphlet to YMCAs around the country, including the one in Herkimer, New York, Basloe's hometown. But in his controversial 1952 book, *I Grew Up with Basketball*, he advances Lambert Will, the Herkimer Y's volunteer physical director, as the game's first real prime mover and gospel spreader.

Unfortunately some of Basloe's dates appear to be 2 years off. Apparently working backward from an 1898 Utica, New York, news story (when Basloe was 11), he assigns "1890" to Herkimer's first game while Dr. Naismith's invention date is inscribed in stone as "December 1891." But historical dates slightly misremembered by old-timers six decades after the fact should cloud neither individual nor regional contributions. Basloe credits the area around Herkimer, whose population at the turn of the century was 2,700, with the first high school team, the first pro team, the first five-on-a-side game, the first use of the name "Celtics" (in nearby Utica), and the first use of "Globe Trotters," the label newsmen hung on Basloe's touring Oswego Indians, who claimed the world's championship in 1914. Lambert Will is portrayed as a driver who organized "the first real game," played the game himself, experimented with it, called regional parleys to standardize it, and took it on the road. According to Basloe, Dr. Naismith never replied to Will's progress reports or requests for guidance; "Herkimer was on its own." In any event, the Mohawk Valley—from Utica to Schenectady—was one of basketball's earliest hotbeds, and Will, then Basloe surely had plenty to do with this phenomenon.

Joe Lapchick started playing basketball in the Yonkers parks and streets, using a soccer ball stuffed with a cap. A score was achieved by throwing the ball onto the roof of a shed. His first semipro team paid him $5 a game, out of which he had to pay for meals and transportation. On the Hollywood Inn team, he was the only non–high school student. By age 18, considered a giant at 6′5″, he was playing with the famed New York Whirlwinds at the then fabulous salary of $7 per game clear. This, in addition to his apprentice machinist wage, made him affluent. From the Whirlwinds he gravitated to the forever touring Original Celtics on which he, Dutch Dehnert, Nat Holman, Pete Barry, and Johnny Beckman became basketball immortals. From 1920 to 1928 they compiled a 720–75 record. Later as a coach, Lapchick had two stints at St. John's University (1936–47 and 1957–65), during which he won four NIT championships, including one in his final bench appearance. In between, this local boy who never went to high school guided the New York Knicks to nine straight NBA play-offs and three appearances in the finals. It must have seemed eons from the crackerbox floors waxed for "The Varsity Drag" to giant Madison Square Garden.

Let those who deplore home-floor advantages and crowd demonstrations in 1987 consider some of the realities of Lapchick's early days. At best, the single referee had little authority. At worst, he was a cop, the natural object of hatred. Play was rough. Instead of a defensive style, "press" meant the two-man crush administered an errant official after he allegedly blew a few calls. He usually got the message. Referees had little control over hometown fans who often used mirrors, lighted cigarettes, or stove bolts to intimidate the invaders. Courts were only 60′ x 40′. Backboards were flush with walls, making the drive-in or fast break a perilous venture. Sidelines were inches away from front-row fans, subjecting the invaders to kicks and hat-pin jabs on throw-ins. The "coach" was either the oldest player or the club owner. Lapchick called it the day of "dance floors, thick smoke and lopsided ball."

In a day when sixth graders are more concerned with video games and how braces will affect their social life, the entrepreneurial beginnings of sixth-grader Frank Basloe in 1903 will boggle the mind. Bored with school and in love with the new sport, "basket ball," he marshaled his paper route profits, borrowed $10 from his mother, and launched a dream venture. He had stationery printed bearing the slogan, "Herkimer Team—Champions of the Mohawk Valley." He didn't yet have a team, but he set out to recruit the best Herkimer high school–age players at a $5-a-game ceiling and bought a $12 suit befitting his new station. He booked 6 games in 6 days—at Ogdensburg, Malone, Tupper Lake, Saranac Lake, Lake Placid, and Fort Covington—telling his mother he was visiting a friend in Utica for a few days and keeping the trip completely secret from his shopkeeper father. The Herkimers came home with a 6–0 record, but Father, enraged at his son's suspicious week-long absence, was waiting at the door with a cocked broomstick. Father's anger subsided quickly, however, when he learned that the tour netted $300, a 2,900 percent return on Mother's investment and more than he could make in 2 months at the store.

Come 1904, the 17-year-old mogul parried the higher salary demands of his players by looking elsewhere for talent. His new team was the Utica Celtics. This was also the second of two fabulous seasons recorded by Little Falls High School, 7 miles east of Herkimer. Untouchable at the prep level, LFHS sought competition at the independent, college, and semipro levels, such being permissible in those days. Its crowning achievement was winning two out of three games from national AAU champion Company E of Schenectady.

The zany events of 1906 could keep a TV sitcom writer in material for weeks. With the team now named the 31st Separate Company in deference to its new home floor, the National Guard armory in Mohawk across the river, our hero soon experienced the bane of all promoters, a double booking. There were only seven players on his roster, including himself, and he had inadvertently scheduled games at Cortland and Watertown, 100 miles apart, on the same night. He tried to cancel one but couldn't. Frantic, he went on a recruiting foray. He hornswoggled a friend in Utica to play in this hour of need, then took a train to Syracuse where he picked up three University players for $5 apiece during lulls in their workout. The coach spotted the action and called Frank to task. Made to feel properly guilty at the prospect of destroying three amateur careers, Frank glibly said he'd return the money, and that if he ever got married and had children, he'd send them to Syracuse. The coach, barely able to stifle his laughter, reinstated the players. What could a sixth-grade dropout possibly know about college eligibility rules? The short-term result of this chicanery was victory in both games. The long-term result was that Frank did send his children to Syracuse—all four of them, two boys and two girls.

Until now, virtually all Basloe's opponents had been of high school age. Indeed many of the good teams of this early day were of that age bracket. But there was another stratum of play, gradually developing, and it crept up on Frank. Offered $35 to play the famed Pastimes in Syracuse, he jumped at the chance. He didn't realize how good these fellows were, and this was to be his most humbling experience. The Pastimes, 7 to 8 years older per man, won, 102 to 10. Local humorists were to comment that the game wasn't as close as the score indicated.

A month later Basloe promoted a game in Richfield Springs, 17 miles south of Herkimer. For $5 he hired the Springs town team, and for another $5 he booked a five-piece orchestra for the customary postgame dance. For halftime entertainment he engaged two wrestlers. He chartered a special trolley car for $20 to transport sixty Herkimer fans to and from the game. He even shortened the playing court in order to pack in more spectators at both ends. They sat on the floor. Unfortunately, only one wrestler, a 220-pounder, showed up. Although he had just played 20 minutes of basketball, Frank, who weighed a strapping 145, volunteered as cannon fodder.

Buffeted about for a seeming eternity and remaining unpinned only "because of my rounded shoulders," he was mercifully rescued by the referee who bade the second half of the ball game go on. Fearing that he had made a public fool of himself, particularly in the eyes of his girlfriend in the stands, Frank instructed his teammates to feed him. He scored all 18 points, thus saving face, he thought, as his charges defeated Richland Springs, 18 to 12. After expenses, our entrepreneur, still only 19 years old, pocketed $102.50.

The best was yet to come. In 1909 Basloe's team handed the famed Buffalo Germans their first defeat in 111 games. In 1912 they beat the Germans twice in one day. Two years later the Basloes, now known as the Oswego Indians, claimed the "world's championship" and started a series of barnstorming tours that would carry them 95,000 miles through the East and Midwest. They spread the gospel to places like Fond du Lac, Lima, Fort Wayne, Muscatine, Bismarck, Duluth, Rockford, and Carbondale, Pennsylvania, as well as Chicago, Minneapolis, and Detroit, earning the media name "Globe Trotters" in the process. Even Abe Saperstein's latter-day Harlem Globe Trotters would respect the Basloe Trotters' nineteen-season record: 1,324 victories against 127 defeats, a .912 percentage.

In 1944, when Frank Basloe was 57, Paul Williams of the *Utica Daily News* wrote a poetic tribute to the original Trotters. It included this stanza:

They trotted from Vernon to Kankakee;
They'd play any town for a guarantee,
And if Bas figured "the game's on ice,"
For another purse they'd play the same town twice.

The kids of today don't know much about the Joe Lapchicks, let alone the Frank Basloes, and it's too bad. History limits its accolades, and time dims the contributions of pioneers, leaving their "discovery" to apple-cheeked researchers several generations later. It is hoped the evidence will survive.

Paraphrased by the author from Joe Lapchick, *50 Years of Basketball* (New York: Prentice-Hall, 1968) and Frank Basloe, *I Grew Up with Basketball* (New York: Greenberg, 1952).

'BAMA DRAMA

Four decades of any state basketball tournament reflect the overriding social, economic, and technical changes that regulate our lives. Highlights from William J. Plott's book State Champs! *weave such a trail through Alabama history.*

It's no big thing for a dyed-in-the-wool basketball fan to have seen 25 or 30 state high school tournaments without a miss. Neither snow nor wind nor the ordinary pressures of life can stay the regulars from this annual community-based madness. Every team, large or small, urban or rural, black or white, regardless of season record, starts even. Unlike baseball, a paradise for statistics lovers, basketball is most often remembered in sweeping strokes—for a style or flair of play or for comeback drama—and every state has its legends. At tourney time they're retold by the old-timers while the youngsters listen with reactions ranging from rapture to skepticism. Typical is Alabama, where the state play-offs originated in 1921 as a twenty-three-team single-class boys-only invitational at the Birmingham Athletic Club and today involve every school in the state with boys' and girls' champions in four classifications crowned before packed houses in Tuscaloosa.

Veteran railbirds will tell you about the night in '76 when Bradshaw High of Florence, playing without head coach Eddie Frost who was called home by the death of his father, came from behind to win the 4A title from Parker of Birmingham, 79 to 73. Instead of the customary celebration and stay-over rest, the boys made a long-distance call to Frost, asking him and his family to "meet us in the school parking lot." They drove the 125 miles from Tuscaloosa to Florence and presented the trophy to their coach at 2:20 A.M.

Also in '76 came an all-time dramatic moment. With seconds to play and Birmingham Glenn safely ahead of Huntsville Sparkman, a 5′3″ senior guard named Sandra Murray entered the game, the first female in tourney history. She later received a women's basketball scholarship to the University of Alabama, thus becoming the third member of her family to play in the Southeastern Conference.

Again in '76 there was the 1A team from little Loachapoka, a Macon County village seven miles west of Auburn down State 14. In only its third year of basketball the school had no gym of its own, could only occasionally borrow the facilities of another institution 20 miles away, and was shackled with a 1961 bus given to engine breakdown and light failure. "Traveling was always an adventure for us," Coach Tony Thompson sighed. "We never knew if we could make it through a trip." Loachapoka bowed in the first round to Rebecca Comer of Eufaula, 72 to 62, but persevered to win the 1983 Class A championship.

In '41 there was the Bibbs Graves High team of Millerville, which had only one basketball and reached the single-class final wearing outdated uniforms and sneakers held together with adhesive tape.

A decade later it was Priceville, a Morgan County hamlet not even on today's map, which won the Class A (smaller school) title with twenty-seven eligible boys in the student body. In '53 and '57–59 there was Austinville, which captured four A championships, then was consolidated out of existence.

Memories flash the great teams from Geraldine, which fashioned three straight championships in 1931–33; Chilton County of Clanton, which won three in four years ('39 and '41–42); and since-consolidated Parrish of Selma, which compiled an awesome six-year 150–13 record, including unbeaten title seasons in '45 and '46. Also etched in memories are Alexandria's four-overtime 30 to 29 victory over Parrish in '60; future NBA star John Drew's 68-point performance in a 91 to 90 loss in '71; and the '66 tourney, which saw the event's first black player, Danny Treadwell of the championship Huntsville Butler five.

There were the many outstanding black teams that came to the fore after the '68 federal court decision leading to the merger of Alabama's white and black high school associations, hence complete integration of the state tournament. Sometimes the effect of desegregation decisions was simply the combining of schools, as with Parrish and Hudson in Selma. Sometimes it meant the closing of an all-black school such as R. R. Moton High of Tallassee, which despite a male enrollment of thirty-eight and lack of a single six-footer won Class A in '69, only to go out of business the following year.

In '77 there was Robert Miles of Montgomery St. Jude, who left his team after its semifinal victory because of his father's death. Back home, however, his six brothers and sisters persuaded him to return. He did, scoring 12 points and making the all-tourney team as St. Jude defeated Montevallo for the 2A crown.

Lore from the pioneer days makes great Hot Stove League reminiscing. In '21 most of the teams had never played indoors before, and the boys from Haleyville solicited tourney expense money from local businessmen. One of the newcomers to indoor play, Alliance Agricultural School, with all five starters named Vines, took third place that year. In '29 Evergreen High, from the far southern part of the state, couldn't get through torrential rains and had to forfeit its first-round game.

Still invitational, the '22 tourney, with forty-two entries, got out of hand. On the first day, they crammed twenty-six games into thirteen hours. At halftime the next two teams would start their game so no time was lost. The game was catching on fast. The *Birmingham News* reported send-offs for the Greenville and Bay Minette teams thusly: "Everybody from the family cat to the birds in the trees saw their teams off from the station."

There was the World War II manpower drain, dramatized in '44 when Luverne High made the state with nineteen-year-old John Davis as coach. And there was the poignant '78 scene when the entire Birmingham Parker bench rushed out to console their star, Eddie Phillips, who had just missed two crucial after-the-gun free throws. With both conversions Parker would have won the 4A championship. Instead, crosstown rival Carver did. Phillips rebounded beautifully from adversity. He became all-SEC at the University of Alabama.

Besides Phillips, famous names from past Alabama state tournaments include Andrew Toney, John Drew, Leon Douglas, T. R. Dunn, Ennis Whatley, Bobby Lee Hurt, Eric Richardson, Alfonso Johnson, Cedric Hordges, Wendell Hudson, Allen

Murphy, baseball stars Ben Chapman, Jim Tabor, Mary Breeding, and Milt and Frank Bolling, football stars Harry Gilmer and Pat Trammell, and two-sport collegian Raymond Odum.

They also include a revered name, football coach Vince Dooley of the University of Georgia. His tourney memories from playing days at McGill Institute (Mobile), as expressed in Mr. Plott's tourney history, *State Champs!* stand in eloquent testimonial to the honor and thrills surrounding a great event: "Of all the athletic contests I participated in as a youngster, none was more exciting, colorful or memorable than the state tournament in Tuscaloosa. We were never state champs, but we were runners-up twice and third once. In reading about those days, I find myself replaying all of those final games and saying aloud, 'If we had done this or that, we could have been state champs!' "

With integration changing the face of basketball in Alabama, the high school fervor has finally flooded into the college realm, previously an almost exclusive football preserve. Prior to 1982, you probably couldn't have given away tickets to a preseason college basketball game in the Heart of Dixie. But on November 26, 1982, just hours before Auburn was to meet Bear Bryant's Alabama football team on national TV, almost 17,000 fans watched UAB and Auburn play basketball in Birmingham's Jefferson County Civic Center. Six years ago college basketball was one of the least desirable beats on any Alabama daily newspaper. Now it's one of the most coveted. The cycle is complete.

Paraphrased from William J. Plott, *State Champs!* (Troy, Ala.: Troy State University Press, 1978), 1–32, 40, by permission of the author.

THE SIXTH MAN

Basketball is whipped to glorious frenzy in Hobbs, New Mexico, an oil town of 35,000 near the Texas border. Coached by a living legend named Ralph Tasker, who had 886 prep victories in 41 years, including 829 at Hobbs, the Eagles are perennially one of America's highest-scoring teams. In addition, they have won more state titles than any New Mexico school through 1986—nine. Ponder these national scoring records: highest season average, 114.6 in 1970; most 100-point seasons, seven; most consecutive 100-point games, fourteen; and most game points by a losing team, 121. Nine prep all-Americas include Bill Bridges, later a Kansas and NBA star. Manny Marquez captured the local spirit in this 1983 story entitled "Sixth Man."

The wall-to-wall crowd at Ralph Tasker Arena is buzzing in anticipation. It's a big-game night for the Hobbs Eagles, and the people without reserved tickets had to hurry to claim seats in the 3,500-seat gymnasium on the Hobbs High School campus.

Suddenly a door on the east side of the gym flies open . . . out step seven little-bitty guys with a basketball . . . they're followed by 12 not-so-little guys in black-and-gold uniforms . . . the drummer in the Taskervitch Band strikes a cowbell three times . . . HHS pep bands break into a familiar tune . . . and the crowd goes bananas.

Ladies and gentlemen, it's showtime!

From the second the Eagles set foot on the floor until the final second is erased from the scoreboard clock and another victory is safely tucked away in the history books, the "show" in the arena named for the Eagles' legendary coach defies description.

"You have to see it to believe it," says Barry Sollenberger, publisher of the Southwest Sports News Service in Phoenix, Ariz.

Sollenberger, who published the Hobbs Holiday Tournament program for several years, was so impressed with what took place between the walls of Tasker Arena that he asked for and received permission to use the Ringling Brothers/Barnum and Bailey Circus logo in the 1978 and 1979 programs.

The logo reads, "The Greatest Show on Earth." Nobody who has ever seen this show will argue the point.

What makes it the "greatest" is a perfect blend of out-of-this-world basketball on the part of the Hobbs Eagles and the reaction of one of the most basketball-educated crowds to be found anywhere. Throw in the mascots, cheerleaders and the Taskervitch Band—"They make the sweetest music this side of heaven," Coach Tasker proclaims—and you have what Tasker fondly calls his "Sixth Man."

Together, the Eagles and their Sixth Man are a tough combination to beat.

"It's like trying to play the Lobos in the Pit in Albuquerque," claims Clovis coach Jimmy Joe Robinson, the last coach to beat Tasker and the Eagles in Tasker Arena.

That was 'way back in 1978. Going into this season, the Eagles had won 42 home-court outings in a row.

While for opponents it may seem like trying to scale Mt. Everest, the thrill-a-second style of play is a turn-on for first-time viewers.

Ross McKeon, a sports writer from San Jose, Calif., who came to Hobbs' 1980 holiday tournament to cover Amador Valley High School, wrote this: "Once you're inside the gymnasium, it's a circus atmosphere. The crowd seemingly electrifies the players with its constant noise. You would be hard-pressed to find better support for high school athletics anywhere around the country. Going from a Hobbs basketball game to one in the Bay Area is like going from a party to a funeral."

Nobody loves it more than Ralph Tasker.

"It's rewarding when you play a little team like Canutillo and our fans turn out as they do," he said. "I didn't expect there'd be 30 people here for that game. So I came out of the dressing room for our warm-ups, and I couldn't believe it. The gym was full. Seeing all those people come out for a game like that makes it all worthwhile."

Then there are the big games.

Many a time the Hobbs fire marshal has had to order the doors at Tasker Arena closed to keep people from jamming into a structure where there are no more empty seats. It has happened several times during the holiday tournament when the Eagles have hooked up with the likes of East Phoenix, St. Mary's of Phoenix, South Oak Cliff of Dallas and Amador Valley.

The games against the two Arizona schools stick most in Tasker's mind as examples of how the crowd got the Eagles off on the right foot.

"That Sixth Man was really something when we played St. Mary's and East Phoenix," Tasker said. "St. Mary's was a fine team. The excitement in that gym . . . I've never seen anything like it, not even in the state tournament. That's one game that will always stand out in my mind because of the way our Sixth Man responded to the challenge. It really pulled us through that one."

This isn't the only game Tasker can remember in which the Sixth Man came to the Eagles' rescue. There was one against Carlsbad in 1967 in which the Eagles wiped out a 15-point deficit in the final quarter to win. And there was one at Clovis in 1981 in which Hobbs was down 17 points to the state's No. 2 team in the final four minutes and somehow managed to come back and win, 103 to 102, in overtime.

The Eagles didn't do it by themselves, Tasker insists.

"Our fans brought us back in that Carlsbad game," Tasker declared. "And at Clovis they wouldn't let us quit. We weren't playing inspired basketball. We weren't hustling. But they got after our guys until they started playing like the Hobbs Eagles. The Carlsbad and Clovis comebacks are so clear in my mind. I can still hear those fans encouraging us.

"We certainly would have lost by 20 points both times had it not been for our Sixth Man."

Ralph Tasker and longtime followers of the Hobbs Eagles can remember when it wasn't quite like that.

"The night we dedicated Eagle Gym (he won't call it "Tasker Arena") we were playing Lubbock, and we got beat by 12 points," Tasker recalled. "We didn't even have to pull out the bleachers upstairs."

Tasker credits State Representative Harry McAdams for helping spread the word about the Hobbs Eagles in the early years of the Tasker era. McAdams did the play-by-play of Hobbs games over Station KWEW (now KUUX) from the late 1940s until he retired from broadcasting a few years ago.

"Harry did all our games when nobody came out," Tasker said. "He said he'd just keep doing them until the people did come out. He used to say to me, 'We'll keep telling 'em about the Hobbs Eagles until we make 'em want to come out and see for themselves.' "

Jim Rawls, longtime photographer for the *Hobbs News-Sun*, has been around Hobbs since Tasker arrived on the scene.

"About 1955 or 1956 they really began to draw the crowds," recalls Rawls, who photographed all HHS games until retiring recently. "People like Ray Clay, Bill Bridges and Kim Nash were big drawing cards. They were hellacious players, and they gave people their money's worth."

Count Hobbs City Manager Joe Harvey among the devoted Sixth Man. He's been hooked on Hobbs basketball, and Hobbs sports in general, since he got his first glimpse of it 23 years ago.

"The first game I saw in Hobbs was one of those Hobbs-Roswell overtime affairs in 1960," Harvey remembered. "I was a policeman working the game. It just flat turned me on. I haven't missed one since."

Well, he *has* missed one or two but not often.

"I had to miss a couple of those games they play on Tuesday nights in Abilene, and I didn't make the last trip to Oklahoma with them," confessed Harvey. "I usually take some vacation time and go wherever they go. Sue and I don't miss any of the home games in any sport. We're fond of them all. I don't know what gets you started. It's not just basketball either. It's all sports in Hobbs. Like anything else, it gets in your blood."

Indeed, the athletic program at Hobbs High School may keep Harvey from leaving town any time soon.

"I have enough years with the city right now to take early retirement, and people ask me why I don't do it," Harvey disclosed. "The thought of leaving the Hobbs Eagles is really the No. 1 reason for not wanting to leave Hobbs."

Rawls can tell you first-hand how the enthusiasm created by the Eagles and their Sixth Man can get to anyone.

"Back when I had some spring left in my legs, I sometimes had to contain myself while covering them," he said. "I just couldn't keep from getting excited. They get you caught up."

There may be some fans in Hobbs who take the atmosphere in Tasker Arena for granted. It takes a newcomer or somebody who was involved in it before to notice just what the Sixth Man does for the Eagles.

Take the case of former Hobbs standout Gerald Coppedge, now an assistant coach at Abilene High. He remembers a 1981 game at Tasker Arena in which Abilene was giving Hobbs a good run for its money in the first half.

"They had gotten a jump on us, but we started to make a run at them in the second quarter," Coppedge said. "Then the Sixth Man started firing up, and the Hobbs players started responding. It just kept building up, and Hobbs kept playing better and better, but we were still in the game.

"Then when I looked up in the stands and saw my mother leading the cheers, I knew we didn't stand a chance."

Hobbs won the game, 101 to 84, and the Eagles and their Sixth Man lived happily ever after . . . or until the next game.

From Manny Marquez, "Hobbs Eagles: Sixth Man," ***Hobbs High School Basketball, 1959–1983*** **(Midland, Tex.: BPI Sports Publications, 1983), 35–37. Reprinted by permission of the publisher.**

THEY CALLED IT EDDLEMANIA

This is about a high school player so storied that AP and UP would receive a rash of complaints from all over the state if they didn't run his individual point total alongside the team's line score. It's about an athlete so versatile they named an era after him. And it's about his storied philosopher-coach and their 1941 Centralia Wonder Five that some observers fantasized might finish .500 in the Big Ten. They were getting carried away, of course, but this was an electric team out of the Illinois hotbed. "Even better than Lou Boudreau's Thornton teams of 1933–35," the old-timers said. Here's how it was, as I wrote it in 1984.

Dike Eddleman was probably the most publicized high school athlete in world history. Though there's no way of proving it, the 4-year, three-sport aspect of his fabulous 1938–42 career at Centralia, Illinois, along with special media and sociological factors never to be duplicated, will make the claim extremely difficult to top.

Dike had every imaginable ingredient going for him. Such were his impact and charisma in this Age of the Hero that players hundreds of miles away copied his style, walk, and dress. If you lived in Illinois and had the choice of watching a Big Ten game or Dike's Wonder Five, you probably would have picked the latter. The era was called "Eddlemania." Some of the ingredients follow.

All-state eight times, Dike was an electrifying basketball player whose scoring heroics and general flair were mealtime subjects throughout a basketball-mad state. Years later he would be a charter electee to the Illinois Sports Hall of Fame, along with such titans as Red Grange and George Halas. He is the only athlete in history to participate in the football Rose Bowl, the All-Star Basketball Game (a collegians versus pro champions event long disbanded), and the Olympic Games. More later.

He lived in the circulation crossfire of ten daily newspapers—four in Chicago, three in St. Louis, two in Champaign-Urbana (home of the University of Illinois), and one in his hometown, population 16,000.

He had a revered, always quotable history-teacher coach named Arthur Trout, a longtime media darling who had been at Centralia for 27 years, had state championship teams way back in 1918 and 1922, and would eventually set the existing national record for most coaching victories at the same school, 809. Dubbed "King Arthur" and "The Sage of Little Egypt" by the writers, Trout was a master psychologist with a glorious vocabulary and a repertoire of Latin, biblical, and poetic one-liners to fit dramatic game situations. Among other incredible things, he required all his players to use the "kiss" shot for distance, an outrageous two-handed delivery of super-high trajectory fired face-high from a closed-foot stance. More later.

Dike was depressed southern Illinois's answer to Chicago football's Bill deCorrevont, the triple-threat halfback who had led an Austin High School juggernaut to an undefeated season of lopsided scores in '37 and drawn a national record 110,000 crowd to the Public versus Catholic play-off in Soldier Field. With the Depression lingering, war clouds gathering, and uncertainty everywhere, heroes were particularly welcome.

Eddleman was the central figure in what some down-home philosophers called a "morality play" or just plain "destiny." With the Wonder Five he suffered a stunning 30 to 29 upset at the hands of Morton (Cicero) in the '41 semifinals; then, with a relatively ragtag supporting cast and a string of squeaker victories in the record, he led a seemingly outclassed team to a classic uphill triumph over unbeaten Paris in the '42 final. The enormity of the '41 upset can best be dramatized by comparative scores: Morton nipped Urbana in the final by 1 point; Centralia had beaten Urbana by 40 just a few weeks before. No one begrudged the "destiny" references in '42. Centralia was 14 points behind with 6½ minutes to go, and Paris, apparently lord of all it surveyed, prepared to celebrate the state's first perfect season since 1911. Then it happened. Centralia scored 18 of the next 20 points—with Eddleman laying in the final 2—and snatched the title, 35 to 33. Nobody ever figured it out. Whatever the explanation, it seemed a Sunday School road from the overconfidence of '41 to perseverance's reward in '42. In the *Champaign News-Gazette*, T. O. White wrote, "The condemned ate a hearty meal, then went out and slew the executioner."

Dike would have received more wintertime media exposure than modern counterparts if only because basketball schedules were not limited in his day. The Wonder Five's record was 44–2. The champions of '42 were 34–6. The fourth-place '39 team, on which freshman Dike set a state tourney single-game scoring mark of 24 points, was 29–14. Seasons such as these helped Centralia become the nation's first institution, high school or college, to reach 1,500 victories. It happened early in the 1981–82 season, the school's seventy-sixth, and all spectators received certificates of attendance.

In high school basketball the 6′2″ Eddleman averaged 21.5 points per game when nobody else averaged more than 17. His career total of 2,702 is still a school record, 4 decades later. He hit 40 or more several times when 30 was almost unheard of. He was virtually unstoppable on a drive, he rebounded in double figures fifty-six times, and people would drive miles to see him fire "kiss" shots. In college basketball—after 3 years of military service—he won three letters as a University of Illinois regular, leading his team to the Big Ten title and third place in the NCAA as a senior. He made a few all-America squads and graduated to four NBA seasons with the Fort Wayne Pistons and Tri-City/Milwaukee Blackhawks, averaging 12.1 points over 266 games. In his final college appearance in Illinois's Huff Gym, he tallied 23 in a victory over Indiana. With a prep and college career spanning 11 years and including at least fifty games on that floor, it seemed as if he had been there forever. As the clock ticked off the final seconds, the ball in Dike's hands, the cry went up, "One more time!" He fired a long one, which went in, and when the cheers subsided, the announcer called out, "A fitting end to a great career!" It was like Ted Williams's home run in his final time at bat.

In high school track Dike high jumped 6′6″ or more numerous times—in the Western Roll era when only one human being had ever cleared 6′11″. He won the state championship three times and, as guest at the then annual Big Ten–Pacific Coast meet at Northwestern University, outjumped the collegian winner by 2 inches. In college track he won five letters (a neat trick made possible by military service), most of the high jump titles in relay and AAU meets from coast to coast, and a second-place tie in the 1948 London Olympics.

In high school football, an activity he had to abandon for 2 years because of a freshman-season injury, he gained more than 1,000 yards as a senior while punting for a 40-yard-plus average. In college he won three letters as a halfback-punter, becoming the team's leading rusher and a top receiver by his junior season and an NCAA-leading punter as a senior with a 42.9 average on 60 boots. He would have been drafted by an NFL team as a receiver or defensive back, but he chose pro basketball.

At least one major league baseball club was said to be interested in Eddleman, but while he had demonstrated some potential in this his fourth sport, he had too many proven irons in the fire.

Coach Trout was good copy even in a bad season, of which he had only five in thirty-seven. He often started his shortest player at center, reasoning that "it's more important who gets the ball when it comes down than who can best tip it up." At the jump he placed three men in the backcourt and only Eddleman in the forecourt, reasoning that "this gives us an extra hand on defense while the state's best scorer-jumper ought to be able to hold his own on the other side." He liked "kiss" shots, authorized with seemingly reckless abandon, because "we can make 'em, and even if we don't, we'll get more rebounds than our opponents because we know better how the ball will come down." In football he had a guard-around play, in which the left guard, lining up on the flank, would take a handoff and circle end instead of leading interference. Trout never gave the officials a hard time.

When the Sage inherited a basketball squad of sensitive types, ten of whom were on an approximate par, he alternated two "first fives." He called one the Alphas, the other the Betas. He'd give clinic listeners this difference between the two major school sports: "In football you diagram what you want to do and then try to do it. In basketball you do it, then sit down and try to diagram what you did."

Either because he wanted to prove to the various elements of his Wonder Five that they couldn't get along without each other and/or was seeking a sly way to get a potential "undefeated" monkey off their backs, he started Eddleman and four reserves against powerful Taylorville in an early-season home game. In the second quarter he inserted a new unit composed of the other four regulars and another reserve. Centralia lost by 12, but the point was made. This was the Wonder Five's only regular-season defeat.

Like greyhounds, Trout players had legs taped halfway to the knee. The Merthiolate usage must have been tremendous. The likely theory was that a taped leg was more springy, but some wags applied "extrusion" reasoning—that tape could squeeze an extra, say, quarter-inch of height for each boy.

Not the least dramatic aspect of the Centralia Story is the team nickname, "Orphans." History is fuzzy on its origin. One yarn has Trout, who'd seen Lillian Gish in *Orphans of Storm*, affixing the label himself when the team vehicle was stalled in a snowstorm upstate. The real instigator may have been a Chicago reporter at the Pontiac holiday tournament who allegedly wrote that the Centralians "looked like orphans in their bedraggled uniforms, tired and dirty from a long trip, but they sure could play basketball." In any event, Trout the psychologist did his part to ingrain the name. As time went by, it prompted some uninitiated city writers to characterize Centralia as a boys' home or an otherwise small school when in fact it had an enrollment of more than 1,200. By the same token, they labeled Dike's high-top street shoes as a Li'l Abnerism when in fact they were oil-field boots, a cherished symbol of the Centralia-area oil boom which was keeping the Depression at bay.

As a member of the *Chicago Daily News*'s all-state board, Trout wrote area roundup stories periodically. They were a joy. A good youngster who had moved in from another town might be "a peripatetic treasure." A small player who constantly hustled might be cloaked with the Latin phrase, *multa in parvo* ("much in little"). A particularly deep squad constituted "infinite riches in no small room." When his own charges prepared to face the region's most powerful team, his final paragraph read, "Angels and ministers of grace, defend us!"

Beneath it all, Trout was sound. He took ten teams to Illinois's "Sweet 16," and his three titles (1918, '22, '42) and four final-game appearances (including 1946) are still records although they've been tied. He produced enough all-staters for two teams. Dolph Stanley, another Illinois coaching dean who used the "four corners"— considered a modern development—as far back as 1929, says he got it from Trout.

These were simpler days when unemployment was high, spending money was scarce, and diversions were few. They were also days of Grantland Rice poetry and greater tendencies to rhapsodize sporting events. After Morton upset Centralia in the '41 tourney, one reporter penned this quatrain:

Ye scribes of note, we heed your words;
In lore ye do abound,
But Morton beat Centralia,
Not the other way around.

Old-timers recalled the local daily's banner headline after the 1918 championship game: "We Won, We Won, by Golly We Won." At some point after the '42 title game, Trout probably blurted, "Sic vincit Centralium." Arthur Trout retired in 1951 after suffering a paralytic stroke and died 4 years later in Oaktown, Indiana, a few miles from his boyhood home.

Both Trout and Eddleman are throwbacks to simple but elusive ideals. The mentor sought only to teach as much history, basketball, and football as he could to high school youngsters in a small city in mid-America. The pupil was respectful, unassuming, and low-key. When it came time to select a college, he picked the University of Illinois over hundreds of institutions because, believe it or not, he loved the Huff Gym floor and wanted to stay reasonably close to home so his friends could see him play. No agents. No press conferences. He never tried to become part of high society or to capitalize on his name via the insurance or PR routes. When his playing days were over, he took an industrial-relations position at a food-processing firm near Fort Wayne. He married his high school sweetheart (the cheerleader), bought a modest home, learned to play golf because that was the only adult recreation around town, and eventually sent his daughter to the old State U. He relishes being asked to speak at awards banquets on the relationship between sportsmanship, hustle, and sacrifice in sports and on the battlefields of life. His are the old-fashioned virtues, and they stand up as well as ever.

Nobody who takes on personnel, labor relations, safety, training, and workmen's compensation in an industrial plant is looking for an easy ride. No human event leaves more scars than a brother-versus-brother labor strike in a small town. And so when they painted "scab" on the side of Dike's house one night, he must have felt millions of miles from the adoring throngs in Illinois gyms and known what his elders had meant by "the cruel world." Today he's back in his element—as director of the grants-in-aid program of the University of Illinois Foundation.

Years come and go. New Lochinvars replace the old. Players get bigger, faster, quicker, more accurate. But the Dike Eddleman story stands out like Paul Bunyan. He generated a respect bordering on adulation among his peers, including those who to this day are unconsciously emulating his springy walk, as well as those whose shoulders may still feel bruised from under-the-basket confrontations. His was a year-round household name as a high school student. Given new diversions and the trend to sport specialization, this will never happen again.

By Nelson Campbell.

ONCE IN A LIFETIME

There's a college anecdote from another, more impressionable era—about the Harvard football coach preparing for the big game. "Gentlemen," he said solemnly, "this will be the most important day of your lives; you are going to play football against Yale." For high school basketballers, most of whom will not play in college, the state tourney is a comparable juncture, a glittering climax yet a regretful end. In a selection from The Best Sports Stories of 1967, *Paul Hemphill of the* Atlanta Journal *tells how it affected one team. His subjects were from Cordele, Georgia, but they could just as well have been from Winfield, Kansas; Houlton, Maine; or Flagstaff, Arizona.*

There were a dozen of them, in identical blue blazers and gray slacks, and they hunched over in the eighth and ninth rows with their elbows on their knees and tried not to think about it. Their small blue overnight bags said "Crisp County High School Rebels" on the side. On the floor they could look and see Cedartown and Headland blurring up and down the polished court under the yellowish glare of the lights of the 75-foot ceiling of the huge coliseum, the biggest coliseum any had ever thought he would see. They tried to keep their minds on the game, but they could not. One hour to go. All they could think about was the crowd and that huge floor and the smoke clinging to the ceiling.

Ben Rogers, their coach, sat 10 rows behind them, studying the two teams on the floor. If Crisp won its 9 o'clock game against Hart County, it would meet the winner of this one the next night. Rogers looked for strengths and weaknesses, and it helped keep his mind off his own game.

"How are they?" somebody asked.

"Scared," Rogers said. "First night's always like this."

"How many have played here before?"

He thought for a minute. "Three. No, it's four. Four of 'em were with us when we came up last year."

"What'll you tell 'em?"

"What can you say? You just try to tell 'em it's no different from playing back home."

This was the first night, the opening round of the state Class AA high school basketball tournament at Alexander Memorial Coliseum on the Georgia Tech campus. Sixteen teams from towns like Blue Ridge and Cedartown and Ringgold and Waycross. And Cordele, home of the Crisp County Rebels.

If you are accustomed to going by the coliseum every time Georgia Tech plays, and you are used to the lights and the crowds and the size of the place, it means nothing to you. It is the way basketball, big-time basketball, is played. But if you live on a farm like, say, Gib Williams does, this is it. This is the end of the line, the highest cloud. This is the place it led to, and this was the place it ended before you settled down and went to school and never again heard your name called out over a public-address system and had people cheer for you all at the same time.

For Gib Williams, 6-foot-3, this was the big one. He was the starting center for the Crisp County Rebels. He lives on a farm outside Cordele. When he was cut from the squad before the 1965–66 season began, it was one of the worst things ever to happen to him. He fooled around with a basketball all summer and then gave up football so he could keep working through the fall. He wanted to make the basketball team. And he did. He was a substitute during the early games, and then he made the starting five, and now—on this night in the big city, Atlanta, 160 miles from home—here was all of it boiling up inside him.

They were not talking. It was 8:30, and they were dressed now. Their ankles and wrists had been wrapped with white adhesive tape and they wore their gray warm-up jackets and they sat quietly in the dressing room, in the caverns of the coliseum. The dressing room was a small concrete cubicle, with gray steel lockers against the walls. Two bare light bulbs emitted a harsh light. Coach Ben Rogers stood next to the only door and looked at them. They were all staring at the floor.

Rogers turned to the manager, a thin boy with a crew cut. "How much time to play?"

"Three minutes."

"Gib," Rogers said, "we've got to keep this Hill running. Wear him out."

Gib Williams nodded.

"This McCollum talks a lot," Rogers said. "He'll try to make you mad. Be sure you don't let him."

Nobody would so much as clear his throat. The tension had peaked out. If you swallow, everybody hears you. Rogers had to do something.

"There'll be more people out there than we ever saw."

Heads dropped.

"It's a big place. Bigger than any we've seen." It was wrong. Rogers knew it was wrong. He began walking from one end of the dressing room to the other. His heels clicked on the concrete. The manager came back in. He said there was two minutes' playing time left in the Headland-Cedartown game.

"Look," Rogers blurted. "It's no different from playing at West Crisp. Play it just like back home."

One of them yelled, "Don't give 'em nothing."

"Don't give 'em nothing but a hard time," another said.

Then Ben Rogers told them, softly, "Let's ease out of here."

The tension went quickly. There were the introductions. Then the tip-off. Hoke Hill, the gangly 6-foot-6 center for Hart County, easily beat Gib Williams for the opening tip. It was 2 to 0, 2 to 2, 9 to 2, Hart, but by the end of the first quarter Crisp was ahead by 14 to 12. Crisp still had the lead, 42 to 41, and was on its way to a big upset when the third quarter ended. But Hart's Alan Richardson found the range in the last period, and Hart County burst ahead and won it, 67 to 58. For Gib Williams and his teammates, the ones he had practically lived with for all these months, it was over, and the ramp to the dressing room seemed longer than before. And tomorrow morning there would be 160 miles between Atlanta and home.

Gib Williams wandered out of the dressing room. He had on his blazer, and the blue overnight bag was dangling from one hand. Coach Rogers had told them they had done a good job and could hold their heads high, but that did not help.

"You're a great basketball player," another player told Williams.

He mumbled thanks and walked down the hollow hallway.

"We did our best," he said.

"You gonna go to school, to college?"

"Probably to Cochran. Cochran Junior College. Then Tech."

"Play basketball there?"

He said, "Naw, I don't think so."

"Scared tonight?"

"Yeah, plenty. You get used to it, but it scares you."

Perhaps 100 fans had come up from Cordele for the game. Gib walked out of the narrow corridor leading from the dressing room, and he saw his folks. His father is a lean, suntanned man and his mother a pleasant housewife. His sister, a nurse in Atlanta, was with them.

"You boys did just wonderful," his mother said.

"I'm so sorry you lost," said his sister.

His father shook his hand. "Good job, son."

"Thanks. We tried." Gib looked at the floor.

"We're going to have to head back home," Mrs. Williams said.

"Okay."

"You want me to leave the car out for you, son?" she asked.

"Uh-huh. Yes'm."

"I'll see you Friday, Gib," his sister said.

"Yeah. Okay."

And that is how it ended. For Gib Williams, it is over. There will be other good days. There will be a wife, perhaps, and children. And business deals and vacations and grandchildren and better cars and a big house and moments that have big meanings. But they will be different. Nothing will ever be like it was last week, during March of '67, when the Crisp County Rebels played for the state championship and over the public-address system they were telling 3,000 people, ". . . at center, No. 50, Gib Williams . . ."

THE WEIRD AND THE WONDROUS: VINTAGE IN-BETWEEN

Superlatives, oddities, and memorable anecdotes I've collected over the years from communities with populations between 5,000 and 100,000.

The 1953 Indiana final, won by South Bend Central, 42 to 41, over Terre Haute Gerstmeyer, is remembered as "The Game of the Foul Mix-up." Gerstmeyer's stars were identical twins Arley (number 34) and Harley (number 43) Andrews. Early in the contest, one of Harley's fouls was, in the opinion of all media people present, given in error to Arley. The Gerstmeyer coach immediately protested, but the referee would not order the correction. Arley, the stronger twin, fouled out early in the fourth quarter, setting the stage for a cliff-hanger ending. Harley went the entire game without a foul call. Toward further confusion Gerstmeyer had a third regular named Andrews—Harold, the twins' uncle.

The Little Falls (New York) High teams of 1903–04 were so superior to aggregations their own age that they sought and did extremely well against pro and college competition. Little Falls once won two out of three against national AAU champion Company E of Schenectady. Some of its other opponents were the famed Buffalo Germans, the New York 23rd Streets, the New York Knickerbockers, the Syracuse Pastimes, the Paterson Crescents, the Cortland Athletics, the All-Troys, and six colleges—Syracuse, Colgate, St. Lawrence, Hamilton, Union, and Potsdam. The rubber game against Company E, played in neutral Amsterdam, New York, went into overtime. With just a few seconds remaining and Company E ahead by one point, Little Falls forward Bert Schell hurled a desperation pass the length of the court, hoping it would fall into a friendly hand. It was too high for that, but it hit the wall and slithered through the hoop, a legal maneuver in those days. Little Falls High had won, 27 to 26, and taken a series from the national AAU champions.

Two Montana high schools, Anaconda and Helena, had a game that night, but Anaconda officials misread the schedule. Fortunately the buses passed on the highway and stopped. The Anaconda bus wheeled around, wasted 150 miles of driving, but got back home in time and won, 58 to 53.

Few state champions have borne the "melting pot" stamp more indelibly than the 1940 team of Granite City, Illinois, a steel town across the Missis-

sippi from St. Louis. Led by Andy Phillip, later an all-America at the University of Illinois, a several-time assist leader during eleven NBA seasons, and a Hall of Fame electee, the Warriors climbed uphill to nip Herrin, 24 to 22, in the final. Phillip was the son of a Magyar steel worker whose original surname, Fulop, had been anglicized in deference to Hungary's alignment with Germany in World War I. Also on the squad were four of Armenian descent, one of Bulgarian, one of Yugoslav, two of German, and one of Scotch-Irish. Pearl Harbor was still a long way off, but the war in Europe was 6 months old. Just before the final game the boys received this wire: "If the nations of Europe were as cooperative as you are, there would be no war. You're together, boys. Win."

Following the victory, Pat Harmon's lead in the *Champaign News-Gazette* read: "There is joy tonight in Granite City. Joy around the Vartan Market and the beauty parlor of Eftimoff. Joy down where Kirchoff's Grocery lies hard by Mitcheff's Market, with Stoyunoff's Dry Goods not far away. For Granite City won. . . ."

When the victors got home, they were paraded through the main business section, but the procession stopped at Lincoln Place, heart of the neighborhood where the Fulops, Eftimoffs, Parseghians, and Hagopians grew up. This was the American Dream.

You can argue all night about "the greatest" prep teams, but try these two 1971 candidates as measuring sticks: Mt. Vernon (New York), featuring Gus Williams, Earl Tatum, and Rudy Hackett, later of USC/NBA, Marquette/NBA, and Syracuse, respectively, and Washington (East Chicago, Indiana), featuring Junior Bridgeman, Pete Trgovich, Tim Stoddard, and Darnell Adell, later of Louisville/NBA, UCLA, North Carolina State, and Murray State, respectively.

In a single 1984 performance Boone County High won the highest-scoring game in Kentucky prep history and equalled the low-scoring record. Here's how:

On January 24 Boone County defeated Newport, 117 to 111—an astronomical tally made possible by a slow-running clock that went undiscovered until after the start of the second half, and thereafter was simply allowed to run its course. Hence the record, albeit tainted. Later it developed that Boone County had used an ineligible player. Result: the high-scoring game was forfeited and went into the record books as a 1 to 0 victory for Newport.

Led by an all-state playmaker standing 5′4″ and weighing 121 pounds, the Astoria Fishermen won their second straight Oregon title in 1942, outscoring four opponents by an aggregate 64 points. Those were itchy times on the Pacific shores. With Pearl Harbor only 3 months into history, an army sentry fired on a police harbor-patrol boat off Portland, a "guerrilla" army was organized in Tillamook, and the region's football standard bearer, Oregon State, *had its Rose Bowl game with Duke moved from California to the "safer atmosphere" of Durham, North Carolina.*

In the record book of West Virginia's Kanawha Valley Conference there are these individual scoring championship entries:

1958—Gary Justice, 23.4
1959—Gay Elmore, 27.9

Justice played for Nitro, Elmore for Stonewall Jackson. Each had an outstanding basketball-playing son with the same name. Hence readers may do a double take when they see these entries further down the list:

1980—Gary Justice, 23.1
1981—Gay Elmore, 25.0

While big-city and suburban schools find all the competition they need within a 10-mile radius, Key West (Florida) High, 130 miles from nearest rival Homestead and 160 from Miami, averages about 3,500 miles a year traveling to and from Dade County gyms. Its bus legends abound with such trials as a tire blowout on a bridge, an 8-hour mechanical problem, a rattlesnake on board, and the "road legs" the players often have during the first quarter after a long drive. Key West won the state AAAA title in 1968.

Granite City was a heavy favorite to eliminate West Frankfort in a 1960 Illinois supersectional at East St. Louis. Merle Jones's story in the Southern Illinoisan *suggested that the latter lads might attend the state finals at Champaign but "will not have to take their uniforms." A West Frankfort fan thereupon wrote Jones, challenging him to ride a donkey down Main Street in the Franklin County town in the event the Redbirds won. Jones accepted. The Redbirds did win, 64 to 62, in two overtimes, and because the weather was cold and snowy, they stayed the night in East St. Louis. Arriving home the next day, they found a parade had been arranged, with Jones, on donkey, serving as "marshal."*

The South has a virtual lock on high school coaching records. It boasts four of the first five on the boys' national career-victory honor roll and two or three of the top three on the girls', depending on whether Oklahoma is classified as "South." Eric "Fessor" Staples of Perry, Georgia, owned the top win total among boys' coaches with 924 from 1933 to 1965, but still-active Walter "Buck" Van Huss of Dobyns-Bennett High, Kingsport, Tennessee, was only one behind as of mid-1986. Next were Charles Womack of Hawley, Texas, 896 from 1947 to 1979; still-active Ralph Tasker of Hobbs, New Mexico, 886; and O. W. Follis of Lamesa, Texas, 857 from 1946 to 1982. National Hall of Fame member Bertha Teague of Byng High, Ada, Oklahoma, whose girls' teams compiled

1,152 victories from 1928 to 1970, is believed to have the highest prep total in modern history. Recently retired Thednal Hill of Highland High, Hardy, Arkansas, was second on the girls' list at 1,063 from 1951 to 1986, with still-active Jim Smiddy of Bradley Central, Cleveland, Tennessee, close behind at 1,040. Dolph Stanley, still coaching an Illinois private school team at 81 after 51 coaching seasons, had a combined high school–college total of 952.

Who hasn't fantasized about keeping a high school wonder five together through college? It happened once—in Franklin, Indiana, from 1920 to 1926. Led by future National Hall of Fame electee Robert "Fuzzy" Vandivier, the high school won three consecutive state championships in 1920–22, the only Indiana institution ever to do so. When the coach, Everett "Griz" Wagner, transferred to Franklin College down the street during the summer of '22, Vandivier and three other members of the prep team followed him, joining a fifth, a veteran of the '20 team, who had been there 2 years. Another two came later.

Franklin College, which today has an enrollment of about 600, compiled a 51–5 record and earned national recognition during the three seasons the Wonder Five remained intact. Its victims included Notre Dame four times, Wisconsin three times, Marquette and Purdue each twice, the professional Indianapolis Omars (who owned a victory over the Original Celtics), and three in-state teams—Butler, Wabash, and DePauw—which were major powers in those days. Injuries ended the Franklin dynasty a year too soon, but the players were reassembled in 1931 for a Christmas charity game against the current college varsity. Shaking off the rust of the years, the Wonder Five wowed the crowd with some of the old-time precision, winning, 32 to 28.

Vandivier coached Franklin High with great success from 1926 to 1944. Teammate Burl Friddle coached state champions at Washington (1930) and Fort Wayne South (1938). Indiana basketball lore contains many rhapsodies of the great Franklin teams. Bill Fox, Jr., of the Indianapolis News *wrote, "Dust off the word 'wonder,' for little Franklin has the team." An anonymous reporter commented, "Basketball may have originated in Massachusetts, but it was perfected in Franklin, Ind." When Vandivier left the floor after his final college game—for approximately the two hundredth time—he was asked, "Now that it's over, which part was the best part?" Unhesitatingly he replied, "The high school days."*

In 1904 Flushing (New York) High played five games in one day at Madison Square Garden and won them all.

Most high schools have never won a state championship, hence the thought of the band playing "Happy Days Are Here Again" in recognition of revived glory is only make-believe. But that's what happened on March 14, 1981, when Greeley Central defeated Broomfield for its eighth Colorado title but first since 1962. Five of the titles were under Coach Jim Baggot, whose teams failed to make the state tourney only twice in 22 years. None of the '81 players were born in '62, but fans and bands know about tradition.

A few of the noted high school officials have been sportswriters. Illinois had one of the most respected, whom we'll call Sam. He enjoyed holiday tournament assignments because they were vehicles for catching up on old cronies. At the scorer's table at halftime one year, he was asked whatever happened to a mutual acquaintance who once worked on the Rock Island Argus. The question set Sam's wheels in motion, but memory was hazy. The second half started, and after a little preliminary pass work, the ball handler drove into the lane, where he collided head-on with a defender. The action was in Sam's territory, but there was no call. Spectators screamed: it had to be a foul on somebody. Sam walked calmly over to the scorer's table. "I remember now," he announced. "He's working for the Denver Post."

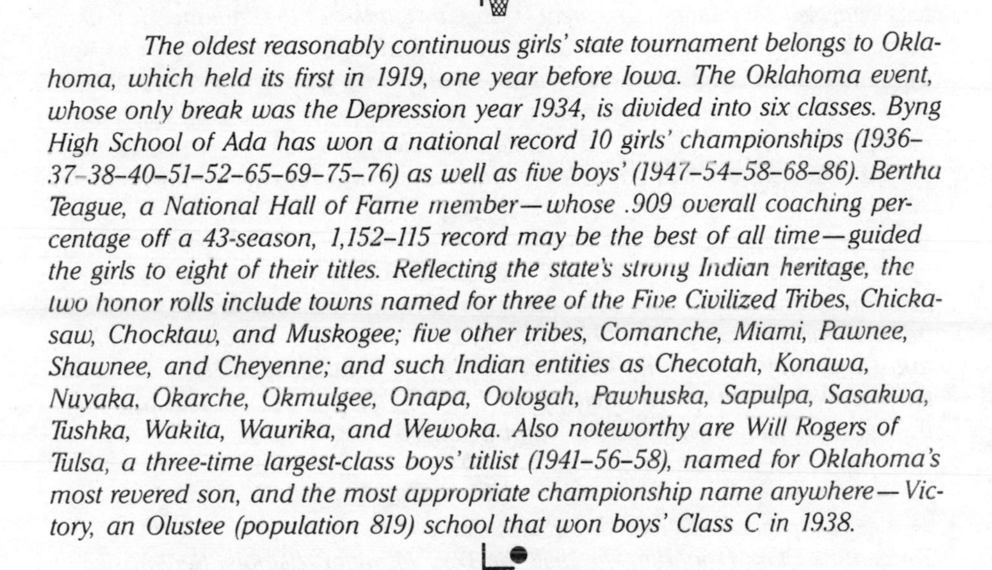

The oldest reasonably continuous girls' state tournament belongs to Oklahoma, which held its first in 1919, one year before Iowa. The Oklahoma event, whose only break was the Depression year 1934, is divided into six classes. Byng High School of Ada has won a national record 10 girls' championships (1936–37–38–40–51–52–65–69–75–76) as well as five boys' (1947–54–58–68–86). Bertha Teague, a National Hall of Fame member—whose .909 overall coaching percentage off a 43-season, 1,152–115 record may be the best of all time—guided the girls to eight of their titles. Reflecting the state's strong Indian heritage, the two honor rolls include towns named for three of the Five Civilized Tribes, Chickasaw, Chocktaw, and Muskogee; five other tribes, Comanche, Miami, Pawnee, Shawnee, and Cheyenne; and such Indian entities as Checotah, Konawa, Nuyaka, Okarche, Okmulgee, Onapa, Oologah, Pawhuska, Sapulpa, Sasakwa, Tushka, Wakita, Waurika, and Wewoka. Also noteworthy are Will Rogers of Tulsa, a three-time largest-class boys' titlist (1941–56–58), named for Oklahoma's most revered son, and the most appropriate championship name anywhere—Victory, an Olustee (population 819) school that won boys' Class C in 1938.

Officials called a national high school record 110 fouls in the 1954 West Virginia debacle between Weston and Grafton, 59 against the former and 51 against the latter. Assuming no overtime (the National Federation of State High School Associations record book indicates none), that's approximately 3.5 fouls per minute or 1 every 17 seconds. At 5 fouls for disqualification, at least fifteen players must have been whistled to the sidelines. One hopes the visitors brought enough bodies.

January 15, 1927, was a night of misery for Logansport, Indiana. The bus carrying its undefeated team to Frankfort stalled for several hours near

Michigantown, and the varsity game didn't start until almost midnight. Frankfort won the game with another kind of stall, 10 to 7, after which fights broke out both inside and outside the gym.

Frankfort began its stall after 5 minutes of the first quarter, with Logansport holding a 7 to 6 lead. Since Logansport was ahead, it let Frankfort hold the ball near center court till the end of the half. Logansport got the tip at the start of the second half and went into a stall of its own. After 3 minutes one of the officials, seated by now in the first row of the bleachers, called Logansport for traveling. Frankfort then took the ball and stalled until 2 minutes remained in the game, at which point Coach Everett Case gave the start-playing signal. Dick Pearcy thereupon hit from the center of the floor, giving Frankfort an 8 to 7 lead. Logansport got the tip but missed five straight shots. Finally, with rebound in hand, Frankfort set up its Pearcy play, and he hit again from center floor, this time off the backboard. Frankfort led, 10 to 7. Logansport got the tip but missed several shots as the game ticked away.

The Logansport rooters were incensed. The return game at Logansport was canceled by mutual agreement. Case, a member of the Indiana Hall of Fame, winner of four state titles at Frankfort, and later a storied coach at North Carolina State, apparently felt this was the only way his charges could beat a physically superior team. Logansport was coached by national Hall of Fame member Cliff Wells, who won two state championships before moving on to Tulane. The controversial game led to adoption of the 10-second midcourt rule.

The longest prep field goal ever? Steve Patterson of Central High in McMinn County, Tennessee, sank one measuring 79 feet 2 inches in a 1976 district tournament game. The 1978 effort by Duane Wood of Licking Valley (Newark, Ohio) may or may not have been longer. One publication reported his distance at "88 feet," the ball having been heaved "from under the opposite basket." A regulation high school court is only 84 feet long.

Despite a 4–17 record, DeSales Catholic made the final four in New York's 1982 Class D tourney. In 1953 the West Frankfort (Illinois) Redbirds wound up their regular season at 5–18, finishing last in their conference at 2–10. Then they got their act together, won seven in a row and reached the Elite Eight where they lost a 2-point thriller to runner-up Peoria Central. In 1960 Wausau won the Wisconsin title going away, a feat requiring eight straight victories, after finishing its regular campaign at 9–9. In 1983 Salina Central took the Kansas 5A after a 6–13 record.

Behind one point with 2 seconds to go, Schlarman High of Danville, Illinois, qualified for the "Sweet 16" in 1961 when its star, Bryan Williams, sank an old-fashioned chest shot from the opposite free throw line. The ball swished, giving Williams 42 points for the evening. Later, when the excitement had sub-

sided and the gym had cleared out, Coach Paul Shebby ran an adrenaline test. He brought Williams back to point "X" to see if he could shoot the ball that far again. He couldn't—in numerous attempts.

Nice guys do finish first.

It was said of Paul Hustad, coach of the unbeaten 1975 Colorado AAA champion Westminster Warriors, that he had never incurred a technical foul in 22 years. Moreover, none of his players had even been penalized for unsportsmanlike conduct.

Hustad's basic tenets were reflected in quotes compiled during the title year by Mark Wolf of the Arvada Citizen Sentinel *and Don Miles of the* Sterling Journal-Advocate. *They included:*

> "We tell our players that when we can limit our mistakes to one or two during the course of the game, then maybe we can question the official's one mistake."
>
> "Basketball is a very emotional game. If the coach cannot control himself, how can he expect the players to control their emotions? Spectators should be watching the players on the floor, not some coach trying to lead the cheers or boos."
>
> "You have to come into a state tournament with your homework done. If not prepared, you'll lose. You're not going to work any miracles on the bench. My job is done in practice; the players do theirs in the game."
>
> "Sometimes I'm too demanding of the players, but I never cuss at 'em or raise my voice. They are men, so we treat them like gentlemen at all times."

Indiana has more than thirty high school gyms seating 5,000 or more. New Castle's capacity is 9,325, and several schools can seat more than their community populations. At least one town allows its jail inmates to watch the state tournament on TV. To deprive any live Hoosier of this opportunity would be "cruel and unusual punishment." John Wooden, whose UCLA record will be a college coaching yardstick for eternity, remembers the Hoosier high school atmosphere of 1927, the year he led Martinsville to the state crown: "In those days you couldn't grow up in Indiana and not have basketball touch you in some way. It was the homeroom teacher's job to see that everyone had a season ticket. If a student was too poor to afford it, the teacher had the responsibility of finding a way to get him one." In 1966 a pair of sectional tourney tickets was the rental fee for a $6,000 tractor that rescued a farmboy player from Lebanon in a blizzard.

"Cut Day" always bears trauma, some of it to affect personalities for a lifetime. Farm boy Dick Motta, the future Weber State and NBA coach, was cut

as a senior at Jordan (Utah) High, and admits today that he has never completely recovered. He stared at the list over and over, but his name simply wasn't there. All of a sudden he hated the school and the world. He had to psych up just to go home. Weeks later it helped a little when the coach explained his action by way of Motta's ankle injury and a new system that might have been difficult for the seniors to adapt to. Years later it helped a little when the coach sent his son to play for Motta at Weber State. But the hardening had set. Today Motta admits that he trusts only a few select people, and he traces the attitude back to Cut Day at Jordan High.

An eastern coach was called for jury duty. He begged to be excused on grounds that he couldn't afford to be away from his team.

The judge scoffed, "I suppose you're one of those people who thinks the world couldn't go on without you."

"No, your honor," replied the coach. "I know very well that my players can get along without me. But I can't afford to let them find it out."

EPILOGUE

While the pros and collegians clearly have more talent and enjoy much wider news coverage, neither can match the high schools in buzzer-to-buzzer excitement or local fervor. *The Agony and the Ecstasy* wasn't written about prep basketball, but the expression fits.

Nothing stirs the pulse of springtime quite like a state tournament, whether in Indiana or Vermont, Alabama or Oregon. It is a ritual that reaches into city and village with equal force, touching heartstrings as no other sport can. Many old-timers, having witnessed World Series, Kentucky Derbies, Olympic Games, and Super Bowls, each with a special brand of far-reaching drama, unhesitatingly pick the state tournament in any basketball hotbed as the greatest show of all.

In some eyes, hoopla at the secondary school level represents over-emphasis, an undue community burden on teenaged shoulders, and a pandering to the sophomoric instincts of entertainment-starved adults. Given proper academic priorities, however, the benefits of high school competition as we know it far outweigh the abuses. Against a background of apathy, drug presence, and nuclear confusion, we ask 18-year-olds to shoulder a gun, to vote intelligently, and in many cases to start earning a living. When *should* they start confronting the pressures of life?

This book was compiled in an effort to capture some of prep basketball's universal spirit and to help develop a national literature/lore on a subject where little now exists. May it stimulate more such research. And soon. The survivors of the early days are well past 80 now, and the trail is getting cold.